EAR

02/23

We hope you enjoy this book. Please return or
renew it by the due date.

You can renew it at www.norfolk.gov.uk/libraries or
by using our free library app.

Otherwise you can phone 0344 800 8[...]
please have your library card and PIN [...]

You can sign up for email reminders [...]

KU-750-730

Also by Andy Davidson and available from Titan Books

The Boatman's Daughter

THE HOLLOW KIND

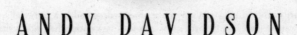

ANDY DAVIDSON

TITAN BOOKS

The Hollow Kind
Print edition ISBN: 9781803362755
E-book edition ISBN: 9781803362762

Published by Titan Books
A division of Titan Publishing Group Ltd
144 Southwark Street, London SE1 0UP
www.titanbooks.com

First Titan edition: February 2023
10 9 8 7 6 5 4 3 2 1

The Hollow Kind: A Novel by Andy Davidson
Copyright © 2023 by Andy Davidson
Published by arrangement with MBD, an imprint of
Farrar, Straus and Giroux, New York. All rights reserved.

A CIP catalogue record for this title is available from the British Library.

Printed and bound by CPI Group (UK) Ltd, Croydon CR0 4YY.

For Crystal

Tell me a story of things hoped for, things dreamed.
I will convince you, it is a story of horrors.

James Green
The Nameless Traveler
1939

THE
HOLLOW
KIND

1988

✦

SEPTEMBER 7

SOMEHOW, HE LIVES. FIFTY-SIX YEARS AFTER THE EXPLOSION, what should have been the end of his story. The fight has all run out of him and his mind is gone, each step slow and hitching up the long gravel drive from motor home to house, a plastic gallon jug in hand, clear liquid sloshing inside. Leather boots laced tight over a pair of threadbare chinos. The old crescent ax dangles from his belt, its moon-shaped blade honed sharp again, though he can barely lift it, let alone swing it. Up the board steps, onto the farmhouse porch, where the door has long been nailed shut with old planks from the barn. With the tip of the ax, he struggles each board loose. When at last the heavy door swings inward, the house almost seems to give out a sigh. A moldy death rattle.

Inside, Redfern stops at the rotary phone on the hall table, hooks out 9–1–1 with a gnarled finger. To the dispatcher, he says, "It's the goddamn *Hindenburg* out at Redfern Hill. Whole place is going up. Best send a truck." He doesn't wait for an answer, just drops the receiver in the cradle and walks to the map room at the end of the foyer, where he works his way into the junk, years upon years of garbage and forgotten things, the crinkled, rolled maps he once drew. Above his old oak desk, the twin crosscut saws bare their rusted teeth. A long time ago, they felled the trees that framed this house. He stands in the center of the room and takes it in, one last time. No sentiment, just weariness. He will not be sorry to see it burn.

He looks down at the jug in his trembling hand. No gloves today. No gloves ever again. The scars and the mottled, waxlike fingers are a remembrance of the one brave act he ever committed. Today, please God, he will be brave again. He will not fail. He thumbs the plastic cap from the jug, and the oily, piney smell of turpentine fills the room.

Beneath the floorboards, in the darkness of the root cellar, a faint, sickly light begins to stir.

He upturns the jug of turpentine over his head, the liquid spilling over his thin white pate, his ears, washing into his eyes. He cries out, his throat a rusty hinge, and fumbles a single kitchen match from his shirt pocket and, with clumsy fingers, strikes it on his thumbnail.

Below him, the light brightens, glitters like the sea, shot through with sun.

Nigh a century you've been here, old friend, old enemy, old god upon your throne of dirt and blood. Your voice, the wind in the pines to me. Are you weak from all these lean years of hunger, ill fed on possums and rats, snakes and toads? Will you beg me now, when you speak my name? Oh, if I had more time, I'd starve you right out of the goddamned earth—

The match flares between Redfern's fingers, as out of the heaps of old furniture and twisted-up paper and columns of musty books, it rises, a dark blur coalescing into blue gingham and brown curls, those eyes like glowing sapphires, smell of pine and loam. It speaks: "Papa."

A voice that breaks loose a lifetime of guilt and shame, like shards of glass in his chest.

"Have you come to hurt me, Papa?"

"You are not my child!" he cries, but still, the match flame wavers, as Redfern's legs begin to tremble.

Creak of wood as the thing before him soughs and sighs, reaches out with a small, pale hand.

The match gutters.

The hand wavers just beyond his grizzled cheek and he feels the warmth of it.

A hungry heat.

He drops to his knees and in an instant its hands are no longer hands, its face something slick and wet. It's unraveling, reknitting itself, little brown shoots that creep and grow, thin as monofilament. Licking tenderly at what few patches of his old man's skin aren't wet with turpentine, searching for a chink, a weak spot. Its blue eyes fusing into one, as Redfern opens his mouth to curse it, one last time, but suddenly, he has no air, no breath with which to scream, because his throat is full of plunging, eager tongues.

He fumbles at the ax, works it free of his belt, but it only clatters to the floor, one more piece of him gone, now, here in this room, where all charts and fortunes have led. Choking, he's choking, he cannot breathe, he—

A light flares, blue and big as the sea. Filling the room as Redfern's skull explodes with the sound of crashing waves and the high-pitched scream of gulls, and time becomes a collapsing star, a folded map. A tide washing in, washing out. He convulses. Feels a snarling in his chest cavity, searching out the seat of his regret—

(it was not supposed to end this way it was always going to end this way)

—where shoots with nodes, nodes with tendrils, tendrils with teeth that chew and chew and chew expand, bloom, and there is darkness now, at the edges of his sight. He closes his eyes, seeks out a memory. A girl of sixteen wearing an old cotton shirt and jeans, traipsing after him in a man's boots through dense woods and wire grass to that dark and rotten place that is the source of all his family's suffering. She is his granddaughter, sad and lonely and strong, and his final thought is her name.

Nellie.

Its teeth find the center of him.

From hell's heart, to his own: no great distance, in the end.

I

1989

JUNE 30

Nellie Gardner stiffens in the lawyer's plush chair and thinks: *Condescending prick*.

Meadows rears back a behind a massive cherry desk, hands clasped at the base of his neck. He wears a gold watch and a short-sleeved pink polo and a pair of pleated khakis. Boat shoes, no socks. He smiles at her from a round, red face, knowing the answer to his question, which only makes his having asked it all the more infuriating.

"No," she says, plucking at a torn thread on the knee of her jeans. "My husband won't be joining us."

"Just you and the boy then."

In the waiting room, through the open door, Max—mop of brown hair, big hazel eyes, red Batman T-shirt—sits by a picture window, a *Reader's Digest* from the coffee table open in his lap: "I Survived a Great White Shark Attack." Behind him, through the window, the town square is empty and the sun falls in golden sheets over the courthouse steps.

Nellie crosses her leg over her knee. "Just us," she says. Picking at the rubber heel of her high-top sneaker—

(Idjits fidget.)

Wade, always in her head.

She moves her hand to her lap, anchors it to the other. Doesn't even think about it.

"How old is your son?"

"Eleven."

"That's just the best age, isn't it?" The lawyer reaches a framed picture from his desk, hands it to her. "I've got two."

Nellie pretends to be interested: Meadows in full camouflage with a scoped hunting rifle, hunkered in a pickup bed over a big buck, two boys seated on the tailgate, round apple cheeks thumb-smeared with blood, the deer's head sprung between them.

The lawyer's eyes, like two black ticks, crawl over her. He sees a girl—women are always girls to men like Meadows, Nellie thinks—long limbed and hollow eyed, peroxided hair going dark at the roots. Sleeve of a denim jacket riding up to flash the beginnings of a long white scar above her left wrist. She hands the picture back, smiling.

"One thousand thirty-three acres," he says. "Be a chunk of change if you were to sell." He rummages in a drawer for a Starlight mint. Doesn't offer her one. The peppermint clicks and clacks in his mouth. "To be frank, Mrs. Gardner, the house needs work. Your grandfather hadn't lived in it for over twenty years."

"He was still on the property, though?"

"That's right. The Winnebago. Conditions there, well, they weren't much better."

"I remember."

"It so happens"—Meadows tears a piece of paper from a pad on his desk—"there is a highly motivated party who would like to make you an offer, whether you plan to sell or not." He scratches out some numbers in pencil on a paper, then passes the note to her.

Nellie stares at it, poker-faced. She counts the zeros twice. Calmly, she pushes the offer away and speaks slowly, carefully, keeping the tremor from her voice: "I know it's strange, Mr. Meadows, but for some reason, my grandfather wanted me to have Redfern Hill. I don't think—"

"Have you considered property taxes? Won't be cheap, that much acreage. There's also the issue of land management. Forests like that require a certain vigilance to maintain their value. As for the house itself, the wiring's ancient. I know the coal furnace was replaced with butane about thirty years back, but I can't speak to the plumbing. And there is no air-conditioning, not even a window unit. Summer in Georgia? Just the money you'll have to sink into the place to make it livable, you'll burn through the cash he left you"—Meadows snaps his fingers—"like that."

Max looks up over the *Reader's Digest*.

"Fifty thousand dollars may seem like a fortune, but it really isn't."

Nellie swallows, face flushing red.

"Even your grandfather was scraping by, Mrs. Gardner. Living on peanut butter and saltine crackers. What you didn't inherit, he sold off piecemeal, five, ten acres here, twenty acres there."

"To your highly motivated party?"

Meadows smiles thinly, and the smile does not reach his eyes. He breathes deeply, folds his hands together over his blotter. "Corporations, mostly. I don't know how much you know, but Mr. Redfern was not . . . well, a popular man here in Empire. Historically. I don't mean to be indelicate, but a lot of bad blood got spilled early in his career, between landowners like your grandfather and certain folks around here who, let's just say, didn't think the terms of their agreements were fair."

Meadows takes up his pen. He crosses out the old offer, writes a new one in its place. This time, he doesn't bother to pass the paper back, just holds it up so she can read it. "That's more than fair, ma'am. That's generous."

She drops her leg from her knee and sits forward in her chair. "You have keys for me."

Meadows moves the peppermint around in his mouth, breathes heavily for a space of ten, fifteen seconds.

She waits him out.

He smacks the slip of paper with his middle finger. Crumples it, throws it in the trash. From a desk drawer he passes her a brown manila envelope, REDFERN KEYS printed in black Sharpie across the seal.

"There are no copies?"

He smiles thinly, cracks his mint between his molars. Ignores the question. "Should be the house, RV, plus a gate or two on the property. The main gate, you have to jiggle it a little bit."

She stands.

In the waiting room, Max tosses his *Reader's Digest* back onto a pile.

Meadows's high-backed executive chair creaks as he pushes out of it. "Sorry I can't drive out with you." He glances at his watch. "Truth be told, I'm late for supper. But I went out this morning, made sure everything was switched on."

I bet you did, Nellie thinks. *Had a nice long look around, too, didn't you? On behalf of your interested party.* She offers her hand. "Thank you, Mr. Meadows. We'll manage."

The lawyer makes no secret of taking in, one last time, the scar that begins crosswise at Nellie's bangled wrist.

He shakes her hand limply. "Welcome home, Mrs. Gardner."

The Ranger rattles past a nail salon, a consignment store, a barber's pole, still and dark. A shuttered movie theater, on its side a sun-faded mural, the town's history mapped on cracked brick. A lumber mill with a huge whirling saw. So many pine trees. A family is picnicking on the banks, and Max twists in his seat: the father is stern faced and his hands are fists, his belt undone; the mother sits slump shouldered in a dowdy dress. On the blanket before her, like a beetle on its back, a diapered baby, screaming. The mother stares off, across the river, at the whirling blades of the saw.

"'Mrs. Gardner,'" Nellie says.

They pass an Amoco with broken windows and Nellie points and says she used to buy cigarettes there, after school.

"How old were you?" Max asks.

"Not old enough."

A cluster of mobile homes drifts past, backyard clotheslines still as death. A boy in a weed-split parking lot bounces a red, white, and blue basketball. Rusting cotton trailers snagged with rotten cotton. Wrecks in driveways, pink and green asbestos siding, little tin awnings. A stand of concrete-block apartments where a woman in a housecoat sits on her porch, shelling peas into a bowl.

Soon, they pass out of Empire into a patchwork of farmland and pine thickets, a world made molten by the dipping sun.

Max wilts into his seat, thinking of home back in South Carolina, how it is not home anymore. He thinks of his stuff in the pickup's bed, as much as they were able to carry: a suitcase full of clothes, a laundry basket wrapped in a black trash bag and filled with *G.I. Joe* and *Star Wars* toys, a plastic Batmobile, a collection of Little Golden Books. *Lord of the Rings* paperbacks and a dozen cheap movie novelizations he's read three times over. In a cardboard box, the lid taped with silver duct tape, a stack of spiral-bound Meads dotted with stickers from movies and cartoons. A sketchbook and pencil box. A Swiss Army knife. A Panasonic VCR trailing cables and half a dozen TK 120 tapes labeled in his own small, adult hand. *The Karate Kid. Gremlins. Jaws.*

All Nellie brought was a duffel bag, stuffed with whatever underwear and jeans and T-shirts she'd managed to grab from her bedroom chest. Before she woke him. Before she took him.

I was kidnapped, Max thinks.

But that's silly. A mom can't kidnap her own kid.

Can she?

A galvanized-steel gate bars the road onto the property. They get out of the Ranger to a blue-hour chorus of crickets. No mailbox, only a road sign knocked into the ditch and overgrown with kudzu: REDFERN ROAD. Tractor chain coils around the gate post, secured with a heavy padlock. Beyond the gate, a dirt road curves away into the wooded gloom. Max looks over his shoulder, to where the blacktop stretches east and west, no houses in sight, just a herd of cows lowing in the pasture across the road, white runners of mist creeping out from the trees. The air is warm and light with the scent of bushhogged field grass.

"How far is the house from the road?"

"About a mile," Nellie says. "Let's see those keys."

Max opens the envelope and turns out a blue plastic key fob. A teardrop, stamped GEORGIA LAND & TIMBER, four keys on the ring, three small and one large labeled with Scotch tape and Bic-writ letters small and crooked: *house.*

"Do the honors," Nellie says.

Max bends to the lock. Tries one of the smaller keys. Tries another. It slides in, but it won't turn at all.

"You gotta jiggle it," Nellie says.

He presses his lips together and, after a second or two, the padlock springs open and the chain rattles free of the fence and drops in a heap in the grass.

Nellie gets into the pickup. Max tugs open the gate, metal scudding over uneven gravel, and when the truck is through, he pulls the gate shut and wraps the chain back around it. He pockets the key and stares ahead, beyond the reach of the Ranger's headlights, the way veiled in shadow. The pickup's taillights bathe him in red. He remembers a snatch of song, has to still his hands from stuttering out the rhythm on his thighs: *A big dark forest . . . can't go over it . . . can't go under it . . .*

Nellie thumps her arm on the door, calls back, "Wagons ho!"

He runs to get in.

She drives slowly. For a while, the ruts are deep, Bahia grass between them whispering against the Ranger's chassis. The road narrows and the trees thicken overhead into a canopy that blacks out an already darkening sky. Yellow POSTED notices are hammered into the pines. Ahead, there's a turnout on the right, barred by a second chained gate, a NO TRESPASSING sign.

"That's the road to the old turpentine mill," Nellie says.

Max shifts in his seat to watch the gate recede as they drive on.

The woods rise up around them, tree roots breaking through high shoulders of red clay. They crest a rise and Nellie takes her foot off the gas. Far ahead, down the hill, the slope bottoms out into a shallow creek bed, and the road, briefly, becomes a wash of pine straw and limbs. She downshifts and they roll to a stop and idle.

"Can we get over that?" Max says.

Nellie does the math. Maybe they can, maybe they can't. It's dark, they're alone. There's a ratty motel back on the bypass, near the old tire factory. Been there since she was a girl. But she's not sure they can even afford that. Their cash is almost gone, whatever's left of a twenty after truck-stop cheeseburgers in Brunswick. In the envelope Meadows gave her, there's only a bank executive's business card. No checkbook, not even temporaries. She has no credit cards. All of those are in Wade's name and Wade's wallet, back in South Carolina.

"How does a shark stay alive?" she asks the boy.

"It keeps moving."

She fastens her seat belt. A quick, decisive click.

Max does the same.

Nellie puts one hand on the gearshift, pops the clutch, and stamps on the gas.

They hit the creek bed and the back tires slew and the wheel jerks in Nellie's hands. Max grabs his seat belt and clings to it, and for a brief, perilous second, Nellie feels the truck slow, spin, begin to claw the earth. Time for a single breath, as the pine limbs hang up beneath the truck and the back goes soft in the wet sand, but then the little Ford chews its way up and out of the creek. Nellie lets off the gas near the top of the hill, struggles to get the shifter out of third. The road rises as she glances down—

"*Mom, look out!*"

Her head whips up.

Something huge looms in her headlights.

Nellie yanks the wheel, tromps the brake.

The pickup slides. The world pitches. A metal crunch from the right rear fender and a slow-motion blur of trees, and suddenly the truck's rear axle drops into the ditch and the engine dies and they come to a teeth-rattling halt, facing back the way they came from in a cloud of their own orange wake.

She moves without thought, all instinct. Clicking free of her seat belt, hands roving over Max's arms, shoulders, the crown of his head. "I'm okay," he says, pushing her away. "Really, Mom, I'm fine."

Ahead, the dust settles and they can see the big, dark shape of something crumpled in the road.

"What is it?" the boy breathes.

She fishes a Maglite from beneath the bench seat. "Stay in the car." The truck's door gives a dry squall as she steps out, sneakers sinking in a drift of gravel. Overhead, the sky is a peach-gold swath where the night's first bats are swooping. Whatever she's hit, it's huge and hulking in the high beams. Nellie walks slowly toward it, a cold sweat beading her scalp. She clicks on the flashlight and her breath catches in her chest. Its eyes are dark and glassy, its claws long and obsidian-gleaming. Blood in its nostrils, flecks of crimson in the fur of its muzzle.

"Mom?"

Max stands outside the pickup, silhouetted in front of its grille.

"It's a bear," she calls back. "A goddamn bear, Jesus Christ."

The boy comes running.

Nellie catches him. "Whoa, kiddo. Whoa. Stay back."

"Is it dead?"

"Looks like."

He inches toward it, bending low. Reaching.

"Max," she warns, but the boy runs his hand through the thick wiry fur.

"It's a black bear," he says, voice hushed.

Back at the truck, she sink-steps into the ditch to check the damage to the fender. The panel is caved, but the tire is good, so they climb back into the cab and Nellie cranks the engine, but when she puts the truck in gear, it only spits gravel. *Stuck*. She hooks the shifter into neutral and the engine cuts out. She puts her head in her hands, closes her eyes. Kneads the space between them as the silence ticks. From the dark woods, a bright sawing of crickets, followed by the low drumming of frogs in the distant river. It'll be full dark in ten minutes, and they've come half a mile. At least another half to go—

"We can't just leave him in the road," Max says.

Nellie kicks out of the truck and snags the boy's suitcase from the Ranger's bed. "We'll have to walk the rest of the way."

Max slides after her, across the seat, hangs in the door. "But what about the bear?"

"Goddamn it, Max, I can't do anything about the bear!"

He shrinks back into the cab.

Nellie stares up at the night sky. Swallows it, this anger. It's not the boy's to take.

Damn you, Wade Gardner.

She reaches into the cab and takes Max's hand. He jerks away, crossing his arms to face forward, eyes locked on the distant hump of the broken creature in the truck's headlights. She reaches again, takes his wrist, firmly, then eases up. "Bring one thing," she tells him. "The house isn't far, but we don't want to haul more than we can carry. We'll come back tomorrow for the rest."

Please, God, let there be power up there.

Nellie tilts the seat forward, grabs her duffel, unzips it. She opens the boy's suitcase and transfers his toothbrush and toothpaste into her bag. Max, meanwhile, climbs into the pickup's bed and fishes around in his cardboard box, comes up with his sketchbook and pencil box. These, and Nellie's purse from the seat, go into the duffel, and she zips it all up. Max asks if he can carry the light. She hands it to him. Shouldering her bag, she reaches through the open driver's door to switch off the Ranger's headlamps, and there she hesitates, staring at the dead bear in the road.

"Mom? You okay?"

She cuts the lamps, and everything is lost to the night.

Max clicks on the flashlight and they start walking.

Fifteen minutes later, they're breathing heavy, sneakers crunching on the gravel, the road a steady incline. Overhead, stars wink out behind a wall of clouds. An owl sings from the tangled brush, stopping Max in his tracks. He's heard owls before, but never so loud, so close. He pictures the Great Owl in *Mrs. Frisby and the Rats of Nimh*, yellow eyes peering out through a mask of cobwebs. That huge, shuffling girth.

"How did your grandfather die?" he asks.

"They said his heart gave out."

Max thinks of his aunt on his dad's side. How they'd visited her in the hospital last year in Myrtle Beach, then got ice cream at the Boardwalk. A treat to drive away the memories of that close, dim room, the wires and tubes and needles trailing out of her. Dad's idea. It hadn't worked. "Was he in the hospital, like Aunt Violet?"

"No. He died suddenly. At home."

"In the house?"

"Yeah. But he had a motor home. He was living in that."

"Why wasn't he living in the house?"

It takes a few seconds for her to answer: "Maybe it was too big, too lonely."

"Where is he buried?"

"There's a family cemetery, somewhere on the property."

Max glances beyond the flashlight's path, into the black pines standing against the blue night. Somewhere out there, among these trees, are graves. Dead people. Rotting in boxes.

Nellie, too, goes quiet. Not one of her easy silences, like when Max used to lie on the floor of her studio and color while she painted, and it was raining outside and David Bowie was on the radio. No, this is a different, darker silence. Heavier. A smothering blanket.

He thinks of the spare bedroom in their little blue house in Conway, dozens of Nellie's paintings propped along the wall, large and small. Covered in dark greens and violent reds and pools of black. Crumbling brick buildings, vacant lots, a city park where she used to take him to play. Empty swings in shafts of sunlight, a trash can on its side, spilling garbage. "It's not really the park though," Max had said, about that painting. "The park is a happy place. Isn't it?"

Her answer had been as mysterious to him as the painting itself: "The places I see, kiddo, are up here." She'd tapped her head.

"You should try painting happy trees," he said, "like the man on TV."

Nellie's answer was to grab him and make pig noises against his neck, and he'd wriggled away, laughing. But later, he was still thinking about it, how that painting made him never want to go to that park again.

———

They walk on, rocks rolling beneath their shoes. Thunder, to the west. In the dark, his mother is little more than a shape beside him, a presence without form. "How big is this place, anyway?" he asks, just to hear her voice. To ward off the eerie feeling they're two balloons untethered and drifting into the night.

"About a thousand acres."

"A thousand acres," he says softly. "And it's all like this?"

"Most of it."

"You used to come here, when you were a kid?"

"No. I spent some time here, one summer. That's it."

"How long?"

"Four days." A pause. Then: "I ran away from home."

Max lets this sink in. Once, he'd run away from home himself, but he'd only gotten as far as the grapevine at the grammar school, six blocks away. Mom and Dad were yelling in the living room and there was the sound of glass breaking, so he packed his little blue suitcase with the train conductor on the side, the one that said I'M GOING TO GRANDMA'S HOUSE, and climbed out his bedroom window and through a crack in the board fence and down a narrow dirt alley that spilled him onto Cleveland Street. It was spring and the grapevine was greening, so he slipped in among the shadows and the bees buzzing with their fairy wings and sat on his suitcase and thought about where he was going to go. But he was already hungry and the only place he could think of was the Gay Dolphin at Myrtle Beach, where they sold snow globes he liked to look at. So he doesn't ask her why she ran away. He only wants to know how old she was, and how far she got.

She tells him she was sixteen.

"Sixteen?"

"If I'm lying, I'm dying."

"So you spent four days here when you were a teenager, and he left you his house and a thousand acres?"

"It's a mystery to me, too, kiddo."

"He must have loved you."

"I don't know anything about that."

"Did you go back home after that?"

"No."

"How far'd you get, then, before you did?"

A tightness in her voice. "I'm still running, kiddo."

The road curves sharply, and suddenly, he feels it. Like a dip in temperature before a summer storm. They're close. Just beyond the bend, the next unseen spill of thorns and briars, the black trees will break—

Ahead, a pair of canted pines blot out the violet sky. They angle over the road as it becomes a long drive between grassy fields, off to the right the shape of a big dilapidated barn. To the left, beneath a huge hardwood, is the long, boxy shape of an old Winnebago, overtaken by the grass. The drive rambles uphill and hooks around like the eye of a sewing needle, and there, silhouetted against the evening sky, where lightning dances, is their destination.

Max stops in his tracks, as if the old house rearing up before them has teeth, claws, is a thing alive. A dragon in the midst of a long slumber. *It sees us.* A fresh sweat springs out beneath his clothes. Above the roof, bats loose themselves like stones from slings.

Ahead of him, Nellie turns. Calls out to him. "You okay?"

Max's tongue is dry in his mouth. It's inexplicable, the dread that freezes him, shrivels his scrotum, makes his legs weak. Doesn't she feel it?

Pressure in his skull, building—

"Max. Max, are you okay?"

His ears pop, and the whole night goes silent.

Beneath his feet, an unexpected shudder, as if the ground itself were stirring.

He reaches up, touches his nose. A single drop of blood trickles out.

Nellie walks back to him, takes the flashlight, and kneels before him. She shines it between them, so the light spills up, onto both their faces, and he can see she's scared. Not of the house, but of him. Of his forever bleeding nose. Bleeding since February, anyway. She's scared of what it means: that it could all be wrong. That *she* could be wrong. That she hasn't saved him—or herself—from anything.

Quickly, Nellie tugs her T-shirt up from her waist and wipes the blood from his face. "Tilt your head," and he does. "It's just a little nosebleed. Nothing new, right?"

No. Nothing new. He gets them all the time. Ever since that day, outside the garage. With Dad. He tastes blood, spits. Closes his eyes and imagines a bright and sunny place, a beach with broken shells to pick up and sift through. A shore where waves roll in that steady, easy way, where gulls cry and maybe a dog barks, goes splashing into the surf. A place where all pictures painted should be happy—

The bleeding stops. He puts a finger beneath his nose, drops his head.

"Good?" she asks.

He takes a deep and calming breath.

Lightning flashes in the clouds as Nellie Gardner turns and looks up at the house. "Well, this is it, kiddo. We're here."

Two mercury-vapor night lamps light the property, one near the drive at the corner of the barn, the other farther up, behind the house. Nellie and Max pass under the first of these, above them a swirling galaxy of bugs and moths. Over Nellie's left shoulder, the road is bordered by thick johnsongrass, a barbwire fence, and beyond the fence a hayfield that doesn't look to have been cut in decades.

They walk up the long drive, to the eye of the needle, where Nellie shines the flashlight along the front-porch balustrade, tracing its crooked, rickety line until the porch wraps out of sight. Tall windows gleam darkly. Two huge columns of mortared river rock flank the high brick steps, a riot of leggy azaleas on either side. She plays the beam higher, over the tin roof, to the second-story windows and, above these, a single attic dormer.

Beside her, Max sniffs back a lingering trickle of blood.

She starts up the steps, wide and steep. At the top, Nellie passes the light over a porch ceiling that might have once been haint blue, lets the beam rest in the center pane of the glass transom above the front door. Stretched over the glass, a web of cocooned, desiccated bugs. At the center of the web, a fat brown orb weaver.

"Got those keys?"

The boy doesn't move. He's staring up at the spider.

"Max?" she says gently.

Slowly, eyes locked on the transom, he fishes the key fob from his pocket.

She trades him the Maglite and jerks the screen door loose from its swollen frame.

Overhead, the spider retreats to some unseen reach.

The front door is heavy, windowless, the dead bolt stubborn, and Nellie's heart leaps when the key refuses to turn. If they can't get in, she'll have to break a window; otherwise, it's a long walk back to the Ranger to spend the night in the hot, cramped cab, and *oh, wouldn't that just be the perfect end to a perfect day*—

But then the lock clicks and the door swings inward.

Nellie takes back the light and shines it down the long, central hallway, over wide-board walls painted white. A coatrack, empty of coats. Hardwood floors of heart pine, wide cracks between the dark planks, runners of dust like cotton rows in each.

Max stares over his shoulder, back down the narrow, rutted lane that brought them here.

A sudden, oppressive wave of loneliness washes over Nellie. The two of them here, in their little island of light, could be the last two people in the world. Max's fingers—light and warm—interlace with hers. *He's a sponge*, Wade once said. *Soaks up everyone's misery.* Hate flares, briefly, in her chest. That old blue flame that never dies. But then she remembers: there are discoveries to be made here, in this house of their own. And those discoveries are theirs, and theirs alone. Wade will have no part in them. Nellie squeezes Max's hand.

Two deep breaths, and into the house they go.

The foyer opens into a long hall like a throat, cavernous rooms on either side. At the far end, a shadowy kitchen, its windows bright with lightning. Between the two rooms on their left, a narrow set of stairs climbs for the second floor, carpet tacked down over it like a threadbare tongue. The balusters are square and plain, and the light fixtures overhead are hammered out of brass and tin. Doors hang on creaky hinges and the walls look slightly out of true.

Nellie sets her duffel on the floor. Near the molding is an old-fashioned rotary switch. She turns it, and overhead, a pendant flares, a single dead wasp suspended in the frosted globe of the lamp. A spindly antique table stands just inside the door, atop it a green telephone. Nellie picks it up and hears a dial tone. She sets the phone back in its cradle, runs a finger over the tabletop, rolling up a rime of dust.

In the first room to the left of the front door, a dull candelabra lights the ghostly shapes of a sheeted antique sofa, an upright piano. No other tables, no chairs. A rock fireplace dominates the wall opposite the door, above it a hand-hewn mantelpiece. Carved in relief and stained darkly against lighter wood are the jagged, saw-toothed shapes of pine trees.

"This is the parlor," she says to Max.

They drop their bags by the sofa.

Max goes straight to the mantel, traces a finger along the lines of the carved wood.

Nellie hears a creak, turns, and sees the door across the hall drifting open. Some trick of pressure, gravity, yet she goes to it right away, as if invited. Remembering the colored squares of glass in the tall windows, leaded panes that caught the sun and turned the room into a kaleidoscope of yellows, reds, and greens. Floor-to-ceiling bookshelves of red cedar line the walls, sheeted over, brimming with books and cobwebs. A tall, crude ladder leans in a corner, no rail or tracks to hook it on, just bits of pine hammered together with square-cut nails. Nellie shines the Maglite around. As with the parlor, there's not much furniture in Redfern Hill's library, just an old wingback chair covered in a dirty towel, the arm spitting stuffing, beside it a floor lamp, its antique globe home to a spider. Lightning flickers through a crack in heavy, dark drapery. The windows, colored or clear, are all hidden. Nellie's light falls on a Victorian writing desk at the east-facing window. A woman's desk. *Euphemia*, Nellie thinks. Her grandmother. Long dead before Nellie was born. *I stood here that summer. This was* her room—

"Mom?" Max, ashen faced, stands in the hallway. "I thought I had to pee. I don't now." He points to a door just down from the library, a narrow bathroom.

When Nellie steps inside it, the smell hits her like a hammer. Something foul, something dead. One hand over her mouth, she toggles the light switch.

"It doesn't work," Max says. He clutches his spiral-bound sketchbook to his chest like a shield.

Nellie's flashlight catches a jagged hole in the ceiling of the small room, like the empty socket of a tooth, a tangle of wires hanging down, each wire a curl of shadow. She plays the beam down to the sink, the toilet in the corner. A chain pull with a black iron box mounted high on the wall, two black pipes running down, corrosion at the joints, the toilet itself like some weird toadstool, sprung out of the cracked tile floor. The seat is up.

She gags, one hand over her mouth. "Jesus."

Inside, a rat spoons the shallow bowl, half-submerged in rust-colored water. Its eyes are empty sockets, its lips drawn back from its teeth. Spindly fibers—mold, hair, guts—trail and corkscrew beneath the bloated tuber of its body.

"Give me a sheet of paper," she manages, stuffing her face in the crook of her elbow.

Max tears a handful of pages from his sketchbook.

Swallowing her gorge, holding her breath, doubled-up sheets of 60 lb. 400 series in hand, she reaches, slowly, into the bowl. Eyes fixed on a fat gray tail, curling up the porcelain.

At the parlor window, Max draws back the heavy drapes to watch Nellie in the bright, electric day of the lightning, rat in hand, arm thrust away from her, plank straight, as she heads for the barbwire fence. Beyond it the hayfield and the old, forlorn motor home slumped beneath the boughs of a black walnut tree. What was it like to be an old man and live all alone in an old RV? To die alone, too. Would his own dad die alone, now that he and Nellie were gone? Max's stomach churns, just thinking about it. In the lightning flashes, he sees his mother toss the rat over the barbwire and start back for the house.

A peal of thunder causes the sheeted piano behind him to hum a single, faint note.

It makes him whirl, raises gooseflesh on his arms, until he realizes the phantom note was a trick of the thunder. Like glass shuddering in a window.

Slowly, he crosses the room and tugs the sheet from the piano to the floor.

The casing is black, flawless, gilded with the letters of a German name he can't pronounce. He runs a hand over yellowed keys and plunks his index finger down far left of middle C. A bass note thrums in the silence of the house.

The front door opens.

He takes his finger away. Listening. There's a sound, a faint scrabbling in the walls. Brief, then gone. What moves in the innermost parts of a house, Max wonders, the places we never see? Scuttling among wire and web?

From the parlor door, Nellie says, "Let's check out the other rooms."

He turns back to the piano, strikes a key an octave lower, but the key is broken, makes only a soft clack. "Sure."

Moving deeper into the old farmhouse, Nellie remembers. The summer of 1975. Wandering through the house, her grandfather off in the woods, who knew where. Fourteen years later, the place is just as hot and stifling and empty of life, but there's something else now, something worse: it feels as if each room has been ransacked, pillaged. Stripped?

Devoid. That's the word she's looking for. Each room is *devoid* of . . . something.

In the dining room, for example, down the hall from the bathroom—

(rat-room)

—there is no table and there are no chairs, just four varnished legs in the center of the floor like gnawed bones in an animal's den.

At the end of the hall is a cased opening into the kitchen, where the hardwood floor gives way to uneven brick. Nellie turns on the overhead light, a whale-oil lamp wired for a single bulb. Here are cabinets missing doors. Iron brackets studding the walls, empty of shelves. An old Frigidaire stands unplugged in a corner, the door cracked open and spilling a litter of dead bugs. The only remaining evidence that once this was someone's kitchen? A Formica table and two chairs in front of a picture window.

A peal of thunder—getting closer now—rattles the glass.

Like astronauts exploring a derelict spacecraft, they drift on, back into the hallway. On their right, a door so narrow Nellie misses it. Max doesn't. He pulls the metal latch, and the door swings open on a closet not much wider than the boy's shoulders. Nellie shines her flashlight into the space. A pantry. Shelves missing here, too. A few ancient cans of Vienna sausages scattered on the floor.

The door to the room behind the stairs—the last of the downstairs rooms they've yet to enter—is shut. Nellie's about to open it when Max asks, "What about that?" and points at the back of the stairs.

A little half door is cut into the boards there, held shut with a simple eye hook and latch.

Nellie stares at the tiny door for a long time. Ghost of a memory: her grandfather's gloved hand falling on her shoulder as she stood on this very spot, fourteen years ago. Like her feet had grown roots. Staring at the door. Heart pounding. Listening. *Listening for what?* For a—

(Did you hear it?)

—voice.

"That's the cellar." She looks away.

She turns the doorknob of the last downstairs room, half expecting it to be locked. But it swings in with a long creak. Lightning stutters through tall, bare windows, revealing misshapen, unnatural forms. As Nellie fumbles for the rotary switch, a thought skitters through Max's head: *This room will tell the story.*

Overhead, a wooden candelabra flares to life.

Nellie gasps.

Max says, "Holy shit." Then: "Sorry, Mom."

"It's okay. You took the words right out of my mouth."

The room is a labyrinth of junk. Heaps of cardboard boxes stacked three and four high along the walls, packed with screws and rusty nails and electrical cords, lengths of chain and bits of twine, hoops of metal. Scattered across a long, wide table at the center of the room are upended drawers of forks, spoons, knives. The kitchen's missing wooden shelves and cabinet doors, books from the bookcases in the library, strewn over the table and floor. Crates of dishes, pots, pans. A stack of big band records, a Victorian phonograph, wire egg baskets filled with apothecary bottles. Two rosewood armchairs, broken and gutted. The dining room's missing table, upended against a window. Beneath the windows: six plastic five-gallon buckets, each filled, inexplicably, with pine cones. A jagged hole in the wall, where the boards have been pried loose, frame wood visible through the gaps, pearled with resin, and tufts of vermiculite insulation.

"Was it like this before?" When Nellie doesn't answer, Max looks at her, and finally, she shakes her head, eyes fixed on the floor.

She bends over, picks up something from beneath a heap of old magazines.

An ax. Short handled. Its blade curved like a crescent moon.

Along the inner wall, behind a fall of beer cans and trash bags filled with pine straw, is a high, unfinished shelf of cubbyholes, each packed with rolled paper. Max touches the end of a roll, the paper yellowed, brittle. "What are these?"

"Maps. Architectural plans. Drawings."

"Drawings of what?"

"Forests. The land."

They forge a path to the wall that abuts the piano room, to an old oak desk heaped with ancient issues of the *Empire Courier* and *The Baxter County Shopper. National Geographic, Life. The Georgia Journal of Land Management*. Fixed to the wall above the desk is a framed map, hand drawn on yellowing paper, and above this, two massive crosscut saws. Max has seen similar saws at craft fairs and antique malls, either dull and rusted or painted with barns and cows to look friendly. But these are neither friendly nor dull: both gleam as new as the day they were forged, each a shark's grin of teeth. Looking at them, he can almost hear the crunch of bone, see the cloud of blood.

Nellie uses the crescent ax to rake the newspapers and magazines off the desk onto the floor. Max dances back as they all come avalanching over the side.

"Mom? What the heck?"

But she's already turned and is reaching up to lift the big framed map from its nail. It's heavy, unwieldy. She wobbles it down to the desktop and lays it flat. Bends over it to brush dust and blow it clear. Max sidles up beside her and she drapes an arm over his shoulders. "Your great-grandfather drew this. It's more than just a map, see?" She points to the house and barn, the hayfield. "See the details?"

Little chickens in back of the barn.

Tiny rocks stippled on the porch columns.

"To the south, the turpentine mill." She points to inky-black smoke rising from the distillery's chimney, where it's nestled in a grove of hickory and sycamore. "You can practically count the bricks in the furnace."

A cluster of men are rolling barrels up a ramp, and it all reminds Max of the picture books he loved as a child, cross-sections of buildings where little cartoon people live their lives, watching TV and cooking meals and reading books with their feet up. Turn the page and there they are again, in miniature, their stories each but one small part of the story of a whole city, where a few streets over, firefighters are saving kittens from trees and policemen are arresting bank robbers.

"This is Camp Road," Nellie says. "Along the river." Here, a mule pulls a cart of steel-hooped casks out of a grove of longleaf pines, where tiny men in overalls are hacking at the trees. "They're cutting cat faces. They call them that because—"

"Because they look like cats," Max says, peering closer.

Nellie traces Camp Road with her finger, to a cluster of cabins in a clearing, where there are cook fires and pigs in pens and a girl at a well, her hair drawn back and tied.

"Isn't it beautiful," Nellie says.

Heading up the narrow staircase is like passing through a blast furnace. At the top, Max turns another rotary switch, and the walls along the low-ceilinged corridor flare to life, studded with high brass sconces. Nellie tucks the Maglite into the waistband of her jeans and hangs her denim jacket on the newel at the head of the stairs, then pinches her T-shirt beneath her breasts to flap a breeze. Four bedrooms here, two on the left, two on the right—an exact replica of the first-floor footprint. A long master bath at the head of the stairs connects to the master bedroom.

"Mom? I've gotta pee. For real this time."

She finds the light in the bathroom. Mold streaks the walls and there's mildew in the sink, but nothing dead in the toilet or tub. "All clear," she tells him, then walks on through to the master bedroom.

A four-poster bed dominates the room, at its foot a wide cedar chest. An oak armoire stands on the inside wall, a dressing table beneath the window. Both are sheeted, cobwebs like bunting across the ceiling. Nellie draws the sheet away from the dressing table, finds only dust rings beneath—shapes of perfume bottles, a mirrored tray, a hairbrush. All missing. Removed. The fireplace mantel is bare of trinkets, and the windows that look out on the yard are shuttered. She opens the armoire. It's empty, save for half a dozen wire hangers.

On the far wall, an adjoining door opens into a nursery. Two cribs in clear view of the poster bed. A framed child's prayer hangs over them, embroidered on a square of fabric. "Now I Lay Me Down to Sleep." A prayer Nellie's own mother taught her when she was little. A prayer she sometimes still recites, on nights when her mind cannot rest. Wade in bed beside her. *If I should die before I wake—*

Briefly, she feels a phantom itch from wrist to elbow. Her scar.

In addition to the cribs, she remembers a hutch of folded quilts, a floor scattered with building blocks, a rocking horse made of pine. But now the nursery is as barren as the downstairs dining room—

At the far end of the hallway, the toilet flushes.

Nellie rubs her arm, crosses to the bedroom opposite the nursery.

Immediately, she sees the rag doll on the floor. Hair of yellow yarn in pigtails, black button eyes. She bends to pick it up, brushes the dust from its plaid skirt, holds it to her chest. A room as plain as all the others. Bare board walls and an iron-frame bedstead, its feather mattress sagging. Twin hurricane lamps on a pair of rough-hewn bedside tables, each furred with a decades-old layer of dust.

She walks through an adjoining door into the next room and realizes, suddenly, what bedroom she's in. She clutches the rag doll to her breast, heart beating so hard she can hear it in her temples. She had the same reaction when she was sixteen—

A deer's head is mounted above the armoire, a coonskin cap

dangling from a horn. Strangely, the narrow bed is made, an afghan folded across its foot. A row of hand-painted metal soldiers stands in a crooked line along the sill of the room's one window, cowboys and Indians, sailors and doughboys. A pair of boy's boots—scuffed and worn—are set upright beside an old cedar chest. The laces, she remembers, how thick they were, how stubborn.

"Whose room was this?" Max, from the doorway.

"My dad's," she says, trying to imagine the boy who once sat at the little rolltop desk in the corner, where a crooked stack of canvas-backed primers waits to be opened. Hank Redfern, the maudlin drunk, once her son's age? Impossible, it seems. The room offers no explanations, no insights. She looks down at the doll in her hands. "He had a baby sister. Her name was Agatha. I think it was her room, next door."

Max crosses to the window, looks out where the porch roof extends, the branches of a huge magnolia tree within reach of the eave. A sudden clap of thunder rattles the glass, and in the lightning that follows Max says, "Hey, what is that out there? It's huge!"

"You mean the fire tower," Nellie says.

She flicks the twin latches, raises the sash, and together, they peer up at a latticework of steel even taller than the great magnolia, Max's eyes gleaming with the light of a boy doing boy geometry, figuring angles and squares and degrees of daring. It's a light she hasn't seen in a long time. A light Wade Gardner had all but snuffed—

"When do I get to meet your dad?"

Nellie stiffens a little—she can't help it—then kisses the top of his head roughly. Wishing, briefly, for a world without the burden of fathers. A world especially made for mothers and sons. "We'll see."

They stand together in the storm-cooled breeze, waiting for the rain.

Later.

The lights in the house are off, save a mismatched pair of midcentury lamps Max brought into the parlor and set on the floor. He'd found them in the map room. He'd promised, through a yawn, to find tables, come the morning. Now, he sleeps on the sofa with his head on Nellie's thigh, and Nellie sits staring at the contents of the manila envelope, emptied onto the hardwood floor: deed to the house and property plus a small stack of papers signed and resigned and notarized, one house key, one RV key, two gate keys, and two business cards, the lawyer's and one belonging to a VP at First Empire Savings and Loan.

Nellie opens her purse, takes stock of what's there: a tube of lipstick, a compact, her driver's license, three emergency tampons, and nine bucks in cash.

First thing in the morning, get the truck out of the ditch.

After that, burn up the last of her cash on coffee, orange juice, and Egg McMuffins. Then the bank.

A plan, but still: she can't sleep.

Nothing new. It's been this way for months, every night lying awake in bed as if some terrible tide's at work in her, drawing her in, drawing her out, a ceaseless, restless stirring. The fear of waking to a new day only to find it's the same as yesterday. A prisoner in her own skin. That old chestnut. But things are different now, aren't they? Here, she isn't a prisoner. It's no palace, sure, just a farmhouse built when the century was new. But it feels huge, if only because her own world has been so small for so long. How many shitty two-bedroom apartments and rental houses had she and Wade lived in, over the years? Once, when things were good and he still had his job in Savannah, they had a trailer, before South Carolina—

Scritch-scritch-scritch.

The sound comes from inside the wall, near the fireplace.

Scritch-scritch-scritch. Like the twisting of a pencil in a child's pencil sharpener.

She sighs. Cocks an ear at the air. She could get up, sure. Investigate. Press her ear to the boards. But Max is fast asleep and she's tired and under no illusions about the number of rodents she's going to have to deal with in the coming weeks and months. Mice, squirrels, trapped birds. Bats in the chimneys. Suddenly, she feels very small and alone in this old house, in a soft circle of lamplight she and her boy have set down like fire in a cave.

One last *scritch*, then the sound stops.

She twines her fingers in Max's hair.

Max's sketchbook is on the floor, beneath the deed to Redfern Hill. She picks it up and flips through it. The first few pages are animal figures, copied in pencil from a how-to book she gave him a few years back. An elephant charging in a flurry of dust, head and shoulders of a tiger. Childlike, but with an eye for what counts, those places where expression and heart reside. Did she bring his oil pastels? She can't remember. Back home—

(Back in South Carolina, you mean, because here *is home now, Nellie.)*

—his art supplies were stored in trunks and boxes and closet bins. She'd grabbed what she could. The last few pages are all He-Men and Beast Men, superheroes flying, leaping, crouching, punching. Muscles and capes, swords and axes, the odd machine gun: aggression channeled from the heart to the fist in service of good. A boy's fantasy of manhood.

The reality?

Wade Gardner.

What had she told Wade, about her past? Even now, was he lying awake, dredging those long-ago, late-night conversations from the early months of their courtship? Stuff about her mother, her father? Was it enough to find them? She doesn't think so. Several months back, she'd found Meadows's letter in a stack of bills less than half an hour before Wade got home from teaching. Just long enough to read it, throw up, read it again, and hide it inside the frame of a painting, a portrait of Max at six or seven. That's when the sleepless nights began. When suddenly there were possibilities, choices, and with them all the traps and dangers of what could go wrong.

But what if Wade isn't the problem anymore?

What if running with Max is just the first in a scree of mistakes, soon to become an avalanche that will bury them both?

(And when the dust settles, it'll be you, Nervous Nellie, his own mother, standing at the edge of the cliff. The one who set it all tumbling down.)

Beneath her breath: "Bullshit."

Life with Wade Gardner had been its own ten-year rock slide, hadn't it, culminating in that awful day last February, a week or so after Meadows's letter came, when she wasn't home. The day of the Lesson. The day that made up her mind, once and for all, to get the hell out. She remembers how, that week, when Wade was home watching sports or grading papers or pounding out poems on his IBM Selectric, Max had spent hours on the swings in the backyard, nose stuck in some paperback he'd no doubt read ten times before, as if some new conflict could emerge in a story he already knew by heart. His nose and face still bruised and swollen. She thinks of all the things she wants for Max, has hoped he'll have since the day he was born—

(Really, Nellie? Since the day he was born? Is that what we're telling ourselves nowadays? Even when that long scar on your arm starts to itch, and you'd like nothing more than to make it a matched set, you're still singing that tune?)

—but he's already eleven, and eleven is a fulcrum, when the balance tips, and everything changes.

Just like it changed for her, here in Empire—

(Empire, I never said that name to Wade, did I?)

—when she was sixteen and her mother died and her father lost all hope at the bottom of a bottle. But here, now, in this house, this *sanctuary*, things will be different. Here—

(Will they?)

—she won't make the same mistakes.

(Won't you?)

Here. In her house.

She switches off the lamps, and soon after, sleep does find her, as outside, the storm rumbles on by, without shedding a single drop of rain. And somewhere in the dark of her dreams, she hears that sound again. Steady as the metronome of her own heart.

Scritch-scritch-scritch.

1917

✦

NOVEMBER 2

AUGUST REDFERN DREAMS THAT EUPHEMIA IS LOST. LOST IN the old forest, above North Creek. He's stumbling among the tangled hammock and moss beds, calling her name. Catching, by and by, fleeting glimpses of her, white and apparition-like. A crane taking wing as the land gives way to swamp and the Altamaha floods inward, alligators lurking primordial, watching him pass as he staggers up, up, up the rising slope of the land, to a wire-grass clearing where, in the upper reaches of a high lone pine, he finds her: naked, trim, beautiful. She stands in the remnants of a giant bird's nest, in her hands something small, something wriggling. Helpless, he calls to her, but her eyes are cold, the color of hardened resin. The thing in her arms, bloody and slick and spasming, cries out like a bird. She lifts it to her mouth. Pushes it in, one pale leg at a time—

He wakes. The mattress beside him empty.

Christ. His eyes are gummed. Was he whimpering?

The ache of a full bladder drives him to the edge of the bed. On the table, his pocket watch tells the time as half past six. The light outside is faint but growing, the pine tops beyond the meadow rimmed in amber. He sits naked, looking out through the muslin-draped window to the yard along the southern side of the house, where half a dozen wooden planks are sunk end to end in the mud, bridging a path from the workers' carts to the front-porch steps. The carts are piled high with milled lumber and river rocks.

He sees her, in her housecoat and mud boots, at the edge of the meadow. Peering down into the lens of the Kodak Brownie, which rests upon the swell of her belly. He imagines the photograph she's after: the farmhouse bathed in morning sun as the world forms itself anew.

Redfern walks into the bathroom, white hexagonal tiles cold against his bare feet, and urinates. He pulls on a pair of trousers and an undershirt, walks down the hall, looks in on the nursery, at the progress she's made. A piece of embroidery recently framed. Wooden blocks, a rocking horse. A paper mobile above the crib and a cubby in a corner where little quilts are folded. *A steadily growing cairn beneath which I will one day be buried*, he thinks. It isn't supposed to feel like this.

He'll never tell her about it, his fear of this sunlit space.

Downstairs, he pours two cups of coffee and walks them out onto the porch. By then, Euphemia is lining up a shot in the newly graveled drive. The barn, maybe. He holds her coffee aloft and she waves. Seconds later she's barefoot on the porch, muddy boots set neatly at the bottommost step. She stretches, hands in the small of her back, belly pushing at her buttoned housecoat. The camera hangs from a strap around her neck. She's smiling as she takes her coffee. "Your beautiful bride. Swollen ankles, swollen fingers." She walks barefoot across the boards and slips his free arm over her shoulder, curls it across her breasts. Draws him to the balustrade and grips his arm in a slant of sunlight, his muscles hard and satisfying to hold. She sips her coffee.

Redfern drinks his own, dropping his arm to run his hand over the swell of her, so close now. She leans back into him, breathes in his scent: yesterday's pine and smoke.

"You smell like some wild thing."

"It'll fade."

"I hope not."

"Pretty soon I'll smell like money."

"You were dreaming again. All night, it seemed. Do you remember any of it?"

He says, "Some of it was about you," and kisses her ear before he steps away to the far end of the porch. "I like to look at them," he tells her, meaning the woods. Smoke curls from the tree line, yesterday's burn the first of many they'll make. "I was thinking of putting in a tower, behind the house. So we can see it all. We'll burn more, after the thaw. Between the camp and North Creek. Way up there, you know."

Way up where I dreamed you were a bird, nesting in a tree, devouring your child.

"What time is Barlow due?" she asks.

"Soon."

She puts her coffee on the railing and slips behind him, slides her hands into his pockets.

"Fishing for change?"

She presses her cheek into his back.

He turns to look at her. Her dark hair falls to her shoulders in rings, framing a face that's oval and flushed. Seventeen years old. Beautiful and lonely. He eyes her belly. She won't be lonely much longer. But the thought brings little comfort. She's a sober, smart girl, so *alive*, too alive, maybe, to be saddled with this—

"Who needs money," she says. "You're all the rich I need."

"Lucky for you." He kisses the top of her head, then takes his hand from the small of her back. He steps away from her, tosses the rest of his coffee. "Busy morning," he says, a half apology.

"Wait." She grabs her camera from the porch floor. "Take my picture."

"I don't know anything about that contraption."

"I want you to have a picture of me, to carry with you." Her smile is tentative, fearful he'll refuse, call her foolish.

He remembers his dream, the terror of crashing after her through the underbrush, no sign of her anywhere. "What do I do?"

She extends the bellows, shows him where to look, what to push.

She stands by the rock column, where the sun can hit her, one hand beneath the curve of her belly.

He peers at her through the lens, which makes the world around her fall away, reduces her to a single point of focus: Euphemia Redfern, his wife, and Redfern Hill behind her. A world of his own making.

The shutter clicks.

He hands her the camera, kisses her cheek, and goes inside.

Euphemia watches dawn break fully over the trees, tries to imagine what it will all look like from high up, if August builds his tower: the woods, the river, the fires her husband has set to clear the land and make way for the cutting, the scraping. One thousand acres. She holds her belly and wishes to be more than what she is. Not to be August Redfern's wife, mother of his heirs, but to be his partner.

She hears the distant clop of a horse down the gravel lane.

Barlow.

She goes inside and shuts the parlor windows against the smoke.

_____

Upstairs, in the bedroom, Redfern dresses before a full-length mirror. Pulls on an umber twill shirt, over it a vest, a union suit coat. The clothes are laundered, pressed. He does not wear a tie. His jaw is set, firm, shadowed with razor stubble. His mustache thin and oiled. From a cigar box on the bureau, he removes a gold watch and chain and threads the chain through his vest.

He is twenty-six years old, soon twenty-seven. Not Southern by birth, so he holds no convictions about heritage, no entitlements through myth. All the legacy he knows is that of a drunken, gambling father who died alone in a Boston street, trampled to death beneath an oxcart, and an Irish Catholic mother who nightly prayed for the old man's lush soul until a blood vessel burst in her head and she keeled over in the kitchen of a lawyer's house, where she'd cooked three meals a day, six days a week, for half her life. Redfern was sixteen, no brothers, no sisters. Had a shitty job as a dockworker unloading freight. After the funeral— a dismal, lonely affair at a dockside crematorium—he signed on with a whaling crew and sailed the North Atlantic, saw Newfoundland, Nova Scotia. Harvested blubber in the corpses of sperm whales. By nineteen, his knuckles were knots of rope and his hair was bleached by the sun and salt air. At twenty-two, he fell out with a girl in New Bedford and made his way south by land, working odd jobs as a bricklayer, a carpenter, a tinker. In North Carolina, he took up with a rich widow and lived six months in luxury, gaining a taste for Kentucky bourbon and sherry and smart polished boots. In Tennessee, he got on with a stonemason's outfit and helped build an amphitheater in the side of a mountain where a band of Holy Rollers set up church. By the time he arrived in Georgia at twenty-four, he wanted something solid beneath his boots, a place to call his own. He wanted land. What he would do with it, he had no idea.

He went south from Savannah by horse, over coastal plains and marshes thick with mayflies that hung upon his eyelashes and bit his neck. He caught a fever in a boardinghouse that overlooked the port at Brunswick, and there, in the throes of delirium, he saw two thousand barrels of distilled turpentine waiting to be shipped, a king's ransom heaped on the docks.

Not long after, he journeyed inland, over vast tracts of longleaf wilderness, the very pines that had produced the turpentine that had sparked his imagination. He apprenticed, for a while, at a mill in Jesup, where he learned the trade: notching, cutting, boxing, harvesting. Distilling. Later, he settled quietly into a job at Baxter Millworks in the nearby town of Empire.

There, he caught George Baxter's ear. They shared New England, the open sea. The old man had been a steamship engineer in his twenties, had sailed the Atlantic from New York to Miami. He had what the washerwomen at Redfern's boardinghouse called a Yankee's imperial bearing. Notions of dynasty. And while Redfern himself came from nothing like that, he did possess a young man's simmering contempt for any who did not respect the gleam of his own convictions, and in this, perhaps, George Baxter saw their kinship.

He invited Redfern to his home, and it was there, in a wifeless mansion upon a dismal, muddy river, that August met Euphemia Baxter, her nose in a book. She was young enough to know nothing of the world but savvy enough to be wary of men who did. August claimed knowledge of nothing save his own heart. She fell in love with him quick enough. Soon after, August Redfern rode out on horseback with the man who would become his father-in-law, some miles from town, along a virgin stretch of the Altamaha. They walked among the pines that would be Euphemia's dowry, and at long last Redfern's own heart was snared and settled, here in this old dark wood.

The last few hours of that day, above North Creek, climbing out of the trees onto a sandy ridge where low turkey oaks grew among the odd longleaf pine, George Baxter said: *Roots. Roots here go deeper than you can imagine, August. Appease them and you'll recoup your money soon enough. I promise you that. In these woods, there's no end to the riches a man can know.*

In the bedroom, August snaps open the watch on its chain. It's time.

Downstairs, Euphemia meets him in the foyer. He kisses her sweetly.

"Barlow's here," she says.

"I love you," he tells her.

He snags his fedora from its hook by the door, inspects himself in the mirror above the little hall table. He tucks his head into the hat, pulls it tight, then slides a hand along the brim.

Out at the barn, Barlow—short, stout, in a gray suit and tan bowler—sits on his horse, eating a banana. He's already saddled Redfern's mount, its reins looped around the pommel of his saddle. Barlow eats the banana with his good hand, hands over the reins with his left, from which the middle three fingers are missing.

Together, they head off down a new wagon trail, into the smoky woods.

The camp is a little over a mile from the house. It consists of a dozen two-room cabins, built in concentric rings of six in a stump-strewn clearing. Among the stumps are two dozen men, congregated loosely by race, all eyes on Redfern, who sits on the largest stump in a shaft of mote-spun sunlight. He peels a length of hickory with a pocketknife, the toes of his calf-high boots covered in shavings. Waiting, as Barlow goes among the men, taking down names on a clipboard balanced on his thumb and pinkie.

Like Redfern's house, the cabins are cut from the pines of these thirteen acres, each with a little porch and a stovepipe and a ready stack of split wood along its eastern wall. There are no windows. Behind the second row of cabins, where the woods give way to the old forest, are three outhouses, each with a carved half-moon in the door.

When Barlow finally tucks his pencil behind his ear, Redfern puts away his knife. He brushes the seat of his pants where the resin has stuck and mounts his stump and stands there, as the men fall silent. He speaks in a loud, clear voice, Adam's apple working like a piston. From time to time, he gestures, points, with the stick.

"I am August Redfern and I do not pay by piecework. I pay by the hour. To men of all colors, I pay the same. I am not a Southerner by birth, nor in practice, and I do not hold with the separation of the races. I come from New England, where I sailed the waters off Nantucket and once cut open a whale from the inside out. I've worked a rope until my hands bled alongside all manner of men, men whose worth was judged by the work of their hands. Their hearts. A man's dignity is his own to earn by the sweat of his brow. Because I believe this, there will be no company store to return your wages to. No gambling tents. No whores. What you earn, you keep. You may, of course, spend it however you see fit, but I do not contrive to rob you. If you wish to be robbed, the town of Empire is not so far away, and the river yonder runs right to it."

"Goddamn a-men," someone says.

"These woods will be home to you—and to your families, if you have them. You may cultivate small crops on my land. Corn, tomatoes, collards, yams. Buy a coon dog and hunt bear and deer and boar, if you like. Or raise pigs. All I ask in tribute is a full day's work. Six out of seven in spring and summer. Five in fall and winter. It's three men to a cabin, or one family per. Those of you without wives or daughters will be gentlemen around the ladies. Those of you with wives will be all the richer, for the wife of the man who works for me will have far softer hands than she who's bent beneath the pines a-chipping and dipping. Softer hands to work the bread. And other things."

Laughter, like a charge set off among them.

"One other thing, gentlemen." Redfern lets them quiet before he says, "These woods are old. So keep to the paths you know and do not, under any circumstances, venture beyond the North Creek. There are no paths there. Men get lost in these woods. Any questions?"

Silence. Then: "How'd you come by em?"

"What's that?"

A man in dirty field clothes and an old Confederate coat, too big for him, steps forward. His hair is stringy, his face long boned. His eyes pop like peeled eggs. "I said how'd you come by these woods?"

Redfern smiles. "I married the right woman."

A ripple of laughter passes among the men.

The man with the long hair doesn't laugh. He makes an antsy shuffle, hands in his coat pockets. "I know these woods." He points across the clearing, toward the river. The woods beyond it. "My daddy had fifty acres here. Was in my family since the country was new. Then George Baxter come down like the carpetbagging jackal he is and took it. Paid my daddy ten cents per acre, after the war. Said we could stay on our place as long as we want. Then came that sawmill, and George Baxter says we got to go." The man hops up on a stump himself and turns to address the crowd. "So I come here today to let you all know, this is who you're signing up with. This man here, he talks about dignity, but where was my daddy's dignity when he put a shotgun in his mouth two winters past? When ever dime he ever earned was spent on lawyers and courts just as crooked and rigged as them what won the war?"

Redfern's eyes slide over the men. They're tense, like a smattering of birds at seed, sensing a cat in the grass. He speaks softly. "What's your daddy's name?"

"Hawley."

"And yours?"

"Jasper Hawley. Folks call me Catfish."

"Well, Mr. Hawley, I'd say your quarrel is not with me but with my father-in-law."

Hawley shakes his head. "Naw, sir." His left hand leaves his coat pocket, gripping an old cap-and-ball revolver. "My quarrel is with *all* you bastards."

The men scatter, but Redfern doesn't move.

The pistol is cocked. Hawley's finger trembles at the trigger.

Redfern has a macabre impulse to check his watch, note the time.

The finger tenses, moves—

Barlow, Redfern's cat in the grass, rears up on Hawley's left and jams the curve of his maimed hand between the hammer and the percussion cap, and with his right lays a blackjack across the base of the man's skull, a blow that lands him on his knees in the mulch. Barlow slips the pistol out of Hawley's hand, tucks it into the waist of his trousers.

"This is Mr. Barlow," Redfern says to the men. "He is my horseman and will oversee your work."

Mutters and stirring, as the men regain themselves.

Apart from the rest, a tall, dark-skinned man with white hair settles his hands in the bib of a pair of threadbare overalls, one strap held with a safety pin. The old man watches the goings-on like a hawk on a wire. His two teenage sons stand beside him, the oldest watching Barlow, the blackjack that slips deftly out of sight.

"I may own the land," Redfern says, "but you men possess the hearts to work it. Poor Mr. Hawley here has alluded to the rotten truth of it: it's all about money. I can't change the past, friends, but I can promise a better future. Set up your own operation, you'll cut boxes, chip and dip all day, and at the end of a week of such days, you will owe your dollars to the son of a bitch who rented you the trees. It will be cash lost at every stage of the enterprise, as you are forced to pay a cheat to bring your heart's work to market. And if you float or cart your gum and scrape to a buyer like me, I will have none of it, because it will be inferior in quality. So, I say to you, is it not wiser to work for the man who owns the land, out of which grow the trees, out of which bleeds the gum? He who promises men like you fair and equal treatment, along with decent wages and steady work? The difference between living and subsistence. In a word, gentlemen, dignity."

Redfern's eyes pass over the men. He has them. They will all sign up.

"Two of you," Barlow barks, "to help me throw this load of Catfish in the wagon."

In the end, the taller of the brothers is the first to answer. His father's eyes slide sideways, watch him step out. "Eli," the young man says to Redfern. "Eli Green."

"Who will join Mr. Barlow and Mr. Green?"

A young boy, rangy and dimpled and pale skinned, with hair the color of straw, steps up. "I'm Marcus," the boy says, then adds: "I'm Swedish," and just like that, in the weeks ahead, he will be known, simply and fondly, as the Swede.

Marcus and Eli each take up an arm, and they follow Barlow into the trees, where the flatbed wagon that brought the men from town waits to return any who decide not to stay. In its seat, an old-timer sipping whiskey from a bottle. Ahead of it, a team of mules cropping the dry fall grass. They heave Hawley into the bed, roll him faceup, and leave him.

"Today," Redfern says, "we get you settled. Tomorrow, we start."

1989

JULY 1

THIN, DISHWATER LIGHT STEALS BETWEEN THE DARK DRAPERY, touching Nellie's cheek. Her socked feet hang over the edge of the sofa, where Max's head is pushed up into the corner, his nose buried in the musty green fabric. Nellie sits up, yawns, springs creaking beneath her. She pads from window to window, drawing drapes and raising sashes. Max doesn't wake, so she laces her sneakers and steps out onto the porch. She puts her hands in the small of her back and stretches, then drops to the boards on palms and toes. Fifty push-ups, each morning, to kick the self-pity and self-doubt in the ass. She counts them down, arms and shoulders working like pistons. After, she sits on the steps to catch her breath and looks out at the dewy yard, the hayfield waist-high, draped in mist. Beyond it, the Winnebago and its rickety, homemade porch.

Heart rate ticking down, she walks out into the drive and looks up at the house, sees white paint flaking, gray board showing through. Rotted eaves. Shrubbery wild and ragged. Scant patches of centipede grass choked with alien stalks of thistle and weed. Ropy green briars along the western corner, pushing between boards and bowing them out. A beard of poison ivy rims the windows, all the way up. She remembers a spring back in South Carolina when Max was little and the old man next door had burned poison ivy, the smoke wafting through their yard as Max burbled on a blanket outside. At supper that night, his eyes were red. After midnight, he woke Nellie screaming in his crib. Eyes crusted shut.

She walks the footprint of the house. Under crape myrtles and past a fat butane tank to the tower, fifty feet of rusting steel, anchored in concrete with an open observation deck at the top. The magnolia tree beside it, making the backyard a litter of leaves that crunch like tiny bones. Around to the northern side, where the porch wraps and long, narrow windows are set into the brick, just below ground level. The cellar. She passes these quickly, not even a sideways glance.

Out at the barn, she hauls open the heavy door on a row of wide, gloomy stalls, a corncrib in back. She pushes through the rear door, and there, among the weeds and tangles of rusty wire left over from an old chicken coop, she finds a stack of weathered lumber, grown over with cross vine. She pulls several boards free, finds the two sturdiest, and hefts them onto her shoulder across the road and into the field, her plan to angle through the woods and cut the trip to the Ranger in half. A path that carries her, inevitably, past the black walnut tree and the Winnebago.

Here, she stops and leans each board against the Winnie's front right fender. Staring, unbelieving, at the small patch of dirt that was her grandfather's world. A ten-foot square of Astroturf covers the ground beneath the porch, a hole cut in the center where he planted his potbellied stove and ran a pipe from the tin-covered roof. Near the stove, his old recliner, covered in rags and duct tape and set on a threadbare Turkish rug, the broken carapaces of palmetto bugs caught in the fringe. Firewood stacked alongside the RV, beetles and termites working unseen in the rotten bark, little copperheads sleeping in tight balls. Overhead, a network of electrical wiring is strung through frame boards, terminating in a hanging outlet and a light bulb backed by an aluminum pie plate.

Nellie reaches for the latch of the Winnebago's door. Expecting it will be locked. The key ring Meadows gave her, she left it at the house—

It opens.

Rank smell of old carpet. The light dim. Front windshield still blacked out with aerosol paint and the captain's chair piled high with old clothes and bath towels reeking of mildew. From the galley to the bedroom, the linoleum is littered with broken peanut hulls and lozenge and foil gum wrappers, cigarette ash and crumpled cellophane and, here and there, the cigarette boxes themselves. The ceiling is yellowed and the air reeks of Vicks VapoRub and years of nicotine-laced smoke—smells that take her back, instantly, to her mother's sickbed. In the rear of the RV, she can see a bedside table brimming with little glass bottles of Bufferin, Mercurochrome, Formula 44. Well-thumbed jars of Vaseline and Mentholatum and half a dozen crusted bottles of Caladryl.

She remembers how she'd cleaned this place, her second day here. Took out all the clothes, hung them on the barbwire. Swept. Washed. Even cooked. She'd really pissed the old man off. Now, in the galley sink, there's a heap of dishes in black sludge. On the narrow dinette table that looks out onto the porch: a jar of crystallized honey, an open package of saltine crackers, and a small dead spider, its legs curled inward. A coffee cup, green milk glass, the bottom yet silted, perhaps the last coffee August Redfern ever drank.

She remembers what Meadows told her, how the old man's body was found in his study. *Damndest thing. He used the hall phone to call in a fire, but there never was a fire. Just that bad turpentine smell. He was covered in the stuff. A struck match lying next to him. You'd almost suspect—*

The lawyer's eyes, cutting to the scar on her wrist. The words drying up.

On the dinette table, beneath the coffee cup, is a yellow spiral-bound stenographer's notepad, bent and cracked and coffee ringed. She remembers this notebook. Remembers traipsing behind him in the woods, over fallen logs and green lichen, back humped beneath an old army-surplus pack. He'd stop every fifty, sixty yards, and out would come this notebook. As if it were a watch, or a compass, some precise instrument of measurement. She picks it up, flips through it, sees the creaky lines of crude maps, nonsensical arrows flying in all directions. Far from the elegant, wistful maps he'd shown her from his youth. Squiggles and numbers and unreadable words scrawled in an old man's hand. Dates and years and meaningless letters at the bottom of each page. She comes to a page torn out, bits of fringe still in the rings. She'd written him a note, her last morning here. Sneaking away as he slept. She threw it away. Here, the ghost of it, fourteen years later, no memory of what it was she'd meant to say.

One word is scribbled in the center of the next page.

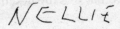

She flips the page.

NELLIE

NELLIE NELLIE

NELLIE NELLIE

NELLIE

NELLIE

NELLIE

And the next page, and the next. Every line, every corner, every centimeter of space.

Her name. As if the old man were desperately trying to remember who she was.

Inside the cardboard back of the notebook, a single image is drawn.

No, not drawn. Smeared.

In red that doesn't look like ink.

She sets the notebook back on the table.
Happy to leave it there.

Boards under her arms, she passes through a thin line of pine and sweet gums onto Redfern Road. She walks quickly, hoping Max snoozes long. Every now and then, off in the woods, the odd crackle of leaves. She ducks a horsefly that pursues her most of the way. After what seems like a long hot time, she rounds a curve and sees the Ranger slumped on the shoulder, back right tire drifted in gravel. Something strikes her as wrong, unexpected. Her gait slows. Then it hits her: the road is empty.

The bear is gone.

Nellie stops. Listens to the still, silent woods. Thinking of the bear zoo Wade took them to when Max was little, some Alpine mountain town. It wasn't a zoo. Just a series of concrete pits that reeked of piss and shit and sad, trapped animals. A man came out, tossed fish from a bucket. The bears looked away. Max was silent the rest of the day.

If it's dead, where is it? Had it crawled off, broken and bloodied?

(Or is it watching you, this very second, from the trees?)

Don't be stupid, she scolds herself.

Still, she walks faster.

When she reaches the Ranger, she works fast, digging out gravel with her hands and chocking the first board behind the right rear wheel, the second in front of it, pausing only to inspect the damage along the fender, where the bear left a dent she'll never be able to bang out herself.

(You deserve worse.)

Wade's voice, or her own?

After eleven years of marriage, it's sometimes hard to tell.

In the woods, a twig snaps.

Nellie spins, gooseflesh breaking out on her arms, hackles on her neck rising.

Ahead of the truck, a doe and her fawn step out onto the road where the bear lay the night before. The fawn's spots are pristine white. It turns its head, just for a second, and locks eyes with Nellie. The mother flicks her ears, and an instant later they've hopped the ditch into the trees.

(Nervous Nellie.)

She gets into the truck, the cab hot and still.

Once the Ranger's unstuck, she digs the boards out of the mud and throws them in the pickup's bed, then makes a U-turn for the house.

At the last bend, before the road angles up to the house, she slows, then stops in the sun-dappled curve. She gets out of the Ranger and rounds the front grill, stands at the edge of the ditch, where she can just make out a narrow path, overgrown with seed grass and knee-high stalks of blue sage, not yet flowering. It's thirty, forty yards through the pines and sycamores to the low stone wall that surrounds the old cemetery. Easily visible from the road, if you know to look for it. Easy, too, to pass right by.

She enters through a break in the wall.

The grass is a tangle of weeds and dandelion stalks, shot through with wild purple verbena. A breeze moves through the treetops, stirs up the scents of pine and honeysuckle.

There are three graves.

The first is marked by a small square of white marble.

CHARLES ELIOT REDFERN

DECEMBER 24, 1917–MAY 4, 1923

Christmas Eve, she thinks. Also her father's birthday.

All she knows of Hank Redfern's twin brother is a name, Charlie, gasped in her father's fitful dreams, him twisted up on the living room couch in the vampire glow of the television. An empty whiskey bottle wedged between his shoulder and the seat cushion.

Farther back, like sentinels standing watch over the smaller grave, are two white obelisks. One features a longleaf pine in relief, at its base the still-mounded earth of her grandfather's grave, covered by a blanket of wild roses. No date is chiseled in the stone.

AUGUST REDFERN

DECEMBER 7, 1890–

Nellie makes a mental note: check the yellow pages for a stone carver.

The inscription at the base of the second obelisk is faded, hard to read. She has to pull away a handful of Virginia creeper.

EUPHEMIA BAXTER REDFERN
MAY 19, 1900–OCTOBER 15, 1932
BELOVED IN LIFE
DEEPLY LAMENTED IN DEATH

She touches the stone, warm with the sun. Runs her fingers over her grandmother's name.

What was it like, to bury your son?

A black-and-yellow grasshopper crawls out of the weeds and up the marble.

Nellie draws back.

The grasshopper sails away, over the wall.

1917

✦

DECEMBER 24

BARLOW ON THE PORCH STEPS, LICKING A HOMEMADE cigarette. Redfern hunkers nearby in the yard, suspenders off his shoulders. Sifting rocks. Lightning jumps among heavy winter clouds. The night is cold, has teeth. Sounds of the birth going hard from the upstairs master bedroom. An Irish woman, one of the camp wives, has come to assist, she and the doctor making a shadow play in the lamplight. A cry from inside makes Barlow flinch, as he draws hot, searing smoke into his lungs. He fishes a flask from his coat pocket. Redfern keeps his eyes fixed on the dark woods below the field. Even when his wife begins to scream.

The midwife's teenage daughter rushes out onto the porch and calls for him.

He plunges past Barlow into the house. Up the stairs and into the bedroom, where the midwife holds out a swaddled twitching lump.

"Here is the first," she says, smiling. Streaked with sweat.

"The first?" Redfern looks up from the baby's face and peers past her, to the bed, where the doctor's arms are thrust beneath a sheet tented over Effie's knees, and Effie's face is a contortion, a terror.

"She's been carrying twins," the midwife says.

Effie screams again.

Euphemia Redfern's mother, a gentle, religious woman, died of typhoid fever when Effie was ten. Her parents had traveled to New Orleans, leaving Effie in the care of her aunt. A second honeymoon, they'd joked, since the Millworks and the building of a house and then, later, a town had never afforded them a proper first. When they returned, Helen Baxter was feverish, and three days later, she wore the telltale rose-colored spots. Effie prayed, nightly, with her mother, and on her own, too. On her knees at her bedside, head thrust down into the quilt, wringing tiny fistfuls of it. "God does not burden us with more than we can bear," her sick mother told her on a Saturday, looking for all the world like a husk, a shell. By Sunday, she was dead. George Baxter's hollow cry carried from her bedside down the stairs and into the kitchen, where the maid clutched Effie as if some mad animal was broken loose in the house.

She made no friends among her cousins who came to visit once or twice a year, or the workers' children at the annual Millworks' picnic. She played alone, read books. Among them the Bible, which, by thirteen, she had read twice. Searching the New Testament through only to realize that her mother's words were not true. Nowhere could she find any guarantee of forbearance. See the example of Christ, who prayed His burden would pass; it did not. In fact, it seemed to Effie, the opposite was true: life's only guarantees were suffering and loneliness and, ultimately, death.

Life's what we make of it, she came to believe. *Nothing more.*

Soon after, she met August, a man dependable and whip smart. Driven, George Baxter remarked to his daughter, like a hurricane bearing down on a stretch of coastline. "Watch out for that one," the old man said. "Anything he sets his mind to, he'll accomplish—or die trying."

To which Euphemia, not yet seventeen, had thought: *I can set my mind to things, too.*

And set her mind, she had, to August Redfern.

Her attraction to him was undeniable. He was handsome, with coarse, strong hands. He walked with them in his pockets, back straight, eyes cast on the ground ahead, as if the immediate future were a constant calibration, the horizon itself impractical to consider.

Those long summer evenings, she kept an open novel or volume of poetry in her hands, drifting past her father's study, August sat there in his threadbare coat, holding a tumbler of bourbon, always the same brown tie, her father extolling through a fog of cigar smoke all the secrets of his lumber trade. August listening like the acolyte of a Greek master. Asking, every now and then, "What other uses? What of turpentine?" Effie, in a high-collared cotton dress with cashmere cuffs, passing endlessly back and forth until, one evening, August's eyes darted her way and she, forever finished with her mother's Bible, turned a page in Shelley. Pretended not to see.

They walked together, along the river, and she wondered, at first, how her father felt anything but lonely around the boy. *He doesn't listen*, she thought. When she said his name, a gentle tug at his attention, he would look at her, crack a wry smile, and ask her to repeat herself. And she would, and this time he would hear, would ask questions or answer hers, and then talk about his seafaring days, the ships he had worked, ports and cities and exotic people, and for a while after, in the quiet they shared, he would be hers and only hers, and in those brief moments she felt as if she could live a lifetime with this man. In these, the loneliness that had enclosed her heart since her mother's death was banished, as a sky clears of thunderheads in the afternoon and the day ends in a cast of gold and red.

Their courtship was brief, the span of a season.

When the redbuds began to bloom in March of 1917, they wed.

They spent their honeymoon overseeing the excavation of the cellar on Redfern Hill, the felling of trees. The planing of boards and the hammering of frames. The house was finished and the roads were plowed. She walked beside him through his woods, grew aware, eventually, that he had once again stopped listening. He had a business to build. Redfern Turpentine would not grow overnight nor would it grow itself. Effie knew this. She made allowances for it. Feigned her part as the blushing young bride, eager to win his affections. A quick smile. A flirtatious caress.

But marriage, she would come to think, in those weeks after the house became livable, was perhaps the greatest lie of God and fathers everywhere: that a woman must be part of some mystic, binary equation, only balanced by a man. There was no balance with August. Pleasure, yes. He was careful, tender. But not long after their courtship, passion was absent, and so was he, most nights, even when he lay beside her. He had fitful dreams, and when they shared the curious, cautious treat of conversation, he would not talk about himself. Only the weather, or the latest numbers from the mill. Soon, she came to loathe the sound of her own voice, flat and dead sounding in the cavernous silence of their new, pine-board house, the scent of resin heady in the emptiness, the long days he was gone, when it was only she and the gloom and the groan of trees in the wind.

In the end, it was the trees August loved. The goddamned trees. Then came the pregnancy.

A nursery took shape. Nesting became her daily hobby, but it was a nest of thorns she was building. One to hem her in behind colored panes of window glass in the downstairs library, where she spent most of her lonely days, reading, staring out at a world she was beginning to believe no longer existed.

Pretending that when the baby came, everything would change.

It did. It got worse.

Later, when the doctor is gone, Redfern kneels at the bedside, touches the back of his rough hand to his wife's soft, damp cheek. Her hand trembles at her firstborn's fontanel. She's pale, blood smeared. She has no smile for August. The midwife passes him the second child, small and wriggling, and when he holds the baby up for Effie to see, she turns her face away, presses her lips to the other's head. Her eyes slip shut. Her pale face streaked with recent tears.

"Charlie," she whispers. "My boy. My baby boy."

Redfern looks down at the other child in his hands. Henry, he supposes, is a good name. He looks back at Effie and asks her what she thinks of it, but she doesn't answer. She won't look at him. He looks over his shoulder at the midwife, whose face is round and flushed with heat and exhaustion. Her daughter hangs a step back, a bundle of blood-soaked sheets in her arms.

"It will take time, sir," the midwife smiles. "It can be quite the shock. You'll see."

The daughter—she's sixteen, maybe seventeen—speaks up. "Henry is a good name, sir."

"Is it?" Redfern stands, holding the child. Feeling its weight, insubstantial as air.

Behind him, Effie shushes the newborn at her breast.

"A strong name," the midwife says.

Christmas Eve in the camp, starbright and cold. At the center of the clearing, a bonfire blazes, the pines surrounding the meadow like a gathering of dark, benevolent giants come to huddle around the flame. A few of the woodsmen and their wives sip cider from tin cups, a barrel of it tapped on the back of a cart. Children toddle. A fiddle plays. Ned Sullivan's wife and daughter return from the Hill with news of twins, and fresh cups are poured all around.

All throughout the fall and early winter, five days a week, the woodsmen have formed a fellowship of sorts. Boxing trees with concave and broad axes, a hundred to every acre. Emerging each morning from the cabins, tools in hand, wrapped like bedouins against the cold and sun. Half their number work construction on the distillery and the Camp Road along the river that will, come spring, carry wagonloads of raw gum and scrape back to the mill's furnace. When it rains, they congregate at the distillery and hoop barrels inside the cooper's shed and tell jokes. Their hands blister, crack, and bleed, and the wives make poultices and salves out of plants and roots. At five o'clock each day, Barlow calls "Time!" from his mount, and every man straightens from his task and sets off for the cabins, where the women cook meals five days a week, and supper is taken on porches, or inside by oil-burning lanterns. On Sundays they fish together, play cards.

Some even worship on half-log benches on a little grassy knoll by the river. Pigs are fattened for spring butchering. Enclosures are built for goats and chickens. Daniel Two Fists, a Cherokee of the Eastern Band, tends bees at the northern edge of the clearing, shares the honey with everyone. Among them are out-of-work Savannah Irish, a Scot or two. A stout Mormon and his wife and three daughters. Marcus the Swede, whose day-off job it is to cut the men's hair for a dime. He sings a song about a land where the water flows in silver streams beneath tall shady pines and, if you drink it, you forget your troubles. He sings it in Swedish and the men all laugh.

Redfern Hill, he likes to say, must be that place.

Lanterns burn on porches all around the circle of cabins. Ishmael Green sits in a rocking chair on his own porch, wrapped in a quilt, old meerschaum pipe in his mouth. His sons, Eli and James, are on the stoop, passing a cigarette back and forth. Shivering—not unpleasantly, as the heat from the bonfire drifts their way, every now and then—in threadbare flannel and denim.

"Say it might snow tomorrow," James says.

Ishmael grunts.

"Who say?" Eli says.

"The Swede."

Eli laughs. "Hey, Pop. Marcus says it's gone snow tomorrow."

"I wouldn't lay money on what that boy says."

"Be nice if it did's all," James says.

"Sure," Ishmael says. "Little more cold's what we all need."

They fall silent, a sudden, ethereal cast of song as, out by the fire, the Mormon daughters take up "Hark! the Herald Angels Sing."

"What it all must look like from way up there," James says, meaning the stars.

"Eli," Ishmael says around his pipe. He takes it from his mouth. "Run and get them presents."

"Yeah?"

"Why not."

Eli is up and moving.

"Beats Arkansas, don't it, Pop," James says.

In Pine Bluff, they'd worked cotton fields out of a sharecropper's shack with three other men. There was one son of a bitch there, Cummings, liked to fire his pistol in the air to start and stop the day. Sometimes, Cummings thought it was funny to aim that pistol over James's head.

"Whips Arkansas like a dog," Ishmael says, though his thoughts are far from here, as far from here as the cold stars shining in all that black. It cannot be their lot forever to serve men on land not their own.

Eli comes back out with three small, newsprint-wrapped packages. Hands one to James, keeps one for himself, and gives the last to his father. Ishmael smiles at the obvious pipe shape of his, says around his meerschaum, "Now, I wonder what this could be."

By lantern light, they open their gifts.

Ishmael packs his new pipe with old tobacco.

Eli finds a leather scabbard, in it a new skinning knife with a bone handle.

James unwraps a green canvas-backed book with gold trim, on its cover a sailor with a sextant, sighting his course. "'*Twenty Thousand Leagues Under the Seas*,'" he reads softly, running his fingers over the title. "What's it about, Pop?"

Ishmael smokes his pipe and says, "What the world looks like. From underneath."

"James?" a voice calls softly. A girl's voice, that Irish lilt.

The men's heads swivel as the young, pretty girl steps into their circle of light. She's changed out of her soiled dress, washed up her arms and face with a bucket of water. She wears a homespun dress and shawl and her auburn hair is swept back in a bun. James stands, book in hand. Ishmael glances at his other son, sees the flinty look in Eli's eyes, where the firelight dances. That hard, Green-boy set of jaw. Already standing, the older brother cocks one leg against the cabin wall and looks down at the knife in his hands. Turns the blade and thumbs the edge.

Shrugging out of his quilt, Ishmael gets up from his chair and steps to the porch rail. "Miss Sullivan," he says, though he looks past her, really, to the bonfire, to her father—the broad-shouldered Irishman, Ned Sullivan—who, in turn, watches her. His wife seated on a log bench beside him, all but dozing off as the hour creeps toward midnight. Ishmael lifts a hand, and Sullivan lifts his own in return. "Y'all been busy tonight."

"Yes, sir," Frannie Sullivan says.

Ishmael smiles. Nods.

"We was wondering if James might want to come over and have some cider? Tell a ghost story or two?"

"Sure," the boy says. But he looks at his father.

Ishmael says to Frannie, "You tell your family merry Christmas for me."

"I will, sir."

James starts off, book in hand, then remembers he's carrying it and sets it on the edge of the porch.

"Son," Ishmael says.

Frannie waits, just beyond earshot, hands clasped at her waist.

Father and son share a look, and the boy says, "I know. I love you, Pop."

"Love you, son."

James walks away to the bonfire, hands in his pockets, pretty Irish girl beside him.

"You know that ain't good for us," Eli says.

"Well"—the old man settles back into his chair, into his quilt—"it ain't Arkansas neither."

"You trust em?"

"Irish folk got it a hair better than we do in this world. But just a hair."

"How long, Pop? How long before it all goes south again?"

"It's Christmas, Eli."

"Redfern, you remember what he said, that first day? Right after Barlow clipped that cracker in the head?"

"Not particularly," Ishmael says, though he does. He knows where this is going. And he knows Eli is right. Deep down, Eli Green is as right as Marcus the Swede is wrong. As surely as the stars above died ages ago and what lies beyond them is no land of silver fountains.

"Well, I remember. And you know what 'fair and equal treatment' means to me? We *all* got a sap to the head coming. Man talks of what's his, what ain't, I don't care what else he says. That's old talk, Pop. Nothing new about it."

Ishmael sighs. "Can I just smoke my pipe?"

Sullen, silent, Eli slides down the wall and sits. He takes his knife out. Jabs the point into the wood. "Goddamn Arkansas everywhere," he mutters.

In bed, later. Holding little Charlie to her breast, the tug and pinch of his feeding. Numb with pain and shock and the end of a journey that was never remotely her own. In the rocking chair by the window, near the radiator, August sits with the other, Henry, in his arms.

Parasite. That's the name for what her husband holds.

Little Charlie was a shoot inside her, setting down roots for nine months, laying claim to her heart, but all the while a second shoot grew in secret. Leeching life from her heart's stem. Life she had not willingly given. It all makes sense now: the vomiting, the misery. The sense of something spoiling inside her.

"You have to feed both," Redfern says into the silence.

She makes no answer.

Later, after August has laid the other at her breast, she feels it latch on, and she begins to cry. The house is silent. Voices drift up like smoke from the porch. Redfern and Barlow. Their weary laughter.

Here, alone with her babies in the Christmas dark, she feels the working of two sets of tiny lungs against her, each a weight upon her heart, and thinks: *If I squeezed both . . .*

But what peace would it bring?

It should frighten her, this thought, but it doesn't. After all, it would free her, wouldn't it? Unchain her from this reality August Redfern and George Baxter have made for her, Euphemia the fattened calf, Euphemia the gifted bride, Euphemia the price of a Yankee sailor's dynasty.

Tired, she thinks. *You're only tired. Tomorrow's Christmas, after all.*

She sighs and wipes her tears and feels the ghost of her husband's rough hand on her cheek and damns herself for ever wanting this, for believing the lie she has whispered, every night before bed, her secret prayer: *Your life is yours and no one else's; your life is yours and no one else's.* In truth, she's a thing passed from one man to another, that's all. From George Baxter to August

Redfern, and now to a second baby boy her husband secreted away inside her, when there was already nothing of herself left to give.

Vampires, one and all, the men who claim her.

She drops her hands to the bed, away from the twins.

Little white slugs at her breasts.

II

1989

♦

JULY 2

LONNIE BAXTER SITS IN HIS IDLING BEAMER AND CHEWS TWO Percocets while staring straight ahead into his daddy's nursing home window, where he can see the old man slumped in his recliner like a bug in a jar. It's lunchtime at Pine Ridge and a female nurse is spooning Alonzo Baxter Sr. applesauce from a foil cup. Lonnie's daddy's head is tilted to the side so the food runs out of his mouth onto his robe if the nurse isn't quick enough to catch it, and because she's heavy and tired and life is hard all over, she's not always quick enough. Her gaze wanders as she speaks small, meaningless comforts, and Lonnie figures, *Yeah, it all comes down to this: we come into the world and go out the same, spoon-fed and shitting ourselves.*

He picks up the car phone, dials the house. It rings eight, nine times before he gives up and thumbs END. If Linda isn't answering, it's Todd. Could be she's changing his diaper, or could be she's forcing anti-seizure meds down his throat so he doesn't bite his damn tongue off. Lonnie glances at the white paper bag on the passenger's seat. Inside, freshly filled prescriptions of everything a growing boy needs. Beneath the bag, photocopies of Lonnie's own morning X-rays, red circles drawn around the disks of his spine where the goo is pushing out. Even now, that numbness down his right leg, like his nerve's some idiot song singing to itself. He caps the Percocet, aka Lonnie's Little Helpers, and tucks the bottle in the right hip pocket of his jeans.

Lonnie shuts his eyes. Cranks the AC. Waits for his daddy to finish lunch and for the pills to put out their feelers, the first of that long, mellow relief to come. Followed by a kick that's nothing but Old Lonnie, the Lonnie he remembers, the Lonnie he wants to be forever. And finally, when all's said and done, he won't feel anything, and the only song will be the one his engine's humming. And when he's there, in that place of needlessness? Goddamn, it's the best part of his day.

Inside the nursing home, the halls are empty and stink of bleach. From an open door at the far end of the corridor, a woman moans in the grip of some terrible dream.

Alonzo Sr. perches on the edge of his recliner, legs spread, fly of his boxers a gaping mouth. Applesauce on his undershirt. Lonnie pulls up a chair. His father's dick flops on his thigh like a dead sea creature. Lonnie covers it with the tail of the old man's robe.

"Mule's out of the barn, Pop."

The old man grins. He wipes his mouth with the back of his hand. "How's it, Herman?"

"It's Lonnie, Pop."

The grin wilts.

"How have you been?"

"Terrible. They're no good here. The fat one's a thief. I had a hundred dollars in my pocket." He fumbles at his robe, hands trembling. In about two seconds, the elevator stalls, and he forgets what he's doing. His face slides into a kind of vacant nowhere land that repulses Lonnie, makes him look away.

"Shoot," Lonnie says. "Wish I had a hundred bucks in my pocket."

"Ask Lonnie. He never hurt for money."

Lonnie sighs, glances at his watch.

"They paid him off, you know. After he sold the mill. Paid him good."

"I'm not Herman, yeah? I'm Lonnie. Herman went out to California to be queer, remember. And for the record, they didn't pay me so good."

"What?"

"They kept me on, though. I'm still the boss. For what it's worth."

The old man grunts, won't look at him.

"Remember way back, when I ran for mayor? Had two terms in office. You even voted for me."

"I never."

Lonnie reaches into his pocket. Pops two more pills from the bottle, gulps them down. He's got a whole afternoon to get through, back at the lumberyard.

Eyes wide, the old man says, "He'll kill himself, before it's done. Pills and booze, booze and pills."

Lonnie remembers the doctor's advice: *It's best, sometimes, to just play along.* "Why would Lonnie do that?" Lonnie says.

"He's got nothing left, that's why. Nothing to hold on to. Your mother, she'd have helped him. She always helped him."

Jesus.

"Yeah, well, Mom's not here."

Suddenly, the old man's eyes fill with waterworks. They fix

on Lonnie. His hands shake violently. When he speaks, his voice is a whimper. "Where's Barbara?"

Lonnie starts to sweat. "Mom's dead. Almost thirty years."

"She never came to see me." Then: "You always were a funny boy. At least Lonnie played sports."

Lonnie gets up and goes to the window and looks out at the parking lot. Hands in his pockets, he jingles some change, rolls the pill bottle. *I can hold on to that*, he thinks. The old man whimpers, cries a little, so Lonnie wanders the room. He lingers at his father's chest of drawers, the pictures there. Lonnie in his football gear, Lonnie pushing Herman on a tricycle. His mother's portrait. Long red hair, bright eyes too alive for Empire, Georgia. All he wants out of the old man is a single moment of clarity, a moment when Alonzo Sr. can remember what it is Lonnie needs him to remember.

"I was good to her," the old man's muttering now. "She never knew how good."

Lonnie listens to his heart drum two, three, four times. "Old man Redfern died a while back," he finally says. "You remember him?"

"Redfern." Lonnie's daddy's eyes sharpen. Like they always do at the mention of Redfern's name. Like this conversation's new. "Your great-uncle George give him that land."

Lonnie pulls his chair close to the old man's. Sits. Licks his lips. "He did."

"One thousand acres. Baxter land."

"Longleaf pine. Burled heartwood. Rare as—"

"Honest women," Alonzo Sr. finishes. He grins at his son. His son grins back.

Lonnie leans in, takes his father's hand. He's been this far and no further, always on the precipice of knowing. Their patter like random variations on a script, a kind of Mad Libs changing out words and greetings and topics, always arriving here. With the old man on the verge of some remembrance, some churned-up truth set to surface in the swirl of his mind, and today's the day, Lonnie can feel it, and so he asks the question. The one that's been plaguing him ever since August Redfern died, when Lonnie first made his discovery, first knew he wanted Redfern Hill.

"Why'd he give it up, Pop? Why let go of something like that?"

"It?"

A flicker of something, behind the eyes.

He knows.

Lonnie squeezes the old man's hand. "It," he says again. "You know what I mean."

"Oh," Alonzo Sr. sighs. "Oh, Herman . . ."

Lonnie shoots up so fast his chair turns over. He hooks a thumb against his chest. "Goddamn it, I'm Lonnie! For Christ's sakes—"

The old man's hand snares Lonnie's wrist in a dry-claw grip. He hauls Lonnie close. Sour breath like the rot in his brain. "You're a coward, boy, and your fortunes are numbered, do you hear? Numbered! You know what you need to do so *DO IT!*"

Lonnie jerks his hand away. Rubs his wrist.

Spit drips from his daddy's chin. His eyes smolder, until suddenly they dim and he slumps in his chair, wheezing. The springs in his La-Z-Boy creak and pop. "I'm sorry, Herman," he whimpers. "Please don't go, don't leave me alone, don't go . . ."

Lonnie drops to his knees beside the old man's chair. "It'll be okay, Pop." He takes his daddy's hand. "We'll own those woods again. When we do, you'll get better. You, Todd. Everything will be better. I promise. I'll do whatever I have to do. Whatever it takes."

"Whatever?" Alonzo Sr. says, and he begins to cough—a hard, chest-cracking hack. He pitches forward in his chair and coughs into his hand until his face is purple and his tongue hangs out. Lonnie gets up and goes to the door to call for the nurse.

"Boy!" the old man gasps, behind him.

Lonnie, who is sixty-two years old this month, turns. "Yessir?"

"Feed it," Alonzo Sr. rasps. "You get that land, and you—"

But the cough starts up again, like shattered glass in the old man's chest.

Lonnie stands in the doorway, certain the old man's going to bust something inside. Then he remembers himself and rushes out and grabs a nurse by the elbow, tells her his old man needs help. He waits outside until she's in there, lets the heavy door swing shut behind her, and then it's all too easy to just turn and leave, cut and run, like Lonnie's been doing most of his life.

All the way down the hall, he can hear it, that cough.

He's still hearing it when the Beamer cranks and the AC roars and he peels rubber out of Pine Ridge's parking lot.

"Better eat," Nellie says, brushing at a fly that's found the boy's sandwich half-eaten on the porch swing between them.

It's noon and they're taking a break from the day's sorting and scrubbing. Inside the house, the new washing machine churns and the new dryer thumps. That morning, two men from Sears delivered them, along with a riding lawn mower and a seventeen-inch Magnavox cabinet television. Max sat on the stairs, Skeletor in hand, watching the men roll the machines down the hall and into the kitchen on dollies. One of them winked when they brought the TV into the parlor. "Bet this one's yours, am I right, big man?" To which Max only shrugged. Now, he sits with his sketchbook in his lap, legs dangling. He makes a final adjustment with his eraser, brushes away crumbs, and passes her the book. He reaches for his bologna and cheese.

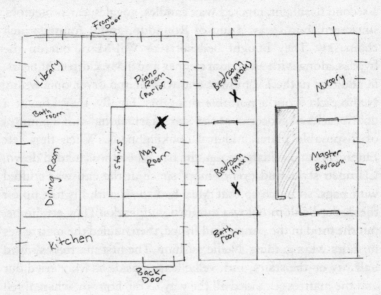

Nellie studies the map. She's asked him to do it, to create a floor plan of the house. She hopes it'll spark something, a bond with the place. She points at the map room, the bedrooms. "Why are these x-ed?"

"They're cleaned." He pushes bologna back between his bread. "We've put furniture back in. New mattresses in the bedrooms. Mopped the floors. Dusted. That sort of thing."

Early yesterday morning, after leaving the bank in Empire with a sheaf of temporary checks, they went to the furniture store and bought two box springs and two mattresses and loaded them into the Ranger's bed. Next, they went to the hardware store, where they filled a cart with Old English, Murphy Oil Soap, Pledge, shop towels, cleaning rags, a broom and dustpan, a mop and bucket, yard rakes, screwdrivers, a hammer, garden shears, a second flashlight, tapered wax candles, goggles, ear protectors, sunscreen, bug spray, a jug of Roundup, and a fourteen-inch chain saw. They bought bedsheets at Wal-Mart, out on the bypass, along with a vacuum cleaner and a Mr. Coffee. At Sears, in addition to the TV, mower, and washer and dryer, on a whim, Nellie picked out a portable turntable. Finally, they bought a dozen sacks of groceries at the Star Mart, along with a handful of disposable plates and foil cooking pans. When they left Empire around midafternoon, the truck's bed was loaded down, Clampett-style, and every empty space in the cab was stuffed with bags, so much so that Max had to sit with his feet up on the dash, the floor below crammed with sacks. They got home, put the food in the pantry and fridge, then hauled the mattresses upstairs, Max guiding, Nellie pushing. The first mattress slipped halfway up the stairs, and Nellie leaped aside as Max cried out and the mattress thudded all the way to the bottom, where it fell over on its side with a great, dusty *WHAP*. Later, after the beds were made with new sheets, Nellie and Max trashed, scraped, and scrubbed Redfern Hill until damn near midnight.

Mostly in August Redfern's map room, currently the only *X* on the first floor.

First, they opened the huge bay windows and backed the truck up between the crape myrtles and filled its bed with three loads, drove each to the county dump a few miles east of town. The heartwood pine table in the center of the room was old and scarred, so Max attacked it with Pledge while Nellie took lamps and footstools and chairs and tables out into the hallway and cleaned them and set them throughout the house. They found nothing dead underneath it all, thank God, just a minefield of rat droppings, which Nellie swept up. Her grandfather's ax she set by the back of the stairs, just outside the door. She was thinking of hanging it somewhere in the room. They played Redfern's old big band records on the turntable, singing along to the chorus of "Pennsylvania 6-5000," only Max sang, "Transylvania 6-5000."

Once the room was clear, Nellie got down on hands and knees with a bucket of Murphy Oil Soap and water and inched her way across the floor with a rag. Max gathered up the boards Redfern had pried from the wall—the ones they found, anyway—and by the time they collapsed at the kitchen table for a dinner of Totino's Party Pizzas and Dr Peppers, Nellie's knees and back were throbbing, her hands were red and raw, and she was deliriously happy.

That night, she lay awake in her new bed and marveled at how, before today, cleaning meant little more than picking up after Wade. Holding the chaos of life at bay. Laundry, especially, she'd always hated—not so much the washing, but the folding. Baskets emptied and piled on the bed, only to be refilled each night and shoved in a corner, to be dressed out of for days, until Wade lost a pair of socks, and suddenly a basket was upended on the floor, its contents strewn down the hall, and he was yelling: *WHAT THE FUCK DO YOU DO ALL DAY!* Dishes, dusting, changing out the Hoover's bags—she hated these things because Wade expected her to do them. She had played the parts of housewife, mother, maid. Had endured thrown plates, fists through sheetrock. Once, a knife—

No, she thought, drifting off, *no more of that. That's over.*

"You're missing a room," she says.

"Where?"

Nellie taps the stairwell. "The cellar door. Remember?" Max clamps his sandwich in his mouth and takes his sketchbook and draws a door behind the stairs. They finish their lunch in the warm shade of the porch, Nellie guiding the swing with the tips of her toes, Max hunched over his pad. Drawing the barn, the trees beyond. The road and the meadow. The Winnebago.

"What was your grandfather like?" he wants to know.

Nellie has closed her eyes, is dozing, one hand gripping the chain, head against it. She sits up straighter. Considers her answer. "Brilliant, I think," she finally says. "But a little crazy. A little scary."

"Like, just old-man crazy? Or seriously crazy."

She laughs. "Old-man crazy, mostly."

"Was he a good person?"

This stumps her. "As good as anyone, I guess. I didn't know him that well. Why?"

Max shrugs. "You said you and your dad didn't get along, right?"

"Did I say that?"

"Like you and Dad didn't get along?"

"No," she says quickly. "No, me and your dad, that's different. Whole other thing, kiddo."

"Did you like your grandfather?"

"Sure. I was looking for something that summer, when I came here."

"Did he help you find it?"

She gets up and walks to the far end of the porch and leans her bare shoulder against a sun-warmed column. "Maybe."

"I get why you left him."

She feels every muscle in her body tense. She doesn't turn

around. She doesn't want him to see the terror that grips her, the fear that if she turns, she'll start talking, and she won't stop in time to save him from the worst of it, and he'll know that she didn't leave because she was strong, just scared shitless of the man she married, his own father, and maybe she'll keep on talking until that last, terrible truth spills out, the truth behind the scar upon her wrist—

"But this place," Max says, "it's not home."

She sighs. Relieved. This one's easy. "If it ain't here, pal, where the heck is it?"

His answer is quick, certain: "We're still looking."

Lonnie steps out from the lumber stacks at the eastern corner of Baxter Millworks and marks the golf cart beelining for him. His secretary hunches over the wheel. She's a broad-shouldered woman with a face like a rat. In the passenger's seat, the lawyer wears an orange hard hat stamped with the word VISITOR. A log truck belches and shudders along the Ring Road, forced to crawl past the cart. The afternoon's hotter than the morning, and Lonnie's sweating beneath his own hard hat. He's rolled his shirtsleeves but saddlebags are spreading beneath his arms. The heat draws his back pain up through his nerves like poison. He takes off his hat and sweeps a hand over his bristly scalp and flings the sweat on the concrete floor of the shed. Flexes his hand, puts it in the small of his back, and kneads the muscles there, beneath his checked cotton shirt.

Meanwhile, the cart wheels into the lot and the log truck speeds by in a pissed-off cloud of dust.

Lonnie tugs a pack of Salems from his shirt pocket and shakes one out. He lights it, snaps his Zippo shut.

Meadows walks up fanning air with his hard hat.

"You oughta keep that on," Lonnie says. "It's dangerous out here."

"It's no good, Lon."

There's something oily in Jim Meadows's voice, something Lonnie's never liked. He doesn't know the word, but if he did, the word would be *obsequious*.

"You met with her?"

"Night before last."

"And you made the offer?"

"Made the first and the second, like you said."

"And?"

Meadows shrugs the shrug of a man who's exhausted all possibilities, a posture Lonnie knows to be 100 percent, grade A bullshit. "She won't sell. She's got it in her head to make a home out of that place, if you can believe it."

Silence. Punctuated by the steady clamor of the debarking chain in Shed Three, the high shriek of a saw biting pine. The soundscape of Lonnie Baxter's furious, buzzing brain. He shuts his eyes. Wills it away.

"We could make an offer to lease a portion, for logging?"

"Shit." Lonnie flicks ash, squints into the sun. "Then she gets smart, makes a call down to the ag school, and they send up some peckerhead with a PhD? No thank you. My forebears bought that land and sixty-nine thousand acres like it for ten cents on the goddamn dollar. Now you're telling me I can't even swing a thousand acres from a divorcée?" Lonnie turns away, paces in the shade of the shed. Inside, stacks of lumber curing. Sweet, bright scents of red, white, and yellow pine.

"Oh, she ain't divorced. Not yet." Meadows stays still, watches Lonnie pace. "My man in Savannah, that private investigator I told you about? Well, he says the husband's a real piece of work, a real A-one shit bag—"

"You didn't sell her on it. That's all."

Meadows bows up. Points his hard hat at Lonnie. "All due respect, Lon, I am not a salesman. I am your lawyer."

Lonnie stops pacing, rubbing his lower back. Cigarette clamped between his lips, he says, "What's wrong with you?"

A few sheds away, the saw screams on, chews up another log. "Pardon?"

"What's. Wrong. With. You."

Meadows flushes from neck to cheeks. Calmly, he answers, "Not a thing, Lonnie. Not a thing."

Lonnie spits out his cigarette and says, "You follow me, lawyer," and sets out across the Ring Road into the raw-timber stacks. He doesn't have to look back to know that Meadows is hoofing it right behind him. When he stops, the two men are deep in a mountain range of fresh-cut timber, jets of water arcing overhead, broken rainbows in the air above them. The spray falls as a fine mist around them. Lonnie takes off his hat, lets it cool his head.

"Look around you, Jim. What do you see?"

Meadows, trying to stay out of the spray, says, "Trees. What are we doing, Lonnie?"

"You see money. Do you know whose money?"

The lawyer's polo—a turquoise Ralph Lauren—is getting wet. He tugs at it. Wipes his face. "Georgia Land and Timber's?"

"That's right. And who owns Georgia Land and Timber?"

"Hell, I don't know. Not you, I reckon. Can we—"

"Not me. That's right. And that's been the case for a long fucking while. So everything you see here, it's worth spit to me."

"Lonnie—"

"The truth is, I could give a flying fuck at a rolling doughnut about timber. Timber-wise, August Redfern's land is shit. Sure, once upon a time, there were no forests like it. Trees with huge old hearts. But he bled those hearts dry cutting cat faces and hacking at em until they were half-dead. I don't want his rot. What I want is older than trees. Its roots go deeper. It's my birthright, as a Baxter. Do you understand that? Before my people came here, this place was a fucking mosquito farm!" Spittle flies from his lips. Water drips from his chin. He's soaked through. They both are.

"Look, Lonnie, I can appreciate your position—"

"We have planned this, and we are in it. *You* are in it—"

"Lon. Think about Linda. Think about your boy—"

Lonnie stabs a finger into the lawyer's chest. "You don't talk to me about my son," he snarls. "You ever talk to me about my son again, I'll drop one of these goddamn logs on you."

Meadows goes stony. "Don't threaten me. I've stuck by you until now, but, man, you're obsessed. You know what I think? I think you don't have the first clue why you even want that land. You just want it because you want it. And you don't like someone telling you no. Even though that's all your life here in Empire amounts to, Lonnie—one big *NO!*"

The cords in Lonnie Baxter's neck tighten. He strikes fast and hard, driving headlong into the lawyer's gut with every ounce of old Linebacker Lonnie he can muster. Briefly, beautifully, there is no pain, no tingle of the nerves nor seizing muscle. He is nerveless. Meadows pitches up and sideways, lifted out of his loafers. His head strikes the end of a log and he goes down in the bark-littered mud. Knees of his khaki pants and one side of his Ralph Lauren shirt streaked brown. Bleeding above his right eye, his visitor's hard hat spinning on the ground like a turtle on its back.

Lonnie balls one fist, other hand holding his own hard hat, as his heart rockets adrenaline. His back isn't hurting at all anymore. It's a miracle. No need for Lonnie's Little Helpers, not right now. Right now, he looms over Meadows, a madman, white heat flaring at the edges of his vision, and Meadows cringes, even cries out, and Lonnie's grinning, grinning through the mist that runs and drips from his nose as he thinks about how good it will feel to tear this son of a bitch a new asshole—

Across the yard, a shift whistle shrieks, and something in the sound cuts through Lonnie's rage. His eager, bloodthirsty grin slips, and there's a bit of drool on his chin mixing with the water. He unballs his fist and runs his hand over his scalp and sets his hard hat—still in his hand—back on his head. He bends over, picks up Meadows's hat. Bits of timber and bark in the bowl. Meadows is moaning, rolling in the slop like a pig. Lonnie hauls him up, sets the hard hat on Meadows's head. Pats it twice.

"Now"—Lonnie thumbs a smear of blood from above the lawyer's eyebrow—"you tell me everything your man in Savannah told you about this Gardner gash's husband."

The invisible cellar door in back of the stairs might just as easily open onto a cupboard or a closet—the kind of space you'd stow a mop and a bucket, or a box of Christmas decorations—but one look at the dark sliver where the boards misalign and Max knows that door leads down. Down, down, down. Nellie gives him the Craftsman flashlight bought at the hardware store. She carries the Maglite. "Ready?"

Heart a rabbit, he nods. "Ready as I'm gonna get."

The top corner of the door has to be yanked, and when Nellie swings it wide, a breeze wafts up, rich with earth and age and sealed-up autumn dark. They stoop and shine their lights down the stairs, through shining white membranes whorled between the frame boards of the wall, all the way to the bottom, where their beams are swallowed by the shadows.

Nellie has to duckwalk a few steps down before she can stand hunched over in the low space beneath the hallway stairs. She steadies herself with a hand on an overhead two-by-four. Max follows suit, thinking of Frodo and Sam and the pass of Cirith Ungol. Max looks neither right nor left, certainly not up, where the webs thicken. Only down at his own two feet. Nellie's already reached the bottom when he hears the sound, a skittering-scratching in the dark. Like the first night, in the piano room, that noise in the walls—

Three steps from the bottom, his ankles tangle and he pitches forward.

The cellar floor is packed dirt, hard as concrete. Max goes down on his right knee, and the floor grates a patch of skin right off. Flashlight still in hand, he's pushing up from the floor when he feels his mother's hand close around his upper arm and lift him, right him. Steady him. "Ow," he says.

Nellie shines her own light on his knee. "It's not as bad as it looks." She licks her thumb, swabs the dirt away gently. "Think you can soldier on, or do we need to go up and put a cloth on it?"

"I'm good," he says, and means it.

An old apple barrel stands at the foot of the cellar stairs, its lid askew, the barrel empty, though a whiff of fermentation lingers. Beside it, several empty crates that might have once held potatoes, onions, turnips. Despite the damp smell, the air is cool, almost pleasant.

Nellie finds a pull string that does little to dispel the dark.

The only other light comes from a pair of narrow, grimy windows set high up, at ground level.

Max shines his Craftsman on a musty canvas drop cloth in a far corner. Nellie pulls the drop cloth away and they paw through the wooden peach crates beneath, wiping cobwebs on their jeans. Right away they find two big coils of thick rope and a few rusty contraptions that look like spurs to Max, only with sharp, pointed toes. "Tree-climbing gear," Nellie says. She rummages in another box, comes up with half a dozen empty mason jars and an olive-drab backpack, tattered and dusty. At this, a ghost of recognition crosses her face.

Farther back, in the rear corner, beneath the floor of the map room, is the furnace, an iron monstrosity of ductwork and dials that likely hasn't been used in over fifty years. Its grate hangs open like a slack jaw, broken lumps of coal on the ground beneath it. Beside it, abutting the foundation of the house, is a brick wall built up to the joists above. The bricks are large and tumbled, no chinks or gaps between them, just heaping gobs of mortar that spill out from the joints. At the center of this wall is a heavy iron door skinned with cobwebs.

"It's another room," Max says.

"It's the coal closet. To keep the dust contained when the coal was delivered. Not too common down here in the South, but then again, August Redfern wasn't from the South."

"How'd they get the coal down here?"

"There's a chute outside, leads straight in. Look for the little *Alice in Wonderland* door, next time you're outside."

Max gives a tug on the iron door's handle. It doesn't budge.

Nellie yanks it, too, bends to inspect the keyhole. "Well, it's an old-fashioned lock. Looks like a spider home now. I'm sure we'll find the key in a drawer upstairs." She moves on, looking for pipes.

Max wonders, briefly, if the coal chute outside the house is wide enough for a kid to shimmy down. But he's no dummy. He's seen all those public service announcements between commercial breaks on after-school specials, the ones featuring *G.I. Joe* characters like Snake Eyes and Roadblock telling stupid kids not to play around downed power lines or put out grease fires with water. He figures it's a sure bet you could add shimmying down strange coal chutes to that list.

Around the corner, Nellie's found a modern water heater on bricks, above it a network of newish copper snaking through the joists to join a matrix of old pipes.

Nearby, along the bare framework of the stairs, wooden shelves are nailed into the studs, each crowded with small fruit crates and water-stained cardboard boxes. Max plays his beam among the boxes, opens one. Old baby clothes. In another, a heap of corroded batteries. His light catches something in the dirt beneath the shelves. A book, thick with dust. Probably fallen off a shelf. He picks it up and blows dust from it. A wide leather cover embossed with an elaborate tree, its roots extending into the flat golden curve of the earth. He fumbles at a metal clasp on the side and the book falls open to a front page that reads ALBUM in sweeping, ornate letters. He turns the page—the edge is speckled with foxing—and a sheaf of photographs spills out. He bends to pick them up.

Behind him, something stirs. A clattering of rocks.

Max jerks his head round at the heavy iron door.

Now, another sound, faint. Like scratching. But not like before, the scratching in the walls, no, this is different. Like fingernails drawn slowly over metal. A sound that freezes Max's blood and sets his heart to thudding like a drum.

Then comes a whisper, little more than a sigh.

... *max* ...

He jumps, like someone's put the tip of nine-volt battery to his tongue.

A girl's voice.

"Thank Christ the plumbing's solid," Nellie says as she rounds the stairs.

Max gathers up the last of the pictures and stuffs them back into the album and snaps its clasp. He clutches the book to his chest and backs slowly away from the coal closet.

"Let's head up, kiddo. Lots to do."

Behind him, Nellie tugs the pull string, plunging the cellar into darkness.

Out of which the windows in the foundation peer like rheumy, yellow eyes.

Recorded from a television broadcast, complete with commercial breaks, *Jaws* plays on the VCR while Max and Nellie clean the parlor floor. They move into the dining room—big and empty, not much to do—and finally, by the time Chief Brody's shouldering a rifle to climb the mast of the sinking *Orca*, they've worked their way back to the library at the front of the house.

Nellie pulls down the sheets from the shelves, drags them out onto the porch. Flaps them. Hangs them over the railing. She finds Max in the center of the room, staring up in awe at the books.

"Was your grandfather a big reader?" Max asks.

But Nellie doesn't answer.

She stands over the writing desk by the front porch window and lifts the angled lid. Inside are a fountain pen, an old inkwell, long dry. A stack of stationery, each page inscribed with dark ink: BY THE HAND OF EUPHEMIA REDFERN.

Max: "What happened to her?"

Nellie bites the inside of her cheek.

The boy sees it. She's deciding what to tell him.

"She died when the mill burned down," Nellie finally says. "A long time ago."

"She died in the fire?"

Nellie nods. She puts the stationery away, closes the desk.

Max has more questions—who wouldn't—but he knows she doesn't want to answer them right now, so he looks at the shelves instead and says, "We'll need to reorganize all of these. Plus, there's the books we found in the map room. I stacked them by the stairs. We'll have to move them back in here and reshelve them."

"Yeah, I'm going to leave that job to you."

"Ha. Thanks."

"If you're up for it. How's the knee?"

"Fine." He's already walking the ladder over to the nearest shelf.

"Be careful on that thing. It looks rickety."

In the hall, she picks up a bucket of vinegar and soapy water and goes out onto the porch, where the day is dry and bright and her nose doesn't burn with the stink of Clorox. "I think I'll work in the yard," she calls through the screen door. "Come out in a bit?"

"Sure," Max calls back, arms already spilling books.

Nellie slings dirty water over the porch rail.

But Max never makes it outside. Instead, he works in the library for hours, stacking armloads of canvas-backed books in the center of the floor and ordering them alphabetically. Most of the books in the library are stodgy nonfiction: the complete *Encyclopaedia Britannica*, English and American dictionaries, tomes on weird things like sailing and how to raise chickens. He finds a few novels by long dead writers like Nathaniel Hawthorne, Herman Melville, a book of short stories and poems by Edgar Allan Poe. Poets he's never heard of: Elizabeth Barrett Browning, Christina Rossetti, John Keats. Some nit named Lord Byron. There's an old copy of *Frankenstein*, too, which Max is happy to see; the book's been a favorite of his ever since he found it on his dad's bookshelves back in Conway. He prefers the book to the movie version with Boris Karloff, if only because there's something so much scarier about a monster who can plot and scheme, a monster who's smart.

Midafternoon, he comes across a slim book called *A Boy's Guide to Rope*, tucked on a shelf next to nursery rhymes and fairy tales. He finds an inscription on the inside cover, written in a precise, careful hand: THIS BOOK BELONGS TO HANK REDFERN. AND NO ONE ELSE.

Hank Redfern. Mom's dad. His grandfather.

Max turns the pages slowly, sees such words as *bowline*, *clove hitch*, *cleave hitch*. *Anchor* and *sheepshank* (*sheepshank* he knows from *Jaws*). Illustrations of knots, descriptions of their uses, watercolor pictures of children in brightly colored shirts and shorts making tire swings and tug-of-war pits and even bridges. In fact, there's a whole section on rope bridges. Suspension bridges and hanging bridges and catenary bridges. Max flips back to the title page, checks the publication date: 1930.

He tucks the book under his arm to take upstairs and goes to the kitchen to wash his hands. At the sink he runs a glass of water, his "glass" a red plastic Solo cup because they've yet to sort the three boxes of dishes recovered from the map room. In a week or two, the paper plates and the foil pans will run out, and they'll have to wash dishes. He knows how much his mother hates washing dishes, but it's starting to bug him, all that stuff not washed and put away where it belongs. *Maybe*, he thinks, *I'll just do it myself.*

He glances out the kitchen door and down the hall through the open fly screen, where Mom's going at the azaleas with the garden shears. Her hair is pulled back in a ponytail and she's rolled her T-shirt sleeves to her shoulders and her freckled arms are turning red in the sun. *She's beautiful*, he thinks. *Beautiful in a way nothing else in the world will ever be.* Not even a sunset over the Grand Canyon. He feels a bizarre, irrational fear, having such a big thought. Her mouth is a tight line, her brow drawn down into a furrow of concentration. Each snap of the shears is a grunt. He's seen her like this before, when she's painting. Seeing the shadows he can't—or doesn't want—to see.

He's just finished gulping his water, is running himself a second cup, when upstairs there's a muffled thud. The sound of something heavy dropping. He glances up at the beadboard ceiling. His room directly overhead. Hank Redfern's old bedroom. Is it his imagination, or is a slight sprinkling of dust drifting down from the boards?

Clutching *A Boy's Guide to Rope*, Max goes out of the kitchen and into the hallway and mounts the stairs. Halfway up, he stops. Cocks his head. Listens. Almost immediately, he hears it: that skittering-scritching sound. Fainter than before, but that's it. Like rats in the walls. Or giant rats, like the ones in that movie he and Dad stayed up late to watch, where the rats ate that baby right out of its pajamas—

Max climbs to the top of the stairs, one hand on the balustrade. He holds his breath to hear. Scrape of cardboard?

Rustling paper. A page being turned. The hairs on his neck dance.

"Hello?" he calls.

Silence. Followed by a sound he knows well. The sharp, unmistakable, fart-like rip of spiral-bound art paper tearing loose. A clatter of plastic, then silence again.

Max creeps toward the open door of his room. He's only a few steps away when another sound springboards his heart into his throat: laughter. Like the twitter of a morning bird, short and girlish. The bedroom door is cracked, revealing a slice of wall, a corner of cedar chest. It gives away nothing.

Suddenly, Max is scared. Not scary-movie scared but *really* scared, cold-sweat scared, like the time Leon Miller caught him on the playground and shoved him up against the monkey bars and made him eat a clod of dirt. He remembers the way it tasted, hot and gritty and brown. Max never told Dad about this. Dad would have said it was Max's fault, that size had nothing to do with taking a beating or giving it. *You're a scared little sissy* is what Dad would have said. Max feels it then, like the first night here, outside the house, that sudden, telltale tingle in his nose, taste of—

(No, no, you don't, sissy!)

—pennies. He tilts his head back, sniffs once, twice, counts to thirty, between each number repeating in his head, *Don't bleed don't bleed don't bleed don't bleed.*

One last, deep breath to screw his courage, and Max yanks open the door.

The poison ivy winds up the corner of the house from behind the azalea, beneath the parlor window. Nellie rakes out behind the bush and grabs the jug of Roundup from the Ranger's bed in the driveway. After spraying the roots, she buttons the sleeves of her painting shirt, old and thin and rainbow spattered with oils, then tugs on a pair of gardening gloves and returns to the vine. She imagines what her mother might say, wry and amused, like the time Nellie was four and wanted to feed an alligator a piece of beef jerky on a fishing trip, the alligator huge and sunning itself less than ten feet from the bank where Hank was fishing. *Well*—Ruth Redfern laughed, pushing up her cat-eye glasses, cigarette ash a shade too long in her right hand—*this is ill-advised.*

Nellie grabs the poison ivy and tugs. A length of vine pops free of the boards.

Slowly, surely, she unstitches it from the house.

Max sets *A Boy's Guide to Rope* on the nightstand and stares at the bedside floor.

The laundry basket Mom filled with his toys the morning they left South Carolina is overturned. Action figures, books, comics, coloring books, a dog-eared copy of *How to Draw Comics the Marvel Way*—all dumped and scattered. He picks up his special mail-away Clark Kent ("Yours free with five proofs of purchase!") and turns him upside down. A pearl of something that looks like spit drips from the figure's head, thick as melted caramel. Or Elmer's rubber cement. He touches it, rubs it between his fingers. It's sticky. He sniffs it, and the stink is sharp and familiar: pine sap. In the sunlight streaming through his window, he can see little flecks of something, dark and wriggling in the white.

"Gross." He wipes it on his bedspread.

A trail of the stuff drips from his toys over the hardwood planks to the cedar chest, from the edge of the lid onto the floor, and finally onto a sheet of drawing paper, torn from Max's eleven-by-fourteen tablet. His downstairs map, brought upstairs after lunch and tucked away in the chest. But the drawing's changed. The cellar door is now a gaping black hole in back of the stairs. A ragged, hungry mouth, scratched into the page by a heavy graphite lead. Max gets down on hands and knees, picks up a pencil where it's rolled between the cracks in the floor. The tip is blunted and the shaft is sticky.

And, of course, there is what's beneath the paper.

Max lifts the drawing, and the little rag doll stares up at him with smiling button eyes.

The first yellow jacket hits Nellie before she even knows what's happening. A flash in her periphery, followed by a needle-bright pop just below the ridge of her cheekbone.

"Shit!"

She dances back, a runner of poison ivy in hand.

Wasps boil up from the ground, flying at her as she flees for the Ranger. She leaps into the cab and slams the door and watches the bugs bat their bodies against the windshield like Nellie-seeking missiles. She pulls off her gloves, touches her cheek, which is reddening, throbbing. Something moves in the collar of her shirt. Nellie slaps it, feels a piercing sting on her right middle finger.

"Jesus fuck!"

She shucks her painting shirt and kicks open the passenger door. Bare armed and furious, she forgets about the can of Raid bought yesterday at the hardware store, stowed inside in the pantry.

Instead, she snatches the spare gasoline can from the pickup's bed and stalks back to the azalea at the corner of the house. "Let's dance, motherfuckers!" she says, and drenches the ivy, the bed, the exposed roots where the bugs swarmed out.

A root *moves*.

She leaps back, gas can in hand, thinking she's roused a snake bedded down in the leaves, but then she sees the slim, wormlike tendril, retreating lazily into the ground, in a wheeze of dust and leaves. Leaving behind a bright, silver slime like that of a garden snail. Later, she'll try to convince herself that it was a snake all along, harmless, more scared of her than she of it. But then she'll remember that it had no scales, that it was a long, slender thing burred with tiny little hairs, a ground root come to life.

In the woods across the meadow, a crow rips the day.

Nellie sets the gas can down. Edges closer to the azalea, toes the leaves aside. There, beneath the lanky shoots of the azalea and the last clump of poison ivy, is a perfectly round hole in the earth, big as a shotgun barrel.

A yellow jacket crawls out, dizzy with the fumes.

Nellie stomps it.

Rosy cheeks, hair of yarn.

He remembers the doll in Mom's arms, their first night here. He wants to run out of the room, out of the house to his mother. He wants to shut his eyes and open them and see everything in its place. Instead, carefully, he touches the tip of his index finger to the doll's cheek. Prods it. Picks it up.

The laughter, it was a girl's.

There's a story here, he thinks weirdly. *Something I should see but I don't—*

A creak. He jerks his head at the door that adjoins Nellie's bedroom. The door is cracked.

Did it move? Yes, it moved.

"Hello?"

No answer, but another smell is in the room now, beneath the scent of pine. Garden-like, the smell of after-rain on a humid day. Damp and fetid. Like leaves churned up in search of earthworms. Suddenly, the room is stifling hot.

Max turns the doll over. Does what any boy might do. He lifts the skirt.

Sewn across the doll's bottom, like a kind of undergarment, is a white cotton tag. Initials are embroidered there, in bright orange thread. E.A.R.

Nellie sets out across the field for the Winnebago, face and hand swelling. Nothing in the house save a cold washrag to ease the pain. Redfern, however, left behind a whole drugstore, and if she can scrounge a few Tylenol or Bufferin before her eye swells shut, she and Max can drive into town for the rest. With any luck, she'll stumble across the Holy Grail: a tube of hydrocortisone.

(Of course, a good mother would have had these things in the house. A good mother—)

"Fuck you, Wade," she mutters.

Inside, she swallows four anti-inflammatories, then sifts through the rest of the bedside stock, holding up bottles to the open blinds to read labels. In the table drawer, beneath a stack of Louis L'Amour and Max Brand westerns, she turns up a blue tin of Penaten, three years expired. Beggars can't be choosers, so she rubs it in. First the hand, then the face. Afterward, she sits slumped at the foot of the bed, sweating through her T-shirt in the stuffy gloom. Her hands are shaking. *It's not supposed to be this way.* She's alone. Way out here. *No one to see—*

The first sob hits her like a sledgehammer.

The second she draws in, tries to hold like a breath, but it only explodes, and suddenly Nellie Gardner finds her tears, and she sits on the end of her grandfather's bed and cries. She cries for Max. For herself. For the last dozen years, and the years before those. She cries like the rain pours down on a summer day.

The Winnie roars with it.

Seven miles east of the Millworks, Lonnie Baxter's Beamer turns onto a paved county road that winds through pine thickets to a pair of heavy iron gates that roll open on fifty wooded acres. Half a mile of asphalt through beard-silvered oaks brings him to the house itself, late Victorian, part Gothic Revival, part Queen Anne: two stories with long sloping angles, exposed trusses, elaborate scrollwork. Frankenstein's Mansion, Lonnie calls it. The house that his great-uncle built in 1891 for the woman he married. Like nothing anyone in this hick corner of Georgia had ever seen.

At twenty-nine, Great-Uncle George came down from Connecticut to work for his brother at a manufacturing firm in Albany. By thirty-one, he was a land baron. Twenty years later, Baxter's Mill—the village that sprang up north of George Baxter's sawmill, today the Georgia Land & Timber's Millworks—became the city of Empire. Baxter had hair the color of snow by the time he married a twenty-five-year-old schoolteacher named Helen Gross. *Just like a Yankee to get it backward*, folks said. *First he builds a town, then he builds a house.* By 1924, Great-Uncle George was dead of a stroke, and the mill and the house went to his brother's boy over in Dougherty County—Alonzo Baxter. His kids: Herman and Lonnie. Lonnie the quarterback. Lonnie the lumberjack. Lonnie the mayor.

Lonnie the joke.

He parks in the carriage house and weaves across the gravel drive and up the steps into a high-ceilinged foyer. A carpeted staircase climbs the wall to a second floor of five bedrooms, only two of which have been in use since Todd was born. The rest are outfitted with stodgy antique furniture and beds that no one will ever sleep in. The wallpaper throughout is golden silk, frayed around the edges. The windows are tall and leaded blue and cast the house in permanent gloom.

Linda's in the kitchen, chopping onions. A flank steak set out on a wooden cutting board, beaten tender. The last of Lonnie's Little Helpers are all holding hands now, singing a little song in his heart and head, so he sidles up behind her and nuzzles the back of her neck, hands on her waist.

She sags against him, relieved he's home to share a bit of the burden of standing, delivering. "We had a Not So Good One."

"I'm sure you did," he slurs into her hair.

She stiffens. "What?"

"Nothing."

"I tried to call you after your doctor's appointment this morning. Did you get my message?" She wears the same tattered housecoat she wears every day. Rarely changing out of it, except to put on sweats or one of his old football jerseys and leggings to make a grocery run—and only then when she can get the caretaker to drop by.

"Yeah, and I tried to call you," he mutters.

"What did the doctor say?"

"He said I'm a candidate for surgery, and if I don't get it

done, I'll likely be shitting my pants in two or three years. How about that."

Linda slides the knife into the onion. Tears springing to her eyes.

He drifts away—practically floats, if he's being honest—to the bills on the little desk beneath the nineteenth-century wall-mounted phone. They're stacked, unopened. *Nope. Not the day for that.* He sets them aside, sifts through the rest of the mail.

"I had to call Patrice. She's upstairs with Todd. I know what we talked about, the expense and all, but—"

"It's fine, babe." Lonnie slips away through the dining room to the den, where he pours himself two fingers of Jack Daniel's from the sideboard. He sits for a spell in a leather rocker, closes his eyes, just for a second. When he opens them, the shadows outside are longer and it smells like onions and gravy in the kitchen.

He climbs the stairs.

Todd's room is at the end of the hall. The door stands open.

The boy sits in his recliner by the window, where the evening sun falls streaming and he can turn his face to it. He sits on bare feet, legs folded beneath him. His head is large and heavy and hangs forward and he rocks back and forth in the chair and makes soft, happy sounds that are not quite words. Across the room, in her own chair, knitting in her lap, Patrice says hello and Lonnie smiles and asks her how that new grandbaby is, and Patrice smiles back and says he's just fine.

"He'll outgrow that blanket before you finish knitting it."

"Don't I know it."

"How is Todd?"

"We had it rough, Mr. Lonnie. He had himself a big one, just before noon."

A seizure. They're coming more frequently these days. The first time it happened, decades ago, Todd was six months old, in the crib. Little body curled like a new leaf. The doctors said he wouldn't live five years. *Quacks, what the fuck do they— Shit.* Todd's new meds, he'd picked them up today, along with his refill. He'd left them in the car—

"Life is long, Patrice," he mumbles.

"Sir?"

Lonnie doesn't repeat himself. He goes over to the boy's chair and kneels beside it. Todd's head turns at his father's touch, and his left eye rolls toward Lonnie and blinks. Lonnie squeezes his son's thin arm. "How are you, champ?"

Todd smiles, laughs. A line of saliva slicking his chin. His teeth are small and crooked. They look like baby teeth. Baby teeth in a thirty-three-year-old man.

"We took our medicine," Patrice says. "Then we was better."

Lonnie's eyes slip shut. *We took our medicine all right.* He opens his eyes. Looks up at his son and thinks, as he has so many times before, that he is looking into the face of God.

The boy laughs, a sudden, strangled bark.

Bedtime. A warm breeze shifts the curtains in Max's room and magnolia leaves chatter outside the window. Hair damp from his bath, he lies atop his covers reading *First Blood*. He's in his underwear and a long T-shirt two sizes too big. The T-shirt's from a summer trip to Myrtle Beach. A grinning shark and a pair of scuba fins, goggles, a tank. "Send more tourists!" the shark says, licking its lips. "The last ones tasted great!" Worn so much the silk screening is cracked and flaking. Dad bought it for him at the Gay Dolphin. They'd laughed over that shirt a long time, all through dinner at a place called Crabby Mike's. Mom had only rolled her eyes, but it made her happy, Max could tell.

In the bathroom next door, the claw-foot tub gurgles, begins to drain.

Rambo's on the cliff and the cops are shooting at him from the helicopter when the bedroom door eases open and Nellie, hair wet, the rest of her wrapped in a towel, says, "Thanks, kiddo."

"For what?"

"All the hard work. The house is shaping up, don't you think?"

He keeps his face in his book, doesn't answer.

Nellie bends over him to kiss him good night, and her wet hair drips onto him, onto his book. "Mom!"

She laughs, grabs a length of her hair, and wrings it on his head.

He cries out, ducks under the covers.

She drops on the lump of him, grabs at his knees through the sheet. The knees always drive him crazy, he doesn't know why. He begs her to stop through the laughter, so she slaps his arm and says good night. He feels the weight of her leave his bed, hears her bare feet padding into her bedroom.

He pops out from under his sheet, relieved to see she's left the adjoining door open.

An hour or so later, his mother's beside light winks out—she's reading a book on Romantic painters Max found for her, down in the library—and shortly after, when he hears her breathing deepen into sleep, he switches off his own lamp and opens the drawer of his bedside table and slips out the photo album he'd found that morning in the cellar, along with his flashlight. He tents the bedcovers over his head and clicks on his flashlight and opens the album.

On the inside flap, his fingers trace a faded inscription.

> *To Effie, who sees all . . .*
> *Merry Christmas, August*

The yellowed pages of the album are blank.

Max spreads the loose photographs, begins to sift through them. They're small, old, and delicate, and so he holds each as if it might crumble between his fingers. At first, there are no people in the pictures, only angles on the house being built. A wooden frame, the porch columns half-mortared. The barn. Some of these have dates written on the back, *1917* mostly. He comes across a ring of cabins in a meadow, beyond the meadow a river. Remembers the map downstairs, drawn by August Redfern: the cabins and the woodsmen and the pigs and chickens, the girl at the well. The first picture of a person is a wide view of the cellar and foundation, the house itself nothing more than a hole in the ground and a few bricks. Standing at the center of that hole, hands on his hips, face shadowed beneath a wide-brimmed hat, is a man who must be his great-grandfather. The back isn't labeled.

He comes upon a picture of a dark-haired woman, slight shouldered and bright-eyed, hair curly, like Mom's when she doesn't straighten it with the iron ("Daddy likes it straight, kiddo . . ."). She wears a housecoat, has a big, pregnant belly. One hand on the rock column by the porch steps. He flips the picture over: *August's First Day—November 2, 1917.*

Max fans the pictures out in stacks, sorts them by dates, and pretty soon they're telling a story. The story of Redfern Hill. And the pictures are good, too, not like the Polaroids Max used to snap randomly with the camera he got for Christmas a few years back, pictures of grass or road signs or the kitchen countertop when the beans spilled and Mom said, "Fuck!" and they both laughed (Dad broke that camera when he was mad, threw it across the room). The one common thing they all share, Max realizes, is that Effie isn't in them. Which means she's taking the pictures. Which means it's really *her* story.

Boxing the pines—November 1917: row upon row of huge pine trees bleeding thick black ribbons of sap, bark shorn away by coarse, heavy-browed men with long-bladed tools.

Distillery takes shape—January 1918: the wooden framework of a roof and a platform and stairs and a giant barrel, going up at the edge of a clearing around a massive oven and chimney that look for all the world like a big brick heart about to beat.

At the camp—March 6, 1918: men with hard, lean faces posing next to grim-faced wives and half-naked children on the porches of cabins, the cabins all clustered in a clearing. Gardens and laundry lines and women feeding chickens.

Gus and Barlow and the team—March 7, 1918: a wagonload of small barrels, standing by it two men, one a scowling bulldog of a man in a suit coat, watch chain, and tiny bowler hat, the other with eyes set close together, features sharp and flinty in that Indiana Jones hat and jodhpurs, bare hand snagged in a mule's harness.

Here is another picture of the same wagon, five men in baggy denim. They're ragged, sweaty. Each man wears a white bandanna over nose and mouth. In the wagon, rolled in a tarp, are three bodies. Max can see the bottoms of their shoes sticking out. He flips the picture. *October 22*, the scrawl reads. *Spanish*

Flu takes three more. Bodies will go to Brunswick, to island off coast. Mass burial site. Below this, apropos of nothing, a single fragment: *Not well.*

He keeps sifting.

March 8, 1920—The Twins, Charlie and Henry. Again, his great-grandmother, this time seated in a chair Max recognizes from the library, downstairs. Posed in that stiff, unsmiling way old-timey people pose in old-timey pictures. She's heavier, stouter. Not quite three years since the picture of her pregnant, but she looks to have aged ten. Balanced on her lap are two little boys in cloth diapers. Mirror images of each other. Effie's eyes are dark and cold.

One of the babies is Hank, Nellie's father. Max's grandfather.

He picks up the empty album, thumbs the first few pages. Stops at a hand-drawn tree, like something out of a fairy tale, its branches wide, the ink faded. Names written on every branch: his great-grandfather, his great-grandmother; beneath their branch, *Charles Eliot Redfern* and *Henry David Redfern.* Charlie's name slashed with a violent scrawl. And, on the lowest branch of the tree, a third name.

"Eleanor Agatha Redfern," Max whispers, remembering the initials sewn onto the rag doll (which is tucked away at the bottom of his cedar chest right now, where it will stay forever, thank you very much): *E.A.R.*

Outside, in the hallway, a board creaks.

Max looks up.

A second creak. Closer. In his doorway.

He clicks off the flashlight. Sound of his breathing loud, so he holds his breath.

Listens.

Nothing, for a while.

Then: that dry scrabbling sound. Like mice in the walls—but at the foot of his bed. Suddenly, the lid of the cedar chest creaks open in the dark, and the sound trips his heart like a school bell. Rummaging next, the shift and clatter of action figures, rustle of paper. He tastes the first drip of pennies. Swallows it. Then clicks on his light and hurls back the covers.

He's alone.

The flashlight throws its spot on the wardrobe beyond the foot of the bed. The deer head mounted above it, shadows of antlers long and crooked.

The lid of the cedar chest is raised.

He glances at the open door that adjoins his mother's room, listens, but nothing moves beyond it. He leaps down to the end of his bed, shines his light inside the chest.

The doll is gone.

1918

✦

SEPTEMBER 16

MARCUS THE SWEDE SETS OUT FROM REDFERN HILL AT HALF past three, collar buttoned to his throat, hair slicked back with pomade. In one pocket a list of groceries and supplies, which includes a new pair of scissors for barbering. In the other pocket, a week's wages. He's just crossed the narrow, one-lane river bridge when he hears a sputtering-ratcheting behind him, so he walks backward a while along the shoulder, staring hard to where the road dwindles to a heated point. Soon enough, an open-topped Buick clatters over a rise, and Marcus stops and stands in a drift of gravel to watch it pass. Instead, it pulls alongside him with a squeal of brakes. Behind the wheel is a man in a seersucker suit and straw hat, sporting a politician's smile. In back are two ginger-haired boys in army fatigues, duffels heaped on the seat between them. They're sunburned and dirty and the one on the far side looks pale and hollow eyed.

The dust settles, and the driver in the straw hat says, "This the road to Empire, friend?"

"Straight ahead." Marcus points.

"Ever ride in a car, boy?"

Marcus shuffles his long, stork-like legs, looks down at the sole of his right brogan flapping loose like a dog's thirsty tongue. "No."

"Well, hop in, son, and meet the modern age."

The ride is jarring but the seat is softer than the iron-sprung seat of a wagon, and the boys in back are friendly enough. They introduce themselves as the Lasky brothers, Tom and Terry, on leave from Camp Gordon. "We home to kiss our mothers and hump our girls," Tom says.

Terry just watches the trees crawl by.

The driver shakes the Swede's hand, says his name is Minyard Gaskin, says he's running for state senate and is personally delivering such boys as these to their families in order to make a Christian impression on the electorate, come November. "Assuming, of course, we still got an electorate, come November."

"What you mean?" Marcus says.

"My fair-haired friend, is there a rock you south Georgians all share to shade y'all from the news of the world?"

"I don't know what in the hell you're saying."

"That socialist Woodrow Wilson, boy! If that speechifying peckerhead goes unchecked, why, all us God-fearing folks down here in Dixie will be choking on humble pie with the Hun! League of Nations, giving women the vote. Next thing you know, this flu gets down here, hell, we'll all be ordered to mask up like a passel of Night Riders at a Mardi Gras Ball!"

"I heard tell about the flu," Marcus says. "But it's not here yet."

From the back seat, Tom Lasky leans forward. "It's here, son. You just don't know it."

Terry watches the trees. Dark moons under his eyes.

Minyard Gaskin shakes his head. "Goddamn German aspirin. League of Nations."

Tom Lasky spits over the side of the car. "We taught the Hun a thing or two, though. That's for sure."

Terry puts a fist to his mouth and coughs into it twice.

In Empire, when Gaskin pulls up to McCann's drugstore and idles, Marcus climbs out and thanks him for the ride. Before he heads into the store, he shakes all three men's hands. Again, Terry Lasky sputters, but this time he swallows it. Flinches when his brother slaps him on the back.

"You all right?" Tom says.

"Sinus."

Marcus watches them drive off, lifts a hand.

When he turns to go into the store, he sees a hand-lettered sign hanging in the window. The words are simple, words he'd agree with on any given day, but somehow, the news of the world as told by Minyard Gaskin angles new light on the phrase, and the sign strikes him as ominous, unsettling: WE FEAR NOT. Marcus looks up and down Main. A few horses tethered, a truck or two—the Ford kind, like Mr. Redfern's thinking of replacing the wagons with. A cool wind blows and a scrap of paper sails along the curb, and suddenly Marcus feels eerie, like he's the last man on earth.

He unfolds his list from his pocket and goes over it on the sidewalk, reading each item under his breath. Moving his finger down the list, so as not to lose his place. He always forgets something if he doesn't go over the list. He'll have the paper right in front of him, then he'll get to talking with Mr. McCann or put down a dime for a soda or a malt, and soon enough he'll breeze right out with a happy stomach and be halfway home to Redfern Hill before he remembers the thing he forgot: a razor blade, a bottle of aspirin, an ink pen for James Green, or a sewing needle for Mr. Sullivan's wife. The last item on the list, that's the one he'll forget this time, sure as shooting: *The Saturday Evening Post*, for Mrs. Euphemia herself. *It has a new Edith Wharton piece*, she'd said, pressing a quarter into his hand and winking, as if to say, *Get yourself something, too*. That wink Marcus has carried in his heart ever since walking away from Mrs. Euphemia's porch. "Magazine, magazine, magazine," he repeats, head down as he starts into the store.

The shop door rings and Marcus looks up just in time to avoid crashing into the man coming out, a man wearing shabby clothes and clutching a half-gone Dr Pepper.

Marcus catches the door and slips in and the bell rings as it shuts behind him.

On the sidewalk, the man with the Dr Pepper stops. He turns and looks after Marcus, eyes squinting. He steps back to the shop door, peers inside to where the Swede is handing the pharmacist his list and pointing at something on the paper, and the pharmacist is taking out a magazine from a shelf behind the counter, and the Swede is grinning like a fool.

"Son of a bitch," the man with the Dr Pepper says.

He's grinning, too, only it's a very different sort of grin.

Nothing foolish about it.

The spring day is warm and windy and blows pollen out of the pines in huge green clouds. On the return walk, Marcus stops twice to rest, both times fishing out the bottled root beer he's tucked into a corner of the old lettuce crate, among cans of pork and beans and potted meat and boxes of Lux soap flakes. The first time he stops, it's to sit on a tree stump at the edge of a cow pasture and watch a swayback horse crop johnsongrass. He takes a green apple from his crate, lets the horse chomp it from his palm. Then he's moving again, until the one-lane river bridge appears in the distance through a caul of heat, and Marcus realizes this is his last chance to rest. So he finds a spot of shade at the edge of the woods and settles down with his back to a sycamore to finish his soda. He doesn't mean to close his eyes, but the day's warm, the soughing of the branches overhead so pleasant.

When he wakes, the sun has moved in the sky.

Ants have found a sack of rock candy he's brought back for himself. He flicks them away, one by one, then pops a chunk of strawberry into his mouth—a *suck-upon*, his mother used to call such things—and sets out quickly for the bridge, beyond it Redfern Road.

A man perches on the bridge rail, a man with a Dr Pepper bottle. Long, greasy hair swept back behind his ears. Cheap boots, frayed jeans. His shirt is off, his bare chest covered in angry red welts.

Marcus's gait falters at the sight of him.

The man cracks a grin over a mouthful of gray teeth. "How do."

A wild smell of woodsmoke and unwashed skin hangs about him. His welts are chigger bites, weeping and infected. Even now, he's scratching one beneath his nipple, dirty fingernails raking flesh.

Marcus walks on, keeps his head down.

The man sucks his Dr Pepper through a straw until the bottle's empty and it's just air he's sucking. "Hey," he calls after. "I know you." He pushes off the rail. "You know me?"

Yes, Marcus knows him, remembers him from that first day at Redfern Hill almost a year ago. And because Marcus remembers him, he keeps walking, makes only a half turn to say,

No, sorry, friend, afraid I don't, but he doesn't get a single word out before the loose tongue of his brogan snags a risen nail in the boards and he goes down hard on his left knee. Something tears, pops. He cries out and the lettuce crate flies from his hands and everything in it scatters in the dust.

Behind him, the man cocks his head and tongues the paper straw in his bottle. He clamps his teeth around the straw and draws it out, chews it briefly like a stalk of grass. He hurls the empty bottle into the river and slips the straw from his mouth and tosses it, too, all the while fixing the boy's back with smiling eyes.

Marcus gets stiffly to his feet, then bends down to pick up his crate.

"You work for August Redfern," the man says to Marcus's back.

The Saturday Evening Post lies open at the edge of the bridge, its pages fluttering in the wind. Marcus picks it up and slaps the magazine against his thigh to shake off the dust. Puts it carefully back into the box.

"Yeah, you know me. Say who I am."

Marcus holds his crate and stares ahead at the distant turnout of Redfern Road. Gauging the distance, wondering if his left knee will give out if he runs. Wondering if the man behind him is faster than he is. Marcus is tall, quick. His stride is huge, but he isn't graceful. He'll trip again or run out of breath. There will be no dignity in what happens to him if he runs. So he turns to face the man. "You're Jasper Hawley. People call you Catfish."

Hawley—the man Mr. Barlow sapped for pulling a gun on Mr. Redfern, the man Eli Green and Marcus himself tossed unconscious into a wagon back in November—puts two fingers in his mouth and whistles. Directly, three other men in overalls and pants held up with rope belts, shotguns slung over their shoulders on baling twine, come trudging troll-like up the grassy embankment from under the bridge.

"These my cousins," Hawley says.

Knee throbbing, legs aquiver, Marcus sets his crate down. He makes sure Mrs. Euphemia's magazine is rolled and tucked tightly into a corner, between two cans of peaches in pear juice. Then he stands up straight.

Barlow and Daniel Two Fists and James Green carry the boy down the hall and into the dining room, where Euphemia and Frannie Sullivan set out two wide enamel pans of heated water. The men lay him on the table, and Frannie dips white rags into the water and washes the boy's hands, which are swollen, the knuckles pulped, the fingernail of his right thumb missing. Euphemia washes his head. One eye is swollen shut, the other red with burst capillaries. A whole plug of hair has been torn away above the boy's left ear, leaving behind a blood-crusted scalp. His lips are split. His left cheekbone is shattered. Through it all, he remains silent, watchful. His tears make clean tracks down cheeks orange with road dust. Rags go back into the pans, are wrung out, and the water is red. "Heat more," Effie says to no one, and James Green peels himself from the far wall, where the men stand with hats in hand like mourners before a casket. James takes up one pan, Frannie the other. "Be quick!" Effie hisses.

Within the hour, Redfern brings the doctor from town, whose first task is to set a broken left leg. It's then that the boy's silence finally gives way to screaming. Effie retreats from the sound, taking the pan of cooling water out the back door and dumping it at the edge of the field, where the spring grass is tall and the stalks bend beneath the weight of fat black grasshoppers. Great white clouds hang unmoving in the sky, frigates on a windless sea. She looks down at her apron and sees the Swede's blood smeared there and thinks of the twins, asleep upstairs in their cribs, while below a boy not much older than Effie herself lies broken and bleeding on her dining room table.

Behind her, the screen door slaps, followed by the sound of August's boots as he descends the back steps. "How is he?" she asks, when Redfern stands beside her.

"Doc says he'll heal with rest."

August's hands are in his pockets. He wears no hat and the wind plays through his hair, which is graying at the temples. Effie takes a folded piece of paper from her apron pocket, passes it to her husband. Pushes her own hair out of her face, where the wind has blown it. "It came this morning. Addressed to me, same as the others."

He opens the letter. Reads it.

"Pretty soon they'll be writing to the boys instead of me," Effie says.

There have been four such letters since the New Year. Crude, unsigned ruminations of what a buckskin knife could do to a young gal like her, what a bootheel could do to her babies' skulls, if her husband won't fold and get out of Baxter County forever.

As if that could happen.

Sometimes, standing very still in the empty house, or gathering eggs in the coops out behind the barn, while August is in the woods or down at the turpentine mill, Effie remembers her dream, the one she always has, night after night. A dream that should be her husband's, but is somehow her own. She is in the belly of a ship, rowing giant oars among men, hands blistered, as the sea presses and the hull creaks. The rumble of some leviathan's

passage in the dark, stormy waters stirs them all. The ship begins
to shudder, to leak. A man cries out and water bursts through the
boards and the ocean rushes in and the ship plunges, quickly, for
the seafloor, so fast that Effie cannot tell whether they are flying
down to meet it or it is heaving up from countless fathoms, and
just before waking, she understands: it is the land that her husband
craves, come to claim her.

"Hawley trash." Redfern crumples the letter.

"They did this, August."

A single, tight nod. "Barlow found him down by the mill
road. They'd lashed him to the gate, length of twine around his
neck." August takes his hands from his pockets, rubs his palms
on his trousers. Haltingly he adds, "I saw a man once, hanged by
a yardarm," and he seems to want to say more, but doesn't.

The wind blows, and the clouds finally seem to move. Their
shadows crawl.

"You see the sheriff, when you went for the doctor?"

"Wasn't time."

"But you will."

Silence, like heat from an oven. He doesn't like it when she
presses him. "Your father—"

"My father," she barks.

All-seeing, all-wise George Baxter, who has always believed,
like a proud, foolish king in a children's tale, that Baxter County
was a land of his own making, as if the trees and the river and the
fields, the people themselves, had not existed until he came along
and spoke them into being. *We're paying the price now*, she
thinks, *for the woods he's leveled, the families he's swindled.*

"Your father says," Redfern goes on, "it was the same in the
early days of the sawmill. They're cowards, these men."

"And how do you think my father dealt with such men?"

"What would you have me do?"

"Hire men to protect what's yours."

"Hire them with what? We haven't even turned a profit yet, Effie—"

"You can't lay claim to a thing, August, then refuse responsibility for it. Defend us. Defend this place. Defend your men."

He stares at her, but she only looks away, out at the field. Her jaw set.

He reaches something from his back pocket, holds it out.

Effie takes it, unrolls it.

The Saturday Evening Post.

On the cover, a woman in profile, clad in a charcoal dress and hat, in her hands a pair of binoculars. In the bottom right corner, a bloody thumbprint.

Redfern slides away, toward the house.

"Cowards are men of action, too, August," she calls after him. "A man has to be willing to go all the way, to see a thing through, no matter the cost!"

Clouds pass over the sun, and the world goes briefly dim. Again, she thinks of the twins, sleeping upstairs in their cribs, oblivious of the terrible things at work in their lives. Effie rolls the magazine, picks up her pan, and goes back inside to heat fresh water.

1989

JULY 3

NELLIE, SORE AND STIFF AND COVERED IN HER OWN SWEAT, opens her eyes. The end of a nightmare playing over in her head, something fevered and strange: she and Max are passengers in the Ranger on a twisting, narrow tongue of blacktop, and Wade's behind the wheel, driving too fast. The road dips and the truck careens toward a guardrail, beyond which there is only mist and darkness, and Nellie cries out to Wade, *Slow down, goddamn it*, but he insists, in that reasoned, handsome way he has, he isn't even speeding! The road turns to gravel and something huge and vague speeds ahead of them, kicking up dust, its brake lights flashing red like eyes, only Wade doesn't see, isn't stopping, so she thrusts her foot against the floorboard and hauls Max to her, turning his face away as this behemoth fills the Ranger's windshield—

She sits up in bed. Touches her cheek, gingerly. It's puffy, feels hot, her right middle finger likewise, swollen like a sausage. She pries the damp second skin of her David Bowie tee away from her stomach, sheet damp beneath her. She slides out of bed and onto the floor, to her hands and toes.

"One," she counts.

Wake the acid in your muscles . . .
"Two."
Pain in your finger, but your arms are strong . . .
"Three."
So strong you had to wear sleeves around Wade . . .
"Four."
Sleeves he made you wear anyway, to hide the scar . . .
"Five."
Your secret strength . . .

It's 1977 and Nellie Gardner is eighteen years old, telling people she's twenty, and living in Savannah in a roach-infested dump of an apartment, taking night classes at community college. She waits tables at a dive off Abercorn, tends the bar on the weekends when the regular guy's too hungover to come in. It beats the bars on River Street and Broughton, where tourists and frat boys get hammered and the girls have to blow the owners to keep work. Here, between a used-car lot and a window-service barbecue shack, the customers are all too dispirited or too drunk to be any real trouble, even during the wee hours of a Friday or Saturday night. Nellie wonders, sometimes, what they go home to, whom they're hurting, besides themselves. She does not drink and never will. But work is work, money is money.

Tonight, Nellie's English professor sits drinking a cherry Coke in a booth, smoking cigarettes and reading a James Cain paperback. A stack of sophomore lit essays untouched to his left. Her own among them. Hawthorne, "The Birth-Mark." Aylmer the alchemist and his new bride, Georgiana, that evil mark upon her cheek. To kiss it or cure it?

What the hell's he doing here?

He was polite enough when he first came in. He smiled, asked how her night was going. Ordered his drink.

"That's it? A Coke?"

"A cherry Coke. Is that not an acceptable thing to order in a bar?"

"It's fine. Just a little weird."

"Why is it a little weird?"

"Well. See that lady over there?"

"The one by the jukebox, talking to the wall?"

"That's Mary O'Meary. She's a regular here. And she never orders anything but Pabst Blue Ribbon. So, yeah, it's a little weird that the lady over there talking to the wall, like she does on a regular basis, understands that bars are for ordering booze, while you, Dr. Gardner, with your PhD and your keen knowledge of American literature, show up at this fine establishment on a Friday night and order nothing more than"—she pretends to check her notepad—"a cherry Coke."

"Call me Wade. Please."

"Okay. One cherry Coke, coming up. Wade."

An hour before last call, the place has emptied out, except for poor Mary, who's over by the window, wagging her finger at people who pass on the sidewalk. Nellie knows Wade knows she's been watching him, biting her thumb until the nail is ragged. He sips the last of his Coke until his straw burbles, puts his book down, digs into the stack, and starts reading essays. No pen in hand.

Nellie pours herself a ginger ale and goes to the jukebox and drops in a quarter for "Wish You Were Here." The jukebox whirs. The song plays. Wade reads. She takes off her apron, throws it over the bar. Ginger ale in hand, she slides into the booth opposite the man she will, in only eight weeks, marry. A man she knows nothing about, save he is not of her world. He is not Hank Redfern. He does not drink at a bar on a Friday night. And while Savannah is not even two hours from the house on Elm where she grew up, Nellie Redfern figures this dingy hole might as well be the moon if men like Wade Gardner come here to *not* drink.

Typed on a giant office IBM she bought for ten bucks at a pawnshop off Victory Drive, her essay's about scars, scars that run unseen like caverns cut by rivers in the earth. Internal landscapes forever changed—and unseen—by men who murder women just to prove they're nothing more than the sum of their flaws.

She doesn't hear it, but his breathing changes when she sits down.

So does hers.

Behind the essay, he smiles.

Later, the sour smell of restaurant garbage drifts through her open bedroom window. She smokes a cigarette, bedsheets bunched at her navel, one arm folded over her bare breasts, the other cocked behind her head. He's told her about his father, a Baptist preacher from some cinder-block church way back in the swamps of Horry County, South Carolina. A man who believed the answer to everything was prayer and pain. "The Father, the Son, and the Holy Whipping Post," Wade says. So she tells him about Hank, the late-night wake-up calls, lights thrown on, bedcovers torn away. Hauled out by her bare ankle and dropped on the floor like she was a fish he'd caught, no wherewithal to clean or cook her. Just left there on the floor. Some deep stirring satisfied, it seemed, at the sight of her there, still alive beneath his roof. Next, inevitably, his own bedroom door would slam and a gibbering arise behind it, her mother's arms around him, her voice soothing, calming. More madness than drunkenness, as if some key piece of her father's soul were missing or stolen. A thing irrevocably lost he went searching for, every night, in a bottle. She listened outside the door. Cracked it one night and saw her mother on her knees beside him, holding him, rocking him like a child. What had been torn from him, that he was this way? Rudderless in a storm that never ceased. He drifted through its ever-moving eye by day. Every night, he capsized beneath its waves.

"What that must have done," Wade says, lying naked beside her, "to your poor mother."

Nellie ashes into a seashell on her belly. "When she got sick, I moved her into my room. Stood watch over her. Her sister helped some, but it was mostly me. Bowls of canned soup heated in the microwave, spooned into her mouth. She went crazy from the pain, near the end. He was never there. Some juke joint out at the county line. Cockfights and deer camps and who knows what. Drove his truck into a lake once. Spent the night in jail.

"I slept nights in a chair at the foot of the bed. She had oxygen, a little tank. Hose that ran into her nose. After they brought her home from the hospital, I went through all the drawers, found her stashes. Her lighter. I kept it all for myself, tucked in a little cigar box high up in my closet. Every cigarette I smoke now was one of hers. One day they'll run out. I guess then I'll quit."

The tip of her cigarette flares, burns.

"It's a nasty habit," Wade says, trailing a hand along her shoulder, down her arm.

Later, she'll remember this, tell herself she should have known. Right then, she should have known.

"One morning, I wake up. Mama's dead. She'd been awake the night before, trying to talk. But I was so tired, I fell asleep. You know how people say, 'Well, she went peacefully, at least,' or 'She died in her sleep.' It was funny. It's like she died in *my* sleep."

Forty-four push-ups now, nearing the end.
After you told him your story, he kissed you . . .
"Forty-five."
He kissed one pale, smooth arm, just below your elbow . . .
"Forty-six."
You flinched at his touch, remember? . . .
"Forty-seven."
Cried softly. Grateful . . .
"Forty-eight."
That a man could listen, that a man could care . . .
"Forty-nine."
How could you know he was an alchemist, the worst kind of man? An Aylmer, all along . . .
"Fifty!"
Out of breath, right hand throbbing, Nellie gets up and goes to the window. Yesterday she'd raised the sash to let in air, and overnight the screen has caught a host of little black bugs. She thumps them, one by one, watches them fly away.

She edges open the adjoining door but the bed is empty, the covers mussed, cedar chest open.
"Max?" she calls.
He's tacked up his own pencil drawings of superheroes. His pencil box and sketchbooks are open on her father's old desk.

A line of action figures along the windowsill. Above which the window is cracked. Curtains rustling in the breeze.

How quickly a place becomes familiar, she hopes.

She pulls on a T-shirt and jeans, ties her hair up in a red rag, and slips downstairs to look for Max. She finds him in the parlor, asleep on the couch, still in his underwear and T-shirt. The Magnavox is on, one of his tapes. *The Karate Kid*.

She leaves him long enough to make coffee. After it's brewed, she pours herself a cup, then stares at the styrofoam in her hand. Abruptly, Nellie dumps the coffee back into the pot, throws the cup away, and goes into the pantry, where she rummages a milk glass mug out of a cardboard box. She washes it in the sink and pours herself a proper cup, then goes back into the parlor and sits down beside her son.

Shakes his shoulder.

He opens his eyes.

"What's the matter?" she says.

"I couldn't sleep up there."

"Why?"

"Mmm." He rolls over.

She leaves him, goes upstairs into the old nursery.

She takes down the embroidered prayer, tosses it into one of the dusty cribs. Later, she'll drag the crib out into the hall. Right now, she's thinking of her brushes, her paints. All of it left behind in South Carolina. She likes the way the morning slants through the front windows here. The opposite wall, wide and blank, where the light lands, is the best place for an easel.

Sipping coffee, she has ideas, and they're good ones.

The healing kind.

———

They're making a late breakfast of Hot Pockets at the kitchen table when Max asks if he can climb the fire tower. Get out of the house, work his muscles, not his brain. Forget . . . whatever last night was.

"Tell you what," she says. "Tomorrow, we'll both climb it. Maybe we can see the fireworks from there."

In Empire, while shopping for supplies, they'd seen banners hung on Main Street, flyers in every shop window: INDEPENDENCE DAY CELEBRATION! PARADE 4 PM / FIREWORKS DUSK.

"Can we go into town for the parade?"

"If you want. I need to buy some paints. An easel. A few canvases."

"You also need medicine."

She holds up her hand, her fingers slightly less swollen. "They're looking better."

"Mom"—a warning in his voice.

"Okay, you're right. Lots more yellow jackets where those came from."

"What's the Boy Scout motto?"

"Wear a rubber," Nellie deadpans.

He doesn't get it.

Nellie sees the look on his face and bursts into laughter.

So Max laughs, too, happy she's happy.

After lunch, Nellie works upstairs while Max, feeling unmoored and aimless, sorts August Redfern's maps. He's not sure why he's doing it or what he's looking for, but it kills a chunk of the long, hot afternoon. He pulls out rolled paper by the armloads and piles it all on the wide pine table. Always careful of the brittle edges. What he learns right away is that not every rolled piece of paper is, in fact, a map. Some are architectural plans, like the original blueprints for the turpentine mill. Others are sketches of custom tools, like gauntlets made of stovepipe tin to protect the workers from snakebites. One of these includes an illustration of a coiled rattlesnake striking at a woodsman who's wearing the gauntlets. The woodsman's smiling, laughing, like the joke's on the snake. There's one sketch for a special clay cup to catch the gum, one for an ax with a curved blade to fit the shape of a tree, just like the ax Nellie found on the study floor, their first night here. The maps are mostly studies of the property, much like the one framed above Redfern's desk, only close-ups of things like the turpentine mill, or the woodsmen's camp. Little half-moons on outhouse doors, wire-grass fields billowing black smoke as rabbits flee the fire lines. Maps of the longleaf groves, too, notes scrawled in the margins about when to "chip" and "pull" and "dip." And finally a single map of a shadowy section of woods—deep whorls of charcoal-dusted trees and heavy dark pencil—above something called North Creek, where something in the center of the drawing has been scribbled out, a black slash of graphite.

Immediately, he thinks of his own drawing: the cellar door scratched into the paper, the pencil blunted. Suddenly, Max is sweating all over. He can feel it dripping beneath his arms. He wants to run out into the hallway, to stop Nellie on the stairs, to help her wrestle that second crib into the yard and, oh yeah, blurt out everything that happened yesterday: the cellar, the noises, the laughter, the gross sticky sap in his room and the creepy doll and the cedar chest opening on its own last night, how it drove him downstairs to the sofa. But he doesn't. Instead, he takes two, three, four deep breaths, even as his gaze drifts to that ragged hole in the far wall of the map room, boards ripped away, furring strips exposed like ribs, like the old man was looking for something *inside the walls*—

No, he tells himself. *You can't ruin this for her.*

After all, she's about to start painting again, and that's a good thing. No matter what, it's a good thing. *So forget your own misgivings, your own fears. Mom's happier than she was, and that's enough for now.* Besides, whatever the mystery is, Max has seen enough movies and read enough Stephen King to know: kids go it alone. That's the rule.

Just like Conway, he thinks.

Long afternoons spent hanging on swing-set chains, head down in a book, while things broke inside the house and his parents flashed back and forth in the windows like trapped birds.

In the last few hours of light, as the day cools down and the sky turns molten behind the trees, they go outside. Nellie teaches Max how to operate the riding lawn mower. He stands quietly by, listening. She tells him twice to stay away from the bushes, and when the time comes for him to climb into the saddle, he does so eagerly. He sets the choke and turns the key, and the roar of the tractor seems to clear his head for the first time that long day. He puts it in gear and lets off the clutch, and Nellie sets him off with a slap, like he's lit out a-horseback in some old western.

Meanwhile, she fetches her gloves from the Ranger's cab, where she left them yesterday, and goes at the crape myrtles with the chain saw. The grind and bite of the teeth through the wood, the way the new blade falls through without much resistance, is entirely satisfying.

Out by the barn, the boy caroms around on the John Deere like a crazy bullet.

A little while later, she's dragging severed tree limbs to the open tailgate of the pickup when she hears, on the far side of the house, the lawn mower cut out.

A heavy silence rises as the dust in the yard settles.

Unease tugs her around the porch to the long shadow of the northeastern corner, where Max sits astride the mower, both hands gripping the wheel. He stares up at the second-floor windows. Their bedrooms. The boy's eyes are narrowed.

"Everything okay?"

Max doesn't answer, just keeps watching the glass, opaque with shadow.

"What's up there?" She ruffles his hair.

After a long while, he simply shrugs. "Just us."

1918

OCTOBER 27

Dawn.

Redfern cuts east of the second firebreak, out of understory thick and snarled with smoke and embers that dart like fireflies. Far behind him, the fire teams shout and call, their voices fading after he fords North Creek and the land rises up to the sandy ridge where the turkey oaks stand no taller than a man. Beyond this, the wire-grass meadow. In the hollow of a lightning-struck pine are two small casks of turpentine he stowed there yestereve. Sweating, trembling, he shakes a blue bandanna from his trouser pocket and ties it tightly over nose and mouth. He takes up a cask under each arm and carries them into the pine-studded meadow. Here, the trees are tall and reaching, like the spires of a vaulted cathedral.

The sick tent is pitched in the center of the clearing, its canvas blazing white in the early-morning sun. Inside, the light is scant and the air is foul. There are thirteen cots, in each a woodsman, thin and wasted beneath coarse blankets. A few are old, most are young. All are dead. Marcus the Swede, his busted leg still encased in plaster, lies near the entrance, right hand hanging over the edge of his bedding.

Redfern stares at the boy's hand.

A thick brown root—or something like one—has broken through the soft earth below the Swede's fingers. It's put out five shoots, and these have bored *into* the fingers. The hand itself is swollen near to bursting, though the rest of the boy is shriveled and drawn.

Redfern looks around the tent. They're all as he found them yesterday, in the twilight hour when the fireflies were flashing. Their pot of evening soup set down outside the tent, prepared by anxious wives and brought up from camp by Redfern alone. He'd stood and called to empty air. Listening. Hearing only the buzz of flies. And so, cinching his bandanna tight, he'd lifted the flap and peered into the gloom—and afterward went reeling into the meadow to tear the bandanna from his face and vomit. Now, he swallows his gorge, beholds it all again, tells himself it was no nightmare. No dream from which he will wake.

Roots. Bursting through the ground, boring into ears, out of nostrils, blood and fleshy pulp clinging to every shoot. One man's stomach is a sunken pit, shreds of shirt and intestines and a mass of something like snakes coiled inside it. Another man's head is a broken nest, bits of skull caught up in the fibers like scraps of paper. Every last man is stitched to the ground.

A fly lands on Redfern's nose.

Effie was right. That day, when Marcus was brought to the house, he should have done something then, he should have *listened*—

"I'm sorry," he says to them all.

He sets one cask at the entrance of the tent and edges between the cots with the other, sloshing everything with turpentine. The fumes are dizzy making. When the first cask is empty, he drops it and is about to break open the second when he hears something, a rustling beneath the cots, like the whisper of leaves on a windy day.

Something clutches at Redfern's leg.

He whirls and looks down and sees the Swede's hand, flopping, climbing, grasping now at Redfern's wrist. The dead boy's throat begins to bulge, and Marcus—pale, shriveled, dead Marcus—opens his mouth and suddenly the tent and Redfern's skull explode with a great prehistoric shriek. It comes from everywhere and nowhere as a dark, wormlike thing flops out of the boy's mouth. The corpse jerks upright in the cot like a marionette, and the dead boy's eyes open and Redfern sees in them waves of shimmering blue that break in starbursts, and these are not the boy's eyes, but the eyes of something else inside him, something vast and terrible, and then the eyes explode as tubers filmed in mucus erupt from the sockets and the boy's jaw cracks down, like a drawer yanked from its track, and blood begins to gush from his mouth.

As all throughout the tent the corpses of the woodsmen are jerking and rattling as the thing moving inside them withdraws, like some hideous, unimaginable worm threading them all, and now the only sound in Redfern's head is the sound of his own screaming, as he pinwheels backward out of the tent, into the bright, indifferent day.

Not long after, the fire roars and the canvas blazes. Redfern sits in the grass, dizzy and sick to his stomach. He tears the blue bandanna from his face. He opens his left hand, and the matchbook is there, crushed in his grip. That scream, reverberating behind his eyes, jangling the very nerves—

(roots)

—of his teeth.

The turpentine. It's the first clear thought he has. *The turpentine set it to screaming.*

After a while, the fire spreads to the grass, so he gets up and staggers away, into the trees. Looking back only once, at smoke rising into a blue sky. *It will work.* No one will suspect anything but another controlled burn. The wind simply blew in the wrong direction. A terrible tragedy. He walks on, steeling himself, as that horrible shrieking fades and the roar of the flames falls away. In its place, a softer, kinder voice speaks, and the word it speaks in the sunlit clearing, as the fire licks the bristled stalks of wire grass to bring new blooms, is gentle, loving.

A language entire, in a single word.

. . . *august* . . .

The moon breaks over the river, luminescent shards of bone. Redfern slumps in a camp chair on the upper deck of the distillery, a bottle of Scotch on the boards beside him, half-empty by the time George Baxter's mare chuffs from the road's shadows. Old snow-beard sits his horse and calls up to his son-in-law in a sonorous baritone broken by age and phlegm: "You'd better be sober enough to explain yourself."

Redfern bends down for an empty tin cup between his boots. Baxter wraps his reins around a hitching post and mounts the steps. "I heard about the fire." He pulls up a chair. "Tragic, but it's no reason to put my sore ass in a saddle at one in the morning."

Redfern grasps the neck of the whiskey bottle, smacks it against the cup. Sloshes whiskey across the boards.

Baxter snatches the bottle. "Don't piss away good Scotch."

Redfern tips back his cup, shifts in his camp chair. Tries to sit straight. His eyes are bloodshot and he reeks of turpentine and smoke. His eyes mist over. "I need help, George."

"What's wrong?"

"I saw it."

"You saw what?"

"*It.*"

Baxter looks sidelong at Redfern, then takes the cup, too, from his son-in-law and pours himself a drink. "And what did you see?"

"The boy was dead. All of them were. Until they weren't."

Baxter swallows everything in the cup. "Oh, they were dead all right. Did it touch you?"

Redfern's gaze drops down to his wrist, where the Swede's dry fingers clamped. A ring of mottled bruises, at the center of each bruise a tiny red puncture. Half a dozen, at most.

"What did it feel like?"

Redfern glances at the old man, misliking the thirst in his voice.

Baxter sits forward on the edge of his chair. "Did it speak to you, August?"

Redfern puts a hand to his temple, shuts his eyes. Out of the dark, a whisper. Soft as the wind in the pine tops.

. . . august . . .

The old man's voice thickens. "What did it say?"

Redfern opens his eyes. "My name."

A tear drops down Baxter's cheek into the snowfield of his beard. He sits back and looks out at the dark woods, beyond the edge of the lantern glow. "I take it you burned the tent then. The bodies."

"Did I kill it?"

Baxter laughs without smiling, a single bark. "Most likely you just pissed it off."

"I didn't know what to do, I—"

"Oh, but you did, August. I told you, when I entrusted you with this land, what to do. You didn't hold up your end of the deal. You strayed from a path that was preordained. I warned you. And now . . ." The old man shrugs. "There are consequences. Why do you think this sickness spread through your camp? Thirteen men, the bulk of your workforce laid low?"

Redfern tips forward in his seat, hangs his head between his knees. Puts his hands over his ears to block out the distant, alien night song of the frogs.

Baxter stares out into the dark, where a thousand eyes stare back, unseen.

"There are prices to be paid. I bought this land, damn near a hundred thousand acres, from ignorant white trash, and I paid pennies on the dollar. The years went by, they'd come at me, spill some of my blood. I'd spill theirs. When I was your age, of course, I believed I was their better, but now . . ." He shakes his head. "Now, I realize I had my price, too. *It* knew that, the first day I set foot in these woods. And my price was far dearer than pennies on the fucking dollar."

Redfern stands. Takes a few uneasy steps, his pant leg hitched above his boot. He circles the heavy copper kettle. Its burnished, onion shape like some pagan altar.

"Anywhere else"—Baxter stares out at the dark—"a man works hard, that's enough. But this place, these woods, whatever it is that dwells in them, it asks more of us than sweat. I don't know what it is, or where it comes from, but it's been here a long fucking time, and it will be here long after you and I are worm food. I *told* you what you had to do. I *showed* you, years ago. But you didn't listen. You didn't learn, boy. I love you, August, but you are goddamn pigheaded." Baxter turns round in his chair to face his son-in-law. He watches him, this slow, coming-to-grips unfolding. "Maybe I mistook that stubbornness for strength."

"The trees won't bleed," Redfern finally says. "No gum, no resin. Not since March. It'll be my ruin."

Baxter notices an old cap-and-ball pistol snugged in the waist of Redfern's trousers.

"It's an easy remedy, son."

A long, guilt-ridden pause. Redfern's hand touching the hilt of the pistol. "There's more."

Baxter waits.

"Charlie's sick. Effie, too."

Baxter's head, his whole frame, slumps. He stares at the boards between his feet. "Henry?" he asks after a moment.

Redfern shakes his head. "He's fine."

"You can fix it."

Redfern's voice is small. "Help me, George."

"Who will it be?"

Redfern draws the pistol from his waistband. It's the one he took off Hawley last November. He's kept it in the desk drawer in his study. He isn't sure why. Every now and then, he feels the pull of it and opens the drawer to look at it.

By lantern light, they descend the stairs.

The wide board door of the cooper's shed is padlocked. Redfern passes the lantern to Baxter and takes out a key ring. He unlocks the door and swings it wide on a room rich with the scents of sawn wood and iron. Dozens of metal hoops hang from the ceiling like weird bones. In a far corner, hog-tied and gagged with a handkerchief, is a man. His eyes swivel as the light from the lantern reveals him in his threadbare rags. He has long, unkempt hair, a three-day beard. The sole of his right shoe has a hole sealed up from the inside with newspaper. A wound in his shoulder, crusted red, the sleeve of his old Confederate coat soaked. Jasper Hawley kicks and strains against his ropes until the cords in his neck and the veins in his head pop.

"Caught him this very night," Redfern says. "Trying to set fire to the mill. He came up by river as I sat right yonder, drinking. Almost like—"

"Like it was meant to be," Baxter says. "Anyone see him here?"

Redfern shakes his head.

"You sober enough for this?"

"Drunk enough."

"Well, it's a long goddamn walk, so we best get to it, if we aim to be done by daylight."

Hawley's eyes bulge as the men step toward him.

Baxter leads, carries a lantern to light their way. For a while, they take the newly finished Camp Road, which runs along the western bank of the river, Redfern bringing up the rear in the soft gravel, pistol trained on Hawley, who walks between the men, hobbled by a length of coarse rope binding his ankles. Arms tied behind his back, still gagged, he stinks of something old and sour. Eventually, the road turns back toward the woodsmen's camp. Off to their left, little more than half the cabin lights are twinkling in the meadow, the rest dark. Baxter douses the lantern. On the breeze the brief, sad curl of a fiddle. Redfern presses the pistol hard into Hawley's back, warns him against noise. They ease along the embankment, hunkered in the moonlit grass, until the trees give cover again.

Baxter's lantern bobs in the dark as they reach North Creek.

Here, they pause. Listen. A crackle of branches, a rustle of leaves, off to their right.

Hawley moans, begins to grunt, as if summoning air.

Redfern shoves the pistol's barrel against the base of the man's skull and cocks the trigger.

Hawley falls silent.

Seconds later, a doe rockets out of the trees in a slant of moonglow, bounds past them, disappears into the pines.

On they go as the wilderness rises up and the land grows uneven, and they struggle through a maze of brush and gnarled trees with ghostly forms, until finally the forest breaks and they're passing scratched and bitten through the still-smoldering fields and the blackened wire-grass meadow where the tent was burned.

Was only a deer then, Redfern remembers. That first, long ago day in the woods, when the old man showed him Euphemia's dowry, its secrets. Secrets, George Baxter said, that could not be trusted to men without vision. Without heart.

Or need, Redfern thinks.

Once upon a time, George Baxter had *need* of its power.

Redfern's mind is clearing, the whiskey long since sweated out of him, despite the chill fall night.

They'd carried rifles, set up a blind, and when the buck had wandered out to crop the freshly dewed beard grass, it was Baxter who had fired, put a bullet in the animal's breast. They'd tracked it, finished it. *Make a fine trophy*, Redfern told his father-in-law. But Baxter only shook his head. Took the buck by an antler, told Redfern to catch the other, and together they dragged the deer into the trees until the sun shot spears of light through the forest, which opened, after a while, on the very thicket of wire grass they passed through now.

He was easing you into it, Redfern thinks, staring at the vague shape of Jasper Hawley's head, his slumped shoulders. Beneath their boots, the grass is black. *You had no enemies then, the deer was a lesson, a primer—*

They'd walked all morning together, guns shoulder-slung, the old man telling how, when he'd first laid eyes on this ancient tract, it must have been the same as when the conquistadores of old had landed on the shores of South America and stepped into the jungle primeval, how the sacred silence of that place must, at least in part, have seemed like a trap, a trap those conquerors wanted desperately to spring, so the mystery might finally reveal itself, their souls be damned. He'd walked these woods for days on end, camping, hunting. Dreaming, as all men do, of the future. *Of peaceful times of plenty*, his words.

Later, when the deer had grown heavy between them, they ceased walking, sat on logs, and Baxter told the story of the first time it spoke to him. How it whispered his name from beyond the edge of his firelight. *Was my mother's voice, she who'd been in the ground over ten years up in Mystic, Connecticut. The only woman I ever listened to. She who taught me to treat people fairly. To never steal. Borrow no more than you can repay, she told me.* Baxter smoked, offered a cigarette to Redfern. *It spoke my name*, he said, *because it knew me.*

Redfern said nothing.

The deer's carcass by then drawing flies.

It found me before I found it, Baxter said, touching his head. *It was in here the moment I set foot in these woods. For days, it poked around. Learned me. It listens. It lurks.*

Nearby, a black snake made a shepherd's crook on the trunk of a red oak.

It demanded unspeakable things. But the rewards . . . the things it promised . . . so much greater than the cost.

And next, after the silence had lengthened like the day's light: *Has it spoken to you yet?*

Redfern's answer, rough, impatient: *I haven't heard a goddamn thing.*

You will.

It was not long after, they came to the place that George Baxter called the Hollow.

Heat, like she has never known. Charlie in the crib beside her, coughing, leaking, theirs the shared misery of imperiled voyagers shot through a molten star, straight to the surface of a world scorched anew every hour by lightning storms and scouring winds. Delirium. Darkness. Voiding. And always: heat. The fever roams her dreams on stilts, stands tall above ever-shrinking pools of consciousness, leaves only steam behind. Babies, birth, screams, and blood. The doctor is her father and his arms are inside her, ungloved, and she can feel the bones of his hands against the walls of her uterus. His beard is slick with red, his teeth bared, and he has been down there, lapping at her like a dog at a spigot. Charlie is born with two heads and bat wings and flies up to the ceiling and hangs above her to roost and drop vampiric as she sleeps. The forest, the piney woods, where a horned Satan roams tempting August and his woman, Eve, who has Euphemia's mind but no mouth with which to speak it, and so it falls to the man, the naming of all God's perversion, and in ten, fifteen years they are clad in rags and murdering alligators that slime out of the river, eating their fishy meat raw, still naked, still within the dying, blasted borders of a horned beast's kingdom. And last: the island, that place where even now August and her father go, a boil of roots and mud and bones, a black cosmic throat out of which the ocean wells up to swallow the world. The men go to change their fortunes, to feed their god, because a god is like a pet, the old man says: if you feed it, it will love you. But the old man never told her, never told this secret, this black family jewel vaulted away in George Baxter's heart, bequeathed to August, poor weak August, who believes in the dignity of all men, unfit to sate with blood a creature whose very will can change the course of fate for good or ill. And now, she and little Charlie are dying, reliant upon him, and in the dream there is a wretch who will be their salvation, his life for theirs, and out of his death a terrible tide of nightmares will rise up and drown them all, but *I do not want to die, August, Daddy, I do not want Charlie to die, because my baby is not a monster and Daddy you are not a monster and Henry is not a monster, and Gus, Gus is not a monster and I am not—*

A creak from the boards outside her shut door, a passing shadow beyond the keyhole. The wrenching cry of Henry, a shushing lullaby from Frannie Sullivan.

Effie sits up on her elbows, pillow drenched in sweat.

Beside the bed: Charlie in his crib, weak and pale, though his eyes are wide and shining.

Can it be, their fevers have broken?

Effie collapses, and the dream settles, way down among the

rock beds of her heart, where dark shapes slumber, waiting to be roused.

Beyond North Creek, there is a low-lying inlet, and the inlet is crowded with cypress trees that grow out of the shin-high water, and beyond this water there is an island, little more than twice the height of a man. At the peak of this island, out of a dark, black hole, spills a vomitus of strangling vines, as if the earth itself has sicked up its own insides. The banks at its base are laced with dropwort and water hemlock, and moccasins pend spellbound among the twisted roots.

The three men slosh through the cypress trees, edging between them at times, and when Baxter finally steps aside and Jasper Hawley sees the Hollow, rising up from the black water, he looks from one captor to the other, finds in their faces a determination, a resolve, and falls to his knees with a splash.

"Get up," Redfern says.

But he doesn't, so Redfern shoves the gun into his waistband and seizes the rope between the man's ankles and drags him on his back, thrashing, through the shallow water, up the narrow, root-studded ascent. Snakes slide away, cold-weather sluggish.

Redfern's boots are sucked and pulled in the black earth.

Baxter follows like some old acolyte, lantern held aloft.

Halfway up, something moves in the hole.

The men freeze, Hawley wriggling between them like a haul of fish.

Out of the dark, a shifting-squelching-cracking.

"Don't hesitate," Baxter whispers. "Give freely of your heart, August."

Redfern remembers hauling Baxter's deer up this mound,

how the old man had reached for a hunting knife from his belt and slit the buck's throat, how the blood spilled over the ground as they heaved the deer into the maw. How Baxter brushed the buck's stray hairs from his hands and said, *That's how she's done.* The deer sliding only a few feet down the tunnel. Redfern peering in. Leaning closer. *Not so close, August—*

A blast of foul air, and suddenly the deer was torn away into that long, dark gullet.

And out of that black hole came a terrible crunching sound.

What in the name of God did we just do?

Nothing. The old man laughed. *Not in our God's name, anyway.*

What, for Christ's sake, George, is in there?

I've never seen it. But wouldn't that be grand, to catch a glimpse of it, before I die? To know it, the way it knows us?

Hawley sputters behind his gag.

Redfern sets him, knees down, before the hole, a ragged black mouth.

The truth is, August, I'm getting old. It's not so easy anymore . . .

Redfern draws the pistol. Nestles it among Hawley's greasy locks.

. . . but I want you to live well, I want my daughter to live well. And while I can, I want to live well. I've seen too much heartache already.

A dark stain spreads at Hawley's crotch.

One day, at your hour of need, it will come to you, speak to you, and all you need remember is this: fortune follows the faithful. This is its power. Like the moon influences the tides unseen, it shapes our way, so long as we serve it.

Now.

Fixed in August Redfern's mind, the face of his son, the face of his wife, he pulls the trigger, and the powder flash catches, for an instant, something huge and long and glistening, a rind of teeth. Then Hawley's body pitches headfirst into the dark, and the first thing Redfern feels, when the numbness passes, is warmth, warmth at the center of him. He lets the pistol hang at his side, remembering his final question that day, as the two of them had trudged away through the muck of the cypress inlet: *Is a deer enough?*

Baxter's answer came quickly, easily. *Men of great enterprise make enemies, August. Enemies come in handy out here.*

Drained, Redfern turns away.

"It will be okay now," Baxter says. He puts his arm around his son-in-law, guides him down the treacherous path. "Everything will be fine."

1989

✦

JULY 4

THE DAY BREAKS COOL, WOODS AND FARMLANDS WRAPPED IN a mist that burns off as the sun mounts higher. By noon, the sky is bright and blue and the people of Empire line the sidewalks for the parade. Teenagers lounge and strut on the wide stone steps of the courthouse, as the high school wind-and-brass ensemble sets up shop, their sheet music fluttering like wings.

Nellie and Max stroll down side streets where farmers sell homemade whirligigs and fresh garden vegetables. Max disappears into the narrow stalls of the Baxter County Library's book tent. Nellie, meanwhile, thumbs through used vinyl outside the antiques store, twenty-five cents a sleeve. She finds a few albums she left behind in South Carolina—Bowie, the Carpenters. The Bee Gees, *Main Course*, 1975. The summer she was sixteen and her mother was dying and all she had was Barry Gibb singing "Songbird," played over and over until the record was nothing but skips. She hesitates, then buys it. She buys the Bowie and the Carpenters, too, plus a forty-five for Max: Kenny and Dolly, "Islands in the Stream." On the B side, "I Will Always Love You."

"Isn't Dolly wonderful?" the dealer says, making change.

They shop on until a fire truck blasts its horn and the parade rolls through. From the post office steps, they watch it pass, Max eating a caramel apple and paying more attention to the crowd than the floats and the ponies and the Shriners, who weave tight figure eights in their little orange cars. Watching Max, Nellie can't help thinking about her own summers in Empire, all chain link and barking dogs and midnight trains two blocks over from the house on Elm. Dodge's fried chicken from the Amoco, sometimes three, four nights a week after her mother came home from the hospital. Nellie shifts the records so she can put her free hand between Max's shoulders. The boy has caramel on his chin. She thumbs it away.

The last car in the parade is a convertible Mustang, red as Max's apple. Perched on the back is a girl in a sequined ball gown. She wears a tiara and a smile and waves at the crowd like she's on a spring. Beside her is a man in a plaid button-down shirt and jeans. He has a square jaw, looks like a lumberjack. A banner's draped over the side of the car:

TINA GORN
MISS LONGLEAF 1989
SPONSORED BY BAXTER MILLWORKS

Lonnie Baxter, Nellie thinks. She remembers him, vaguely. Doesn't know much about him, aside from the Baxter name. First family of Baxter County. She knows her grandfather married into the Baxters, and that's how he came by the land—

My land. Of course. An interested party.

Baxter flashes a mouthful of white teeth at the crowd and lobs handfuls of Jolly Ranchers. Nellie watches him pass, sees his hand slip down behind Tina Gorn. His fingers settle, lightly, in the hollow of Tina's back. They make a circle there, over bare, freckled skin. Tina, who's sixteen, maybe seventeen, just keeps on waving. Keeps on smiling.

Suddenly, Nellie feels eager to be anywhere but here.

The warm amber glow of a sinking sun, treetops aflame. Nellie and Max climb the ladder to the top of the tower. Max goes first, Nellie behind him, urging him on. He looks down once, doesn't look again. At the top is a wooden trapdoor, about shoulder width. When Max reaches it, he's hesitant to let go of the last rung and push through, so Nellie reaches up over him and punches it open herself. She plants her hand on the seat of his pants and pushes him up onto the weathered platform.

They scoot to the edge of the rail and sit side by side in the vanishing sun. Their legs hang over the edges. Far away, over house and trees, the Altamaha is a golden ribbon unspooling for the coast.

"Is your dad's name Hank?" Max says.

"Yeah, why?"

"I found a book in the library the other day. Had his name in it."

"Yeah, what kind of book?"

"Some old thing about ropes."

The sun disappears behind the pines.

"Do you think I'll make friends here, when I start school?"

"Sure, why not."

He shrugs. Kicks at the air. "I didn't really have any friends back home."

He isn't looking at her, just staring down at the ground. Fifty, sixty feet below.

"Me either," she says.

Max picks rust from the railing. It's a thing she'd do—

(idgits fidget)

—and because of that she wants to tell him to stop.

The ground below is hard and packed beneath the dry, summer grass. A thought comes to Nellie unbidden, like a sudden breeze over water, turning a boat: she imagines the sensation of falling, the wind in her hair. That brief, weightless wonder, when nothing touches her. She closes her eyes. Rests her chin on the railing.

Max scoots closer, puts his head on her arm.

They lean into each other.

Far away, above town, fireworks explode. Nellie shuts her eyes and listens. She listens to the beating of her son's heart against her, a sound so loud, so strong, it might as well be the rending of the night sky above.

That night, they eat burgers cooked in an old iron skillet Nellie finds in a cabinet. Afterward, they watch *Raiders of the Lost Ark*. They sit on the sofa in the piano room. The only other furniture in the room, other than a pair of end tables and lamps, is the piano, polished with Lemon Pledge to a high shine.

Routine, Nellie thinks. They're settling into one. Dinner, TV.

The Magnavox flickers when the tape runs out, turns to snow. Nellie stares at it and wonders if Wade has called the police yet. Or if he even will. Maybe he's happier, without them. Free to chase tail on campus until his heart's content.

Static flickers in their eyes, both their minds miles away.

"We'll be okay," she says.

Max looks up at her.

"We'll make new memories here. I promise."

"I hope," Max says.

The tape cuts off, begins to rewind.

Max grabs the remote for the TV and clicks it off.

"Sit with me a while longer," Nellie says, her arm around him.

"I'll sit with you forever."

Nellie closes her eyes. "Forever's a long time. I'll settle for just a few more minutes."

Soon, they're both asleep, dozing against each other.

SUMMER 1975

FIRST INTERLUDE

DAY ONE

✦

THE DAY OF HER MOTHER'S FUNERAL.

Heaps of casseroles and covered dishes spread on tables throughout the house, the contribution of Nellie's aunt on her mother's side, who had organized everything. Nellie's father, useless from the start. No money for a casket, no money for a stone. Hank sits on a kitchen chair in the corner of the living room, wearing a secondhand gray sport coat and bolo tie and hunched with a plastic fork over a paper plate of green-bean casserole. It has to be the best food he's had in years. Nellie shuts her bedroom door, quietly. Walls decorated scantly with Nellie's own drawings. A Bee Gees poster above a scarred-up dresser that speaks not of childhood but economy. At the center of it all, her mother's hospital bed, the rails lowered. In a few days, the man will come and fold it up and roll it out on wheels, onto a truck, and a bill will come in the mail after that. She sits on the end of the bed, smooths her black knee-length funeral dress over her knees, which peek out over black knee socks like scared white rabbits. It's the first dress she's worn in years and it fits like borrowed skin. Black buckle shoes, bought at Goodwill. All her aunt's doing. Her mother's favorite headband—the tortoiseshell—holds back her chestnut hair. She's cried some, but mostly she's kept silent, said almost nothing. Offered no smiles. No thank-yous. Whatever she's always known about her world is now upended. Whatever she controlled, she has lost. Her aunt means well, but Nellie hates her. She's a busybody, a woman who instructs and prays. The night before, when Hank was drunk, Nellie heard him through the wall, on the phone with her aunt. Promising a new day. A new leaf. "I've gotta do right by the kid," he said.

But Nellie knows better.

She's thinking of the pillow. The one that rests, right now, on the made bed. A little rose embroidered in the corner of the pillowcase.

Three weeks ago. Early in the morning. She came back from the kitchen, a bowl of cereal in hand, to find Hank Redfern standing over her sleeping mother, pillow in his hands. The room reeked of deer-camp smoke and cheap beer and the blood on his T-shirt. Little brown hairs, too, like he'd skinned something the night before.

"Dad?"

He turned his head slowly, looked at her from beneath the bill of his green Miller ball cap. His face was sallow and his eyes were red with crying. A four-day grizzle on his cheek.

She didn't even ask what he was doing. She set her bowl on the dresser and walked around the bed and took her fifty-seven-year-old father by the elbow and jerked him, hard, like a mother might jerk a child in a grocery store, or a parking lot. She thrust him out of the room and slammed the door. Pressed her hands against it as he thumped it with his shoulder, once, twice, before he slid down to the floor, the weight of him heavy against the door, and Nellie, too, turned and sat on the deep pile carpet, watching her mother breathe.

"Nellie, are you in there?" Her aunt's voice.

Bringing her back to this long, terrible day.

She does not speak. She tenses, waits on the doorknob to turn.

Silence, and her aunt goes away.

Nellie gets up and takes off the tortoiseshell headband and sets it on the bed, beside the pillow with the little rose. She looks at herself in her dresser mirror, sees a pimple or two. (A sudden fist to the chest: the memory of her mother teaching her to put on makeup when she was twelve. Covergirl face powder, cream blush, Bonne Bell lip gloss—Hires root beer, her favorite. *It's about finding what's already there, Nellie. Natural beauty. You can buy it for two bucks. Spend any more, you look like a whore.*) Dark hollows beneath her eyes. Her bangs are growing back, finally. She cut them, a month ago. Afterward, they hung short and lifeless. Her mother had laughed and Nellie had laughed with her, until her mother's laughter became a coughing fit, and nothing much was funny after that.

Now, Nellie pins her bangs back with a bobby pin and turns and opens the bedroom window and puts one leg over the sill, then the other, and drops into the boxwood bushes. Leaning against the garage, her Schwinn. She mounts the bike, swings it round, and pedals out of the drive and into the street.

She knows where she's going.

She's known it since the funeral, when she saw the old man at the cemetery.

He stood beneath the shade of an oak tree, apart from the small circle of mourners who burned in the July sun. He was rail thin, his suit too big, the shoulders too wide. He wore a black hat that looked about a hundred years old. His hands hung at his sides in brown leather gloves, the kind you'd chainsaw a tree with, not wear to a funeral. Nellie stood beside her father as the preacher read from the book of Psalms—Ruth Redfern had been religious in fits and starts, but not for a long time—and watched the old man, and the old man watched her, and something in his narrow, hawklike gaze and the close set of his blue eyes told her this was her grandfather, whom she had never seen or spoken to. When the service ended, she broke away and wove through the tombstones and topped a grassy rise just in time to see a rattletrap taxi pull away into the street, the old man's shape dark behind the glass.

She pedals all the way from town, has to walk her bike the last half mile. Too tired, too hot, her muscles sprung. Nauseated from the heat and no food in her belly. Her new black buckle shoes are dusted orange and hurting her feet. When she rounds the curve and sees the house for the first time, she stops. It looms, massive and empty. She stares until the old man whistles like a bird from beneath the shed, off to her left, and she turns and sees him sitting there in front of his RV, in his duct-taped recliner, still wearing his black funeral slacks and a white shirt, no tie. A flask of something in his lap.

She leaves her bicycle against the barbwire fence and ducks under it.

He does not call out, welcome her, or say anything at all. He simply waits, sips from his flask. She steps into the shade of the shed and stands before him, grass seeds and beggar's-lice snagged in her dress.

"I'm Eleanor."

The old man's eyes flash up and down. "I know."

She's staring at the flask in his gloved hand, so he offers it to her.

She shakes her head, slowly.

He blinks at her, owllike.

They sit outside, she on the Astroturf with legs crossed, shoes off, he in his chair. She eats his meager offerings of peanut butter and crackers and Vienna sausages. She's guarded, at first, and he seems to understand this, so they don't really speak for a while. The wind blows.

"Why'd you come to my mother's funeral?" is the first thing she asks.

The shadows of clouds roll like great beasts over the field.

"Ask me something else."

"Why do you live in this shit-box Winnie when you've got a nice house up there?"

"Who says it's nice."

"It's nicer than my house."

"Don't you believe it."

"Did you drive my daddy off from here, when he was my age?"

He cuts his eyes at her. Eyes like arctic ice. "How old are you?"

"Sixteen."

"Then no. Your daddy was fourteen when I drove him off."

She looks up at the old man from where she sits. She takes up a plastic knife, smears some peanut butter on a saltine cracker. Mashes another cracker on top. "How old are you?" She bites into it.

He waves his hand like he's fanning flies. "Hell, I don't know. Over eighty."

"Why do you wear them gloves?"

He forks a Vienna sausage out of the can and pops it into his mouth. Chews.

He has no teeth, Nellie realizes.

"I wear these gloves because my hands are ugly."

"I've got ugly feet." She kneads the instep of her foot.

"They seem fine, as feet go."

"They're knobby. I know a girl in school, Debbie McKee, she's got pretty feet."

"I had no use for school when I was your age."

"Yeah. Well. I hate it, too. Every day you do the same thing, day after day, and nothing ever changes. Plus they write things about you in the bathroom stalls."

"Who does?"

She shrugs. "Girls."

"I don't know much about that."

"Daddy says he dropped out of school when he joined the navy. That true?"

"I don't know much about your daddy either." He drinks.

She pops the last of her cracker into her mouth, licks the peanut butter from her thumb. "I can tell you something I did like about school."

He stares at her. At the field. Looks back at her.

"I made a coil pot in Mrs. Johnson's sixth-period art class a couple years back. I painted it cobalt blue and fired it and brought it home to Mama, and she told me it was beautiful and she used it as an ashtray. Later, that same class, I drew a picture of this girl, Rhoda Carmichael, who sat three desks in front of me. She was like me. She didn't have any friends, and Mrs. Johnson saw the sketch and told me I can see things other people can't."

"You draw?"

She nods.

After a moment, Redfern says, "You want to know who your daddy is, why he is the way he is, you best ask him. He left here, he was right to leave. He was right to tell you never to come here, too. Redferns are cursed."

The old man's words turn the crackers in her mouth to a thick, gummy paste. She washes it down with the last of her Coke. "Cursed to be assholes, maybe."

At that, Redfern looks down at his flask and smiles. Then he begins to laugh. He laughs long and hard, and the sound is dry and creaky, like he hasn't laughed in decades.

That night, she makes a mattress out of the four dinette seat cushions. Redfern gives her a thin, faintly mildewed bedsheet, and she curls beneath it like a wounded mouse. Back in his bedroom, the old man pulls a curtain and sets to snoring. He calls out in his sleep, snatches of unformed words and nonsense. Her own mind a torrent of emotions, some old, some new—fear, guilt, exhilaration—all of it culminating in a simple realization: she has run away from home. Had Aunt Vera phoned the neighbors, the police? Did she even know? Did Hank, or was he too deep in some bottle to care? She lies awake until finally drifting off into a sleep of dreams, dreams of small rooms and wild-animal smells and her mother's ghost drifting beyond the window.

In the middle of the night, the old man shakes her awake. She starts up. He looms over her in a pair of saggy boxers, an undershirt stained with jelly. His gloves are off and she can see, in the moonlight, his hands are nothing but scars and mottled flesh, hooked into claws.

"Aggie? Aggie!"

He clamps her forearm in a hard grip. A mad, fear-struck shimmer in his eyes.

"Grandpa?" The word escapes her lips before she even realizes she's called him that.

"Goddamn Hawley trash, they're back. Get dressed, Agatha."

"It's Nellie. You're having a dream, that's all." She grips his forearm, squeezes.

He lets her go. Like she's a hot coil.

A fly buzzes where the dishes are piled.

"Hank called you something else," he mutters. Then shuffles away, back to his bedroom. "He called you Aggie."

DAY TWO

✦

SHE WAKES TO THE SOUND OF THE MOTOR HOME CREAKING
on its axles, the old man bumping around in the bathroom. She
turns, opens her eyes, and sees him push open the door and set
two, three, four mason jars out onto the linoleum, beside an
olive-green backpack. He bends down, packs them into the bag,
then stands and sidles past her, unaware she's awake. He
disappears through the door, into sunlight. She sits up and looks
through the blinds, watches him wade through the long grass
and struggle over the barbwire. He wears that big hat, a pair of
khaki pants with knee-high boots laced tight. A walking stick
made from a sycamore limb. Gloves. On his belt a canteen and
an ax, its blade shaped like a crescent moon. He vanishes into
the pines, beyond the old barn.

She gets up and steps over a litter of cigarette butts and
cellophane wrappers into the bathroom, which isn't usable. No
water. She looks in the shower and sees, stacked there, at least
a dozen empty Ball mason jars. She goes out into the field and
hikes her dress, rolls down her underwear, and squats in the tall
grass to pee.

Inside the RV, she snoops among the wreckage of the old

man's life. Reads the labels on his medicines heaped and spilling over the bedside table. Nothing she knows. He isn't dying—at least not of cancer. She looks in his closet, finds nothing but empty hangers and an old shotgun, disassembled in two pieces. Up in the cab, the seats are piled with clothes. She sifts through these, finds a few that seem to be her size, but they're old. Really old. A boy's pair of chinos and a red-checked shirt. She takes them out and hangs them over the barbwire in the morning sun, to improve their smell.

The day is pleasant, bright. Not too hot. She looks up at the house, then back to the Winnebago. Remembers, suddenly, the old man's nightmare, his grip on her arm. She checks the flesh there, sees a ring of bruises purpling. Where's he gone? She stares at the tree line beyond the barn. She doesn't want to go home. She isn't even sure she has a home anymore. As for this place, it's only a stop along the way to whatever lies ahead.

Still, there's no reason it has to be foul.

She walks barefoot through the grass, pricked by stickers, and steps into the Winnebago to begin.

With any luck, she'll be done before the old man gets back.

Still wearing her funeral black, she works all day, the door thrown wide and stopped with a stack of wood from the pile. The windows opened, the vents cranked. She begins with the sink, gathers all the dishes into an old washtub she finds beneath the RV and carries it out to a water trough and spigot in back. Nearby is an electric well, wrapped in insulation. Redfern must have sunk it when he moved out here. She turns the spigot and fills the trough and washes the dishes, sets them out on a sawhorse table in the sun to dry. Then she goes back inside and finds a stash of old washcloths beneath the bathroom sink. She cleans the counters, the dinette. Wipes down even the blinds. Sweeps the floor with half a broken broom and gathers up about a hundred dead palmetto bugs and scatters them like seed in the field. She uses the barbwire fence as a clothesline and hangs out the linens from the old man's bed, as well as all of the clothes. She carries these by the armload. They flap all the way up the drive and along the edge of the house. By the time Nellie gets that far up the hill, she's exhausted, and when she's hanging the last pair of pants over the wire, that's when she sees it: a clothesline stretched between two metal poles driven into the ground in back of the kitchen. She's sunburned by then and soaked in sweat. She goes back down the hill and snags the pair of pants and shirt she picked out that morning and goes into the Winnebago to change. The air inside is fresher, smells of sunshine and grass.

As the sun sinks, the old man emerges from a far section of woods across the field. He walks slowly, eyes crawling over the fencing, where the clothes hang like the ragged wash of a scarecrow army.

Nellie greets him at the door, wearing the chinos and the checked shirt. She's swept her hair back and has no shoes on. The pants come to her calves, which are covered in scratches and bug bites.

He stops, startled. Stares at her, as if he doesn't recognize her. Nellie has time to wonder whose clothes she's put on before he comes back to himself, and his brow draws down. He steps inside, hot and sweaty and bringing with him a strong summer-heat reek that fills the RV.

She's set two plates on the dinette table, opposite each other.

She spoons scrambled eggs from a small iron skillet onto the plates.

He glares at her, then brushes past. In the back, he inspects his medicine bottles, neatly set out in alphabetical order. "What in hell are you up to?" Before she can answer, he pushes past her again, kneels down on the turf outside, and unslings his pack.

From the doorway, skillet in hand, she says, "I just wanted to help—"

"Don't need a goddamn nurse. I ain't sick. I ain't dying. I ain't your mother."

Calmly, she walks past him to the edge of the Astroturf and hurls the skillet and eggs as far into the field as she can.

He watches it sail high, disappear into the grass with a *thonk*.

"Who says I'm your fucking nurse?" she says.

He's unpacking his bag. Setting out three mason jars by the iron stove.

"What are you wearing?"

"I needed fresh clothes."

"Nothing here is fresh."

"You can say that again."

The old man gets up and walks toward her.

Nellie takes a step back. But Redfern only brushes by, bends down at the Winnebago's steps, and drags out a plastic milk jug from a crate. It sloshes with clear liquid. He walks it back to the mason jars. He opens one and Nellie sees that all three hold severed roots, cut out of the ground. Each about the length of her hand. He uncaps the jug and fills the first jar with the liquid.

A slick pine smell wafts up.

Arms crossed over her chest, Nellie says, "What in hell are you up to?"

Silence, as the old man pours. Careful not to spill a drop until every jar is full. A fat brown root suspended in each. He screws the lids back onto all three jars. The liquid clouds, turns murky. "Turpentine, tar, pitch, and rosin." He holds up a jar, swirls it in the sunlight. "All come out of these woods. Used to be it was a million-dollar industry. We kept ships afloat. Kept lamps lit. Clothes and houses clean. Some even said it was a cure-all for disease, but take you a drink and you'll learn right quick that's bullshit." He puts the jar down, picks up another. His eyes, his voice, are years away. "Used to be, it was a thousand uses for spirits. Far as I'm concerned, it's only one now." He sets the jar down, picks up the last one. Swishes it. The big root whorls inside the jar. He presses his ear to the jar.

Bugshit, Nellie thinks. *That's what he is.*

"They hate it. You can hear em scream. Listen."

Despite herself, she bends down, and he presses the glass to her ear. His eyes shift from her to the jar, back to her. "I don't hear a thing," she says.

"Then it's just a root." He pours the jars, roots and all, into the belly of his stove.

That night, despite the warmth of the evening, he lights a fire in his stove, and Nellie sits feeding it wood. Old and dry and riddled with termites, the wood burns quickly, popping and shooting sparks onto the artificial turf. The old man leans back in his chair and drinks from his flask. He offers it to her again, but again she shakes her head. Out in the field, there are fireflies and the songs of crickets and frogs. Nellie enjoys the heavy nighttime silence, which is loud and wondrous strange. She's only just begun to hum a few bars of "Nights on Broadway" when something screams, out in the dark woods.

Her blood freezes.

The old man's eyes don't leave the dancing fire.
The howl fades away, a long and furious shriek.
"I hear you," Redfern says to the fire.
Beyond the little stove, all is void.
"Was that a coyote?" Nellie asks.
"No."

III

1989

✦

JULY 5

UP EARLY, A RESTLESS NIGHT. DREAMS OF WADE IN A T-SHIRT and red athletic shorts, roaming the downstairs, tugging sheets from furniture and calling out for Max. In the dream, Nellie doesn't know where Max is. Desperate to find him first, she opens the armoire in his room, and a hand shoves her from behind, slams her shut inside it. She fumbles in the dark, touching wood, touching clothes. At last, touching flesh. Lips move beneath her fingers, as her father speaks her name.

She's having coffee at the kitchen table, staring out the window at a pair of mourning doves pecking in the slope of the yard. Max pads into the kitchen in his knee-length shark T-shirt, a three-ring binder tucked under his arm. He pulls back a chair and sets the binder on the table. He's clear-eyed and ready for orange juice, so she gets up and pours it for him. He waits, both hands on the binder, as if eager to open it, to show her something.

She knows the binder. It's his Garfield photo album, the famous fat cat in sunglasses on the cover, flopped in a beach chair. It's the last thing Nellie remembered to snag on the way out of the house in South Carolina, and there's nothing in it she

179

wants to look at ever again—mostly because it's all pictures of the three of them, vacations they've taken each summer since Max was eight and Wade bought him the album and a Polaroid camera. Pigeon Forge, Tennessee. Myrtle Beach. Dogpatch USA, that stupid amusement park up in Bumfuck, Arkansas. Somewhere in North Carolina, they rode a chairlift up to a "ghost town," which turned out to be bunch of rickety old shops selling tin stars and plastic tomahawks. There's a picture in there of Wade and Max with a bandit, the bandit's six-shooter drawn. Wade's fingers cocked like a pistol, Max ramrod straight like it's a school picture.

She glances out the window. The doves are gone.

"I made you something." Max pushes the photo album around the salt and pepper shakers, toward her. "I figured, in the end, it might be the best way to keep them safe."

She sets her coffee down and opens the album.

Each page holds three pictures in clear plastic sheathes. The pictures are old. Nellie stares at them, realizes what they are—*who* they are. "Where did you get these?"

"In the cellar."

Most of the pictures have writing on the back, a thin, delicate script. Her grandmother's, it must be. *Gus and Barlow*—who else but Euphemia Redfern would call him Gus? "Oh, Max."

"You look like her."

"Like who?"

"Your grandmother. See?" He slides his chair back, comes around the table, and points at a picture. Euphemia on the porch in a housecoat, one hand beneath her belly. Edge of a smile. Nellie draws in a breath. The lips are thinner, the chin rounder, but the bones are the same—and the eyes, large and dark and melancholy.

"Look at this one." Max flips a few pages and points to a ring of stone-faced men, arms around their wives, or hands in their pockets, behind them a cluster of cabins in a clearing, a slip of river in the far right corner. "It's the camp from your grandfather's map."

Nellie kisses the boy where his neck and shoulder join.

"Jeez, Mom." He rubs the spot. Blushing.

"Hey."

"Yeah?"

"You up for a hike?"

"It's not cleaning, I'm up for it."

"So go get dressed." She shoves him off toward the door. "And bring your sketchbook!"

"Roger roger!" he calls back, already on the stairs.

Nellie looks at the album. Turns the page to a photograph of two woodsmen, one on either side of a wide old pine, bark hacked away in a chevron shape. Raw gum oozes from dozens of slash marks that angle up and down the face and end above a metal box jammed into the tree like a lip. The men wear white bandannas tied over their mouths and noses.

It makes the scar on her arm itch, this picture.

She flips the page, reads the inscription.

Sips her coffee.

Into her grandfather's rucksack, Nellie packs a thermos of water, four cheese sandwiches, a can of bug spray, and a bottle of sunscreen. Through the belt loop of her jeans, she slips the crescent-bladed ax from the map room.

"Why are you bringing that?" Max wants to know.

"Bears."

"Why, when we've got this?" Max smiles as he holds up a Swiss Army knife, a present from Wade on the boy's tenth birthday. She knows to smile back and ruffle his hair, even though the sight of the knife strikes a pang of jealousy so sharp in Nellie's chest she has to turn and pretend to fetch something from the pantry so Max won't see it writ all over her face, this petty, sour need for him to love her more than he loves his father. It passes quickly.

At the edge of the woods, near the barn, Max takes out a folded square of paper from the pocket of his shorts, a quickly sketched copy of the framed property map from Redfern's study. She'd had him draw it, after they got dressed. "Should be a wagon trail that leads from the barn into the trees," she tells him, slapping at a fly. "At the end of that trail, there's a camp."

It takes traversing the shin-high grass that borders the tree line a few times, but eventually they find it: twin, hard-packed ruts where the grass grows thinner. They pick their way around briars and nettles along the path. The light begins to fracture as the pines get taller, thicker, and soon it fades. It strikes Nellie, after a time, how the word *quiet* means something altogether different out here. There's noise and movement everywhere, from the rustle of birds among the humus to the eerie creak of younger pines high above, pitching against one another in the breeze. And yet, there is also a sense of absence. No thundering log trucks, no ringing phones. The path just goes on and on, winding toward a snatch of blue sky and cloud. Stickers in the grass make Max hiss and dance. A spider's web spans the path, no spider to be seen. They duck under.

The trail curves left, after a while, around a fallen tree, beyond the tree a clearing where the sunlight hits the grass and warms the wings of a hundred dragonflies among the purple-blooming thistle stalks. Wild lantana grows and flowers in snarls of yellow and pink, butterflies and hummingbirds winging from bud to bud. At the far side of the meadow, wrapped in thick mats of jasmine and rioting wisteria, are the ruins of a dozen tiny log cabins. The field slopes away from the cabins to the wide green ribbon of the Altamaha, sparkling in the late-morning sun.

"This is it!" Max says. And takes off, running for the nearest cabin.

Nellie runs after him.

They tromp onto the porch, where the door hangs from a single rusty hinge. Inside, the roof is collapsed, and there's not much to see save rotted wood covered in vine. A rickety chair stands upright and intact in the corner near the door. A potbellied stove spilling ash and rust in a single room. Nellie can see there was once a loft, up where the remnants of an iron bed frame are jammed among the rafters. A bolt of gingham cloth hangs in tatters from a crossbeam, above it a nest of bristling wasps.

"How many people you think lived here?" Max asks, outside in the grass.

"One family per, maybe." Nellie kicks over a rotten cedar bucket. In back of the nearest cabin is a split-rail corral, grown up with dandelions and milkweed. Someone's pig pen. "Not the best digs, but maybe not the worst they ever saw." She feels a sudden kinship with the men and women who lived here, forging lives out of what they were given, making the best of life's meager offerings. "I guess either way, it was home."

They linger at the last cabin, which has fared better than the others. Its shingled roof, at least, is mostly intact, save the rear corner where a gout of wisteria spills into the room. On the porch are two wooden rocking chairs, the seats collapsed. Inside, at the center of the room, is a table. At the center of the table, in a litter of old tobacco shavings, an old meerschaum pipe. Nellie picks it up, sniffs the bowl. A warm, pleasant scent long cooked into the wood.

A sound.

Dry slithering.

Her eyes dart to the rear corner of the room.

A brief shifting of vines there, purple blooms fluttering earthward in a shaft of sunlight.

Stillness.

Followed by the eerie sensation of being watched.

"Did you hear that?" she asks, but Max is gone.

Her right hand, she realizes, rests on the ax at her hip.

A brief swell of panic, rolling back with a sigh when she finds him outside, on his knees on the broken steps.

"Look." He points at the porch floor. Carved into the planks:

BAD PLACE

GONE TO FLORIDA

E.G. 23

"What's it mean?" Max asks.

"Initials and a date, maybe. Times were hard. Not enough work to go around. Could be they found better prospects in the Sunshine State."

"Why 'bad place'?"

She remembers the men in white masks in the pictures from Max's album. "Probably just means the paychecks dried up. Come on, kiddo. Let's eat lunch down by the river."

She puts her arm around him and they set out for the water.

They haven't gone a dozen yards when she feels it again, a sense of eyes upon her.

She resists the urge to look back, over her shoulder.

Knowing, of course, there's nothing there.

They sit on two flat slabs of rock at the edge of the embankment and eat cheese sandwiches. Nellie slips the ax free of her belt and props it against the rock. Max picks it up and swings it. Sets it down. Takes out his map. "Are we going to the Old Forest?"

Beyond the camp, along the map's far border: charcoal shadows, trees like teeth.

Nellie pops the last of her sandwich into her mouth. Shakes her head as she chews. "Not today."

"How come?"

"No paths."

And yet, she wants to. Remembering, suddenly, that long afternoon she and Redfern spent walking in the woods. Turkey oaks and moss beds in the gloom—

"Mom." Max's sandwich is half-eaten on a square of wax paper on the rock beside him. A fly crawls over the paper. He pays it no mind. The clearing darkens as a cloud passes over the sun. "There's something out there." He points.

Her eyes follow. "I don't see anything." But her hand moves to the moon ax's handle, closes around it. Max is on his feet now, standing on the rock, perfectly still. Nellie sitting below him.

"Near the first cabin." He points again. "See?"

Something ducks low, hides itself in the long grass. A flash of black fur.

"It's a dog!"

"A dog? No, hey, Max, we don't know if it's— Max!"

But Max is already wading into the grass, calling, "Here, boy!" and waving what's left of his sandwich in front of him. Nellie watches, figures she might as well let it go, there's no stopping this. He's always wanted a dog, begged Wade for years to let him have one.

Max stands still for a while and listens. They hear a rustle off to the right, a blur of something that leaves the grass sawing. Max makes kissing noises until Nellie finally calls to him, "It's probably gone," and she watches the boy's heart sink like a stone that only seconds before had seemed to skip across the surface of a bright, shimmering water.

"Sorry, kiddo," she says, and puts a hand between his shoulders.

He sighs, there among the dragonflies and sunlit stalks.

Lonnie Baxter stands in the driveway of Redfern Hill. The woman's pickup is parked at an angle in front of the porch, its bed full of sawn limbs. The property is still, silent. He steps quietly onto the porch and knocks. Waits. Reaches into his pocket and takes out the spare set of keys Meadows made, months ago. He slips open the screen door, inserts the key. Hesitates, listens. Hears only the distant trill of a bird out in the mist-wrapped pines. He turns the key. Calls a hello into the dim hallway, and when no one answers, he goes inside.

The house creaks around him like an old ship. He moves through it, eyes roaming. Lingers in the library, notes the polished bookshelves, the tang of Lemon Pledge. The sunlight beaming through the leaded glass to throw bright squares of red, yellow, and green along the walls. In some ways, he thinks, Redfern Hill could be a sister house to the Baxter home. A plainer sister, fewer frills. The one who steps out back behind the barn, with the older cousins. To smoke. To cuss. Lonnie had a cousin like that, Aunt Irene's girl, Ima. He and she had snuck off into a hayloft once and played house when Lonnie was twelve. It was the first time Lonnie ever saw what nested between a girl's legs, and just the thought of it now, all that sweet and musty-smelling hay, makes him smile. He can still remember Aunt Irene, calling up from outside, "Y'all play nice now . . ."

In the hallway, Lonnie looks up at the long stairs and reaches into his pocket to pop two Little Helpers. He listens, again, for movement, voices.

Nothing yet, he mounts the stairs.

Nellie and Max follow Camp Road south from the cabins along the river, their destination the old turpentine mill. Here, the road is a slightly wider wagon path, graveled over. The Altamaha runs off to their left, green and wide, beyond a break of cypress trees. Nellie kicks a crushed beer can out of the stobs and down the road. The soil is sandy, marred by jagged washouts and potholes. They cross an old wooden bridge where a creek runs inland and turtles dive from logs. On their right, the hardwood thicket that's rambled south beside them gives way to a vast grove of tall, slender pines.

Mother and son come to a standstill and stare.

The trees are dead but for a handful deformed with the residue of old bleeding. Gory black cavities up and down their trunks where, too many times, the bark was hacked and rehacked to extract the resin and the pines, over too many years, were tricked and tricked again into healing themselves. What torture. Nellie crosses her arms over her chest, thumbs the scar on the inside of her arm. Imagines drawing a razor over her own flesh, not once or twice, but year after year after year. Remaking the same old wound to spill fresh blood. Was this why she never had the guts to leave Wade? Because the roots went too deep, so goddamned deep she could only ever stand and bleed? And slowly die.

Max, unsurprisingly, thinks of Wade, too. Of that no-good day in the backyard. Of nosebleeds that never stop. Hurts that never heal.

Nellie steps off the road into the brush and puts her hand on the first trunk she comes to. Runs her fingers over the long, V-shaped scars. At her feet, the sun catches a glint of metal beneath pine straw and grass. She drops to her knees, brushes away the straw, and begins digging out the edges of whatever it is with her hands. In a flash, Max is at her side. Out of the sandy earth, together, they pry a tin box the size of a small bread pan, its bottom rusted through. The inside of the box is crusted with hard black streaks of resin, the outside dented from years of careless hammer blows—

(Nellie is sixteen and traipsing behind August Redfern, far above North Creek, over fallen logs and green lichen, Redfern's back humped beneath his army surplus pack. Her eyes clock to the pendulum of the odd, short-handled ax dangling from his belt loop. Its handle eaten by time, the grip worn smooth. The blade shaped like a crescent moon. Among pines old and ascending, he takes it out to show her. *Set your box with the flat end, see?*

Box? she says.

To catch the gum. And this side here—his gloved finger traces the curve of the moon, before he lays it against the bark of a pine—*gives the tree a smile. So it can spill its gum.*)

Nellie drops the box in the grass. She takes the moon ax from her belt loop. Beneath the deepest slash in the pine's long face, she finds an even older scar. Uglier. As curved and wide as a crescent moon, and into this, she sets the ax blade, and the blade fits perfectly.

It gives the tree a smile.

Lonnie pisses in the upstairs bathroom. Swings his stream wide of the toilet, onto the floor. After he zips, he doesn't flush. On the sink are twin toothbrushes in a red plastic cup. He plucks them up, swirls the bristles of each in the toilet, and puts them back, all the while whistling. He catches his reflection in the mirror, sees himself smiling, and wonders: how long has it been, since he last whistled? When was it he last felt so . . . good?

One week after August Redfern died. That's the answer.

The day he met his destiny, here at Redfern Hill.

It was Jim Meadows's job to oversee Redfern's burial in the family plot, and so, while Meadows directed the backhoe where to dig—and that long, black van rolled up, filmed in dust, and the pine casket was slid out on rails—Lonnie, who had come along for the ride, wandered away up the drive. Enjoying the peaceful quiet of the place, even if it was a shambles. He'd come out of curiosity, more than anything else, no real desire to own Redfern Hill. Not yet. No, that day, he'd only wanted to walk on old Baxter land he'd never seen, where Baxter blood was sewn in the very soil itself. And so he looked upon the ruins of August Redfern's legacy and thought, inevitably, of his own daddy, who was by then already mistaking Lonnie for Herman out at Pine Ridge. He thought, too, of his son, Todd, the bad hand he and Linda were dealt. He thought of Linda herself, the unhappiness that had opened up at the center of her, years back, like a black hole. Had been swallowing her ever since. Swallowing him, too, if he was honest—

Lonnie stepped wrong, foot turning on a rock.

His lower back seized, a giant claw gripping his spine.

He wanted to move but couldn't; any one step might send him toppling.

He cast about, popping sweat. Behind him, about a hundred yards away, Meadows and the funeral home boys in their dark suits were smoking cigarettes and laughing. Lonnie stood paralyzed in the gravel lane between the barn and the Winnebago. He saw the ramshackle shed built onto the front of the motor home. A chair beneath it. So he shuffled off the road and through the field to August Redfern's ratty recliner and lowered himself into it. Palmetto bugs ran out onto the Turkish rug and fled for the woodpile. Lonnie shut his eyes, tried to slow his breathing.

Doc said it would happen when you least expected it, son of a bitch, you're useless anymore—

He gave out a moan. Gone were the days of touchdowns and state trophies, a fistful of some cheerleader's tit in the steamed cab of his pickup, the way she fit him like a warm, gritty glove—

. . . lonnie . . .

He opened his eyes.

A man stood out in the field, watching him from the waist-high grass. He was tall and thin and dressed in brown pants and boots and a red vest and watch chain. He wore a long coat and a broad-brimmed hat, had a beard white as snow that lay upon his chest.

Lonnie knew him from old pictures at home.

The man had been dead since 1924.

Great-Uncle George?

George Baxter lifted his head and stared down a long, patrician nose at Lonnie. Then he turned away and set out walking through the grass, and when Lonnie shoved up out of the chair to follow, he didn't stop to wonder if his back was better. He just went after the man, who had crossed the drive and was passing the barn, heading off down an old wagon trail, into the woods.

As Lonnie crossed the gravel lane, in pursuit, he happened to look down and see what had tripped him. It was not a rock.

It was a root, gnarled and hairy and bursting through the ground.

"Look!" Max cries.

Nellie, walking ahead in the grip of a fierce melancholy, turns.

Max stands a few feet in back of her, pointing to where the dog sits a stone's throw away, back up the road, tongue hanging out. Its fur is black, with tan patches along its legs and belly and muzzle.

When Max calls to it, it scoots away into the brush. Left rear leg hanging limp and close to its body.

"There's something wrong with it," Nellie says. "Did you see?"

Max doesn't answer. Instead, he takes his half-eaten sandwich from Nellie's backpack and tears some bread and cheese and sets it in the road.

They start back walking.

After about fifty yards, they turn, just in time to see the dog lope out of the grass for the scraps. Not a big dog, but it might be bigger, Nellie figures, if it weren't starving. She gets a better look at it, realizes it isn't hurt so much as malformed. The leg's shriveled, hairless from the crook of the joint down to the tip of the foot, which doesn't resemble a foot so much as a pink stump. The dog sniffs the cheese and bread and snatches it up and eats it all in one bite. When it sees them, it sits down, ears pricked, and licks its muzzle.

"What do we do?" Max says.

Nellie watches the dog watch them.

"Strays can be dangerous," she says.

Again, they walk.

Every few hundred feet, Max turns and leaves a snatch of sandwich on the ground, and after another few hundred feet, the dog is that much closer, sitting in the middle of the road, panting.

By the time they reach the mill, both spare sandwiches are gone.

Lonnie passes out of the boy's bedroom—he spent a while in there, digging around for just the right gag, and oh, it's a good one—and into the woman's. He stands inside the doorway, eyes roving until they settle on a chest of drawers. In the top drawer, he finds a handful of T-shirts, some folded jeans. The T-shirts are mostly black. Silk-screened bands and rock stars. A few Lonnie knows. Most he doesn't. Duran Duran, he recognizes. Duran Duran did a Bond song. Next drawer down, he hits pay dirt. Bras with underwire, white cotton underwear. Nothing too exciting. Mostly plain-Jane shit. But not all of it. Here, for example, is a pair of flimsy black panties, more a promise of underwear than the actual thing. The Gardner woman probably grabbed them by mistake, throwing her shit together, the day she left her husband—

Lonnie presses the fabric to his face with one hand, breathes it in.

Chews it a little.

The turpentine mill's footprint is still discernible beneath the kudzu that's overtaken it, at its center a heap of bricks that was once a furnace, a chimney, rising up from the ground through an opening on the second-story platform and, finally, the shingled roof. Now, there is no roof, no platform, no chimney. Rough-hewn cedar pillars jut from the vines, attached to the bones of a set of stairs, broken and slumping. The last recognizable feature is the giant wooden barrel, its purpose to trap the condensation from the kettle. Easily the size of a Volkswagen Beetle, it's collapsed, but Max can still stand inside the shell and be wrapped entire, enclosed in a Kong-size fist.

"Watch for sharp stuff," Nellie says.

Something strange in her voice, Max realizes. She's uneasy here.

"Why do you think it burned?" he asks.

"Mills like this were dangerous. Lots of flammable gases. One spark's all it takes."

Broken turpentine casks litter the woods like the cast-off shells of molting insects. Among the ribs they find masses of rosin, hardened on the ground in glittering, slag-like pools. Max breaks off a honey-colored shard and turns it in the sunlight.

Nellie steps to the edge of a wooden trough, set below ground level, grown over with vine and littered with dead beetles. She crouches at the edge. About the width of a coffin, the trough runs seven, eight feet out from what's left of the furnace. Nellie pulls at the vine, finds more of the hardened yellow rosin crusting the wood. Bits and pieces of a flimsy frame, rags of rotten mesh, like cheesecloth. A sieve.

Max picks his way around the collapsed furnace, where he finds, nestled at its center, the remnants of a copper kettle the size of a small washing machine. It's scorched and blasted, the metal twisted. He recognizes the shape of it from Redfern's drawings. It would have been heated by the furnace to cook the raw gum from the trees, which would have separated it into turpentine, water, and the rosin in his hand.

Nellie knocks her fist against the trough.

"The liquid rosin settles in the bottom of the furnace," Max says, remembering the schematics, the mechanics of the still. "They drained it off while it was still hot." He jumps down into the trough. "Here. They drained it right here." He holds up the golden shard. "And when it cooled, it was this."

"Like lava," Nellie says. Her voice hushed.

Max makes a gushing noise.

"Max . . ."

He spins in a circle, arms akimbo. "Ahhh, I'm melting! Melting! What a world!"

"Stop it, Max." She jerks him out of the trough—

(*Too hard, Nervous Nellie, too rough!*)

—and gives him a shake, then lets go of him.

"I'm sorry, I didn't mean anything . . ."

"People died here. Be respectful."

He falls silent, remembering what she told him, that first night. Her grandmother. A fire. *Here*, he realizes.

"This place is a graveyard," Nellie says, and looks over her shoulder, down the narrow, shadowy lane that leads away from the mill and back to Redfern Road. "Let's get back to the house."

Max pockets the rosin in his hand. He looks around. "What happened to the dog?"

But Nellie doesn't answer. She's already walking.

Max jogs after her, glancing back every now and then at the ruins of the mill.

The last room Lonnie enters is curiously empty, save a dozen or so large white canvases leaning against the interior wall. An easel among them. A blank, pristine canvas on it. Beneath the easel, on the floor, is a plastic tackle box of brushes, paints. Lonnie has a moment of inspiration. He picks up a tube of red paint, squirts most of it out into the upper tray of the box. He takes up a wide, flat brush and dips it in the paint. Touches it to the canvas. He grins, and the brush begins to move.

Soon, he's whistling again, imagining the Gardner woman's face when she sees it, this masterpiece, Lonnie's own pièce de résistance. Her jaw will drop, her heart will hammer. She'll take it for the threat it is. Who knows, maybe it'll even stir something else inside her, something deep, deep down between her—

But then he sees it, the thing he's painting, and his whistle fades, dries up. The brush goes still against the canvas, bleeds runners of red. What is this? What's he done? This isn't the shape he wanted to paint. Not the shape he started, anyway, no, it's something else, summoned up from deep, deep down inside Lonnie himself, a portrait, a memory, from that day in the woods, following—

(the ghost-apparition-Uncle-George-thing along the old wagon trail until the path hooks left into the meadow, past the ruins of Redfern's turpentine camp, into the trees, the old man walking ahead, always, no matter how close Lonnie gets. Slipping through the pines and oaks. Once, stepping over a rotted log, Lonnie feels a tremor in his back like an aftershock and has to stop, and when he does, George stops, too. Waiting, peering down that garden spade of a nose.

"Just where in the fuck we off to?" Lonnie tries.

No answer.

On they go, the land rising and plateauing onto a wire-grass meadow. Here, the old man leaves a trail of bent grass behind, and when Lonnie looks down, he sees that the earth his great-uncle's trod is torn up, as when an armadillo roots for bugs. They pass beneath towering old pines, in the top of one an osprey's nest. The bird's eyes track them until they disappear down a slope of cypress trees that quickly becomes a swamp. George doesn't stop when he comes to the water's edge. He splashes into it, makes no effort to wait on Lonnie, who stands among the stobs like a man caught out between two worlds, the one behind him lacking all wonder, the one before him yet a mystery—)

. . . *lonnie* . . .

He leaps back from the canvas.

A red slick of paint sticking his fingers together.

That voice. That sweet and terrible voice. First heard that day, after he waded out of the swamp and saw George ahead, waiting at the edge of a stagnant stream, beyond it a hillock, an island. Wrapped in roots and thick vines that were nothing like any vines or roots Lonnie had ever seen—

("What is this place?" he asks.

Uncle George does not speak, only lifts his hand and points at the top of the mound, to a hole big as a whale's mouth overhung with a net of dead muscadine, and now, closer, Lonnie can see that the old man's beard is not really hair but moss, and the old man's eyes are not really eyes but wet river stones, and his skin is not skin but the light pulpy flesh of a longleaf pine, its bark sheared away. For the first time that day, Lonnie wonders if he is, in fact, dead. Dead in August Redfern's drive, his back seizure really a heart attack that felled him in an instant, and now, his ancestor, the great Baxter patriarch, has come to usher him across this great and final threshold into hell everlasting. But he can't be dead because a dead man's pulse can't tick like a stopwatch in his throat, as Uncle George's eyes gleam like polished jewels and Lonnie moves past him, up the hill, finding his path made of roots and moss, drawn by a whisper in his head. Reeled in like a fish.

   . . . *lonnie* . . .

He drops to his knees at the summit. A rank sigh issues from that black cave as something huge and old turns in the earth, as if waking from a deep and dreamless sleep.

A root—

no, not a root, something else warm and wet)

—like the paint between his fingers. Warm and wet and sticky. He feels it, even now, here in the hot and empty farmhouse, as a summer fly buzzes against a nearby window. Those gentle, lapping tongues, nuzzling his thigh. Inching up over his crotch and between the buttons of his shirt, licking his belly. That low, gritty heat, pinching skin and pulling hairs where it grips and crawls, out of his shirt and up his throat, and all the while it sighs his name, just as a cheerleader once sighed it, or Linda gasped it the night Lonnie fucked a boy into her, a boy who was born brainless and gibbering.

   . . . *lonnie* . . .

Whispering, now, of the fortunes he can yet possess, and the riches his family has already known in service to its hunger. All he has to do is feed it, help it grow strong, nurse it back to its former grandeur, when its branches were long and mighty and its shoots were many, before the long decades of betrayal, when August Redfern denied it the sustenance, the nourishment, the worship it required . . .

. . . we need you, lonnie, we need you . . .

Words that Lonnie Baxter had not heard in a long, long time.

Words the slithering thing teases at the porch of his ear, until at last it plunges inside, and Lonnie's eyes fly open and he sees in his painting the face of a god, rendered in cadmium red.

They walk in silence, Nellie scratching at mosquito bites while Max fends off fat horseflies that buzz him like dive-bombers. Down the mill road, around the galvanized steel gate, then back onto Redfern Road. Max scuds his feet over the gravel, listless from the day's rising heat.

"We're getting close," she says after a while. "Creek's just ahead. Then it's not even half a mile." She wonders if they should have skipped the mill, cut through the pine groves and back to the house. But just the thought of walking among those wasted trees, like boneyards now, makes her angry. She feels cheated. Her grandfather had used up this land, played vampire to an entire forest until the whole enterprise was bled dry. He'd built no real empire, left behind no legacy save ruin. At least the trees here are healthy, she thinks, looking around at the woods, the land rising and falling in hills of red clay.

Ahead, the road slopes toward the muddy trickle that is South Creek on Max's map. Laid across it, end to end, are several wide planks of lumber from the stack in back of the barn. Nellie and Max had brought them in the Ranger, the morning of their first trip to town, set them down as a makeshift bridge across the shallow wash.

Crossing the first plank, her eyes are on her shoes. Her thoughts faraway.

Behind her, Max cries, "Hey!" and drops down into the creek.

The board wobbles and she slips off, sinks the heel of her sneaker in red mud. "Shit. Max!"

He's already splashing away. "I thought I saw the dog!"

"Max!"

He follows the creek into a bower of saplings, out of sight around a bend.

"Max, get back here!"

No answer.

She scrapes her sneaker on the edge of the plank. Gobs of red clay like cake batter.

He's gone twenty, maybe thirty seconds when Nellie hears the dog begin to bark. Not a single bark, but a volley, loud and vicious.

Then, from somewhere in the trees, her son gives out a sudden, high-pitched yelp.

Without thinking, she plunges into the trees, crying out his name. Her sneakers sinking in the silt of the creek bed, face and hair snagged by branches as she pushes through, and then she sees him: standing ten, fifteen yards away, in the middle of the creek, his back to her, staring down at something.

She grabs his arm, spins him to face her. "What were you thinking, running off like that?"

Her grip doesn't faze him. His eyes are big and wide.

A few yards away, the thin, clear creek water curls around the muzzle of a bear.

Nellie gasps, jerks Max backward, away.

"It's okay. It's dead. Mom, it's dead."

Nellie's hand loosens, goes to her mouth. The bear lies on its side, covered with a latticework of roots, its head and front paws the only parts of it left exposed. The roots have burst out of the earth above the creek and plunged like pylons into fur, into flesh. Above its shoulders, along its forelegs.

She clamps one arm around Max's chest.

"Is it the one?" he says. "The one we hit?"

Jesus Christ, it is, Nellie thinks. But how is that possible? She'd hit it, what, four, five days ago? Mushrooms, weeds, flowers, maybe these could spring up quickly, but *roots*? Like this? One of the bear's eyes has burst from the inside, a gob of jelly crusted near its nose. A brown tendril drops down from the empty socket, moist and glistening with creek water. The bear's tongue lolls from its mouth.

"It was thirsty," Max says.

Nellie hugs the boy close, if only to still her own trembling.

They shamble back up the creek and onto the road. Only then does Max wonder, again, where the dog has vanished to. Down by the creek, he'd heard it barking, but found only a handful of paw prints in wet sand. Nothing else.

Halfway up the drive, having passed the last mile in near silence, each exhausted and wet clear through with sweat, Nellie and Max stop when they see the silver BMW parked in the turnaround in front of the house. "Now what," Nellie mutters, at which point a man walks out of her barn. He wears boots and jeans and a button-down plaid shirt, a slight belly pushing over his belt buckle. He has broad shoulders and a thick neck, a build and bearing that screams high school football hero gone to seed. Short, bristly hair.

"Who's that?" Max says.

"An interested party" is her answer.

They head up the lane, and when the man sees them, he lifts a hand and smiles, as if inviting Nellie up to her own goddamn property.

When they're close enough, she calls out, "Can I help you?"

"Howdy," the man says.

Which infuriates her.

Nellie shrugs off her pack. "Take this in, would you, kiddo."

She hands Max the house key, too, fished from her shorts pocket.

"Whatta-ya-say, pardner," the man says. He throws out a calloused hand, palm up. "Gimme five."

Red paint, Nellie sees. On every finger.

Max eyeballs the hand like it's a cobra. He weaves around it onto the porch.

"Don't leave me hanging!"

Max glances back, and the man winks.

"What can I do for you, Mr. Baxter?" Nellie says.

Lonnie Baxter turns to Nellie and smiles, and the smile does not reach his eyes. He opens his mouth to speak, but then Max calls down from the porch, "Mom? The door's open. And it's got—"

"Just go in, Max."

He does.

Baxter takes a step toward Nellie, fills the space between them. He reeks of cologne and something else, something rough and animal. *Adrenaline*, Nellie realizes. *Cortisol*. She's smelled it before, on Wade: raw male aggression exuded through the sweat glands. *The stink of small-town mean.*

"Y'all been having a walkabout?"

Summer heat bakes off her freckled arms, her T-shirt sleeves rolled to the shoulder. *Don't antagonize him, whatever you do.* "I'm guessing you're the one I was told about. Mr. Deep Pockets?"

Baxter spreads his arms as if to say *you got me.*

"Well, I'm sure Mr. Meadows gave you my answer by now."

Baxter sucks his teeth. "It's a big place. You've done wonders with it so far."

"All it needs is a little love."

"Saw a bit of daylight through the barn roof. You might want to patch that—"

"You're a snoop, Mr. Baxter." But he's big. He's dangerous. So she smiles when she says it.

He hooks his thumbs in his belt loops. "Call me Lonnie."

"Was there something you drove out here for, Lonnie?"

"Just to say hey. Meet you. We're practically family, you know."

Her smile broadens. "Oh, I don't know much."

"Yessum, your grandfather, he married into this place. See my great-uncle, he owned this land. Owned most of Baxter County, as a matter of fact. Long before it was called Baxter County."

He circles her, wolflike. Reaches out, runs his thumb slowly along the dull edge of the moon ax that dangles from Nellie's belt loop, curves down Nellie's thigh. His finger whispers over the fabric of her jeans, Tina Gorn–style, and her placating smile withers, and she steps away, out of his reach.

His grin remains fixed, his gaze drifting across the meadow, over the trees. "Lotta blood been spilled over this land."

Nellie does not look at him. But a slow charge is building in her. Building like thunderclouds in the July sky.

"My daddy, he used to tell stories about my great-uncle George, back in the day. Back before this was even Baxter County.

Said Uncle George had to patrol his property on horseback with a shotgun on account of all the crackers he'd pissed off, stealing their land." Baxter laughs. "No-good white trash never got tired of sneaking onto the home place, trying to burn it all down. Rape his daughter."

Nellie's skin prickles. Her hands make fists at her sides.

"Uncle George, well, he'd just shoot em and hump the bodies out here, Daddy said, to these old woods. What he did with em, no one really knows. There's other stories, too. About your grandfather. How he went crazy after his firstborn died. Folks worked for August Redfern, they'd up and vanish, every now and then. Yessum. Bad things happened here. You can take that to the bank. You sure you want to stay, chance it?"

She forces the tremble from her voice when she says, "I've got supper to start," and strides past him.

"What y'all having?"

She stops. Turns. "Something out of a box."

"My boy, Todd, he's older than yours, but he loves Kraft macaroni and cheese. Kind that looks like wagon wheels? He'd eat it every day if we let him."

He thrusts his hands into his pockets, jingles his keys. Rattles a bottle of pills. He takes out a blue plastic teardrop fob, stamped GEORGIA LAND & TIMBER. "Well, I just wanted to see how y'all were settling in. It's a pleasure to meet you, Mrs. Gardner. I expect we'll talk again soon."

He opens his car door, is sliding behind the wheel, when Nellie happens to glance over at the porch, where Max stands watching like a shadow behind the fly screen, but instead of Max her eyes fix on a smear of red fingerprints on the door latch, and above this a full, clear handprint on the screen itself. And suddenly her stomach churns up a ball of acid that rises into her throat, and it hits her like a wave of heat, this fury, this *need*, to wipe that shit-eating grin right the fuck off Lonnie Baxter's face. "Hey."

He pauses, one boot in the car.

"Did you go in my house?"

Far out on the highway, a log truck grinds through its gears. "Did I what now?"

Nellie steps calmly to the rear of the car. She slides August Redfern's ax out of her belt loop. "You went in my house."

Still grinning, Baxter looks off to where the sun is heavy in the western sky. "Now, why would I do that?"

Nellie shores up a two-handed grip on the ax. "I hope it was worth it." Before Baxter can grin even wider and say *worth what*, she swings the ax into the BMW's left taillight, and the sound of crunching plastic, crunching glass, is the best sound she's heard all day, all week, all year, so she swings again. And again. Until the ground is littered with bits and pieces of Lonnie Baxter's car and the ax hangs heavy in her hands, and she's gasping through a fall of hair.

Baxter is not grinning anymore. His hand grips the doorframe, his knuckles white. The cords of his neck are standing out and a red vein is throbbing at his left temple. His eyes dart from the broken glass to Nellie's ax, then to her face, and now his lips are twisting into a snarl, so Nellie stands up straight and pushes her hair away from her face and prepares to meet whatever comes her way, to go down swinging.

But Lonnie doesn't move. His breathing slows. His snarl resolves into a smirk.

"Shit." He spits on the ground and slams his door.

The BMW grumbles away.

Ax in hand, Nellie watches until Baxter is out of sight, then sets the weapon against the wall of the porch and rubs her sweaty palms on her jeans.

Max finds her in her bedroom, where the dresser drawers have all been opened and the bed—

(someone's been sleeping in my bed)

—bears the impression of a body twice her size. She's holding something in her hand, a pair of underwear, balled up. Staring at the quilt. In a flat, mechanical voice, she tells him to look through the house, see if anything's missing, broken.

"Mom?"

He holds out his pencil box, the one she bought him at an antique store last Christmas. Simple, wooden, two brass clasps and a lock. He opens it and shows her: inside, all the pencils—shades of B and H—are broken. Snapped in half.

"That's the man who wants the house?"

"Not the house," Nellie says. "The land."

"Will he be back?"

"No. No, he won't be back."

But her words, to Max's ears, sound every bit as hollow as they are.

Lonnie glances once, twice, in the rearview. After he's rounded the curve at the end of the drive, out of sight of the Gardner woman, he stomps his boot on the brake and the heavy car skids to a halt. He grips the steering wheel with both hands, heart walloping in his chest. *Bitch*, he thinks. *Bitch bitch bitch*. He ought to turn this boat around, drive back up there, and—

No.

He runs a trembling hand over his scalp.

Thinks, pleasantly, of the walkabout he'd had, inside the house.

The key Meadows made for him in his hip pocket.

She'll change the locks now, but Lonnie doesn't care. He has no business here, after today. After today, *Mrs*. Nellie Gardner is going to be someone else's business. He'll see to that. He surely will. He'd like to be the one to see to it himself, but there's his future to consider. That old state legislature dream, ever more present in his mind these days. Senator Baxter.

You know what you need to do—

(feed it)

—so DO IT.

Lonnie lets up his red-handed grip on the wheel, lifts his foot off the brake. The BMW begins to roll. He eases it over the creek wash where the road is treacherous, and a few minutes later he's reached the highway. He signals left, is looking both ways, when the car phone rings. He about jumps out of his skin. He shoves the car into park and snatches the phone. "What?"

A pause. Then: "Lonnie?" Linda. "Lonnie, where are you?"

Something in her voice. Something wrong. "Just out. Is it Todd?"

"I don't know how to say it, Lonnie—"

"Just say it," he growls.

"Your father is dead."

Click-clock of the turn signal.

The engine's heavy, diesel rumble.

"Lonnie?"

"When?"

"An hour ago. The home just called. They think it was a stroke. Lonnie, I don't have Herman's number—"

"It's okay. I've got it somewhere. I'll be home soon."

"Lonnie, I'm sorry. I love you."

"I love you, too, Linda. I'll see you shortly."

"Come straight home."

"I will."

"Bye, Lonnie."

"Bye, love."

He sets the phone gently back in its cradle. Holds on to it. Picks it back up. Sets it back down. Picks it up again. Sets it down hard. Again. Harder. Again. Harder. And suddenly he's slamming the phone into its cradle, over and over, until finally the plastic cracks and a piece flies off onto the floor and spit flies from Lonnie's mouth and he seizes the wheel and stomps the accelerator and the car roars onto the highway.

From his right, a world-quaking horn blast.

Lonnie reacts, yanking hard left and gunning for the shoulder as a pulpwood truck roars past, bits of bark trailing in its wake. Two short honks as it thunders over the river bridge.

A rock pops his windshield, leaves a divot in the glass.

Lonnie slips the car into park and lets go of the wheel. Drops his hands into his lap.

Off in the field to his right, a bunch of cows look at him.

He stares at his hands, watches them shake until, finally, they stop.

After that, Lonnie drives home to his family.

She can't look away from the canvas.

The cunt—it's the only word for it, really—is wide and gaping, a red, sideways smile. Cartoonish and vulgar, sure, but—here's the weird part—not without charm. Like maybe, just maybe, he was really trying? All around it, to the edges of the canvas,

Baxter's painted swirls of black pubic hair. Huge looping curls. It's the biggest goddamn bush she's ever seen. She puts her hand over her mouth. Has to stifle the laugh. And then she sees the heavy red splotch of paint at the top, dripping down the canvas, like blood.

Nellie cocks her head. Steps forward and turns the painting on its side.

The horizontal orientation makes it something else, altogether.

It reminds her of the last page of her grandfather's notebook, out in the RV.

An eye. But not an eye.

And not so funny as the other thing.

She takes the canvas down, turns it to face the wall.

No. Not funny at all.

1923

◆

MAY 4

ALL ALONG A PHALANX OF CAT-FACED PINES, THE WOODSMEN shuffle like ragged birds from bounty to bounty, so much gum to harvest they can't keep up. Dead on their feet, hands blistered, fingers sticky. Among them, the Green brothers, moving in tandem through the gloom, spade and pail and hack in hand, each man half asleep until Eli gives out a furious cry. James, walking ahead, whirls, heart in his throat. *Snake*, he's thinking, half expecting the telltale rattle of a diamondback, but all he sees is his brother, slumped against a pine, face a grimace of pain.

Eli unbuckles the metal stovepipe from his left shin and peels it away. He rolls his trouser leg to his knee. A trickle of blood, where the pipe has gouged him.

"Reckon you'll live?" James says.

"Fuck you. This shit hurts."

"I believe you."

"I'd rather get bit by a rattler than walk around like a tin of potted meat."

They hear men's voices, harsh laughter, the whinny of a horse. In the distance, a saddled roan weaves among the trees and shafts of sunlight, Barlow astride it in his suit coat and bowler, reins looped around the wrist of his two-fingered hand. With the good hand he points, gives orders, and the men step to.

"Boss man sees you sitting there with your hack in your lap, you'll wish you was up swinging it. That's all I'm saying."

"Well, fuck old Seven Fingers, too. And fuck these trees, and fuck you, and fuck these metal sons of bitches." Eli fumbles loose the second shin guard and slings the pair of them into the brush. He leans back and shuts his eyes.

James looks in the direction they're headed, considers the length of the work ahead. His right arm hurts from thrusting his spade into box after box, slathering and scraping the thick gum into the pail. Sweat drips in his eyes and gnats hang from his lashes. "If you're through"—he gestures down the long row of pines with his spade—"we got a ways to go. And I aim to get my quota, before the day's out. I got a date tonight."

"It ain't a date after five years."

"You know, if you'd bitch less, some gal might want to take you out, too."

Eli, head chocked back against the tree, opens his eyes. "Some white gal?"

James shrugs.

Eli slaps a mosquito at his wrist. "All right, Mr. Poet."

"I ain't no poet."

Eli thumps his chest. "In here you are. Too much, maybe. You need a little anger about you."

"What, I should walk around like a lion with a thorn up my ass?"

Eli fans a fly from his leg. "Yeah. You and Pop. He keeps it inside, too."

The brothers share a look at the mention of Ishmael. No words, though both understand each other; this fear, they've carried it with them into the trees every day these past few months. Ishmael up before the sun even cracks the trees, struggling to make water in a little patch of brown grass in back of the cabin. Hands trembling when he lights his pipe. That long, old-man's shuffle along the river, down to the distillery, his job for two years now simply to saddle the mules and drive the wagon back up Camp Road, haul them barrels of raw gum. Mr. Redfern's got new Ford trucks, but he keeps that wagon, them mules, just for Ishmael—

James feels every minute of the five long years they've spent here. All the men who've come and gone. Those who died from the flu, the tent fire, those who jumped ship not long after. Eli begged Ishmael to leave, head south to Florida so he could breathe salt air, but the old man was stubborn, said he was just fine here. Just fine, of course, meaning already too tired, too sick, to travel. And James, well, he just kept quiet, didn't he? Heart spun up in love with a red-haired Irish girl whose family thought, like Ishmael Green, it was a better shot here than elsewhere. After all, ever since the miraculous recovery of little Charlie Redfern and his mother, Frannie and Mrs. Sullivan have been working as nanny and cook up at the house, and Mr. Sullivan, he's apprenticed to the cooper now. They're all saving up, Frannie says, for their own patch of farmland, east of town—

But things don't last.

That's the lesson James Green knows like a schoolboy knows his ABCs.

For two years, the woodsmen have been replenished each season from rougher and rougher stock. Men less inclined to run from a fight, James figures, and there's always a fight to be had, ever since Jasper Hawley tuned up the Swede on that bridge (*poor Marcus, burned in that awful fire*). And now that production's singing, Redfern's hired new toughs to guard the mill, a passel of crackers brought in on trucks from the train yards at Brunswick, pale skin and mean eyes, a heap of loaded shotguns—

"Pop's plumbing"—Eli shakes his head—"gone bad."

"It's been one shit place after another for him. Here was different."

Florida. James can almost see the word shimmering in the air above his brother's head. "He'll never see the ocean, Eli."

"No." Eli sighs. "But you and me, we can. Frannie Sullivan, too. Like we talked about."

James doesn't say anything to this. He's thinking of the years he and Frannie have shared in these woods, a love nurtured outside of time, outside of reality—as fragile, in the end, as a globe of glass in a trembling hand. Would she want to go? How could he ask her to leave her family? What could he offer—

"Hey, you!"

Barlow's voice flies like an arrow.

James grabs Eli's hack and thrusts it into his hands. Snags his own pail and spade and hauls his brother up, and the two scramble back to scraping, hacking. James half expects a thunder of hooves at their backs, but there is only the heat of a long and studied glare, and soon after that, nothing at all. When he looks around, the horseman is gone. Disappeared among the pines.

Beneath their blades, the trees bleed on.

Frannie spreads the quilt on the library floor and sits down with Charlie and Henry. Each wears blue short pants and a white shirt. Charlie's legs are folded and his chin is in his hands. He's waiting patiently, brightly. Little Henry slumps beside him, shy and reticent. His thumb wanders to the corner of his mouth before it worms its way in and hooks itself behind his tiny teeth. Mrs. Effie wants Frannie to put pepper on it, or castor oil, but Frannie's mother says no. *If the boy wants his thumb, let him have it*, Mrs. Sullivan says. *He'll soon grow out of it.*

Frannie opens a book of nursery rhymes and fairy tales and reads from it as best she can. Sometimes, she stumbles over the words, reading being still new and frightening, even after James has taught her. She's self-conscious, uneasy with the scrutiny her fumbling invites. But James reads oh so well. Frannie could listen to him read all day, could lose herself in the sound of his voice.

Their first night together, on the Altamaha's southern bank, far from camp, he brought a book. His favorite story, which he read to her: "The Black Cat." He read with gusto, and when he closed the book, her freckled face was pale, her green eyes wide. She wanted to be able to read like that. But "What a terrible story," she teased.

"World's full of terrible things."

"And why would you want to read about them?"

"I want to *write* them."

"Stories like this?"

"Maybe. Sort of. I don't know."

"Well. You'd be marvelous at it. You're marvelous at most things, aren't you."

"You ain't read a word I've written."

"Do you actually have any stories written down, James Green?"

"A few."

"Well, I don't suppose you'd tell me one?"

"Maybe you could read it yourself."

"Don't tease me."

"Let me teach you."

"You want to teach me to read?"

"Why not. It's just a matter of—"

And then Frannie Sullivan was kissing him, and he put his hands on her shoulders, and her fingers touched his jaw, and when they separated, she found him staring dumbly at her, and she was staring back, and some days, Frannie thinks, it still feels like that: like they're the only two people in the world. Though their families know—and, oh, how James's brother disapproves—they remain new man, new woman, forever busy with the naming of all creation in this strange paradise.

Suddenly, Charlie's voice interrupts her: "You have to read better if you want us to go to sleep."

She closes the book. "Oh, really?"

"I'm not sleepy at all."

"And what about you, Henry? Are you sleepy?"

Henry grins at her around his thumb. She touches his nose with the tip of her finger. He laughs.

"Would you like to read it?" Frannie says to Charlie, and holds out the book.

The boy takes it, turns it round in his lap, and opens it. Turns to his favorite story. "'Beauty'"—he runs his finger below the title—"'and the Beast.'"

Frannie gathers Henry into her lap and he settles against her, sucking his thumb. Quickly, he's asleep, and soon enough Charlie begins to yawn around the words, exhausted from the effort. Before long, she takes the book from him, shuts it, and sings him softly the rest of the way. After that, she's able to slip away to the kitchen, carrying the book with her, as the children nap. Cookies are in a jar on the counter, and Mrs. Redfern never minds if she has one—

A man stands at the back door.

Framed in the red hourglass window. Tall, no hair. A grizzled face.

She freezes where she stands. Book of fairy tales clasped to her breast.

The man waves at her. He is not a man she knows.

"Is this my house?" the man says.

"Beg your pardon, sir?" Without thinking, she takes a step closer to the door.

"I used to live here." He reaches for the doorknob.

"No, I don't think—"

The doorknob rattles.

"This is the Redfern house. Redfern Hill."

"But I've got this." He holds up a key.

It's then that she remembers the talk between her mother and father, over supper out in the cabin, of the letters Mrs. Redfern's been receiving. Not meaning to snoop, but it was there, on the writing desk—well, in the writing desk—Mrs. Sullivan read one. Horrible, dirty letters. Cruel and threatening. *The most vulgar, awful thing*s, her mother whispered.

The man smiles. His teeth are gray and rotten.

Frannie's heart plummets into her stomach as she realizes what he means to do. She clutches the book of fairy tales to her breast and turns, heading briskly for the hall, as the key slides into the lock and the door bangs open. She runs for the library. *The boys, oh, God, the—*

Hands snag her dress, her hair. Fabric tears.

"No! Please, oh, no!"

The man throws her to the hallway floor. She crawls for the foot of the stairs.

He falls upon her, driving the breath right out of her. Reaches for his belt.

Frannie screams.

A shotgun blast pitches him off her, into the wall.

A few feet away, little Henry hugs the library door in shocked silence. Inside the library, Charlie begins to cry.

Euphemia Redfern descends the stairs, her father's Browning double barrel in hand.

The intruder's bowels are spilling out of his shredded denim shirt. He reaches a bloody hand toward Henry, but Henry does not move.

"Back!" his mother commands, and the boy retreats into the library.

Frannie Sullivan rolls over on her back and lies on the floor, breathless, staring up at the pendant light fixture, the board ceiling. Cobwebs up there, her mother needs to clean.

James follows the river by moonlight to the fallen sycamore, lantern in hand. He goes quickly, arrives early amid the nightly serenade of frogs. He doesn't know if Frannie will even come, the news of the day's terrible events having reached the woodsmen even in the fields, far from the house. The mill. Frannie is okay, this much he knows. Mr. Sullivan himself had brought the news back to camp, as the men washed up down by the river. "Whatever you hear," he'd said to James, "she's fine." After that he went away, across the clearing and back down the trail, toward the house.

The talk, at first, was that someone tried to hurt the twins. Broke into the house.

Little Charlie, the talk went, was murdered.

But Daniel Two Fists and Ishmael Green and half a dozen others were at the mill, as the day wound down, and late that evening they'd returned, a sad, whipped lot who had born witness to a thing so terrible, Ishmael himself had sat down in his rocker and wept. Later, he told James and Eli the whole story. *You never heard such screams*, Ishmael said. *Like a heart being torn from a chest—*

Now, James sits on the tree and waits, heart galloping at every rustle, every snap. An hour passes. Two. The frogs fall silent, as the night closes around him like wings. He watches the dark woods for the firefly bob of her lantern. By the bottom of the third hour, he's convinced she's not coming, so he reaches into his pocket for his matches to relight his own lantern, and that's when her voice slides out of the dark: "James? James, are you here?"

He stands, strikes a match, and she emerges from the pines in her housemaid's dress, hair still up in the tidy bun she wears when working. Her face is wan, grave. She blows the match out before it singes his fingers, then falls into his arms and begins to cry. Hard, stricken tears, the kind you push deeper and deeper until they finally break you open. He holds her, and she burrows into him, hot face pressed into the hollow of his neck.

"Shh," he tells her, and strokes her hair, there on the midnight bank of the river.

Nothing left in her to spill but words, she tells him the story. About the man at the kitchen door, Mrs. Euphemia and the shotgun blast, the acrid smell of gunpowder. How, in the moments after the man died, she felt a strange, unearthly calm. Mrs. Euphemia's command to take Charlie and Henry out the back door and meet her in front of the house. How she stepped over the dead man in the foyer, his insides spilled out like a knot of slick worms. She waited out front, children pressed against her, wailing, as Mrs. Euphemia went upstairs to reload the gun and then came down and they all set out walking across the hayfield, Frannie carrying Henry, Mrs. Euphemia holding Charlie one armed, shotgun slung over her chest on a sash of twine. Through the woods, down the road. To South Creek, where they cut up the wash and came out at the distillery beneath the trees, skirts hemmed in mud and bristling with burrs. The mill was in full operation, the men rolling that day's barrels out of Mr. Ishmael's wagon and up the rails to the kettle, where Mr. Redfern himself stood supervising.

"It was him who spotted us," Frannie tells James. Her voice is flat, as if every feeling she could possibly feel has already been felt, and her tears are the last to be wrung out of her. "We stumbled out of them woods like flushed game."

Henry so heavy, so quiet in her arms.

"Mr. Redfern met us in the road. Mrs. Euphemia, it was like someone cut a cord. She just dropped. Mr. Redfern had to catch her, one armed, and Mr. Barlow, he was right on Mr. Redfern's heels. Close enough to lurch and catch little Charlie. Mr. Redfern, he was asking me all sorts of questions. I couldn't think, my head wasn't on straight, I—"

She stops for a while.

They sit quietly on the sycamore, river whispering down the red-clay embankment.

"I don't know what Mr. Barlow did with little Charlie. How he ended up where he did. My arms was full of Henry, and all of a sudden, the men, it was a terrible commotion. I'll never forget Mr. Redfern's face, he looked up from his wife, he was holding her hand, and it's like he knew—"

"Stop." James puts a hand over hers. "Pop told us."

She pulls her hand away, fiddles with her skirt, smoothing the fabric in her lap. She goes on as if she hasn't heard him, like she has to tell it. Sick the story up and out. "Some of the men, they stood their posts up on the platform, they had to. To vent the gas from the kettle, to open the sieve. Even if the Lord Jesus Himself had stumbled out of those woods, they'd have stood their posts, I reckon. Otherwise it might have all gone up. And when the man up on the platform opened that gate and all that hot liquid come pouring out, there was little Charlie, down in that trough. Mr. Barlow had let go his hand for an instant, I heard him say later. Only an instant."

"Someone screamed. I had Henry in my arms, and the men, they all moved toward that sound like a flock of birds."

"Was it the boy, screaming?" James remembers his father's words: *Like a heart being torn from a chest.*

In the dark, he can't quite see her face, just the shape of her head as she shakes it.

"No. No. It was Mr. Redfern. He put his hands down in there, to drag the little one out. All that hot rosin come pouring over him. And when he took em up, his fingers, they ran like candle wax. I held Henry tight, turned him away. 'Don't look,' I said. Little Charlie, he never made a sound."

Her hands move in her lap, fingers working at each other.

James puts one arm around her, and with his other he lifts the lantern from between them, sets it at his feet. He draws her to him. She moves, but she moves woodenly, resisting even the barest comfort. They sit like this until the moon sinks behind the woods across the water, and then James Green walks Frannie Sullivan back to her cabin, where her father sits in the dark of the porch, waiting to take her in.

———

Mrs. Sullivan, meanwhile, roams Redfern Hill, switching on lamps. On the parlor couch, Euphemia stares with wide, wet eyes at the ceiling, imagines she can see straight through the cracks to the bed where her husband sleeps, drugged with laudanum, hands wrapped in great gloves of gauze. Earlier, the sheriff was at his bedside. Somber face, hat in hand. Voices in the foyer, through the half-shut parlor door. Heavy, as if underwater. The doctor, stinking of horse and sweat. Reminding Mrs. Sullivan of the dosage.

Euphemia refuses opioids. She will not dull the sensations that spark through her like electricity. She will feel them all. Every last one. The buck of the shotgun in her hands. The sight of the man's gut, shredding. The hot-pine-sap reek of the steam and the screams of her husband as he plunged his hands into a molten river of rosin.

She remembers when little Charlie was born, that long night of despair, when motherhood and a life lived at Redfern Hill seemed as deadly as the twin barrels of the shotgun now propped beside the parlor door. How she longs for the surety of that gun in her hands, little Charlie's killer to see the end of a Browning. But she cannot shoot a furnace. Cannot shoot a mill. She can only shoot men—

. . . *euphemia* . . .

The voice speaks. Once again, as before, out of a fevered, altered state.

When the flu almost killed her, it brought her, in a vision, to her father's secret place, the voice of his secret god. So intimate, so strong. *Come to me*, it says. *Bring me your pain, your hurt, your broken heart.* August has failed it. She knows this. He is weak and he has failed them all. *Take me*, she begs it.

. . . *euphemia* . . .

No, she thinks, I *would not give myself to anyone, ever again, save to end this life.*

. . . no . . .

She feels it then, like a thing uncoiling in her chest, waking from its slumber to slip into a great blue sea and swim, as it spreads all through her, and she, too, is drifting with it, in that sea of calm and peace and strength, for hers is the willing, grieved heart it has always lacked in the servants it has sought: a woman's heart, ever so capable of any and all demands.

But I want, too.

Men never have to ask, their desires so predictable, from birth to death: money, influence, control. Her father's heart, were she to dissect it, pin it, diagram it, would show little more than greed tangled up in a monster's plunging roots. August's heart? A sodden, fearful rag of blood and ambition. Land. All the land in the world, and his firstborn to be planted in that very land now, where tombstones have already been erected for each of them, as if death on Redfern Hill were as inevitable as the rising and setting of the sun.

I want—

But what does she want?

What she wants now at twenty-two is hardly what she wanted at seventeen, when she thought being a wife, a mother, could save her from a life without—

Purpose.

True purpose.

Yes. That's what she wants.

Sound of scrubbing, Mrs. Sullivan on her knees in the hall, a sloshing bucket and wire brush. Soapy, bloody water on the boards . . .

Euphemia closes her eyes.

Voices in the foyer, through the half-shut parlor door. Heavy. Drowning. She gasps for air. Sits up in the dark, the silent tomb of her house.

That voice, again, a slither among leaves.

. . . *euphemia* . . .

In delirium and grief, it comes. Knocks. And Euphemia answers.

Out in the barn, in the deepest sounding of the night, she finds the dead man wrapped in burlap bags and planked on wood between two sawhorses. She traces the shape of him with the beam from a Winchester flashlight, then passes him by and harnesses one of the mules in its stall. She leads the mule to the sawhorses, puts a bucket of oats in front of it, and ties one end of a rope around the dead man's neck. The rest of the rope she tosses over the barn's rafter, gathers up, and hauls in to lift the body and swing it onto the mule's back. Once she's tied the corpse to the mule, and the mule has eaten its fill of the oats, she allows herself a rest, then leads the animal out of the barn and onto the narrow wagon path that will take her as far as the camp.

She wears a pair of August's pants, tucked into her own mud boots, and a light canvas blouse with sleeves to protect her arms. The two-cell flashlight casts a weak yellow beam, enough to see by without being seen. Her eyes are red and swollen from the day's long grief, but her pulse is steady, her mind focused to a point.

When she spies ahead the entrance to the camp, she veers off into the thicket, the mule hesitating, until she gives the bridle a yank and bends the stupid creature to her will.

1989

JULY 6

LATE MORNING. MAX STANDS AT HIS OPEN BEDROOM WINDOW, staring out at the magnolia tree, its branches big and wide and resting, elbow-like, along the rim of the porch roof. His eyes track the branch to the trunk, then up to where two long, thick limbs, one above the other, stretch lazily for the fire tower. The lower limb peters out less than an arm's length from the platform's edge. *That's the spot*, he thinks. He picks up *A Boy's Guide to Rope* from the bedside table.

At the end of the upstairs hallway, the nursery door is open. One of the new records is spinning, the Bee Gees (not a group he knew Mom liked, she's always been a Debbie Harry–Grace Jones–Culture Club–Thompson Twins kind of gal). Max stands at the threshold looking in.

Nellie stands staring at a blank canvas on the easel, doesn't see him.

"I'm going downstairs to the cellar," he says, over the music.

She turns, slowly. A funny look on her face, distant. Then she cups one ear.

He goes into the room and cuts the music down. "Are you okay?"

"Fine," she says a little too quickly. She peers at him like he's roused her from a nap. "What are you going downstairs for?"

He tells her again.

"What's do you need in the cellar?" Her gaze is already sliding back to her canvas. He's seen her this way before. When the art doesn't come. Like she's standing upright in her sleep, or the world has somehow slipped away around her.

"I need some rope."

She bends to her sack of paints and sifts through it for a big jar of white gesso. "What are you going to do with some rope?"

"Make a Postman's bridge." Max opens the book to a page he's dog-eared and begins to read: "'One of the most common types of suspension bridge, the Postman's bridge has long been the province of explorers and adventurers. Typically, two ropes are secured between two anchor points, as in trees on opposite sides of a gully or river. Once established, the bridge provides a stable means of crossing a ravine by sideways stepping.'" Max claps the book shut. "So that's what I'm doing."

"Mmm." She pours thinner into a small bucket. "Just be careful, yeah?"

"Sure."

"And, Max?"

"Yeah, Mom?"

"Yell if you need me."

He gives her a salute she doesn't see and slips away. He takes the stairs two and three at a time and yanks open the cellar door.

Before he goes in, the music cranks back up.

Sometimes it can be this way, he thinks. *It'll pass, soon enough. She'll find the picture, tease it out. She'll paint. She'll be happy.* All of this he tells himself as he hunches over and descends.

———————

Max hefts a coil of rope onto each shoulder. They're heavy, scratchy. On his way out, he does not stop to stare at the coal-closet door. Or to listen for the sound of fingernails scraping metal. He doesn't even think about it, truth be told; he's got *rat killing* to do—one of Dad's favorite sayings.

Back upstairs, in the foyer, he turns to shut the cellar door, and a brown spider the size of a dime drops out of the rope and down Max's left forearm. He cries out, throws off the coil, and staggers against the wall, shaking his arm. A second later, the spider goes scurrying across the hall, over the threshold of the downstairs bathroom. Max slaps webs from his skin and drops the other coil and kicks the ropes to be sure no more creepy-crawlies come tumbling out. He's always been afraid of spiders, ever since Wade read him a bedtime story in a book about a girl with a pimple and the pimple burst and baby spiders spilled out all over her face. *Scary Stories*, no shit. That one gave him nightmares forever. He doesn't hate spiders, like some people do. They aren't serial killers or cancer, they aren't—

(*Dad*)

—Leon Miller at recess. All things being equal, a spider's just a spider. Still, Max doesn't want one tap-dancing on his bare skin, or hanging out beneath the toilet while he goes number two. *The elusive pervert spider*, he thinks, and makes himself laugh.

He picks up the rope and gets to it—his rat killing.

Max sits in the porch swing, head down, munching Cheese-Its straight from the box and sipping a grape-juice barrel, *A Boy's Guide to Rope* open in his lap. He's learning his way around bights and figure eights. Every now and then, he dusts orange cheese on his shorts and reaches down and takes up a length of rope and practices bending, curling, tying, like Chief Brody in *Jaws*, that last knot dressed and tight when Quint's reel begins to scream.

Max climbs the tower with the ropes on his shoulders, afraid, at first, their weight will drag him off the ladder. Like Rambo—off the cliff and into the trees, only here there's no tree to break Max's fall, just hard, sunbaked ground fifty feet down, twice as high as the roofline of the house. One wrong move, one slip: *SPLAT*.

Sweating, neck itching from the rope, he finally pushes through the trapdoor onto the platform. Here, he makes his initial set of anchor points. The first rope he secures to the platform railing. Easy enough, though he has to tie it twice before the tension is right. The second rope is trickier. He has to hang down over the edge and tie it off to a support beam beneath the platform, and when he does, all the blood rushes to his head and the upside-down world swims.

Once both are tied, he flings each rope into the upper reaches of the magnolia tree. Then he climbs down the ladder and stops to rest for a while in the shade beneath the tree, thinking of a field trip he took in the third grade to some Revolutionary War village about an hour west of Conway. There, his class picnicked beneath the boughs of what an old plaque said was the largest magnolia tree in South Carolina. Max sat off by himself, eating his peanut butter sandwich and gazing up in wonder at a tree made for one thing and one thing only: to reward a boy's warm blood.

Weirdly, scaling the magnolia proves easier than climbing the tower's man-made ladder. For one, the branches are wide and pebbled, so he never wants for a decent grip. And, too, there are limbs to straddle and rest on, the canopy around him full and green, whereas on the tower it's straight up or straight down, one slip and you're jelly. Here, it's a latticework of boughs to catch him, should he fall. Maybe it's bogus, but in the tree he feels no fear, only the pump and race of blood in his veins, and so he climbs, until at last he reaches the branch where the ropes hang like huge, exotic snakes. He scoots out onto the limb, snags the first one, scoots back. He's about to walk it around the trunk when he sees, just above his head, something small and round stuck in the bark.

It's a metal ring. The tree has grown around it, almost eaten it, like trees do. Max reaches up, hooks his finger through it, gives it a tug. Someone else climbed this tree, he realizes. Drove this ring into this trunk, standing right here . . .

He remembers the tree-climbing gear in the cellar, the inscription in *A Boy's Guide to Rope*: THIS BOOK BELONGS TO HANK REDFERN. AND NO ONE ELSE.

All of a sudden, his heart flutters with the need to tell his mother what he's found: evidence of a secret kinship between himself and a grandfather he's never met—

Keep it to yourself. It won't change the way she feels about you meeting him. It might even upset her. She's got her reasons. So keep it special. Keep it secret.

Just like that: flame snuffed, decision made, moving on.

He runs the rope through the ring, wraps it around the trunk until the slack is gone, then knots it. He's careful. Methodical. So grown-up.

Later. Twilight falling as the yard lamps crackle on.

Max sits back on his elbows atop the fire tower and marvels

at his Postman's bridge. He's crossed it once, from tree to tower. Easy as pie until the last bit, where the magnolia's limb can't support him, so he has to put his full weight on the lower rope for about five feet of empty air. The effort leaves his muscles rubbery, and he can see Nellie in the lit kitchen windows below, setting the table, which means he has just enough time to climb straight down the ladder before she calls him inside to wash up. But he wants to get one more crossing in so he can hop from tree to porch and scamper over the roof into his bedroom window. Just like Jim and Will in one his favorite books, *Something Wicked This Way Comes.*

Max peers over the rail, and a bat flits up from beneath the tower, past his head like a bullet. He staggers back, slapping at the air, but the bat's already gone. "Shit," Max says, to no one, then straightens up. Looks back over the rail. Way, way down. If that had happened out there, on the rope—

Any minute now, the back door will open, and Mom will yell.

He takes a deep breath and throws his left leg over the handrail. He grasps the upper rope and brings his right leg over next, slowly. One hand on the rail, the other on the rope above, he slides his left foot out, onto the bridge. A deep breath and he lets go of the rail and grabs the upper rope with both hands, one foot still on the edge of the tower's platform. The lower rope gives beneath him, and his heart flies into his throat, and before he can think better of it, he settles his right foot onto the rope, and when he doesn't fall, he grins, though he dares not look down.

For a time, he simply hangs there, suspended above the earth. An astronaut on a space walk, a fly on the Empire State Building. Heart galloping, eyes on the horizon above the roofline of the house, where the evening star shimmers in a violet sea. He shuts his eyes and his breathing deepens and he thinks: *I could live here forever. Wherever this is.*

He opens his eyes, and a girl is staring at him from his bedroom window.

Max freezes.

The pale oval of her face oozes darkly from a thousand tiny cuts, like the raw skin of a hacked pine. Horns of rough bark jut from dark tresses that fall over the shoulders of a blue dress. She lifts a hand and closes it and opens it, a windup doll's wave. She smiles, and beetles spill from between her teeth.

Max begins to shake, like the ropes he's holding are two live wires.

Far below, the back door opens and Nellie walks out beneath the bare bulb light.

He opens his mouth to call out, but the words won't come. He has no breath.

He looks down, through the crook of his arm, and at that moment his right foot slips from the lower rope and Max pitches backward, and everything that happens next seems to happen in slow motion, as gravity yanks his hands from the upper rope, and he falls, and he can see the purple sky and the stars and the dark leaves of the trees whirling above, as his mother cries out below—

"Max! Jesus Christ!"

—and there is the brief, weightless sensation of flying, the world spinning, and in that instant, Max Gardner knows he is going to die, to crack down from branch to branch until he hits the ground like a sack of bricks, only to lie staring up at the rope bridge still swaying, as the world turns crimson, and his mother's terrified face fills his vision, a rising supermoon, the last thing he ever sees—

He falls six feet before his stomach hooks a branch, and his arms clamp round it, even as he starts to slide away. Mouth wide like that of a fish tossed in the grass, legs scissoring until his feet settle on a lower branch, where he clings, windless and quivering.

He isn't falling. He isn't dying. And he can hear his mother, already climbing the tree. He tries to call out to her. Tell her he's okay. But all he can manage is a ragged *hork*.

Tears in his eyes, he looks up through the branches to the dark square of his open bedroom window.

The girl is gone.

Cold Tuna Helper at the kitchen table. Chink of forks against bowls. Outside, crickets saw and the night roars.

Max pushes his food around.

It's like a rain settling in, Nellie's slow, simmering anger. "The tower and the tree are off-limits. No more climbing."

He turns over a forkful of food and stares at it like something's buried beneath it.

"Max? Look at me. Look at me, Max."

He does.

"What if you had hurt yourself? I mean, really hurt yourself?"

"I didn't."

"Do you know what that would do to—" But she stops. Swallowing whatever's risen up in her, some terror, some anger, some fear he cannot know. "What if you *died*, Max?"

Like there's an answer he has for that.

"Answer me." She pounds her fist on the table so hard the salt and pepper shakers jump. "What if you died?"

"Then I'd be dead," he snaps.

"Max—"

"You wanted me dead once, didn't you? What's the big deal."

His words are like a fist, socked in her gut. He knows it. He doesn't care.

"You don't know what you're talking about," she whispers.

Max nods at the scar on her wrist.

She tucks her hand away, under the table.

"Dad told me. He said you did that because of me. He said you never wanted me. Isn't that the same thing as wanting me dead? Maybe if you let me climb some more trees you'll get what you want and—"

Her hand comes quick and hard across his cheek.

Stuns him silent.

She opens her mouth. Closes it. Looks off through the windows at the steel legs of the tower in the circle of blue lamplight. She bites her lip. Tears shimmer. She wipes them, quickly. Gets up and yanks back the little gingham curtain that hides the plumbing beneath the sink, scrapes her food into the trash. Drops her bowl in the sink.

Max watches her do all of this with the red blush of her handprint fading on his cheek.

Outside, the crickets have ceased their singing.

No movies tonight, no TV time.

Max takes a bath then shuts himself in his room and rummages his Walkman from the cedar chest at the foot of his bed, an old cassette inside. Something recorded years ago on a Fisher-Price recorder. He climbs into bed and hits PLAY. A second or two of silence, followed by Dad's voice: "Are we rolling?"

Max says yes, and Dad says, "Okay," and clears his throat. "Excuse me," and he clears his throat again, and again, until finally he's hacking and spitting and a long, harsh cough turns into a "Riiiibbet!" and Max can hear himself laughing as Dad says, "Sorry, had a frog in my throat." Then he begins, for real, reading a bedtime story out of an old hardback book of tales they'd read so many times Dad had to tape the spine back together with silver tape.

At first, Dad's voice is light and brave: "'What reward is there for the man who slays the giant?'" Then his voice deepens: "'The giant's treasure, of course.'" To which the brave voice answers, "'Then I will undertake it.'"

Max interrupts, in a little kid's voice that he almost doesn't recognize now, "Dad? Is this a scary story?"

"Son, they're fairy tales. They're all scary stories."

Dad reads on awhile, until Max falls asleep.

"Good night, Bozo." Dad kisses him.

Max fast-forwards to the next part. He's listened to it so many times, he knows just how long to hold the button. He hears his parents' voices, faint in the kitchen. Dishes clinking in the dishwasher. Mom says she'll leave. She'll take Max and go. A clatter of silverware, a crash. Mom yelps, a door bangs. She makes a weird, strangling sound. Dad's voice like a knife through the silence: *Step one foot out that door with my son and I'll cut your motherfucking throat.*

Max hits STOP.

He puts the Walkman away in the cedar chest, glances at his broken pencils in their box. He's taped them back together, but it strikes him now as stupid, useless. When things are broken, they're broken. It's best to move on, start fresh—

A hot lick of shame. The way he talked to her. Surly, nasty.

Like Dad talked to her.

But Max isn't *like* Dad.

That was always the problem, wasn't it?

Like in February.

He doesn't like to think about that day, but he often does. Like a loose tooth you worry with your tongue until it falls right out. Only the memory of that day never falls out, no matter how much he worries it.

Bright daylight of a winter afternoon. Taste of copper pennies at the back of his throat. He takes his fingers from his face and there is blood. Dripping from his chin onto a Darth Vader T-shirt. Rolling away, into the grass, a basketball. Beneath the netless hoop that hangs from the garage, Wade Gardner stands fuming, hands on his hips. He wears no shirt, just cutoffs and a dirty white pair of Nikes. Slick with sweat. Heavy five-o'clock shadow. His eyes are knives and they're stabbing Max.

Dad threw the ball.

Dad hurt me.

Dad's voice, saying his name.

Hot tears coursing down Max's cheeks. Pain, like a string of Black Cat firecrackers *tat-tat-tatting* behind his eyes.

Max, I'm sorry. Max, it was an accident, really—

Mommy, I want Mommy—

Dad's hands on his arms, shaking him. Hard enough he'll bruise the next day, too late for the nurses and the doctor at the emergency room to see. *Jesus Christ, don't be a blubbering baby, Max.*

A broken nose. Head titled back in the Ranger, on the way to the hospital.

Dad behind the wheel, gunning it through red lights. Still shirtless, the hot, angry smell of him filling the cab.

Why the fuck didn't you just catch it, huh? What's wrong with you?

Max puts his hand on his cheek, feels the sting of his mother's hand all over again.

Apropos of nothing, the words *bad place* pop into his head. He looks around the room. Listens to the stillness of the house. He's starting to think every home is a bad place, each in its own way. Dads with their anger, Moms with their masks. Always something hidden. Always secrets.

In a little while, he falls asleep with the light on.

Later, after switching off Max's lamp, Nellie shuts herself in her room and lies atop the bedcovers, rubbing the scar on her arm. The clock crawls toward midnight. The window's up and there's a breeze, but the house is stifling. In her mind, she replays the slap over and over, and every time her hand connects with Max's face, a piece of her own heart breaks away. Pretty soon, there won't be much left.

Moving quietly, she goes down the hall, into the bathroom, splashes water on her face.

Should have taken the master bedroom, she thinks. *Given him more space.*

(*He'll hate you inside a week, at this rate.*)

Wade.

In her studio, she shuts the door and clamps a twenty-four-by-thirty canvas into the frame of her easel. Crouching by the turntable on the floor, she sifts through the half-dozen albums stacked beside it. Among them Max's little thirty-three in its paper sleeve, Kenny and Dolly. She sets it aside, slips Bowie's *Hunky Dory* from the stack, puts it on low. Back to the wall, she sits, arms hung over her knees, staring at the empty canvas, a white square between black windows. She sings along, softly, drums her fingers to the beat of "Oh! You Pretty Things," and stares until the whiteness seems to expand, to pop the staples of the frame and become the slow, years-long erasure of her talent, her vision, her hope. Out of that void, the face of her husband emerges. Itself an emptiness.

This isn't helping.

(You aren't even trying, Nellie.)

Her eyes shimmer. She remembers.

Max in his crib. Sleeping.

Wade's straight razor, opened, balanced in an upside-down V on the rim of the bathtub.

Just beyond her fingertips.

The faucet *plink-plink-plinking.*

The water warm.

The first cut, a blissful eruption of color beneath the surface. A red flower blooming.

(Dad told me.)

Why, why would you tell Max I did that to myself, you horrible bastard?

"No," she says softly.

You can't keep blaming Wade for every problem you have with Max. These are your problems, Nellie. You should have explained all of that yourself. Probably before now, but especially tonight. Instead, what you did, it was the worst, the most shit thing you could do—

"The Wade thing."

Baxter's canvas leans against the wall beside her. She turns it horizontal in her lap, regards it for a while. Then tosses it across the room. She knocks her head once, twice, against the wall, in time with Bowie's piano riff. Just hard enough to hurt, to feel something else. She stretches her legs. Shuts her eyes. And still: the emptiness that is Nellie Gardner stares mutely from the canvas.

Max starts awake to music. He sits up in his underwear and T-shirt, disoriented at first, wondering if the song was in his dream. "Islands in the Stream." One of his favorites. He rubs sleep from his eyes and calls out for Nellie, but she doesn't answer. So he slips out of bed and cracks the hallway door, bleary-eyed, on Kenny and Dolly, cranked to the max. At the end of the hall, the nursery is wide open, music so loud the turntable's speakers pop.

Max calls out, "Mom?"

But Nellie doesn't answer.

Hands over his ears, he shuffles down the hall and into the nursery—

(studio)

—and quickly shuts off the record player. As the music grinds down, his eyes light on the wooden frame of Nellie's easel, the clamps undone. No canvas, but paint oozes from a crimped tube on the drop cloth. There's a footprint in red. A trail of footprints, leading back into the hall and down the stairs.

He follows them, bare and small, his mother's feet.

Nellie wakes on August Redfern's map table. Max stands over her, shaking her. She sits up and the room spins. She puts a hand to her head. The heel of her palm, her fingers, sticky with cadmium red. Slivers of paint beneath her nails.

"Mom?"

The boy's eyes are big with fear.

"What? Max?"

"Mom, are you okay?"

She sits up, edges off the table. A blankness in her head, like television static. Max reaches out to steady her when she wobbles.

She cups his head. "I was in the studio. Listening to music, staring at . . ."

The canvas.

It's at the foot of the map table. No longer blank. Nellie spins it round, where she and Max can huddle over it, study what she's done. Smeared into the canvas like some macabre version of a child's finger painting is a grotesque red eye. Its pupil swims in a white, ovoid pool. Optic nerves trail behind it, dripping crimson down the canvas. Not so different from Baxter's painting, or the red smear in her grandfather's notebook—

Upstairs, the turntable jerks to life, midverse of "I Will Always Love You," and Max actually ducks, like stones have dropped through the ceiling overhead. Heart in her throat, Nellie eases out to the hallway, as the chorus falls like a breeze down the stairs. Her first thought: *Someone's in the house.* Her second, *Who? A burglar, way out here? Not likely. Baxter? Not beneath him,* she figures, paying someone to slip into the house in the middle of the night, terrorize them—

The ax. It's still on the front porch.

"Wait here," she says to Max, and slips down the hall and out the front door and comes back with the moon ax filling her hands.

But as soon as she puts one foot on the bottom stair, the record skids off into silence, and there's a quality to that silence, something heavy, something watchful.

Whatever's upstairs, it's not Lonnie Baxter.

Max hugs the map room's doorframe.

Then. From the parlor. Three, four notes, struck on the piano. Picking up where Dolly left off. A tiny sound, made immense by the late-night silence of the house—

(I just walked by there and the room was empty I swear to Christ.)

—as the tune is picked out, one note at a time. Like the player's learning it.

Wet with sweat, Nellie edges along the wall to the parlor door. Max follows, taking small, silent steps behind her.

Another sound now, from inside the room. A familiar *scritch-scritch-scritch*, only this time it's a mad, furious scrabbling, a symphony of *scritch*es.

Nellie reaches in and snaps the rotary light switch, and everything goes silent save the last note played, which hangs in the air, though the piano stool is empty. Every hair on Nellie's arms and neck prickling. "Stay here," she says to Max, and goes into the parlor. He stands in the doorway, watching.

She touches a piano key. Her fingers come away tacky. Something sticky on the ivory.

It drips, pearlescent, over the black edge of the piano.

Nellie sniffs her fingers. Pine sap.

She drops the fallboard over the keys and leans her ax against the sofa. The sheet that covered the piano is folded atop the cabinet. Nellie unfurls it and flaps it over the piano. It falls gently, taking the ghostly shape of the cabinet, the keyboard.

A jagged, horned head on a child's shoulders, facing Nellie from the stool.

She cries out and leaps backward, trips over the foot of an end table. Goes down on her rump, grabbing at the table and toppling a lamp that shatters beside her. A sliver of glass slices her hand as she scrambles for the door.

Max waiting there, wide-eyed and frozen.

Behind her, that dry, scrabbling noise. Things moving in the walls.

As the sheet slides from the piano, pools on the floor, the stool is empty again.

Even as the notes sound one last time, that careful, pecked-out refrain.

1923

$\blacklozenge$

AUGUST 10

THE BRUNSWICK AND WESTERN ROCKETS NORTH THROUGH unfolding marshlands, cutting a black swath along the Georgia coast. Redfern sits in the crowded passenger car and stares out at the blue curve of the earth, the odd sailing ship or steamer on the horizon. They remind him, fleetingly, of his fearless youth. Now, three months after the death of his oldest son, Redfern's dark hair is turning gray, and though his fingers can bend, the damage, to skin, to nerves, he's told, will never fully heal. He brushes lint from his trousers, checks his watch on its chain. Tasks made clumsy by the brown leather gloves he now wears. His mapmaking days, he figures, are over. Redfern carries no suitcase, just a weeks-old copy of the *Savannah Morning News*, folded to an article in the back. A write-up he's read over and over, detailing certain bizarre occurrences in a small town near Brunswick. In the home of a railroad magnate, pots and pans falling out of cupboards, a family Bible hurled to the floor by unseen hands— garbage and rot. But the article makes mention of a woman, hired by the family. A medium. *A woman whose abilities*, the paper says, *cannot be disputed*. Redfern isn't so sure about that. Then again, he isn't really sure of anything anymore. He reaches a slip of paper from his coat pocket, checks the address written in his now craggy, invalid's scrawl. He speaks the name in his mind: *Delphine Averaud.*

Gradually, the seascape gives way to freshwater inlets and wide green fields and dense groves of yellow pine, understory prickled with saw palms. Past these, clusters of clapboard houses surrounded by picket fences. Sandy soil and mossy oaks. Finally, the city itself, soot-blackened buildings among green live oaks and, along the distant river, the billowing white sails of trade ships.

Newspaper tucked under his arm, Redfern walks from the station to his hotel on Broughton. By this time the sun is lowering and the streetlamps are stuttering on. He sits on the hotel balcony for a while with a flask of whiskey brought from home (he doesn't know where Barlow gets the stuff, but it's a damn sight better than a poke in the eye). A piano plays from an open window. He thinks of Euphemia, the German piano she ordered four months past for little Charlie, due to arrive any day now. They'd forgotten it, in those chaotic days after the funeral. (Henry, he'll have no interest in it. The boy is growing up to be dull. You can see it in the way he sulks, hear it in the words he stammers.) Despair will descend, upon its delivery. Despair without tears, which have dried up entirely in his wife, these last few months. *Pray God it comes while I'm away*, he thinks.

When his flask is half-empty and night has fallen, he goes downstairs to inquire at the front desk about the address. The concierge offers to ring a taxi, but Redfern says no. He follows directions, south along Abercorn, is surprised to find himself utterly alone. Overhead, oaks join hands in a conspiracy of shadow, streetlamps casting pools of soft light among their lower reaches, hinting at the greater dark beyond. Smells of urine and horse and garbage wafting out of alleyways, a screech of fighting cats. He passes Oglethorpe Square and a colonial cemetery, where the homeless shuffle in rags like roosting birds.

Ahead, lamps burn in the windows of the Cathedral of St. John the Baptist, and Redfern stops at the foot of those wide steps, struck with the compulsion to confess. To tell some anonymous priest through a screen of wire every terrible thing he's done, to beg forgiveness from a God he's never believed in, unlike the god Redfern has propped up with malign worship, George Baxter's own Baal, out there in the pines.

Before, he'd only ever believed in the strength of his own two hands. But now . . .

He looks down at his ugly workman's gloves, flexes his fingers inside them. An ache, like rain settling in to stay.

I should have listened.

That night in the woods, with Hawley, what he and Baxter—

(you, August, you)

—did, shifted his fortunes overnight. By morning, Euphemia's and little Charlie's fevers had broken, their color returned. A miracle? It makes him laugh, the thought of calling it that. What's the opposite of a miracle? A bargain? A curse?

By the winter of 1920, Redfern's operation in Baxter County had produced more barrels than the larger plantations in North Carolina, north Florida. He bought trucks, a new fleet of Fords. Had to hire more men.

In his heart, knowing it couldn't last. It was a cycle, a ritual.

But he didn't want to believe it, that he was beholden to this thing. This horror.

Every night, the dream. Standing alone, naked, atop George Baxter's infernal Hollow, a moon-limned figure behind him. Face impossible to see. Cold steel pressing at the base of his skull.

Fortune follows the faithful, comes the whisper. And every night he wakes choking on the taste of mud. Nostrils aflame with the scent of pine resin. The bed beside him empty, more nights than not. Euphemia somewhere else.

Is your favor so short-lived? he'd asked it, one stormy afternoon, in the days after little Charlie was buried. Standing at his study window, staring out at the rain. Waiting for an answer— that soothing voice speaking his name, soft and reassuring. But silence was its only answer.

So, he neglected it. Bitter at its betrayal, he turned his back on it.

At the same time, in the weeks after Charlie died, Euphemia began to change, to shed the trappings of womanhood, dresses and perfume. Little Hank plodding after her in the library. She at her desk, going over his ledgers. Making amendments to his errors. Errors he would never have made, before Charlie died. He's changed, too, it's true. He won't deny it. He's lost the proper voice and manner by which to command. Meanwhile, a competition inside Euphemia began to rage, the woman she wanted to be consuming the woman she'd let herself become.

And so they fight, argue to a stalemate, most days. They fight about money, about woodsmen. About shipping routes and land rights and the counsel of her father.

One thing they never fight about, though, is the man who came into the house that day, what happened to his body in the shed. Redfern's seen that flame blaze up behind her eyes more than once, when the fights turn on their good fortunes fading. A challenge. A dare. *Ask me*, that light flickers. *Ask me what I've done with the man who would have murdered your wife and children. Ask me where he is now.*

Afraid of the answer, he does not.

Redfern walks away from the church into Lafayette Square, where two skinny Irishmen smoke cigarettes behind a palm and watch a whore on her knees before a john, her dress roughed down around her waist. Redfern slows his gait, and one of the men—eyes like black pebbles—stares out from the green and says, "You fucking lost?"

Redfern thrusts his hands deeper into his pockets. Walks faster.

Less than a block and he hears footsteps on the pavers behind him. When he turns, he sees them, shoulders hunched, caps pulled low. He walks on, ever faster, Charlton Street close, the corner in sight. He rounds it and the building is across the street, three stories of gray block, tall and narrow, steep granite stairs to a bright blue door. From within, a rollicking piano, the lights ablaze.

He ascends the steps and rings the buzzer.

A stout, silver-haired man in a black tuxedo opens the door, and a jangle of music spills out around him. Redfern can smell the hooch from the steps.

"Yes, sir?"

"Delphine Averaud?"

"This is her home. Are you a guest tonight, sir?"

"I have an appointment. My name is Redfern."

Behind the butler, a clutch of richly clad drunks spills out of the parlor, followed by the sound of breaking glass.

"There a mix-up?"

"No, sir, Mr. Redfern. We're starting soon. Madame will be with you afterward."

He steps aside, gestures Redfern over the threshold. Waits patiently.

Down the block, the two Irish hoods take up posts against a wrought-iron fence. One smokes. The other makes a pistol of his finger, shoots Redfern a wink.

Redfern goes inside.

The butler, impassive, shuts the door.

Redfern eases into the throng like a man certain of his place, though he feels anything but. The butler has taken his coat. In addition to the gloves he still wears, Redfern has on a suit of brown wool and knee-high boots scuffed with dried mud, whereas the parlor crowd sports the height of city fashion: black ties and tails and polished shoes and heels, short fringe skirts and feathered hair, billowing black gowns and long silk gloves. The air is redolent with smoke and laughter, and the music that rolls out from the piano at the far end of the room is like nothing anyone ever played back in Baxter County. It's light and nimble and the people who dance and lounge and drink here seem in tune, somehow, with its rhythms. Redfern takes up space near the drapery, scans a sea of society faces for the woman he's here to see. When a waiter dressed in a tuxedo offers him a drink from a silver tray, he takes it. The bright burn of bathtub gin.

"Don't I know you, young man?"

In his periphery, an old woman. Drink in gloved hand, pearls around wrist and neck.

"You are that writer. From Appalachia."

He forces a smile behind his mustache, says nothing. Looks away.

"You have a rugged aspect. Tell me, what do you think of this scandal? Far better use of one's savings to invest in the markets, if you ask me. Bless her heart. A shame. The Piper boy was so young. Barely twenty-four and to go like that. The very definition of tragedy: a bullet in the brain from his own war pistol, and heir to a fortune. And now, tonight, a ghost, perhaps. Oh, I do wonder if we'll see anything juicy."

Redfern drinks his drink and sets the glass down on a table beside a hurricane lamp.

The woman reaches out and snags another by the elbow. The second woman wears a diamond brooch, has two drinks in hand. "Do you know, Tippy, this is that writer, the one who writes about the folk who live in the clouds? I believe he may be skeptical of our hostess's claims. He is very silent on the matter."

Tippy laughs and presses close, red-faced, stale breathed, her bosom crushing against his arm. "Now, really"—she winks—"where's the fun in being a skeptic, sir?"

The drunk women drift away, and the music stops and the crowd's chatter dies.

A voice from the foyer calls out, "This way, please."

A mass of bodies, shifting at once into the hall. Halfway up the stairs, the butler, hands like planks at his side.

"Presenting Madame Delphine."

Redfern feels his breath catch as a woman descends in a black sequined dress that stretches like webbing over her torso and pools like ink over bare feet. Her shoulders are small, delicate, her face long and sharp. Her lips are full, her hair pinned in a black satin head wrap that leaves her neck long and bare. Her skin glows in the honeyed light of the chandelier like heartwood pine. Redfern tries to guess her age, can't get a handle on it. He's aware, vaguely, that he's sweating.

"I am Delphine Averaud." The woman clasps her hands at her chest. Her eyes roam the crowd, lighting briefly on Redfern, whose heart quickens like that of a man pursued. "Welcome, true believers," the medium says, "to my house."

An upstairs room, dimly lit, is cleared of furniture save four chairs before an upright, two-paneled screen. Candles burn in bronze sconces along silk-papered walls. The sconces are round and intricate and look to Redfern like balls of snakes fucking. He stands near the shut door, one of about forty souls crowded into the room. Seated in the chairs before the screen: a middle-aged woman in a violet gown and gloves, a simple heart-shaped locket around her neck, and, to her left, an elderly couple. The woman in the violet gown is pale, her face strained. The chair to her right is empty.

Behind the left panel, a match is struck, a lamp lit, the medium silhouetted there in a straight-backed chair. She sits in profile, her back to the other panel, yet dark.

The room watches, rapt, as the butler bends and binds the medium's ankles to the chair legs, her arms to the back, with four lengths of silk. Once the knots are secure, he steps away and disappears into a dim corner of the room.

"Join hands," the medium says.

A wave of motion through the room as all link up.

Redfern, for once, is grateful for the gloves he wears, shielding him from the hot, moist hand of the fat man to his left.

A silence descends over the room, heavy as wool.

"Tonight," the medium says, her voice flat, "we will see. We will hear. We will know. And in our knowledge, we will find comfort for Mrs. Amelia Piper."

The woman in the violet gown bites her lip to hold back tears.

"We ask after the spirit of young David Piper, lost to his own despair. Let us close our eyes and picture his face. Let us open our ears and hear his voice."

Someone coughs. People shuffle restlessly. Someone belches.

"Quiet," the medium commands.

The stirring ceases.

This new, second silence is so deep, Redfern can hear a clock ticking from another room.

Gradually, a chill descends, sets people to shivering. Redfern sees his own breath.

Suddenly, light blossoms behind the second panel, though from what source—lamp, candle—it is not clear. A shadow rises from the bottom of the screen, assumes the shape of a man in a suit coat and trousers.

Amelia Piper lurches to the edge of her seat, calls out the name of her son, a half sob.

"Mother," the medium says, her voice changed. "Mother, I'm sorry, I'm sorry, Mother . . ."

"Oh, David . . ."

"It hurt too much, Mother. That's all. Everything. I had to . . ."

In the shadow's hand now, a pistol. A revolver.

"David!"

Heads strain, attempting in vain to peer behind the panel, to see the actor, the trick at work, if a trick it is.

Madame Delphine's head drops, chin to her chest.

A collective gasp from the crowd.

Her hands and feet remain bound, though her back arches violently, as if she were caught in the grip of a galvanic current. Her chest begins to heave, her head to jerk roughly. When the spasm subsides, her mouth opens. Slowly. And out of her mouth—

What, Redfern thinks, *in the name of God?*

Long and thin as a pipe of blown glass and every bit as fluid, a tendril of some substance extends from her open mouth, emerging inch by inch. She drops her head and the effect is horrible, as the viscous strand grows pendulous, stretches to a wire-thin breaking point, and finally detaches. Whatever the materialization is, it drops into the lap of her dress, as the air in the room is suffused with the scent of sulfur, and there comes an audible *POP*, not so dissimilar, Redfern thinks, from that of a champagne cork leaving a bottle.

The light in the second panel winks out, and the room gasps.

The butler appears in shadow behind the first panel, kneeling before his mistress. He unbinds her feet, her hands. From a nearby table he produces a tray, and with her silk-gloved hand, Madame Delphine plucks an object from her lap and drops it onto the tray.

A metal *plunk*.

The butler steps around the panel and presents the tray to Amelia Piper, her seated companions. The older gentleman beside Mrs. Piper plucks out a monocle from his inner coat pocket and snatches up the object to inspect it. He spins in his seat, holds it up for the crowd.

"It's a bullet!" he cries.

Delphine Averaud, in profile, stands as the room bursts into applause.

She rounds the curtain, takes the bereaved mother's hands, and holds them. Then, beaming, she takes a bow.

August Redfern, who has seen enough, pushes out.

The butler descends the stairs, catlike, sees him at the door, waiting for his coat.

Upstairs, the house thunders with new applause.

"You do not wish to keep your appointment, Mr. Redfern?"

"I know what I need to know."

Silently, the butler helps him into his coat.

Outside, Redfern casts a cautious eye up and down Charlton, and when he sees no one hiding in the shadows or lurking behind palm fronds, he starts off at a brisk pace, the night air misty and hot.

He feels a fool for even coming.

Her abilities cannot be disputed.

Parlor tricks and games, cheap carnival hucksterism.

Goddamn it.

(What did you hope for? What did you expect? Would you really have let some fraud mystic into your head? To see all the horrible, monstrous things you've done?)

"Talk to me," Redfern mutters, alone on the sidewalk, the fog enveloping him. "Why won't you talk to me anymore? Speak my name, you son of a bitch." His gait lengthens, and suddenly he's turning off the sidewalk, into the cemetery, where the oaks lay their branches on the ground like giants kneeling among tombstones and mausoleums, and the vague shapes of hungry people shift beneath tattered blankets. He strides in the gaslit dark, loses his way. "Talk to me!" he spits, once, startling a drunk slumped beneath a tree.

(But it won't. Because it knows you're weak, because it knows you don't have the stomach for it anymore. You never did, but she does—)

"What did I do? What was my sin? Why did you take him?"

Redfern smacks the side of his head with the heel of his palm, as if to jar the voice loose.

"What did I not do? A man's blood was not enough? You had to have my boy, too?"

Eyes, all around him in the dark. Watching from behind stones, beneath blankets.

"How much blood do you want? Speak to me!"

His boot snags a block of granite and he drops to his hands and knees, and when he looks up, he sees before him a white marble cross, glowing faintly in moonlight and mist.

Redfern's gloved, melted hands make claws and tear clods of grass up by the roots. "Why did you take my son?" he sobs.

But the cross only towers above him, mute and without answer as God Himself.

Spent and bleary from emptying his flask into his belly, he finds his way out of the cemetery, back onto the street. He sets out in a direction he imagines will take him back to his hotel. Four, five steps and a hard object strikes him across the back of the head and the world flares red. He stumbles, goes down on one knee.

Voices, *Irish* voices.

Hands rummaging his pockets. A stiff boot buries itself in his gut and he cries out.

A switchblade snicks.

Then, out of the fog, a man's booming voice: "Get back, trash!"

Suddenly, that voice manifests as a black-clad shape swinging a fireplace poker, and the thugs light out into the night, whereupon Redfern rolls over on his back and finds himself staring up into the butler's face, and then Redfern's eyes slip shut.

"Is he alive, Mason?"

"He is."

"Good. When he wakes up, you can throw his ass out."

Redfern opens his eyes. The ceiling overhead swims into focus, vaulted and white. The walls golden silk. He tries to sit up and everything spins.

A thick, strong hand presses him down onto a gold chaise longue.

The butler bends over Redfern with a damp white rag, sponging blood from his neck. His head feels swollen, stretched. The room, he realizes dimly, is the parlor. He sees the piano, a cold fireplace, a pair of Hogarth chairs, and empty gin glasses covering every solid surface.

Delphine Averaud sits on the piano bench. She wears a blue silk robe over a blue silk nightgown. Her feet are still bare. Her hair—a thick, dark fall of curls—is swept back from her head. She wears no makeup and her face is freckled and even more beautiful, Redfern thinks, without it.

She hunches forward, rolling an empty highball glass between her palms. "It's rude to make an appointment and not keep it."

"It is rude to throw a party on a man's time," Redfern says.

"Tonight's sitting *was* your appointment, Mr. Redfern."

The butler moves to help Redfern to a sitting position, but Redfern pushes him away, sits up on his own. A white towel on the couch, rolled beneath his head, stained red. "Is it my head injury or is your accent gone?"

"So what do you do, back in Baxter County?" the medium wants to know.

"I run a turpentine distillery."

Her eyes cut to the butler and the butler shrugs. "That really doesn't help me understand what you want."

"I don't want anything. Now."

She laughs. "And why not?"

"You're a goddamn fake."

"Watch it," the butler says. He looms over Redfern, bloody rag in hand.

"What makes you so sure of that?"

"That boy shot himself in the head with his war pistol, did he? Last I checked, standard issue isn't twenty-two caliber. What'd you do? Shoot your pocket gun into a pillow out in your garden?"

Averaud and the butler share a brief glance. A crooked smile between them. The medium stands and walks across the room to the window and pushes aside the heavy drapes, looks out on the street, where the mist has all but erased the world. "Those men would have killed your ass."

"Wouldn't be the first to try."

"Who is it, then?"

Redfern stares at the pattern in the carpet. Mud from his boots staining it.

She waits, arms crossed. "Who is the dead person you want me to talk to?"

Outside, the bells from St. John's chime the hour. Averaud turns, one thin, dark eyebrow arched, and Redfern looks up into her eyes, bright copper.

The church bells fall silent.

"We could start," he says, "with my son."

"Mason," she orders, but the butler is already on his way out of the room.

The door shuts softly behind him.

———

She drifts from hurricane lamp to lamp, switching them off, one by one. Light from a streetlamp stamps her silhouette against the window as she closes the drapes. Suddenly, the room is dim, has secrets. From a sideboard, she pours straight whiskey in her highball glass. Pours a second in a tumbler and hands it to him. She sits beside him on the lounge, and Redfern draws back instinctively. Away from scents of lilac and vanilla, a fine, unknowable talc. She crosses her leg over her knee, and the knee slits her gown as neatly as a knife through a sail.

"One fall, when I was little, my daddy took me to the circus in Terrebonne Parish. A special circus." She sips her drink. Sets her glass on the end table behind her. "What made it special, my daddy said, was the menagerie." She takes Redfern's gloved hand in her own. "'You ever see a unicorn?' my daddy said. 'Well, they got one.'" She loosens each finger of Redfern's glove. "I told him ain't no such thing. He said, 'Oh yeah. Unicorns. Satyrs. Hydras. Brought em all the way from California by train, right here to Houma, Louisiana.'"

A cold sweat breaks over Redfern as she tugs his left glove free of his hand. She does not flinch at the mottled flesh. Does not stare at the lumpish waxworks his fingers have become. He watches her, mesmerized by her eyes. They glitter with a flame their own. He downs his whiskey and she sets his glass by hers on the table and begins to work his second glove free, as slowly and gently as the first. The room darkens, even as her eyes burn all the brighter.

"You can imagine my disappointment when all I saw was an old white nag in a cage. Some poor whale's horn stuck on her head. 'That ain't real,' I said, but Daddy, he just stood there, laughing with all these other fools." She drapes his gloves over the whiskey glasses. Her hands settle in her lap, her feet crossed at the ankles where she perches on the lounge. "They all knew it was fake, but they didn't care. They didn't come to see magic. Didn't want to believe in anything their pocketbooks couldn't afford. Even it had been a unicorn, if flowers had sprung up beneath its hooves, would they have seen it? Wanted that? Do any of us want proof that the world is a damn sight more mysterious than the price of admission? Do you, Mr. Redfern?"

I require no proof of that, he wants to say, but his tongue is thick, his mouth dry.

"Anyway," she says, "what did any of us ever do, to deserve a unicorn?"

She extends her hands, palms up. Her nails unpainted, her fingers long and delicate.

His hands drop into hers like magnets finding metal.

"Tell me about your son," she says.

"Little Charlie."

"Little Charlie Redfern."

"He was a good boy. Stuck by his mother's side. She meant to teach him piano, when he was old enough."

The medium's eyes close.

Redfern watches her chest rise and fall beneath her pajamas. "Go on."

"He was four when it happened . . ."

Her breathing shallows. "How? How did it happen?"

Redfern hesitates, remembering. Those few, terrible moments that had finally eclipsed the old nightmares, given him new ones. His heart beats faster, as does hers. They're beating in time together. She tightens her grip on his hands. He shuts his eyes, too, and though he doesn't speak the memory aloud, it passes from him to her, like a current through their joined hands, a memory of smoke billowing black, the smell of hot rosin, the shudder of the copper kettle as Euphemia faints and a woodsman cries, *NO FOAM*, the signal to release the boiling rosin through the open furnace gate, down the sluice, two hundred degrees hot, molten pitch pouring through the sieves and into the rough, pebbled wood of the trough, there among the last of the unfiltered leaves and bark, in that pool of yellow amber. His boy, washed beneath it, and there is screaming and old Ishmael Green is fishing at the boy with a dipping pole and Redfern's shoving him aside, dropping to his belly, hands plunging in to claw at little Charlie's bare skin, his arms, dragging him from the pitch and the pitch drips from his hair like blazing hot honey, and Redfern's fingers are blistering as he rolls the boy onto his back and his face, his tiny face, like meat boiled off the bone—

"Papa?" the medium says.

Redfern's eyes jolt open. He tries to let go of the woman's hands, but her fingers have locked his, and her eyes are open, too, and they are no longer copper, no longer bright. Instead, they're twin black holes, and when Delphine Averaud speaks again, it is not with her voice, but the voice of a child—*his* child.

"Papa how?"

"How what?" Redfern says, a hoarse whisper.

"How am I here?"

Trembling all over, Redfern gathers himself. Mind splitting open, he fears, that vast chasm between reason and want. Terror, love, rising up to fill it. "Where are you, Charlie boy? Where is here?"

"It's blue, like water."

"Blue?"

"Blue forever! Where's Mama, Papa? Where's Hank?"

Redfern swallows thickly. "They're home, son . . ."

"I want Mama—"

"She isn't here now, Charlie."

"My friend promised," the little boy inside the woman says.

"Who promised what? Who is your friend, Charlie?"

A struggle behind the medium's countenance, her eyes clinched shut, as the words wrench free of her like a blade from splintered wood. "Your friend, too—" Her hands tighten around Redfern's, and the sensation that passes into him, rocks him, is like a cold plunge into a winter sea. Briny, freezing. Shocking. Redfern gasps, and in the seconds that follow, time collapses like a sinkhole and he sees what she sees, memories that are not his but some other entity's, sluicing out of her and into him—

darkness, a field of stars, expanse of space

one star dislodging, falling through flame into water

(pretty blue, Papa)

light, warmth, consciousness

the ocean's cold arms

a shape, oblong and soft as gelatin, cupped in a plantain leaf, beating, pulsing, withering, fading, passing from hand to hand amid the cry of gulls and the flap of sails, stowed away in a small dark space, forgotten, burrowing into itself and drifting in the cold black of the long sleep until—

hunger awakens it

bursting out of a wooden box, buried in the earth beneath a tree where the greedy, bloodthirsty sailors who found it fed it, meant for it to stay forever forgotten

now into sunlight

to swim through fresh water, the mud beds of the river where giant catfish drift and alligators go eeling through the gloom

but here the blood is cold not warm and it craves the hot
rich earth like a seed
crawls sopping onto land
this bloodshot orb with its long slick body that moves,
wormlike
seeking heat and the blood of things that walk and run
egrets that step unwittingly into its maw and break between
its teeth
dragged down into its nest as
slowly, over time, it grows
ever reaching for the light
seeking those who would stumble upon it
to serve
blood and godhood the only pleasures it has ever known
its massive mind a lockbox of memories
(like mine, Papa, you buried me in the ground but I'm not there
anymore because it's in the ground, too, and it came for me and
now it tells me stories about you and the things you did about all
those men in the tent and the fire and about the scary Catfish man
with the pistol who wanted to hurt you, why don't you do those
things anymore, Papa, why don't you feed it food like you did
once with Grandpa George you try to forget and it says it's mad at
you and now it's found someone NEW to talk to and I'm going to
talk to her, too, Papa, Mama! It's going to let me see Mama again!)
a lockbox of souls
to feed upon
so it can grow even more
dig deep into the earth and put down
—"Roots," the medium says.

Her eyes spring open.

Their hands untangle, Redfern's sweating and pale.

She, too, is drenched. Beads of perspiration along her nose, her chin, her collarbone.

"What is it?" she whispers. "This thing you're feeding?"

But he only staggers up, beneath the weight of this ghastly revelation: his boy, buried in the ground, in a coffin, roots in that ground, roots that are not roots, piercing little Charlie, like it pierced those thirteen men in the sick tent—

(why don't you do those things anymore, Papa)

—eating him? Something worse?

He remembers how the Swede's dead eyes had opened, his jaw unhinged, as if the tendrils snaking through him were the fingers of some hideous hand, thrust inside a puppet—

(it's found someone NEW to talk to)

Euphemia.

(Ask me. Ask me what I've done . . .)

He snatches at his gloves, tugs them on, the medium breathless and horror-struck, as Redfern opens the parlor door, pushes past the butler, and flees into the night.

1989

JULY 7

THEY LEAVE IN THE WEE HOURS OF THE MORNING, THE BOY
still in his underwear, Nellie shoeless in a T-shirt and shorts. She
grabs her keys and purse from the telephone table, and as the
house key turns in the front-door lock, doubt rocks her, almost
topples her. *Are you crazy? You're half-naked, it's the middle of
the night, and this is your home.* But Max is already in the
Ranger, watching her through the passenger window, and one
look at his face convinces her: they have to go. Whatever it was,
she didn't imagine it. Didn't hallucinate it. She *saw* it.

One night. It's just for one night.

Minutes later, the Ranger's thumping over the South Creek
wash, passing the distillery gate, and they're at the highway,
idling, Nellie's foot on the brake, dark road stretching away
toward the lights of town. The pickup's headlights knife into the
field, where fireflies drift among the shaggy roadside grass.

Her hand is bleeding, a shard of lamp still stuck there.

She plucks it out.

"Mom?"

What comes next?

It's your house, goddamn it, this is crazy—

"Mom, where are we going?"

She doesn't answer, just cranks the window down, tosses the sliver of lamp into the grass, then mashes the accelerator with her bare foot and wheels away, while she still can.

Max hugs himself and pulls his knees up and stretches his T-shirt over his legs and tells her about the doll, E.A.R., found beneath the map he'd drawn of the first floor, how the cellar door was torn into a jagged mouth. How the pencil was covered with the sticky residue, like the piano. He tells her about the girl in the window. How hers was a cat face like those cut out of August Redfern's dead trees, how he saw the same horned shape beneath the sheet in the parlor tonight. He tells her that dry, scrabbling sound is downstairs, too, in the cellar, behind the coal-closet door. Nellie listens, eyes fixed on the lights of town ahead. She wrings the steering wheel until it's slick with blood from her palm. She asks only one question—"Why in God's name didn't you say anything, Max?"—and the answer he gives is so obvious she feels a fool for even asking: "Would you have believed me?" *Of course not. Of course not. Of course not.*

By the time they're on the bypass, nearing the motel, Max is staring out the window. Once, he presses a finger to his nose, like he sometimes does when it's about to bleed, but Nellie can't see a single drop.

The old man behind the desk at the Budget Inn eyes her with a mix of curiosity and suspicion as she signs the register with her bloody hand. Cheeks paint spattered, shoeless, braless in a Roxy Music T-shirt, Nellie says nothing, just hands over the cash for the room, takes the key, and pads out through the double glass doors. She feels the old man's eyes until she pulls out from under the broken brick portico.

They cruise past rooms with doors yet open, TVs shedding ghostly light.

Everyone here, she thinks, *is a permanent resident.*

Room 14. The bed's a rickety queen. She locks the door, cranks the air-conditioning, and Max falls straight away into bed, into sleep. Nellie sits on the edge of the tub and washes her feet. Cleans her cut hand in the sink. When she's done, she slides beneath the covers, scoots close to Max.

Her boy in trouble, her boy with secrets, and once again, here's Nellie, thinking it's all about her. The shape of him against her is pleasant, reassuring, so she wraps her arms around him and falls asleep.

Morning, and with it comes a plan. They drive back to the house. Max sits in the car while Nellie goes inside. Upstairs, she dresses quickly, slips on fresh underwear, a long-sleeved shirt, jeans. She gathers clothes for Max into her duffel, along with toothbrushes, toothpaste, and, on impulse, her zippered makeup bag. She pulls her hair back into a ponytail on the stairs and snags a box of Pop-Tarts from the pantry. She does not look at the cellar door or the canvas painting in the map room, but she lingers at the parlor. The air in there still smelling faintly of pine. The piano still sticky, the stool, too. But there are no sounds—no creaks, no scrabbling. No sudden bursts of Kenny and Dolly. This morning, Redfern Hill is just a house shot through with early gray light.

She resists the temptation to stay. To pretend, to ignore,

to convince herself that she's just tired. Mentally exhausted. Traumatized by the last ten years, even. *Excuses*, she thinks. All of them excuses to avoid confronting the problem.

You're good at excuses, she tells herself, on the way out the door. *You've had a lifetime of practice.*

Noon.

One more corner, another block past narrow dirt drives and cinder-block houses, and Nellie pulls the Ranger into the turnout of a house shingled in white asbestos. A sagging front porch and a bald, square yard wrapped in chain link, grass shaded by the wide boughs of a pin oak.

The Ranger idles, fan belt shrieking.

The garage doors are swung open, a rusted Dodge missing its tailgate parked inside, an I SUPPORT GEORGIA LAW ENFORCEMENT sticker on the bumper. The bed of the truck is a mountain of aluminum cans. Garbage bags are heaped by the kitchen steps on the side of the house, one torn open and drawing flies.

She cuts the engine and Max reaches for his seat belt, but before he can unbuckle it, Nellie puts a hand over his. "Hang on. I need a minute." She rolls her sleeves down from her elbows, then buttons the cuffs at her wrists. Then flips the visor down and takes out a lipstick from her bag. Puts it on. Stares at herself. Smears the lipstick away. Shuts her eyes, drops her head.

"Mom?"

"I'm okay. I just—"

The kitchen door opens and an old man in Dickies shuffles out. Tall and long limbed, frame broad, and in it Nellie sees the ghost of a man she remembers, her hawk-nosed and gangly father. His hair is thin and his cheeks are sunken. Heavy half-moons of flesh hang beneath his eyes. He bends over to brush a plastic milk jug back into the torn bag at his feet.

"Is that him?" Max asks.

"That's him."

Hank Redfern looks up from his garbage. Stares. Raises a hand.

That same hand shakes pouring coffee, so Nellie pours it herself. Hank sits at the small round kitchen table where Nellie remembers eating things spooned out of styrofoam, cold biscuits soaked in hot sauce, as her mother slept in a fog of morphine in Nellie's bedroom down the hall. In the living room, Max has plopped himself on the floor to watch TV, a little Magnavox on a wire cart. On a stand beside it, a houseplant thrives, bright green Wal-Mart sticker still on the pot. A window-unit AC blasts cold air above the couch where Nellie slept some nights, when Ruth Redfern lay dying. The house is smaller but brighter, somehow, than she remembers.

"Get me a Coke?" Hank says.

Nellie opens the fridge and sees a shelf full of Dr Peppers. The same shelf where Hank always kept his beer. She sits down across from him. Holds her lukewarm coffee with both hands. Noticing, as he pops the ring on his soda, that his fingernails are as long as ever, a jeweler's hands, but grown ragged, broken, no longer filed and sharp. Once, even drunk, he could turn the smallest of screws with those nails.

"You retired?" she asks.

Hank takes a pack of Marlboros from a zippered pocket and slides a seashell ashtray close. Scrawled on the shell: MY BUTT GOT BURNED IN DAYTONA BEACH! He lights the cigarette with a Bic and draws hard. He scratches at his face, heavy white grizzle a few days out from becoming a beard. "I tinker part-time. Small engines. Gave up clocks. No patience for it anymore. Anyway, what's a digital watch?" He coughs, and the cough becomes a fit that leaves him red-faced. "How long you been back?"

"Few days."

"Divorced?" He says it like it was only a matter of time.

But her voice keeps even, controlled. "Getting there."

He smokes.

"We're up at the house."

Hank's eyes cut her, sharp. "Sell it." He thumps ash in the shell.

She sips her coffee. It's bitter. She puts it down.

"Lonnie Baxter paid me a visit the other day."

"They broke the prick mold when they made him."

"Yeah, well, he's got a hard-on for that place so big you could sell it by the board foot."

Hank grunts. "Sell it to him then. He deserves it."

"And I don't?"

"No one deserves that place."

"When did you get so cryptic, Dad?"

"When I quit drinking." He sips his Dr Pepper.

"How long's it been?"

"I had a bout of appendicitis, about a year back, nearly killed me. I let it go too long, took it for a bad case of beer shits. That was what they call down at the VFW a come-to-Jesus moment."

"All things considered, you look good." Nellie is surprised she means it.

"I look like an old ex-drunk's all."

"What's Lonnie after?"

Hank stubs his cigarette. Reaches into his coveralls and takes out another. Lights up again.

"Maybe you should quit that, too."

"And what, chew gum? I'd sooner blow my brains out."

"I can't sell the house, Dad. Right now, it feels like the only thing I've ever had I can call mine."

"Not the only thing." He nods at the living room, where Max is on his belly in front of the TV, chin cradled in his hands, Shotgun Red on the Nashville Network. "Money you'd get from Baxter, you and the kid could go anywhere."

"You could have gone anywhere. But you came back."

"I didn't have anything, after the war. This place was all I knew. God help me. You don't know about it. That was always your problem, what you thought you knew and what you didn't know at all. You and your m-m-mama—"

"Don't talk about Mama."

He falls silent. Turns up his Dr Pepper. Half of it's gone in a single swig.

"It can't be the trees he wants," she says. "The old groves, they're all dead."

"Lotta dead things in those woods."

Suddenly, she's thinking about the bear in the creek. The empty cabins in the meadow. The words scratched there: *bad place.* "And the house? Any dead things there?"

He eyes her over the rim of his soda. "A few."

"Mr. Hank?"

They look up.

Max stands in the doorway. "Where's your bathroom?"

Hank hooks a thumb over his shoulder. "Hallway, second door on the left."

Max says, "Excuse me," as he slips past them.

"Seems like a good boy," Hank says.

"It's a wonder."

Hank crunches his can. "I reckon you'd know from bad." He pushes up from the table, opens the fridge, rummages out another Dr Pepper.

Nellie jerks at the pop-hiss of it cracking open.

Hank's Adam's apple bobs like a cork as he drinks.

"You're gonna kill your prostate."

"Make a matched set with my lungs and liver." He sets the can down, belches. Picks up his cigarette. Tips the ash.

"Who in the family played piano?"

Hank sucks his teeth. "Agatha. It was bought for Ch-Ch-Charlie, but he . . ." Hank hesitates, takes a breath. "He d-d-died before it got delivered."

She hears it, the old stutter. Had almost forgotten how bad it got, those drunken nights when he was raving.

"Sh-sh-she had an old hymnal, taught herself to play songs out of it."

"What happened to her?"

"Run off. Like me."

Each question now is one step farther on cracking ice. "Where'd you go?"

"Lied about my age, joined the s-s-service."

He's sweating. Big drops rolling down the sides of his face.

"What about Agatha? Where'd she go?"

Hank opens his mouth as if to answer. His lips form the start of something, but whatever it is, it lodges tight behind his teeth, and eventually he only shakes his head and looks away, his eyes gone glassy. They flick to a corner of the kitchen, where a mousetrap is baited, set to spring, and Nellie watches him struggle with the memory of something huge and terrible, a memory that cuts to the heart of who her father is, and why he is, and why he will never be all that she ever hoped he would. It's beyond her. Beyond them both, maybe, to understand. To fix. And so they sit quietly, as the TV mutters in the other room, and ghosts circle the kitchen table like sharks.

Max goes softly down the hall of his grandfather's house. The first room to his right is filled with boxes and junk, its pine-paneled walls painted white. He stops here. His eyes cut to the window, the molding and sill and frame, all the same flat color. No curtains. No shade. Just the faint, old smells of dust and cardboard. He glances at the bathroom door across the hall. It's not a lie; he does have to pee. But there are things to look at in the dim hallway, and so Max goes snooping. He starts with a series of hung pictures, prints faded behind dusty glass. His mother as a girl, in Buster Browns and with a pink bicycle with training wheels. In one, she wears corduroy and a heavy winter coat and a hat and stands beside a melting snowman with coal eyes and a carrot nose. Mr. Hank's there with her, smiling. Next to these, a woman who must have been Max's grandmother, Ruth Redfern. Sitting on a porch swing, leaning forward, limbs long and birdlike, cat-eye glasses. A green flower-print dress and house shoes. A cigarette between her fingers.

Max moves along the wall to the end of the hall, a doorway.

He glances back toward the kitchen, the pop of a ring tab being pulled on a can.

He edges the door open.

Finds himself in his grandfather's bedroom. The bed is made, neatly. A window sheds sunlight over a round antique table, beside it a brown chair. In the chair a thick black Bible. On the wall, a framed, blue-eyed Christ carries a lamb, the shepherd bringing home the stray. On the table, beside a framed picture of Ruth, is the sepia-tinted portrait of a child, not much older than Max. The little girl sits primly on the porch steps at Redfern Hill, back straight. Her neck long and slender. She wears a ruffled dress and polished black shoes and holds a chicken in her lap. He tries to remember the features of that weird, jagged face in the upstairs window. He reaches out, touches the picture. *The smile*, he thinks. *The smile is the same.* "E-A-R," he says softly.

Voices behind him, floorboards creaking.

Nellie and Mr. Hank appear in the bedroom doorway. They stop when they see him.

Mr. Hank says nothing, eyes moving from the boy to the picture, back to the boy.

"Max?" Nellie says.

"Sorry. I must have missed the bathroom."

Mr. Hank takes two steps back, reaches into an open doorway, and flicks on a light. "Here."

Embarrassed red, Max slips inside and shuts the door.

Hank shuffles into Nellie's old bedroom, now a junk room. The worthless accumulation of a widower's regrets, things an old man has little use for but cannot bear to let go. Mostly Ruth Redfern's old clothes, boxes packed and taped and labeled SALVATION ARMY in black marker. Bits and pieces of a life like broken glass in Nellie's gut. She looks at the walls, as Hank riffles through a box or two, notes the paint, which would have covered over the stubborn smells of medicine and sickness. The carpet has been ripped out, too, bare board beneath.

"Here it is." From a high shelf in Nellie's closet, Hank takes down a cardboard box, smaller than the rest, and sets it on the floor at her feet. Nellie hunkers down and digs through it. A baby quilt, her own. A Roi-Tan cigar box full of tattered photographs of her mother. Ruth's Zippo, emblazoned with a crucifix. A snick every time she lit up, before the lighter vanished into her hip pocket like a magician's coin.

Across the hall, the toilet flushes.

Nellie tosses the lighter back into the box. "There's nothing here I want."

"Memory lane, always was a dead end for us."

The shadows are long outside when they say their goodbyes. Max gives the old man a dutiful hug, and Hank seems surprised. After, Max waits in the Ranger's cab, seat belt fastened. Nellie makes no move to show any physical affection, and Hank makes no assumptions. "If you won't stay," he says as Nellie turns away, "at least look out for the boy."

His words feed the dread that's burned in her breast since Max fell from the tree. "I always do."

"There's something—" But he stops.

"What is it?" She steps toward him, her voice low. "What do you know, Dad?"

"Just keep clear of the . . ."

"Clear of what?"

"The suh . . ." He takes a deep breath. "Suh . . ."

"Dad?"

"Cellar," he finally says. Then he turns and goes back up the steps and into his house.

She gets into the pickup and cranks the engine.

"Are we going back to the motel now?" Max asks.

"No," she says, surprising herself. "We aren't."

They turn onto Redfern Road.

Max is quiet. Wiping at his nose, though there is no blood.

Nellie's thinking. Turning over old memories. The last full day she spent at Redfern Hill in the summer of 1975. She and her grandfather had gone into the woods, and he had taken her up above North Creek. Shown her a place. Said some things. Crazy things. He was old, confused, broken by regret and failure—

"It's stupid," Max says suddenly, jolting her out of her thoughts.

"What?"

"It's stupid to come back. In movies, people always go back, and it's never good."

"It's our house, kiddo, like it or not. We live here. And this isn't a movie."

"We saw what we saw. I saw what I saw—"

"I agree. We saw what we saw. You saw some weird shit, I saw some weird shit. We both saw some weird shit. We. Saw. Weird. Shit. No one's denying that. But if you've got termites, or spiders, or rats, or a leaky roof, you don't just leave and never come back. You deal with it. We've got a problem here, and we've got to deal with it."

"A ghost isn't a rat."

"Max, there's no such—"

She hits the brake.

The truck skids to a stop.

Ahead, the shallow South Creek trickles over the road.

The rat. That first night, the rat was covered in something, just like—

"What is it? Mom?"

"Let's have another look at that bear." She opens her door.

But the bear is gone. A hollow where its body lay. The roots are mostly gone, too. All that remains in the orange silt are a handful of husks that crumble like cicada shells when Nellie toes them. All around the creek bed are holes, bubbling as water seeps into them. They remind Max of crab holes at Myrtle Beach. He'd never been able to catch a single crab. Dad said he was too slow. Wade himself had caught four in a green plastic pail. He'd left them on the balcony of their hotel room overnight. By morning, seagulls had cracked them all open, left little claws and bits of shell strewn across the patio. Wade kicked the pieces off the balcony, laughing.

"Mom, look."

Max points to a clump of roots on the far creek bank. Two, three shoots. Young and new and light colored, snared around the small body of a baby rabbit. The rabbit's legs are long, its ears short. Its little head is no bigger than a smooth brown stone. They step closer, the water sluicing around their sneakers.

The rabbit yips and kicks once.

"It's alive!" Max says.

"Do you have your knife?"

He takes his Swiss Army knife from his pocket.

The rabbit spasms as the roots tighten. The rabbit cracks, crunches.

Max covers his ears, but the rabbit doesn't make any more sounds.

Nellie draws close and, at the last second, changes the blade for the scissors. Her hands are shaking. She snips the shoot at its thinnest point, about an inch from where it enters the rabbit's body. The reaction is sudden and fierce. The root uncoils from the rabbit and whips back into the ground.

A piece still buried in the rabbit quivers.

Max stares at it, repulsed and fascinated. It reminds him of a snake Wade killed in the yard. The snake got its head caught in a Coke can, couldn't get out. Wade chopped the body with a hoe, but both halves of the snake kept on squirming, the head still trying to free itself, even as the body went still.

Nellie grabs the rabbit by its foot.

They trek back down the wash and she tosses it in the Ranger's bed. She puts her arms on the rail of the pickup, drops her head between her arms.

"Mom? Are you okay?"

"The day I got stung, I saw something."

The Winnebago.

Nellie brakes in the gravel drive. She cuts the engine. Gets out. Max follows her across the barbwire fence, through the grass. He takes in the stove, the recliner, the pie-plate light bulb. Nellie takes the blue key fob from her pocket and goes into the RV. She comes out with an empty mason jar and a pair of pliers. These she hands to Max, then reaches behind the metal step. She pulls out an old wooden peach crate, which holds several gallon-size milk jugs. They're all empty save one, half-full of a clear liquid. Nellie uncaps it, sniffs. Snaps the pink plastic cap back on. Max watches, silent. He follows her back to the truck, where Nellie lowers the tailgate. She reaches for the rabbit, draws it to her. The root burrowed into its belly has ceased moving. She grips it with the pliers and yanks. Max looks away, but he still hears it, that sucking crunch. Nellie drops the root into the mason jar—slicked in blood and hair—and takes up the plastic jug and says, "Maybe stand back?"

"What's going to happen?"

"I don't know. Maybe nothing. Maybe something."

He takes two, three steps back.

Nellie holds the jar with one hand and uncaps the turpentine with her thumb. She takes a breath, then pours the turpentine into the jar. The root only floats up, hangs perfectly still in a cloud of pink and brown—

(Why wouldn't it? It's a root. *Jesus, Nellie.)*

—but the memory is there: August Redfern's jars.

(They hate it. You can hear em scream. Listen.)

She caps the jar quickly. Then raises it to her ear, holds it there, listening.

"Mom?"

"Shh." Swirling it in the fading sunlight.

(I don't hear anything.)

(Then it's just a root.)

"Mom, you're freaking me out—"

Something shrieks. A tiny cry like a mouse in peril. They both hear it. Nellie drops the jar. It shatters on the gravel and the air fills instantly with the stink of turpentine. Amid the broken glass the thing that is not a root is flapping, a slick worm with an underbelly of bristly legs that push out from its segmented body, each leg trimmed in tiny mouths with tiny teeth that glint like needles.

"Oh, Mom, what is it, what is that thing?"

She feels a wave of nausea brought on by sheer revulsion as the root spasms and rolls like a limbless baby in a film strip she once saw, way back in high school. This baby pitching around and screaming on a blanket, and it's like that now, this thing in the throes of a mad, mindless fury. The shriek ratchets down as its little feelers scrabble for purchase and it uses its teeth to burrow, wormlike, into the dirt.

Leaving Nellie and Max to stand in stunned silence behind the truck.

A warm evening breeze ruffles their hair, as the sun bleeds vermilion over Redfern Hill.

1923

✦

AUGUST 12

REDFERN TAKES THE TRAIN FROM SAVANNAH BACK TO BRUNSWICK and drives the Model T from the docks. It's midmorning when he turns onto Redfern Road and careens toward the distillery. He's well on his way to drunk and hasn't shaved in two days. He stops at the mill and stalks past the men into the cooper's shed, where he snags a shovel. He throws it in the bed of the pickup and drives to the cemetery. There, he hurls the blade into the earth of little Charlie's grave and begins to dig. He digs for two, three hours, until the dirt and red clay are piled high. He takes off his coat and gloves, throws them on the grass, and keeps on digging. After an eternity, muscles burning, legs quivering, ruined hands raw and bleeding, he hits the boy's pine coffin. Or what's left of it. The shovel crunches through the softened lid. Redfern bends down in the grave and clears the mud and dirt from the lid and uses his hands to tear it free, and at last his fingers touch little Charlie's face. Redfern begins to make noises then, noises he isn't even aware he's making, a kind of grunting-whimpering-choking noise. The boy's eyes are gone, in their place a pair of long black roots that twine into him from the walls of his grave, hideous couplings between Charlie's skull and the earth. The roots have grown up from the ground into his body, through the lining of the coffin, through his little dark suit. Penetrating bone and what rags of rotted flesh remain. The smell in the summer heat is rich and horrible. Maggots in the cheeks, the hollows of his boy's collarbones. A crown of roots fanning out from the boy's head like some monstrous religious icon. Redfern slumps in the grave and weeps and clutches his son and hears no comforting voice, no soothing wind in the pines.

Late that day, he staggers into the house smelling of liquor and death. He's covered in dirt, a new and meager resolve in his breast: he will kill it. Somehow, he will destroy it, this dweller in the woods. Even if he has to tear it out of the ground with his own two mangled hands. If he has to spend the rest of his life hacking and cutting and burning, though his business may fail, his fortunes collapse—

Euphemia sits at her writing desk in the library, cast in red by the colored pane. Her pen hovers over a sheet of stationery, the nib bleeding black ink. He stands in the doorway until she turns to look at him. Her hair is pulled back tight, severe. She wears a new chambray shirt tucked in and a belt and field boots fresh out of the box. She's young, red cheeked, beautiful, but her eyes are steely. She folds her letter, slips it into an envelope, and lifts the lid of her desk. Inside, among her things, the Brownie camera he gave her years ago, put away, as if it were a child's plaything. Perhaps he'd meant it that way. A toy to keep her happy, to keep her from causing him trouble—

"I want to talk to you," she says, not yet facing him. She closes her desk and lights a match and holds it over a red candle, drips wax onto the envelope to seal it with a stamp. The letter *R* in a pine cone.

He crosses the room to sit in a slash of yellow, under the north-facing window.

"I've just written my father a letter informing him that we will refuse any inheritance of money, land, or business upon his death." She blows out the match. "I want nothing more of his. From this day forward, our fortunes will be our own—"

Turning, she sees him. The dirt on his hands, his clothes.

"August?"

He fixes his gaze on a knot in the hardwood floor and does not look elsewhere. He takes his flask from his pocket. Drinks.

"What have you done?" A razor's edge of caution in her voice, as if she were speaking to a demented man.

Redfern blinks at her. "What did you do with him?"

"Who?"

"The man in the barn."

"Are you drunk, August?"

"Tell me!"

"I think you know what I did with the man in the barn, don't you."

"It's eating our boy!" Redfern bellows.

"Yes," she says. Cool. Cold. She doesn't move. "But don't pretend it's somehow my doing."

"You would have *both* died if I hadn't—"

"I wish I had," she says plainly. Then, as if there is other business to discuss, she puts the letter to her father, the candle and wax stamp, the book of matches, all away in her desk. "Now, where have you been the last two days?"

He makes no answer. Just drinks.

She sits back in her chair, crosses a leg. Picks at a fingernail.

"You should know, I'm going to be taking a greater interest in our business affairs."

"Are you."

"Yes. For example, Ishmael Green is sick. I spoke—"

"He's not sick. He's dying."

"Yes. He is. I spoke with him today."

"You did."

"I went to the camp and sat with him in his cabin. He's quite bedridden, has been for over a week. I told him that you were away on business and wanted me to ask him a very important question in your stead. That question being 'Have you made plans for your interment?'"

"Oh, Effie."

"To which the old man teared up and said to me that he had never had a home so good as this one. And that he would like to be buried here, if Mr. Redfern would allow it."

"You can't—",

"I told him that Mr. Redfern would be honored. I told him that he would be the first woodsman to be buried in a woodsmen's cemetery. So that no man ever has to endure the indignity of a pauper's grave. I even told him where you wanted it to be, August. Right there on the little knoll that overlooks the river, where the men sometimes worship in the dawn of a Sunday morning. Green Hill Cemetery, we'll call it, I said."

"It's wretched."

"I'm going to take care of us, August. I want you to know that. Because you have proven that you cannot."

"To hell with you," he mutters.

"There is also the matter of Barlow."

"What of him?"

"I need you to find him."

"Why?"

"The man who came into the house the day Charlie died, he did not force the door. He opened it."

"So?"

"Every door was locked, August. As they have been, ever since the threats began. I told you this. I check the doors morning, noon, and night. Someone gave away a key."

She reaches into her pocket and holds up a single key. She tosses it to him.

He catches it, stupidly.

"It was in the lock. The Sullivan girl found it."

"It could have been . . ." But he stops.

"No. It was him. No one else has a key."

"What happened to Charlie was—"

"Not Barlow's fault? He was holding the boy's hand, wasn't he?"

"It was an accident. Charlie's hand just . . . slipped away in the confusion. Jesus, Effie, he's my friend."

"He's your employee, August. One who has sizable gambling debts to Jasper Hawley's uncle. That's right. The sheriff told me, yesterday. I spoke to him while you were gone. On business. The fact is, Barlow had every reason to open that door for Hawley's men. And I have every reason to ask you to do this."

"You horrible bitch. I ought to go out there right now and set those goddamn woods on fire."

"You have to do this, August."

His voice breaks. "Why?"

"Because if you don't—"

Beyond the open library door, a board creaks.

Euphemia's eyes cut to the foyer. Her mouth a tight line. "Frannie?" she calls.

A breath's hesitation, then Frannie Sullivan enters, holding the hand of five-year-old Henry Redfern. The boy is dressed in threadbare corduroy, little suspenders over a white shirt. One thumb is in his mouth, bitten between his teeth. His gaze shifts from his mother to his father.

"Beg your pardon, ma'am, but little Henry here wanted to say hello to Mr. Redfern."

Euphemia sits back stiffly in her chair to wait.

Redfern's eyes stay on the floor as Frannie hunkers down beside the boy and whispers in his ear. When he doesn't respond, she eases the hand from his mouth and dries his thumb on her skirt. Then points him in Redfern's direction. Henry crosses the room slowly, puts his tiny hands on the arm of the chair, and Redfern looks at him. Henry's lips purse as he tries to speak, but no sound comes. "Puh," he finally gasps. "Puh-puh-puh. Papa."

Redfern touches the boy's cheek with a dirty hand. "Go back to Frannie."

The girl has already crossed the room to gather the boy into her arms. She kisses his cheek, whisks him away, up the stairs.

One last drink, and Redfern stands, capping his flask.

Euphemia holds her gaze on her husband like a knife.

He weaves across the room, boots trailing dried mud across the planks.

"Do it, August," Euphemia calls after him. "Or our end will be the same as Charlie's."

He freezes in the doorway. Half turning, like a man who has heard the sound of his own death, hard on his heels. Then he staggers out onto the porch, where he drops to the steps in a heap and hangs his head in his hands.

The hours creep into late day and Ishmael drifts between consciousness and dreaming. It's Eli's turn to sit with him, while James works. They've wrangled a deal with Barlow: one works, the other "plays nurse." That's how the big bastard put it. In truth, it's how Eli feels, because he can do nothing to ease the old man's pain, lying there under a threadbare quilt and shivering in the August heat. The fire burns in the stove and still the old man shivers. Eli drips sweat until his clothes are soaked through and the little cabin fills with the stink of him. Pop can't smoke his pipe for lack of breath, can't read for lack of strength to hold a book. His arms are rail thin. *What can I do in the face of that BUT play? At least James can read to him.* So, yeah, Eli would rather be out in the fields scraping gum into barrels all day than sitting here with a front-row seat to his beautiful Pop's long, terrible end.

Today, when the Redfern woman came round, dressed like she's the boss, the old man actually sat up to greet her, weak as he was. She with her leather boots and her starched collar, lilac scent trailing after her. Bending over the bed, holding Pop's hand like she knew him, him croaking out what words he could, mostly saying how grateful he was for all they'd done. *Him saying that and here we sit, in a hotbox on a white man's land, nothing more than when we got here four years back but calluses and scars.* Half the men they'd started with had come and gone after one season. Most of the rest, men with wives and children, were gone in two. *Except us and them poor Irish suckers.*

Eli listened to her as long as he could, until that shit about "Green Hill Cemetery." Then he stepped off the wall. "Ma'am, beg your pardon, but I believe he might be give out."

"Of course." She stood and bent low over the bed and kissed his father on his forehead.

She offered her hand when she walked out. Eli didn't take it. Just looked off at the door. Sweat dripping. Not a drop on her.

"Mr. Green," she said, and went on her way.

"Green Hill my ass," he said, after she left.

But the old man didn't hear. He was already asleep.

James comes out of the woods along Camp Road twenty minutes after the wagon drops the others. He comes slowly. Eli gets out of Ishmael's rocker and steps out from the eave of the porch to get a look at him and sees James pressing his hand to his head, and Eli knows something isn't right. Eli meets him in the field. Halfway across, Eli can see the blood, dark and crusted on James's scalp, above his right eye.

"Let me look at you." Eli grabs at him.

"Get off. It's nothing."

"Barlow did this?" Eli's steaming. He looks around, as if the horseman could be somewhere in the camp. Woe to him if he is.

"Hit me so hard I saw stars."

"Come on over here."

Eli leads James to the well, draws up a bucket. Dips a handkerchief from his back pocket into the bucket and squeezes it over his brother's head. "We gotta keep that brain of yours safe so it can write them books, yeah?"

James takes the handkerchief. Wets it again. Touches it to his scalp. "How's Pop?"

"Pop's Pop. He ain't worse."

Some cracker woodsmen who's been here about a week hollers from his porch, "Hey, you! Don't you foul that water!"

Eli mutters, "Motherfucker, I'll foul you."

The brothers look at each other and laugh.

"Let's go," James says. "I need food."

They start for the porch, but Eli stops him. "There's something I gotta tell you, before we go in."

"Okay."

They walk over to the knoll to the half-log benches and sit, their backs to the sun, the sky before them darkening with clouds, against them a rainbow making its bow beyond the treetops across the river.

"Lady Redfern came today," Eli says, using James's nickname for her of late.

"Came here?"

"To see Pop. Said she wants him to be buried here on their land. Said she wants to make this spot, right here, into a woodsmen's cemetery. Said she wants to call it Green Hill. 'Where all men may find dignity in death as they did in life.' Her words."

"No shit?"

"No shit."

"What'd Pop say?"

"You know Pop. All he ever wanted was a home."

James's throat tightens.

"Yeah, well," Eli says, "it don't smell right to me."

James wipes his eyes. Looks out at the dark river. "Me neither." He looks over his shoulder at the strangers that now inhabit the camp, the chickens that roam unpenned, fly-covered deer skins drying on racks. Beer bottles lodged in the mud below this very spot, where no one, anymore, comes to pray. Carved into the very bench where they now sit, a word James has not heard or been called since Arkansas. He touches his scalp. Barlow. The man was drunk and railing. Furious. "Things here have turned," James says.

"I'm glad to hear you say it."

"You know Pop can't make a trip. He can't even get out of bed to piss—"

"He's gonna die real soon in that bed, James."

Tears instead of words now, and James looks out at the river as they run down his cheeks.

"Frannie?" Eli asks.

James shakes his head. "She's up there at the house now. Said Lady Redfern needs her to look after the little one. She ain't going anywhere."

"Then it's you and me, brother."

James reaches out, puts his arm around Eli, and Eli puts his arm around James.

The camp at their backs, as the sun goes down.

Rolling in across the river, a shroud of rain.

Evening.

A roar of rain on the tin roof like a stampede of horses as Euphemia brews the coffee, fills Redfern full of it, and sends him off in a slicker, her father's Browning shotgun in a leather sleeve laced to his saddle. The old cap-and-ball pistol in his gunnysack. She watches until the silver curtain envelops him, then goes inside and shuts and locks the door. Henry is asleep upstairs, fed and bathed, Frannie asleep next door in what would have been Charlie's room. Euphemia opens the cellar door and descends the stairs in the dark, guided by the faint, ethereal glow that whispers from beneath the coal-closet door. She reaches into her pocket, inserts a heavy iron key, and opens the door. The light shines out from the hole in the earth, not much bigger than a washbowl. Blue as the ocean shot through with sun. Not very deep. Not yet. She's only just started, last night. She takes up her shovel from where it leans against the brick wall and jams the blade into the hole and shovels out a heap of black dirt.

The light grows brighter.

. . . mama . . .

On into the night, she digs, until the room shines with the promise of good days yet to come.

After the rain, out of the forge of the hot August night, the woods and fields and farmland sizzle.

Willeford's barn slumps at the edge of his derelict cotton field, a harsh yellow light shining out between the slats, as wagons and horses and a Ford truck or two draw up. Doors slam. Backs are clapped. Cigarettes lit. Someone brings a fiddle and strikes a tune, and someone else snatches the fiddle and breaks it against the side of the barn and the night's first violence commences. Fists and motherfuckers and more to come.

Redfern tethers his mount and steps through a narrow side door into a din of men in field clothes and dungarees. He works his way around the outside of the crowd, climbs the ladder to the hayloft, and hangs from it like it's a mast. Toughs line the loft and swing their heavy boots out in space, hand-rolled smokes between their lips. Down below, men shout and yip and jostle and fingers fly bets and numbers are chalked up on a board behind the next pair of sour-faced entrants, holding their birds for inspection. Willeford walks back and forth and inspects the cocks, which must be properly trimmed and without soap or grease. Soon, all eyes and ears and pulses will be trained on the hex-wire pit at the center of the barn, a rough circle framed up by jagged boards and bits of an old house door. The floor inside it a litter of hay and feathers and blood.

Redfern hops down, catches Willeford by the arm, and yells into his ear, "You seen Barlow?"

"He was around. Saw him head out a while ago."

"Shit. All right."

"You best watch it, Gus. There's some boys here tonight, come up from Waycross. More of that Hawley bunch."

"Ennis with em?"

"He is."

"Where?"

"Last I saw, they's all out back, drinking."

Redfern edges on around, past the fighters, one of whom holds his bird upside down and blows cigarette smoke into its face.

Back out the front, Redfern slips around the side of the barn, past an old harrow that hasn't seen use in years. He walks quietly up to the corner, stops when he hears an explosive sputter, then laughter, followed by a voice that cracks adolescent: "Shit!"

"What's wrong, Frankie? Too strong?"

"Too strong?" the boy answers. "Fuck me, that shit'll about strip paint!"

Gagging. Retching. Laughter.

"Give it," a voice says, low and gruff, and Redfern knows it.

He edges close enough to peer around the corner, sees a flatbed wagon and three men piled into it, sitting on the side boards. Passing a heavy jug around. The man who holds it now holds it without the three fingers of his left hand. He wears a bowler hat. "Nothing wrong with that," Barlow says, lowering the jug.

The boy, Frankie, hunches over in the long grass that grows up around the wagon's tongue. He straightens, wipes his mouth. A stain on the belly of his shirt.

The two men in the wagon who are not Barlow elbow each other.

"Little f-er won't be slipping any slit no tongue tonight, will he, Dale."

"Hey, Ennis!"

Out in the field, a fifth voice answers, low and rough and slightly nasal, "Yeah."

Redfern shrinks back.

The cherry of a cigarette flares. Behind it a short man with a half-bald pate and thin white curls above small ears. When the cigarette burns low, he's all but invisible in the moonless night.

"What's that place you said we'd hit?"

"Sally's," Ennis Hawley calls back.

"Hey, Harp, reckon she got a whore apt to swap spit with little Frankie here, after he's done puked up his guts?"

Barlow, Redfern realizes, is tottering where he sits.

I didn't want this. I wanted to let you go. To tell her you ran. But here you are with these men, who came into my home, and now my boy is dead—

A hand falls on Redfern's shoulder, spins him round.

"What's the rumpus, fella?" says the biggest man August Redfern has ever seen.

And suddenly he's flying, thrust backward by huge arms, into the weeds and dirt, and the men all fall silent.

The big man—a mountain of flesh and denim—hauls Redfern up by his belt.

"What you got there, Orin?" Ennis asks.

"A sneak," Orin says.

Ennis smokes as he wanders up, one hand in the bib of his overalls.

The other men—Harp and Dale—hop out of the wagon, circle

round behind Ennis. Barlow remains in the wagon, long enough for Redfern to catch his eye. At which point he turns up the jug for one last pull, then hops over the edge and shambles off around the barn.

Ennis says nothing. Just gives the slightest of nods, and Orin's arms slip beneath Redfern's and haul him up to hang like a man crucified, as Harp and Dale wade in with fists. Three or four blows and Redfern hears a rib crack.

"Let little Frankie take a turn now," Ennis says, cherry of his smoke flaring.

The boy darts in and wallops Redfern's jaw, then dances away, shaking his hand.

The men laugh.

Orin drops Redfern to the ground.

They drift away, back toward the front of the barn. One of the men claps Frankie on the back. "Let's go break you off a piece, boy."

Ennis lingers. Smoking in the dark.

Inside, a roar goes up as one bird ends another.

"That's the thing about a fight," Ennis says. "Always a loser."

He flicks his butt in the mud beside Redfern's cheek, grinds it dark with his shoe.

Redfern shuts his eyes.

He wakes later, when the barn is quiet.

Above, the stars shine coldly.

He staggers up and finds his horse where he tied it, cropping the damp grass. He puts one boot in the stirrup, but can't pull himself up. So he just walks the horse across the field to the county road, and from there to the highway. A mile east, he turns onto a dirt road that snakes beneath a canopy of oaks, off to his right a river-bottom thicket of wild blackberry bushes and kudzu and cypress trees. He walks until he's close enough to hear the lilt of a piano, the twang of a guitar, and he knows, then, to lead the horse into the woods and tie it off.

He snugs the pistol from his gunny into his waist, then draws the shotgun from its sheath. Pats the horse on the neck, whispers sweetly to it, then limps across the road and follows the sound of music and laughter.

The night is hung with stars but moonless, which is how Redfern is able to creep up behind the house. He ducks beneath a window and peers between the tasseled shade and sill, sees a slice of clapboard wall and an old iron bed frame and two young gals and that boy Frankie naked, twined up and giggling. In a corner, seated in a chair, fully clothed, Ennis Hawley holds a glass of hooch in one hand and watches. Perfectly still. The window is open three inches to let in a breeze, and Redfern sets his shotgun against the house and is reaching to push it up a little more when nearby a back door slaps open and the big man Orin staggers out. Redfern ducks behind a chokecherry bush and watches him weave toward the woods, barefoot and naked, a marvel of muscle and flesh.

Redfern hears what sounds like a horse pissing in the leaves, then changes tactics. He moves quickly and quietly to the back door. Slips inside and closes it and throws the double dead lock. He stands in a narrow corridor of bedrooms left and right. The far end opens onto a parlor, where a half-clad redhead passes by like some bony alley stray. Redfern knows the layout. He came here, once, with Barlow, in the weeks after Charlie died. The night was a blur of liquor and soppy sorrow, the stout horseman begging Redfern's forgiveness for not being faster, stronger, braver, when the little boy went under the hot rosin. *Your hands, your hands.* Later, after the words dried up, Redfern let himself be led by the lanky proprietress into an awful, slick harbor that was not Euphemia's.

He eases past the room where Ennis and the boy are, listens outside another until he hears the full-throated laughter of Harp and Dale. Moves on, slipping through a curtain into a closet stocked with cigarettes and quart jars of liquor when a door opens down the hall. Bodies pass, soft padding feet, another door opens and closes.

The piano starts up in the parlor, a sad, wistful tune he cannot place.

He slips out and into the room next door, where he knows Barlow will be. And he is, sprawled facedown, naked across a couch. The woman he favors, for reasons unfathomable to Redfern, reclines in her undergarments in a nearby bed, staring out the filmy window and smoking. Flat dugs and cellulite arms. Sweet Rita, they call her. Sweet Rita chuckles when she sees Redfern. She's halfway to the moon herself, and the chuckle becomes a hack right quick. Redfern slings half a jar of Hawley hooch into Barlow's face.

The horseman twitches, comes to. "Gus? Shit. Well. I'm fired, I reckon."

Redfern sits down on the coffee table, shotgun across his knees. "Yeah, you're fired. But right now I need your help. Say sure."

"Gus, I'm—"

"Say sure, and you might live through this."

Barlow cuts his eyes over Redfern's shoulder.

Redfern whirls and Sweet Rita is rushing him with a straight razor. He swings the shotgun and cracks the stock across her jaw, knocking out two teeth and sending her out cold and jiggling to the boards. He turns the gun on Barlow. "You owe me a debt for this shit. I want you to pay it. Right now. And maybe then we're square. So say sure."

Barlow licks dry, cracked lips like a nervous cat. Then says, "Sure. What I gotta do?"

"Same thing you always do. Watch my back and help me hurt some sorry sons of bitches."

Barlow sits up, puts a pillow over his dick. "I can do that."

"Get dressed."

They wait until the house is dark and all chatter has ceased from the parlor and front porch, and the springs are silent in every room. They move quietly to Harp and Dale's room first. The men sleep in the same big bed with Sally herself lying naked between them. Her eyes flash open and Redfern puts a finger to his lips and she nods. He offers her his hand. Barlow waits with the cap-and-ball pistol in his waistband and holds the shotgun while Redfern helps lift her out of the bed. "Round up all the girls you can and get em out the door without making a sound," he whispers, close in her ear. "Go out the front." She slips into the hall. Redfern takes the shotgun back from Barlow and puts the barrel snug in Dale's open, snoring mouth. His eyes flash open and he tries to scoot up in the bed, but Redfern presses down hard and so he freezes, and Barlow steps up with the straight razor and clamps one hand over Harp's mouth and nose and cuts deep into his throat. Dale gags, whimpers, and tries to twist away, but Redfern only thrusts the gun deeper until the man's teeth crack and he can't breathe, and he's pinned to the pillow as Barlow reaches down and seizes Dale's flaccid pecker and the razor whisks cleanly through and now Dale's trying to scream but he's choking on his own spit and vomit, both hands on the barrel of the shotgun like it's the root of all sustenance. He passes out from shock and they leave him to bleed.

Down the hall now, to Ennis's room. They ease open the door, and there on the bed, in shadow and red light shining from a lamp on the bedside table, are man and boy, snugged together. The girls long gone. Ennis is small and hairy and childlike himself. Redfern glances at the nightstand and dresser for a pistol, a weapon, something the old fox might surprise him with. He finds none. So he nods at the boy, and Barlow steps around that side of the bed.

A floorboard creaks behind them.

They turn and Orin stands in the doorway, naked still, a piece of chocolate cake in hand. Chocolate on his teeth, his lips.

"Where'd you get cake?" Barlow asks.

Redfern lifts the shotgun and fires.

The big man is blown backward into the wall, a red smear of him left there dripping as he slides down to the floor.

They whirl and the boy, Frankie, is kicking out of bed and dashing for the window, but Barlow snags him by the hair and drags him back, throws him to the floor.

Ennis has rolled off onto the floor and yanks a Colt automatic from beneath the bed.

Everything that happens next happens slowly, all at once.

Barlow draws the cap-and-ball pistol and jams it in Frankie's ear. The boy throws his hands up and pisses himself.

Ennis squeezes off two rounds before Redfern has even brought the shotgun around. The first goes high, splinters the doorframe. The second whizzes past Redfern's ear and takes a nick of flesh and cartilage.

Barlow squeezes the cap and ball's trigger in Frankie's ear and it dry-fires, a flat *click*. The powder wet from the rain. Or just ancient.

Frankie screams and twists in Barlow's grip, kicks at him like he's riding a bicycle.

Ennis slides under the mattress as the shotgun swings up.

Barlow flips the pistol in his hand and smashes the boy's face with the butt.

Redfern fires the shotgun into the mattress, and the mattress explodes in feathers and springs.

The feathers settle, as Barlow stops hitting the boy. His face a pulp, bits of hair and flesh stuck on the pistol's grip.

Redfern squats down, looks under the bed.

Ennis's mouth opens and closes like that of a fish out of water. His eyes become glass.

Half his head is gone.

"That's the thing about a fight," Redfern tells him.

They walk out onto the front porch and sit down in the swing. A quart of shine from the hall closet to pass between them.

"Tell me again," Redfern says. "The story of your hand."

Barlow grins. Drinks. "You want to hear it again?"

Redfern takes the jar and drinks a swallow, then closes his eyes.

"They was an old-timer, ran a gristmill. Just up from this camp where I used to stay when I was a boy. He took me on one summer, apprenticed me to grinding corn and flour, making grits for folks come to trade on a weekend. I got these fingers here caught between two millstones the size of tractor tires. Teeth just chewed em off."

Redfern smiles.

"You like that one?"

Redfern passes back the jar. "Not your best."

"Okay. Here, then, how 'bout this one. I knew this old gal, liked to take boys down by the river. Them boys, they go down there in the bulrushes, have themselves a time. Come back missing a finger. Little one, right here. I asked one of them boys once, I said, 'How come you all come out without that pinkie, boy?' He says to me, 'That there is a small price to pay for the finest thing I ever done with a finger.' So I went on down there myself. Come back out. Few days, I seen that boy. He says to me, 'Goddamn, son. You lost three fingers down in them bulrushes!' I say, 'You know it. I'm a big spender.'"

Barlow laughs, drinks, and Redfern laughs, too.

"Small price to pay," Barlow says.

"I believe that's the one."

"You think?"

Redfern nods. "Unless you want to tell me the truth?"

"Shit. The truth ain't near as good as any lie I ever told."

They sit quietly.

Redfern shuts his eyes, tries to picture this thing Euphemia wants him to believe. Little Charlie's fingers, clinging to Barlow's maimed hand. That sluice gate opening wide—

He takes Ennis Hawley's Colt out of the hollow of his lower back and puts the barrel against Barlow's head and pulls the trigger. Barlow jerks. A bubble forms in his nostril. Pops. He slumps sideways, onto the swing chain, and the last thing he ever knows is the color of himself on Sally's porch window. The bottle of shine's still in his hand, not a drop spilled.

Redfern takes it, drinks the rest of it.

Feels the hurt of every swallow in his broken rib.

Directly, out of the woods across the road, the whores emerge barefoot and trembling, like sylvan creatures.

In the cellar of Redfern Hill, Euphemia's hands are blistered and bleeding as she drops the shovel and falls to her knees beside the hole she's dug. Not a grave, as the one August dug up that morning, but a womb, out of which Charlie will be reborn. Dirt and red Georgia clay heaped among the coal, the closet is suffused with the blue shimmer. The hole is shallow, but something has already broken through the ground to greet her, and she rocks back on her thighs as it comes, silently, a single shoot rising out of the blue to bob like some malign sunflower, only brown and slick, at its head a single orb that blinks at her. All along its undercarriage, little mouths open, filled with teeth that flash and chomp. It drifts toward her, caresses her cheek with the back of its long, fibrous body. Thin runners spill up from the edge of the hole and burrow into the dirt mounded there, and soon a sprout grows, as Euphemia glories in its touch, its voice—

(. . . mama . . .)

—and the sprout becomes a stalk and the stalk becomes a nerve and the nerve becomes a spine and the spine becomes a cage to hold the rest of the child's organs. Lungs of fleshy fungus. A taproot heart. And soon the face emerges, eyes of hot rosin gold, a smile she remembers, a smile she knows.

"Charlie," she gasps, and takes the boy into her arms.

He smells of pine sap and heartwood, is brittle in her hands.

The tendril undulates like a charmed cobra above them, emits a low, pleasant thrum.

(. . . i'm hungry, mama . . . so hungry . . .)

"I know, baby, I know." She's laughing, deliriously happy. She lifts a fall of hair from the boy's forehead, sees only chestnut hair over apricot flesh, bright apple cheeks. She does not see the beetle that ticks out of the briars that are his brows, or the bunchgrass that is his hair, or the new green leaves that unfurl from his ears only to wither and drop away almost instantly. But when the boy's brown, beautiful eyes flick over her shoulder, she does register some change in him, like a second exposure over film: one thing layered atop another, neither the same and yet, somehow, occupying the same space and time.

The stalk swivels, its eye a spotlight.

Euphemia turns.

Frannie Sullivan stands some five, six feet beyond the open coal-closet door, awash in the terrible blue light. She wears her nightgown, holds a lit candle. Her red hair is tucked into a bun and her feet are bare. She puts one hand over her mouth. "I heard—" Then she takes a step back and turns to run.

(. . . so hungry, mama . . .)

Euphemia gets her feet under her, catches up with Frannie on the cellar stairs. She finds her sprawled there, halfway up. She's tripped, her candle lost between the risers, guttered. Euphemia mounts the steps behind her, small and quick and eclipsing the blue below. And the shovel in her hands goes up, and the shovel goes down, and the girl cries out in pain, again and again, until finally the edge of the spade divides flesh and severs windpipe, and the only sound after that is the sound of Frannie Sullivan choking on her own blood, even as the poor child drags herself, hand over hand, up the steps to the half door. At last, she reaches for the door handle, but one last strike and the hand falls away, and Euphemia sits back on the stairs and pushes her wet hair away from her face and breathes in deeply the red, metal scent of the shovel's blade.

Night so deep it is not night but a dense and timeless outer dark into which the weary soul is cast, unable to rest, unable to think, unable to feel. The ride back is long, Redfern clutching at his head, every jolt from the road a lightning bolt of pain through his side. Barlow's corpse hangs over the horse's haunch, wrapped in bedsheets from Sally's. Redfern rides right through town, the dead man's hand flopping along the animal's flank.

Ishmael Green dies with a rattle of air in the last scrap of dark. The boys are at his side. James clutches the old man's hand on the threadbare quilt. The cabin smells of sage and leftover stew. Eli gets up and goes out onto the porch and looks around at the quiet camp. A tightness across his shoulders that has become, these last couple of weeks, a familiar complaint, something to rub and grumble about and work with his hands until the muscles release. He tries it now, but it won't let go. He sits down on the steps, recalls the first Christmas they spent here. He takes out his knife from its scabbard, the blade dulled by time and use. He jabs the point into the wood. Scratches something by the bone-pale light of dawn.

Along the riverbanks, the frogs sing to wake the dead.

A horse comes shambling up Camp Road, a man in a hat staggering alongside it. Something heavy thrown over the horse's saddle.

Eli sits very still.

The horse snorts as it draws closer, scenting him.

The man in the hat speaks softly. "Eli."

"Mr. Redfern?"

"How's Ishmael?"

Eli swallows. "Dead. Just now."

"I felt it." Weariness in Redfern's voice. "I felt it, just there on the road. Like the bite of winter at the end of fall. I am sorry."

Redfern sways, leans into the horse. Almost drops.

Eli rushes to catch him, glancing at the horse's flank. A two-fingered hand falls stiffly out of the blankets.

"I've got business tonight," Redfern says. "Up above North Creek."

Eli does not question. He's not sorry to see what he sees. The why doesn't matter.

"Where will you boys go?"

"Florida," Eli says immediately.

"Don't bury him here. It's a bad place."

Redfern moves on, past the cabin, into the trees.

Eli watches him go. Swears he's watching a ghost.

Midmorning by the time Redfern's feet fall heavy on the stairs, like concrete's hardening in his boots. A throb in his right knee. Busted rib grating in his side. The lights in the upstairs sconces are yet extinguished, and he stands for a spell outside his bedroom door, hand on the knob, listening over the quick, steady rasp of his breath for the sounds of Euphemia sleeping. He hears nothing. He turns the knob.

She sits in the rocking chair by the window, clad in a thin cotton nightgown. The window is open and there's a breeze to cool the sheen of summer sweat across her collarbone. She's ghostly. Beautiful. A creature as remote and cold as the moon.

He walks in and begins shedding clothes, trembling hands fumbling at the buttons of his shirt. She gets up, after a moment, and crosses to him, barefoot, soles whispering on the planks. She cups his cheek with her hand, where there is blood, the blood of the men he killed tonight. She helps him out of his shirt and bends to lift his legs out of his pants, and he touches her bare, sharp shoulders to steady himself. The clothes she takes out of the room in the porcelain washbowl, and when she returns, the washbowl is full of clear water, a cake of soap on the rim. She puts the bowl in the stand and helps him to it, her hand enclosing his wrist. She whispers his name and wrings water and soap in a cloth and washes him, and the water is cool and biting against his skin, and slowly, his muscles relax and his hands unfist, and the last thing she cleans before she leads him to bed are his fingernails, where the little crescent moons of dirt and blood have dried. Her own nails dirty, too. Bloody.

He does not ask why.

She leads him to bed and lays him down and draws her nightgown up over her head and climbs atop him, springs of the mattress beneath them groaning. She sits astride him and reaches down and finds him and he gasps, and suddenly, as the springs begin to creak, she whispers his name, and it is not their marriage bed they fuck upon, but an altar, and theirs is no union of mere flesh. Tonight, and forever after, it's a union of blood.

"Do you feel her?" Effie gasps. "Do you feel her, August? We're making the future. We're making her, so that one day, when we need her, she'll be there, she'll—"

She cries out, and he cries, too. Euphemia's name.

A petition. A prayer.

A lament, in the end, as he falls away, into a sleep like death. He wishes it were.

James calls out to Eli from the porch, and Eli walks out to find Redfern's horse tethered to a post, cropping the green summer grass. Saddle unhitched and slung over the rail. Along with half a dozen heavy blankets washed in the river and left to dry. The boys will wrap their father in the blankets and lay him over the horse and lash him there, and they'll walk out by Camp Road. They'll walk out amid the feeding of catfish in the river, come to snatch late morning dragonflies and water walkers among the cattails and cypress stobs. They'll walk out past the turpentine mill and onto the road, and there they'll stand, wondering which way Florida is. In the end, they'll follow the river, and it will lead them to the marshes, and beyond these, the ocean, where they'll sit in the sand and build a raft out of driftwood and small trees, to float Ishmael out to sea, wading out with him as far as they can, the warm waves lapping at them like the persistent memory of the womb. Eli will douse the raft in kerosene, and James will light it. They'll send him with his pipe and a book of poems, like a king of old, the brothers hip deep in the waters watching, until the ocean swallows their father in a guttering of fire and foam.

Then they'll travel on, out of this story forever, and into their own.

SUMMER 1975

SECOND INTERLUDE

DAY THREE

✦

EARLY, REDFERN SETS OFF INTO THE WOODS AGAIN. THIS time, Nellie is awake, waiting for him. Dressed in her scrounged clothes from the day before, hair pinned back with her bobby pin, her black buckle shoes on, she sits outside, on the edge of the recliner. The old man's pack is in her lap, packed with what he'd unloaded yesterday: empty bottles, his stenographer's pad. Plus an extra canteen of water and sandwiches Nellie made from the last of his peanut butter. The Winnebago creaks and rocks as, inside, Redfern riffles through cabinets and cupboards. She hears the clank of pots and pans. Sees a flash of him through the kitchenette window, looking out at her, and suddenly, he throws open the door, eyes bright with fury, and tromps down the steps. "Don't touch my things." He snatches the bag away and sets off into the dew-wet grass.

She marches after him. "I want to come." Her right dress shoe is rubbing her heel.

"You can't."

"You can't tell me what I can and can't do!" she snaps at his back.

They face off in the johnsongrass, behind them the barbwire

fence strung with clothes, the barn, the trees. Behind the trees the sun burning off the night in brushstrokes of crimson and gold.

"I don't care what you do," Redfern says. "Or where you go."

He sets out again, and Nellie wants to follow him, to keep yelling after him, to tell him all Redfern men can go to hell and fuck themselves while they're at it because they're a bunch of cowards too afraid to love with the hearts they're given. Instead, she stands there watching him until he dwindles away, into the pines. Her breathing returns to normal, her pulse slows, and her gaze turns toward the house, where the sun splashes over shabby boards and shines in covered windows. The sight makes her wistful, wistful in a way she'll never forget, in the years to come, if she happens to catch a glimpse of light thrown by the sun in glass, in a ratty apartment in Savannah, in a rental house in South Carolina. Always, she'll remember this feeling and want it again. Want it so desperately that tears will spring to her eyes, as she grieves a love not yet returned.

She looks at the woods where the old man has disappeared, then at the house once more.

"Fuck it," she says, and ducks the barbwire and starts for the house.

The front door is locked. The back, too, but the lock is flimsy, old. She is, for better or worse, Hank Redfern's daughter, the daughter of a jeweler and a weekend locksmith—at least, on the weekends when he's sober. She plucks a bobby pin from her hair, bends it, inserts it, and after a few seconds of turning, twisting, and tongue biting, the lock pops. She turns the knob and steps into the kitchen.

The house is very much as she will find it fourteen years from now. Sheets covering furniture and shelves. Great dark drapery that hides the sun. In the parlor, she lifts the sheet from the piano and does exactly what her son will do, the first time he sees it. She plunks a single note with her finger, listens to it ring in the silence of the house.

In the library, the morning light casts its red, yellow, and green squares through the windows and onto the walls, and she thinks, immediately, of a color wheel—a little paper device Mrs. Johnson gifted her on the last day of school, along with a set of brushes and paints. Nellie had not wanted to leave campus that day, certain she was going home to the endgame of her mother's long illness. It would be a month or more, still, but Ruth was sleeping more and more. Nellie sat at a long art desk in Mrs. Johnson's room and cried as the buses thundered out of the parking lot onto their routes, and Mrs. Johnson sat beside her and put her arm across Nellie's shoulders and told her it would be okay, which was nice but was also something someone like Mrs. Johnson could say, because Mrs. Johnson didn't live on Elm Street under Hank Redfern's roof.

Nellie goes upstairs.

She gets a good look at herself in the mirror—gaunt, dark circles beneath her eyes, hair a mass of tangles—before running water in the sink. It pours out and she fills her hands and splashes her face again and again, until at last she's erased the worst of it, and the smell of woodsmoke and mildew is lessened. She takes the pin out of her hair, shakes it loose, then runs her hands through it, pulling it back, pinning it again. She thinks of the hand pump in back of the RV and wonders, for the first time, what would drive an old man from a house with indoor plumbing. With toilets. Which, in turn, leads her to wonder where the old man is shitting, and that is a thought she does not want to think about, and so she moves on, out of the bathroom, and into a boy's bedroom.

It shocks her—as the remembering will shock her in 1989—the slow realization of where she stands. She moves about the room touching things—a stack of books, among them a copy of Thoreau's *Walden*, the poetry of Longfellow; toy soldiers; a coonskin cap. In the desk drawer she finds a tiny screwdriver, a handful of screws, and a metal toy, a windup monkey in a red coat and fez. The toy is in halves, broken open, its gears loose in the drawer. This, perhaps, is when she knows, without a doubt: she's in Hank Redfern's room. Her father the tinkerer, the jeweler. She sits on the cedar chest at the foot of the bed and stares a long time at the dusty boots set neatly beside his wardrobe. She unbuckles her right shoe and slips it off and pulls her leg into the right boot, which comes to her knee. It fits her snugly. She laces it. Trades her other shoe for the other boot.

Dress shoes in hand, she moves through the rest of the upstairs rooms, feeling keenly the absence of life in each. Objects untouched, air not breathed. Grief hangs in the nursery and master bedroom like old dust.

She's on the stairs when she hears it.

A board creaks, and beneath it a woman's voice.

. . . *nellie* . . .

She stops. Hand on the railing. Looks down between her father's boots at the step on which she stands. It comes again, seeming to drift up from between the wood. And like a plunge into freezing water, that craggy, cigarette-thin whisper almost stops Nellie's heart.

. . . *nellie* . . .

"Mama?"

Earlier, that spring, the day of Ruth Redfern's diagnosis, Nellie and her mother sat together in the hot silence of their station wagon outside the doctor's office. Pattering on the roof and glass, an April rain. The windows fogging up with their breath. Ruth watched the rain run in rivulets over the window, back of one hand against her mouth, the other on the steering wheel. Her pack of Woodbines and silver Zippo on the dash, Nellie staring at a crumpled leaf on the floor mat, between her sneakers.

Ruth turned to her daughter, eyes wet. "I can't think past the next breath."

Nellie wanted to say something, but she didn't know what it was, or how she should say it.

After a moment, Ruth snatched her cigarettes from the dash and snagged one between her lips. Flicked open the Zippo. "Oh, hell." She lit up.

At the bottom of the stairs, Nellie turns left, trails her hand along the stairwell's riser. Behind it, she finds the half door cut into the boards. The cut is crooked and the door hangs out of true, leaving a thin crack out of which wafts a dank, dark smell. She's reaching for the door, certain her mother's voice is coming from down there, beneath the house, when a gloved hand falls upon her shoulder and spins her around. She screams, throws up her fists, and sees August Redfern filling the frame of a dim room she has yet to enter. A room yet to be filled with garbage and junk and all the bits and pieces of a life lived overlong. Redfern's eyes burn holes into her from beneath the brim of his hat.

"Did you hear it?" she says, and turns back for the cellar door. She snags the upper corner to yank—

He reaches out, seizes her arm, same as the first night, where the bruises are.

"Don't touch me!"

He's about to bark something at her, she just knows it, but when Redfern registers what she's said, those gas-flame eyes dim, and he isn't sure what to say, or how to say it. "Did I hear what?" are the words he settles on.

Her head's tossed back, defiant, her posture rigid. She doesn't even realize it, how she's all but dancing on the balls of her feet, ready to bolt through the kitchen door, be gone forever. *Easy, Nellie, easy. Throttle back.* She folds her arms over her chest, nods at the cellar. "I thought I heard—" But she stops. Heard what, her dead mother's voice? She can't even say it. Not for grief, not for sadness. But for the sake of her own sanity.

He makes a noise in his throat. "Mmm." Then says, "There are things to see," and crooks a gloved finger at her as he turns and walks back into what Nellie will, years hence, remember as her grandfather's map room.

She swallows a lump of spit at the back of her throat and follows.

The room is not yet bright, in want of the western sun, but even in the dim morning light she can see that it's unlike the other rooms in the house. Nothing covered over. Everything in its place. Clean and loved. The twin saws above the desk and the framed map of the property, before it the long pine table at the center gleaming beneath the overhead light. The shelves along the wall are packed neatly, four maps to a cubby. He goes immediately to the first and selects a map and rolls it onto the table, drops a small weighted bag on each corner to hold it flat. The map is drawn in black india ink on heavy parchment. It's old and yellow, the ink faded, but the edges are crisp and straight. It's a map of Georgia's Sandhill and coastal regions, the Altamaha River snaking through a score of tiny counties, a central artery flowing into the Atlantic. "We are here." Redfern stabs a finger into Baxter County. "All of this, at one time, was old-growth forest. Longleaf pine, most of it. Today . . ." He thrusts the map off the table, sends it skittering to the floor. "Gone. Wiped out by men like me."

She blinks, bends down to pick up the map, and the old man moves quickly to fetch another, farther down the shelves. He searches for it, ticking a gloved hand along the cubbies. Nellie holds the map and notes the small details, things no store-bought map would show: a train moving along a thin set of tracks, cows in a field, little saw palms beneath groves of towering pines. In the bottom right corner, a set of printed initials and a date: A.R. *1917.*

"You drew this?"

"All of them."

Each map is cinched with a length of grocer's twine. Redfern undoes the knot, spreads the new map, and pounds his fist on it. "North Creek, the Old Forest. Beyond here, this swamp. That's where it started. That's where we'll go. It's safe now. Safer than here, anyway. Remember this place, Nellie. Remember it."

Where he's pointing, there's a grove of inky black cypress trees, and beyond these an island, and at the center of that island a round black well. Beside that well, a man. The man holds a pistol in his hand, has a wide-brimmed hat, like the one August Redfern wears. Another man kneels at his feet, hands bound behind him. She barely has time to wonder what this could be when, again, she hears it.

. . . *nellie* . . .

She whirls.

Right at her ear this time.

Redfern eyes her as he rolls the map and refiles it.

She's staring at the floorboards, the cracks between them. Listening. "What's beneath us?"

Already on his way out, Redfern stops. He hefts his pack. His head drops down, as if he, too, is peering between his boots. "This isn't the place to talk about it."

He walks out the door, leaving Nellie to choose her path. She follows his.

On a ridge beneath a few lone pines that grow tall and lean, a gopher tortoise throws sand from its burrow. She hunkers down in a grove of turkey oaks and watches, sipping water from her canteen. Sweat rolling off her. Hank's boots are chafing and the sun is burning her skin—she'll freckle within days, she has her mother's complexion—but she's happy, the morning's gloom departed after a half hour of hiking steadily upward, beyond North Creek. Behind her, the old man bends over some long, twisted tree root, ax in hand. He runs his fingers over the bark. Gives the root a tug. Satisfied—though what satisfies him Nellie has no idea—he stands and calls to her. She gets up and traipses back through the low scrub, dodging spindly shrubs of scarlet-blooming wild basil and the odd new-growth pine, hip-high starbursts of green needles long as Nellie's arm.

"We're about a mile above the creek," the old man says.

Back the way they've come, the woods slope to the water, old hardwoods that grow in odd, twisted shapes. Sprawling oaks draped in rags of forgotten glory.

"This ridge," Redfern says, huffing, "drops down, then back up into a meadow. Moss beds. After those, a cypress swamp. Not much farther then."

She does not ask what it all means, where they're going or why it matters. She only nods and follows, pleased that the old man has seen fit to trust her with what he's doing out here with his ax and jars and pack and roots. For the first time in a long time, Nellie Redfern feels like she's moving forward, unraveling the mystery of the old man, discovering, too, some secret at the heart of who she is, or who she may yet be. Secrets her father had long forbidden her to know.

They walk on through blooming shrubs and sandy soil.

"What happened to your family?" she asks, as the land begins to climb again. She doesn't expect an answer, just one of the old man's terse silences, a disapproving glance. She's stopped to study an old pine, bark big and rough as dragon scale. Scored by lightning, it's fallen against another tree, twice its size. The larger tree seems to hold the other in its arms, to cradle it. A few years from now, in a college art course in Savannah, she'll see a photo of Michelangelo's *Pietà* for the first time, Christ's broken body draped in Mary's arms, and tears will well in her eyes as she remembers these trees.

"My little boy Charlie," Redfern says, "died in the accident that took my hands."

The old man stands a few feet up the hill, looking back at her. Hat hanging in his hand, at his side. "Boy never made five years." In his other hand, the ax. He looks at it. "It was after that, Effie lost her mind. The mill burned. She burned with it. Hank run off that night. Agatha, she—"

His voice cracks. He looks up at the blue sky.
"She went away, too," he says to the clouds.
He puts his hat back on.
"Anyhow. It was all spoiled, long before that."
He trudges on.
Nellie, stunned, can only stare after him.

They pass through the wire-grass meadow in silence, three tall pines standing sentinel here. The wind blows through the grass and it whispers and something about this place makes Nellie uneasy. She feels as if eyes are upon her, out here in the open, after walking so long in the gloom of the hardwoods. Even the sun seems to hide its face behind the clouds as they stalk through the brown grass. Then she remembers the high, unearthly scream they heard the night before, and somehow she knows: the sound came from right here, beneath the pale moonlight shining down on this wide, empty place.

She is glad when they're back beneath the cover of the trees.

A short time later, Redfern stops to kick a root and cut it from the ground. He sets his pack down, removes a jar, and Nellie takes the opportunity to unpack the sandwiches she made that morning. She hands him one and he does not refuse it. They sit on a fallen tree, and Nellie is about to take her first bite when she sees, stretching away beneath the trees, over the leaves and humus of the forest floor, whole cities—no, whole countries, whole continents—of moss. Bright green and gray and populated with toadstools and mushrooms that seem to smile and bend toward one another, happy congregants in a cathedral of fungus.

"What's it called?"

Redfern, toothless mouth gummed up with peanut butter, only shrugs.

There can't be a name for everything, she supposes.

The bald cypress trees.

Nellie's mood darkens, as does the light.

The old man wades into the water without slowing, some unseen path known only to him. She follows, wincing at the black water that flows into her boots, rises to her knees. The odd pool of sun spreads like blood around the cypress stobs. They navigate the trees like a maze, passing between them, around them, through them. She mistakes a log for an alligator, blood running cold. Fat skinks traverse the limbs, which bulge in strange places, thick with orange fungus. Once, their passing startles something behind a tree. Nellie hears it whip-splash away.

Eventually, they slog out onto semidry land, a bank of rot. The ground spongy with lichen.

Mosquitoes whiz like darts.

Here, at last, it emerges, through a tangle of thorny hammock and fat vines that hang like chains from the scaly trees. The ground is thick with low bracken, and the inlet that flows around it is narrow and sluggish and oily. It rises up like the long segmented body of a worm, a heap of mud and sticks and brittle muscadine vine, at the top that giant black mouth. Dragonflies light along the roots that scrabble up the slope like exposed bone.

"Go on up. It's safe."

"Safe from what?" she wants to know, but the old man only looks at her, waiting.

She hops over sludge water onto the island, has to catch her balance by bending forward and grabbing one of the exposed roots. It cracks between her fingers, rotten all the way through. She brushes it on her chinos. Each step cracking another dry, chalky root.

At the top, Nellie peers down into a long dark well of roots and thorns.

She covers her mouth at the smell, tries not to gag.

A heap of fur and bones, just inside the hole. The fur is gray and tufted around a long thin skull with sharp little teeth. Nellie sees half a backbone, three snaggled ribs like the broken tines of a comb. A bit of pelvis. A tiny paw, five toed. There are no ants, no bugs. Nothing crawls or stirs.

Not even a breeze to rattle the dead, lichen-thick trees that grow all around them.

"Do you hear it now?" Redfern asks, from below.

Hear what? she almost says. But she knows—

(. . . nellie . . .)

—what he means. She shakes her head.

"It was your mother. In the house. That's who you heard, I'm guessing."

A hot lump forms in her throat. "She said my name."

He looks off into the trees. "It always came to me like the wind. And then it left this place to cleave unto her. I always hoped it was me she heard, when it spoke to her. But it wasn't." He looks at Nellie. "Maybe it was her own voice she heard."

Nellie feels something heavy crash down through her chest, crack every bone on its way through.

"It creeps. Like any root or vine. Eats its way to the center of your heart, where the light is best, and the earth is rich. Leaves behind a husk."

She wants to speak, but she's got no spit, no words to force over a sandpaper tongue. She isn't sure what she expected to find out here, what revelation the old man was leading her to, but it's not this. Not that she was wrong in what she heard, or that Ruth Redfern is gone forever, or that Nellie, in turn, is shut of her sick and dying mother, no—

"No wonder it wants you now," he says.

"What are you talking about?"

"To sit beside a dying mother for months? You're a caretaker, Nellie. The brightest of all hearts."

Whatever's falling through her splashes down, at last, in the pit of her stomach, flash-boiling acid into her throat. She covers her mouth, begins to sob. Staggers down the island until her grandfather catches her and holds her, and she cries and cries and cries, cries so hard it seems she will break herself in two from the force of it.

The old man holds her close and smooths her hair. "Your kind burns the longest. Bleeds the most. You brave, brave girl."

DAY FOUR

◆

SHE LIES AWAKE ON THE DINETTE BED ALL NIGHT, LISTENING to her grandfather snore while she plans the rest of her life. Try as she might, she can't see beyond the next twenty-four hours, let alone the weeks or months ahead. In the wee hours, as heavy clouds part and the moon sets the bone-white farmhouse aglow through the window, she understands, at last, that she has been without a home since she was born. That she is, in fact, homeless yet, Redfern Hill no more where she belongs at sixteen than the house on Elm, where even now Hank Redfern lies in a whiskey stupor on his dead wife's hospital bed, curled like a child, sucking his thumb in sleep. She won't go back there.

As for here, well. The old man loves her, at least. She will leave this place, this town, and know what it's like to have been loved by her own kind. Theirs a kinship born less of blood, more of grief. The hollowing out of two hearts by time and sorrow. But there is no monster in these woods. She knows that, having heard the old man's mutterings, having seen the empty hole where supposedly a creature dwelled that robbed him of everything he held dear. Redfern men need no special demons when they make their own through selfishness and weakness. Whatever his secrets are, they are not hers to know.

Also, she is not safe here. She's thinking of the map, the odd drawing of the man on his knees, the taller man behind him, wearing her grandfather's hat. Holding a pistol.

No wonder it wants you now.

Something in the way he'd said it. She turns it over and over, tries to pin it down.

Like he was jealous, she finally realizes. Jealous that some imaginary monster preferred her to him.

The bruises on her arm are still there—that strong, strong grip.

It's simpler, anyway, to believe that what she heard in the house yesterday morning was simply a thing she had wanted to hear for months, just as she had wanted to live in that farmhouse, the instant the sun struck its boards: her mother's voice, free of sickness, free of pain.

It will make it easier, in the months and years ahead, to pretend everything she saw and heard here, in 1975, was born out of plain old ordinary grief. Nothing more. Grief the old man provided comfort for—in his company, in his acceptance of her. Whatever mistakes he may have made in the past, he took her in. She will always love him for that.

But now, like her father before her, she is leaving this place. Running away.

She gets up before dawn, dresses in her black funeral dress and buckle shoes. Leaves her father's muddy boots beneath the dinette table, which she quietly reassembles. Before she goes, she looks in on Redfern sleeping. She takes his stenographer's pad from his notebook, finds a pencil on the windowsill, and scrawls a brief note of thanks. She reads it back, but it's silly, childish.

Wholly inadequate. She tears it loose and crumples it. Stuffs it in her pocket, never thinks of it again.

Before the first sliver of light cracks the treetops, she's on her bike and pedaling.

Imagining that great blue ocean to the east, where all things empty out and wash away.

IV

1989

◆

JULY 8

THREE A.M. THAT DEAD OF NIGHT SO STILL IT TREMBLES.

Wade Gardner sits in the girl's apartment, in the middle of her shitty couch. He sits in darkness, perfectly still. A sliding glass door leads onto a concrete balcony that overlooks the parking lot, and from there he can see any headlights that flash below. Twice, in the last hour, cars have arrived, but not hers. He sits in jeans and old sneakers and a SUPERMAN T-shirt and thinks about what he will do when the girl gets home. In the kitchenette, the refrigerator's compressor kicks in and kicks out. Wade's wristwatch tick-tick-ticks in the silence.

The girl's name is Heather, and she passed spring composition with a B, though for half the semester she ignored the marks he made on her essays, as if screwing your writing teacher was somehow an excuse for bad grammar. Her couch is shitty like everything else in her life: the board bookshelves propped on cinder blocks, her scuffed-up dining table from the Salvation Army, her relationship with her controlling mother. At heart, she's a *Barefoot in the Park* kind of gal, always in motion. At clubs she dances to music that sounds like a big guy banging pipes with a crescent wrench. Of course, Wade Gardner's no music critic.

Still, he worries about Heather. She doesn't have her shit together, and he's afraid, tonight, her choices have led her to a place she can't come back from.

Can't come back from. A place from which she can't come back?

Awkward, both ways.

Tonight, her choices have led her to the end of the road.

Better, even if the language is a little trite.

Bad choices. Like not returning his calls since—

(Nellie, Nellie, Nellie, Nellie.)

—Nellie left.

So. A month ago, he made a copy of Heather's apartment key. Slipped it from her ring while she was in the shower. An impulse. She figured she'd lost it, got a spare from the complex office. That was a Friday. By Monday, the key was back on her ring. A few days later, she was looking at him funny in class. Usually, she hung around after, and they walked by the pond together or even ended up in the back of her old Wagoneer in the commuter parking lot, way over by the basketball stadium (BFE, that's what she called it, as in Butt-Fucking Egypt). But not that day. That day, Heather left with everyone else, head down, books clutched to her chest.

A few days later, Nellie was gone—

(Nellie, Nellie. Oh, Nellie.)

—and things were different.

Headlights, outside. The Jeep's heavy rumble, cutting out.

Fifteen, twenty seconds for the long gathering up of a woman's shit.

Then comes the familiar creak and moan of the Wagoneer's door opening.

Shortly, there will be footsteps in the outer stairwell, then the key, rattling in the door, and in she will step, Heather Wright—*Ms. Wright*, he'd joked the first day of class, a thousand years ago. The line earned him a smile, an eye roll, a brush back of raven-black hair. And, about two weeks later, a note beneath the windshield wiper of his '84 Mazda in the faculty lot, much closer to the English building than BFE: *Wouldn't it be wrong?—Ms. Wright.*

Not wrong, Wade understands now. Just a mistake.

Nellie was gone, after all, and it made him sick to think about it.

Max. My son. She took my son.

His hands are on his thighs. He balls them into fists, feels his fingernails dig into his palms.

Nellie left him and took his son and now Ms. Wright had stopped returning his calls.

Outside, a key fumbles at the dead bolt.

Three a.m. She's drunk or stoned.

The lock clicks over.

Ms. Wright. What a joke.

The door opens, and Wade stands up. To welcome Heather to the end of the road.

Moths pop against the cold blue vapor lamps, and the lamps buzz and an owl shuffles along a magnolia branch. Upstairs, door locked, chairs beneath the doorknobs, Max and Nellie sleep in Nellie's bed, both dreaming.

Dreaming in a house that is not the same. Boards are still boards, the frame is unchanged. Not a piece of furniture is out of place. And yet: earlier that evening, when they walked through the front door, it became the dog that bites. Even Nellie felt it, a shifting within the walls. They went quietly among the rooms, switching on lights, each afraid to creak the wrong plank or darken a threshold overlong.

Nellie buried the bunny at the edge of the field, then microwaved leftover mac and cheese for dinner. They sat at the kitchen table and she told Max about the summer she was sixteen. About her mother, about the things August Redfern said and did. How he mistook her for Agatha. The long path into the old forest and the place at the end of it. She spared him nothing and wondered, in the end, why she had ever kept any of it from him. After all, he was older, wiser, than any eleven-year-old should be. Finally, she told him how she'd heard her mother's name spoken in the house, wafting up from the cellar. A memory she had long since dismissed as some manifestation of grief.

"The cellar," Max said, like it was the answer to a riddle.

After dinner, they searched, helpless not to. Nellie searched Redfern's desk in the map room, Max the drawers in the master bedroom upstairs. They looked beneath mattresses and cushions and in every kitchen cabinet they had yet to open. The object of their search: a key. Iron, most likely. Old-fashioned in appearance. Max imagined one of those big jailhouse keys dangling from iron rings in old westerns. Probably, Nellie said, it's rusting in the county landfill, along with the five or six truckloads of garbage they hauled away, back when she was certain this house was home.

They felt eyes on them as they searched. Peering out from every crack, every dark cubby. Every still space they had yet to invade. It followed them from room to room. They heard it, though they pretended not to. Moving behind the boards, twisting up through the pine bones of the house, electrical wires, old vermiculite insulation. Corroded pipes dripping on the chitinous corpses of long-dead bugs.

Always moving, always watching.
Always hungry.
Scritch-scritch-scritch.

Nellie turns, tosses, twists in bed, itching at her arm until—
. . . *nellie* . . .
She opens her eyes. Max beside her.
Her mother's voice, faint, out of the fog of dreams.
She peels back the bedcovers and sits up. Stands.
Barefoot, wearing only a T-shirt and a pair of cotton underwear, she picks up August Redfern's moon ax from where it leans against the bedside table. She lets it dangle at her thigh.
She crosses to the door and removes the chair from beneath the knob and steps out into the hall and goes down the stairs. At the front door, she turns the dead bolt, opens the door, and pushes through the screen onto the porch.
She moves like a ghost, ethereal, expressionless.
In the gravel drive, by the front right tire of the Ranger, the three-legged dog sits, watching her. The dog sneezes, then lopes away, into the trees, northwest of the house.
Nellie follows, through briars and branches. Bobbing and weaving like a kite, tugged roughly by invisible string and borne on a silent wind.

Max, meanwhile, dreams on.
In back of the house in Conway, in the dirt drive that curves around to the little blue garage, his father, bare chested, slick with sweat in the sun. Max stands with hands clapped over his nose, the blood gushing out between his fingers. The basketball

rolling off into the grass. Wade claps his hands twice. *Max, look here, buddy, Max!*

Max begins to cry, to cry to for his mother.

Wade's face draws down, darkly. *Mommy's gone, Maxie. She's not coming back. Do you hear me? So don't be a sissy. Don't you cry, you crybaby sissy—*

Wade's voice gutters out. His chest and belly ripple. Things move beneath his skin.

Max can hear them, slapping like fish in a bucket.

They burst through in red sprays and fall out in pink-brown knots, burrowing into the earth around his father's feet, and now the ground is splitting open, roots breaking through to twine around Wade's legs, hairy and wet things that throw out shoots and wrap his father's arms and shoulders and neck and face, fattening, pulsing, tightening. They make a sound like rubber balloon animals. Wade Gardner stands faceless, frozen, a man-shaped tree of fibrous worms that sprout little white flowers, but the flowers are not flowers; they're yellow jackets, each petal taking flight as it saws earthward, and the yellow jackets are flying at Max's face, but he does not run. He cannot run, because his feet, too, are rooted to the ground. As the thing that was his father splits, cracks apart like dried mud, and out of this chrysalis emerges a finger, a hand, a face soft and pale. All at once, Agatha Redfern stands before Max. Skinny and slight shouldered in her blue gingham dress. Dark hair, the last dusty fragments of the roots still clinging there. She smiles and puts a finger to her lips and goes to the little door on the side of the garage. She beckons Max to follow her through the door, and he does. Realizing, as he passes into the door, that it is not the door he thinks it is.

Inside, a long flight of wooden stairs.

Far down where the light diminishes, Agatha crooks her finger.

Max descends into the damp-earth dark.

At the bottom of the stairs, he turns and looks back up at a small, far rectangle of sunlight. The door yet open.

Out of the dark, that girlish giggle.

As something coils around his bare ankle. Yanks him off his feet, into shadow.

The dog lopes ahead of Nellie, draws her out of the trees, far west of the old cabins. Here, without hesitation, she splashes into the summer-warm water of North Creek and slogs out into a field of wire grass, tall and thick and bright as salt in the moonlight. A host of strange forms stand mute, thirteen total, as if assembled to bear witness to her passing. Their clothes are rags of old denim and cotton, their bodies humped and torn apart and stitched back together with wet, fibrous strings. One wears a rotten cast on his leg. Their skulls gleam. They point, as one, to the tree line behind them.

August Redfern is there, an assemblage of flesh and bone and root, his face whiskered white. He wears loose-fitting khaki pants, holes in the pockets, the cuffs threadbare. Thick-soled hiking boots, scuffed and cracked. His hands, for once, are bare, his fingertips trailing vines. Out of the breast pocket of his plain white shirt a wiry nest of tendrils blooms and pulses, heart-like. He watches Nellie from across the clearing with eyes that flicker blue-flame-like. Presently, he turns and moves off into the trees.

Nellie—fast asleep and wide-awake at once—moves after him, heart thudding.

The dog is gone. The thirteen men are gone.

She enters the trees, moving on, into the dark.

Max wakes in a fetal shape in his mother's bed, crotch wet and warm. Suffocating in a tide of bedcovers. Heart racing, he struggles from beneath the quilt and rolls over on his back. He touches the mattress beside him. Nellie is nowhere to be seen, the hall door open. He switches on the bedside lamp and sees the urine soaking through his pajamas.

"Shit."

He gets up and removes the chair from beneath the adjoining doorknob, opens the door, and stumble-walks into his own bedroom. Out of the armoire he rummages a fresh pair of underwear. He kicks off his soiled underpants, steps into the clean ones, and goes back to his mother's bedroom.

Propped against his pillow: the rag doll.

He remembers his dream. Hand trembling, he picks it up and his fingers tack in the sticky white sap on its dress.

. . . max . . .

He jumps, almost screams.

From downstairs, a sudden series of knocks, distant, muffled. Like fists against a door.

"Mom?" he calls.

The pounding grows frantic, urgent.

He moves into the hallway.

"Mom!"

Still clutching the rag doll, he starts downstairs.

The Redfern-thing leads her like a shambling Frankenstein's monster across the hip-deep slough and through the maze of cypress trees. Here, her feet slip and stagger among the stobs, and once, something quick and slender darts between her calves. Her bare feet squelch and suck, and when she emerges, soaked through, a score of leeches cling to her pale legs. She follows the old man through the bracken and the hammocks to where the narrow inlet curves back on itself, the island at its center. A gaping black wound spilling vines, an open mouth thrust heavenward in a silent scream.

Or an eye. Seen from above, an eye.

The Redfern-thing wades into the ankle-deep inlet, ascends the mound, and Nellie follows, toes curling over rocks and roots ensnarled in the earth like writhing cables. They roll away from her touch, dart like shy creatures into the ground—

(it's here it's awake it's not safe it's everywhere now alive and hungry)

—and she stands, wavering, before the maw.

A smell of old death and rot belches out.

The Redfern-thing regards her with eyes that are hollows, head creaking on its fibrous neck, the rough, porous bone of its skull. Its mouth is a glistening black cave; its teeth are hardened sap, mosquitoes trapped inside them. Loam and pine bark clog its throat as it speaks, roughly, thickly.

. . . we are old . . .

Its words are like the workings of beetles in wood.

. . . abandoned these long years . . .

Leaves spill out of its rag of a shirt.

. . . we want to be fed . . .

Nellie hears the deep, hacking cough of an animal. She turns, sees only a huge dark shadow lumbering, half-glimpsed, among the twisted hammocks. It gives out a low moan, and the moan becomes an anguished wail, as it throws its wide black head up to the moon and stamps the ground.

The Redfern-thing grins.

. . . feed us, nellie . . .

It seizes her throat, fingers curling, constricting. Little hairs emerging from its fingers and a clutch of tiny teeth drilling into the flesh of her neck. Purple spots at the edges of her vision. Blood coursing over her collarbones, her shoulders. A reek of pine sap and rot.

. . . share your strength with us . . .

The ax still in her hand, but too heavy to lift.

That black maw, rising up to meet her.

. . . or we will have your son . . .

Max, on the cellar stairs, remembering his dream with every step, doll in one hand, Maglite from the hall table in the other, driving back the shadows.

The hammering grows louder, fiercer.

BOOMBOOMBOOM.

At the bottom of the stairs, he rounds the corner and shines the light on the coal closet, the heavy metal door shuddering, skeins of dust billowing, his heart thundering in time with every blow.

"Mom?" he calls.

The pounding ceases.

Max steps forward, makes a fist, raps twice against the metal. Waits.

Softly, from within, the sound returns: two light knocks.

He shines his light through the keyhole. Sees nothing but a thick gob of webbing and, like some horrid treat at the center of a candy, eight black legs, unmoving.

He knocks again, three times.

The knocks come back, a perfect echo.

Then, a small, clear whimper:

. . . max . . .

"Who's that?" he says, forcing a friendly, playground voice out of a windpipe that wants to close.

Agatha, he expects the answer to be.

But there's only a heavy silence.

Until, like a tumble of rocks spilling down a metal chute, something growls.

A sound so huge and terrible Max feels his scrotum shrivel.

He drops the rag doll and flies to the steps. He's five, six steps up when he trips and falls, barking his knee on the riser. The flashlight skitters away between the steps. Max looks up to the top of the staircase, where the cellar door is swung wide. Below, beneath the stairs, the Maglite's beam shows a bright circle of hard-packed earth.

Max puts his right arm between the stairs, stretches for the light. His fingers brush metal, but the flashlight rolls a half inch away, out of his reach. He's pulling his arm back in when something seizes it.

A hand, five hard fingers around his forearm.

He screams.

A woman's face swims out of the darkness beneath the stairs, moaning and slavering, bits of red hair clinging to the white dome of a skull. A jaw that hangs like a broken cabinet door as the woman-thing tries to speak through a sudden well of black blood, and the tongue that comes slithering out is not a tongue at all, but a fat brown worm—

Suction on his arm, pressure, razor-blade teeth as the fingers become tendrils and the tendrils sink little teeth into his skin and the woman-thing yanks him hard, like she's going to drag him right through the narrow gap in the stairs, like meat through a grinder, down into the dark with her—

Max yanks his arm back, claws frantically at whatever this thing is biting into his flesh.

"Pleeeeease," the woman-thing moans.

Max screams one last time and tears his arm free.

A mad scramble on hands and knees, up the steps and into the hallway.

He leaves the door gaping behind him.

Downstairs, in the dark, something slithers over the rag doll.

He finds Nellie in the yard, where he's fled. Staggering down the porch steps in his T-shirt and underwear, he looks up and sees the white, ghostly shape of her at the tree line near the barn. He calls out to her, hobbles toward her, right arm oozing from a dozen tiny slashes. She, too, is in her underwear, wet with mud. Neck and collarbone slicked in red. Legs crosshatched with blood and something else, something dark and sluglike—

(leeches, oh, God)

—and she carries, in one hand, the moon ax, though her fingers are loosening and it's slipping, as she stumbles, then collapses into a heap on the ground.

Max rushes to her, drops on his knees in the grass at her side. Rolls her onto her back.

A necklace of slashes, like the ones on his arm.

He shakes her. Tells her to wake up. Plucks leeches from her thighs.

Her eyelids flutter. She swallows. Says his name.

Fear rears up inside him like a dragon: *SHE COULD DIE.*

So Max does the only thing he knows to do. He goes back into the house.

At the hallway table, her shoulder purse rests beside the telephone. He loops the purse over his arm and snatches the Baxter County phone book from beneath the phone. Flipping through it to the Rs. "Please be in here, please be in here."

He finds it. Hooks a finger in the dial.

Dragging Nellie to the pickup's cab takes longer than he expects. She's dead weight, heavy as a hundred bags of wet sand, which is just long enough for all the fearful thoughts to thump their fists and have their say in Max's skull. He tries to remember what she taught him, a year or so back, how the shifter works. They were in the Piggly Wiggly parking lot in Conway, and she'd set him on her lap so he could work the gears. "Just in case you ever need to know," she said. They'd driven along the edge of the asphalt, down the slope of the lot to the road, Max practicing with first and second gear as Nellie's feet worked the pedals, the truck stalling out over and over. Laughter jostled out of them every time.

Hand on the key, key in the ignition, Max feels a fleeting sense of inevitability: of course this isn't going to work. He's still barely tall enough to work the pedals and see over the steering wheel, especially in his bare feet—

He glances at his mother, curled on the seat, head against the glass of the passenger window. Blood soaking through her T-shirt. His own arm growing hot and heavy, with every second he wastes—

He cranks the key and the Ranger rattles to life. He slides down to push the clutch with his left foot and works the gears by the guide on the stick, grinds them forever, until finally he hits first. He lets off the clutch too quickly, and the Ranger lurches and stalls.

"Shit!"

Once, twice more, and he feels something catch. He eases off the clutch this time, and the pickup begins to roll forward. Max holds his breath and keeps it slow and steady, and the truck shudders down the lane.

Soon enough, they've rounded the corner by the Winnebago and they're picking up speed, so he slides back down and works the clutch again, and now they're in second, and the road begins to slope to the South Creek wash. He ducks down, presses the clutch, and pops it up into third, even as something screams in the gearbox.

Before he even realizes it, they've tromped the boards over sand and gravel, bouncing and sliding through the creek and back up onto the hard-packed road.

Ahead, a pair of headlights set the trees aglow.

Max jams on the brakes, and the Ranger stalls out and skids to a halt in the loose gravel.

The ax slides out from beneath the seat, where Max has stowed it.

The oncoming lights bathe the Ranger's cab in light.

Max puts his head down on the steering wheel and says a silent prayer of thanks, and a moment later, the passenger door opens, and Hank Redfern reaches in and gathers his daughter into his arms.

Not long after sunup, hours yet before his father's funeral, Lonnie Baxter makes eggs and toast. He and Linda eat at a little drop-leaf table in a corner of the kitchen. Before she goes upstairs to wake Todd and feed him, Linda reaches across the table and squeezes Lonnie's hand. After she's gone, he drinks a second cup of coffee and looks out the window at the sloping yard, the willow trees that overhang the river, and beyond the river a forest of new-growth pine, planted in 1975, the year he lost a third term and went back to the Millworks full-time.

Back to a changed industry. Dry kilns and gang resaws and 15 million board feet a year. He'd read up on the new machinery, had the manuals in his office. It makes his head hurt, most days, all those moving parts. Everything he doesn't know, piling up. Like those bills he just can't open. Second mortgage on the house, the fancy car. Todd's medical care. Lonnie's back, insurance complications. Now, his father's funeral. It's like that old poem from high school English, the one about suicide: he's got miles and miles to go. Except the miles are greenbacks, and there's thousands owed. Just the money Lonnie had to free up from the company account to make an offer to that Gardner bitch, the high-wire act he had to do to keep that money off the books? Christ almighty. And now, all that cash, just sitting there in his office safe. More than once, he's been tempted to cut and run, see how far he gets. (*You're weak. You could have throttled her and her brat the other day. Dragged them into the woods. Afraid, Lonnie? To get your own hands red with anything but paint?*) He puts his head in his hands. (*Poor sniveling Lonnie.*) He wipes his nose.

What it all boils down to: Lonnie needs things to turn around, and he needs them to turn around now.

The sun breaks through the leaded glass to bathe the kitchen blue. He glances at the molding along the walls, the doors, the way the heartwood grain gleams, a pattern so rich and varied it seems almost dimensional as the light plays through it. (*Make the call.*) Sure, the call. He would have made the call already, but there were arrangements to be made. His brother isn't coming to the funeral. Herman's got a new job out in San Francisco, something with computers— (*Make the goddamn call, Lonnie!*)

Lonnie fumbles for the phone, reaches a little slip of paper out of his robe pocket, the one Meadows gave him.

Upstairs, his son cries out and Lonnie doesn't even know what the sound means. Is he happy, is he sad? Is there even a difference?

He punches in the number.

Wade wakes, barking out a series of hoarse cries, a dream about his father, a baptism in the little creek that ran behind the old church, cold water washing over him, the old man's hand upon his head, holding him down. A shard of daylight pierces a slit in the bedroom window's pull shade. He rolls over into another hour's sleep, and at half past nine stumbles, shirtless in a pair of gym sweats, to the living room, where he snags the ringing phone just as the machine kicks in.

"Nellie?"

He answers every call this way now.

A rush of air, crackle of static. A man's voice: "Mr. Gardner?"

"Who is this?"

"Wade Gardner?"

"Speaking."

"Mr. Gardner, my name is Lonnie Baxter. I'm calling from Georgia."

"Yeah?" Wade glances at his knuckles, the skin peeled back on his right middle finger. A bit of blood he's missed beneath his nail. *Ms. Wrong, ha.* "And what are you selling?"

"We can help one another, Wade."

"How's that?"

"Would you like to know where your wife and son are?"

The day is overcast, gloomy. Max sits in the cradle of an old tire swing in Hank Redfern's backyard. The swing hangs from the limb of a pin oak, which has all but eaten the rope. Max pushes himself gently with slippered feet. The moccasins are new, as are the sweatpants and T-shirt. Both are black, stamped with the Batman logo from the new movie coming out. Back in South Carolina, the promise of that summer's *Batman* movie had been the center of Max's universe. It's funny to even think about now, how far away that seems.

The screen door opens and Mr. Hank walks out in a pair of denim overalls.

"Is she awake?" Max asks.

Hank Redfern puts one hand in the bib of his overalls and takes out a pack of cigarettes. He shakes one out, leans against the tree. "No, but the fever's down. I cleaned her cuts, like yours. Feet are worse than the neck." He lights his smoke. "I called a wrecker to bring in your pickup."

Max glances at the gauze pad taped on his arm. Old blood beaded through.

Hank coughs. Spits. "Y'all tangle with a bear?"

Max starts at the choice of words. He shakes his head, once he realizes it's just a figure of speech. "I think she was sleepwalking."

Hank's mouth tightens. "She still does that?"

"She's done it before?"

The old man nods. Flicks ash. "Back when her m-m-mama

was sick. She used to walk three, four blocks at a time. Once, I found her as far up as the Amoco on Main."

Max doesn't say anything. He's wondering if she's done this back in South Carolina, too. Remembering how, some days, Mom walked around extra tired, no amount of coffee in the world enough to get her engine started. How she soaked her feet, once or twice, in Epsom salts while Dad was at work.

"What about that old scar, on her arm?" Hank asks.

"That was a long time ago," Max says. "We don't talk about it."

"You ever hear voices? Out at the house?"

Max hesitates. "What kind of voices?"

Cigarette between his fingers, Hank taps his head. "Like someone's talking in here. Only no one's around."

Max stares at the ground, pushes himself in the swing with his feet. He shakes his head. He isn't sure why he lies, only that he doesn't trust his grandfather. Not entirely. Mr. Hank has secrets, things he's not telling, and secrets can get people hurt.

Hank looks off into the yard next door, where a clothesline flaps in the gray light. "You go in that cellar?"

Max doesn't answer.

"I told her not to let you."

"I do what I want."

"Well, that sure makes you hers, don't it." Hank toes out his cigarette and heads for the back stoop, expelling one last stream of smoke over his shoulder.

"What's in that coal closet?" Max calls after him.

Hank hunches, like he's been hit with a rock, square between the shoulders. But he doesn't falter in his stride, and seconds later, the screen door slaps shut behind him.

Overhead, the rope creaks as Max twists slowly in the swing.

Wade makes a scrambled-egg sandwich for breakfast and eats it standing at the kitchen sink. He drinks two large glasses of orange juice, lots of pulp, and when he's finished, he washes his dishes and sets them neatly on the drying rack. He goes to Max's bedroom and sits on the bed, which he's made up, edges of the boy's *Star Wars* sheets tucked drum tight. Wade pictures Nellie, dragging the boy out of sleep. Max beating his fists against his mother's back in protest. Wade was at the office when it happened, grading blue-book midterms from his short-session summer class. He blamed himself.

Nervous Nellie. Scratching her scar, tapping her heels. Twisting in her seat.

But that was wrong. Turns out, she wasn't nervous at all.

She was sneaky. *Sneaky Nellie.*

Wade glances into the spare bedroom, her studio. Her paintings are in pieces, broken frames and torn canvas scattered around the room. Easel smashed, all the paint tubes squeezed out and crumpled. Carpet stiff and brittle. It had helped, doing all that. Sometimes, as now, it still helps, just to look at it. To remind himself of all the things he is going to do to her, too.

Empire, Georgia.

An inheritance.

Son of a bitch.

Sneaky Nellie. He laughs.

Wade Gardner can be sneaky, too.

He packs his Gamecocks duffel, lets the machine take the next phone call.

"Dr. Gardner, this is Dr. Ferris . . ."

He goes into the living room, folded T-shirt in hand, and stands by the machine. He listens for ten, maybe fifteen seconds, long enough to get the gist of it—*can't cancel your summer classes without notifying the department, been absent for days, haven't taken leave, complaints from students*—before he lifts the receiver and says pleasantly, "Hi, Gene. It's Wade."

Over the line, Wade can hear Gene Ferris shifting uncomfortably in his chair, tugging at his tie. "Wade, hi. So, I guess you heard all that?"

"I heard."

Wade's been on the lecture side of Ferris's desk more than once. Grade disputes, off-color remarks to young women. Usually, Wade sits silently, contritely, while Ferris drones on and on. He's a small, bristly turd, and Wade does not like him.

"Well, this is where we are."

"Actually, Gene, I'm going to need to cancel next week's classes, too."

Licking his lips. Adjusting his glasses now. "What?"

"As you know, it's been rough, with Nellie's disappearance—"

"Wade. Man, your wife didn't disappear. Okay? She left you. I think you know that."

Sometimes, Wade imagines hauling Gene Ferris out of his chair and halfway across his desk, right there in the freshman-English suite, in front of student workers and colleagues and the department secretary, whose stubby fingers would stall out over her typewriter at the sound of everything clattering off Gene's desk. Then Wade would punch Gene Ferris until his left occipital bone cracked, and he would hurl Gene to the parquet tile and put his sneaker on Gene's throat and say something like *Fuck you, you little rat FUCK, I quit, and if you ever try to tell me what I can*

*or can't do again, I'll fucking stomp the life right out of you.
I don't give a shit. I don't give a shit, Gene!*

"Like I said, Gene, next week is canceled. I've got to go to
Georgia."

"Georgia? Listen, Wade—"

Wade hangs up.

Whistling, as he rolls a pair of sleep shorts into his gym bag,
a little tune by Dolly Parton, something Max loves. Dolly is a
love they share. Hell, who doesn't love Dolly?

It makes Wade happy to think he'll be seeing his son again,
soon.

One last look around—check the thermostat, check the stove,
check the dead bolt—and he's out of the house and into his
Mazda before 10:00 a.m. He takes 544 for Myrtle Beach and
from there strikes out south along the coast, Peach State bound.

In the dream, which is not like any dream she's ever had—long
and winding down secret paths that lead to secret places—Nellie
listens to the radio for the first forty or fifty miles. The countryside
slides by, lush timberland broken by the odd small town, a few
churches, a courthouse, a factory. Saw palms beneath the trees
and a set of railroad tracks parallel to the highway. Sunlight
strobes over the Ranger's dash, makes her want to close her eyes.
She doesn't remember where she's coming from, or where she's
going, only that there's a reason for the journey. She slows at a
crossroads, to her left Savannah and, beyond, South Carolina,
where the sky is piled with purple thunderheads. Her signal
blinks left, but she turns right.

A massive white suspension bridge carries her over the wide,
open salt marshes that rim the Georgia coast. She takes a narrow

strip of blacktop toward the ocean, on both sides of the road, a rising tide, the sulfurous mud stink of the marsh. The road becomes a rope bridge of wood that sways in the wind as she crosses it, slowly, carefully. Thumping off onto an island of live oaks and palms and old stone ruins. She drives until she sees the place she is meant to be, and there she pulls over and gets out. The front right tire is flat. Above, oak arms wrestle with the stiff sea wind and long yellow spiders hang in webs between them.

She wears a bright summer dress and sunglasses and sandals and her hair is long and blond and swept back and her belly is round and full of the baby that will come any day now. She hikes through the woods and emerges onto a narrow, deserted shelf of beach littered with the bones of trees long uprooted by storms, washed ashore from other islands. Far out where lightning forks pink and hot, she can see another tiny island, where great iron ships with belching smokestacks ferry corpses from the distant lights of Savannah. Men in masks and army fatigues drive heavy equipment to plow trenches, and the dead are poured in.

Wade steps out from behind an uprooted oak as the surf washes in. He's smiling and his shirt is open and his jeans are rolled to the knee. He offers her his hand and she takes it and they walk. He tells her there are blankets down the way, a picnic. He touches her belly, smooths his hand over it. They duck branches, weave among the thick driftwood trunks until at last they come to the largest tree, and this one she climbs alone and stands astride it as if it were some great dead sea beast, and she its slayer.

Ahead, on the beach, she can see Wade's blanket, the picnic basket. Two longneck beers jammed in the sand. She looks back but Wade is gone. In his place the jagged stump of a tree, still and mute.

The tide swirls in, tugs the distant beers, basket, and blanket away.

In their place, as the water recedes, a hole. Water pouring into it.

Nellie doesn't know what's happening, but she knows she has to get there, to that hole, and so she does, hopping down and jogging as quickly as her girth allows. The sand falls into the hole with each new wave that boils over it. Something is down there. Something made of iron and wood. An old-fashioned treasure chest, half-submerged in the slate-gray sand. She drops to her knees and claws around it, digs it out. Water washing around her as, in that sometimes-slow, sometimes-fast speed of dreams, she uncovers a handle and hauls the chest out of the hole and onto the beach. It doesn't weigh much at all. No more than a baby, really.

She hesitates to open it, a sudden break of thunder behind her.

Out on the sea, the waves are thrashing, and a huge, triple-masted ship is anchored along the shallow shelf. A smaller boat rows for it, knifing up and over the incoming waves. Six men, sunbrowned and tattooed, beating a hasty retreat. What have they abandoned here, in this box? What have they left to rule over someone else's fate?

The chest is locked, but there, deep in the shifting sand, is a heavy iron key.

Heart pounding, baby inside her moving, she thrusts her arm into the hole and drags the key free of the sand. With it, she unlocks the chest and throws back the lid.

Inside is the most beautiful, shimmering blue she has ever seen.

It moves like the sea.

As from deep, deep below, something huge rises up to meet her.

The Budget Inn stands on the outskirts of town between a Handy Mart and a vacant lot, behind it the defunct tire factory. Wade checks in around three o'clock under the name Johnson. The carpet's threadbare and the TV is coin-operated and bolted to the dresser, but Wade doesn't notice. He simply throws his bag on the bed and snaps up the toilet lid to piss. Then he hits the Handy Mart to gas up. He asks a pimpled clerk for directions to the sawmill.

West of town, he pulls off the highway and parks in front of a prefabricated log building. In the parking lot, a lone vehicle, a silver BMW, one of its taillights smashed. Beyond the chain-link fence, the mill is silent. No saws, no whistles. No trucks. The log building is unlocked, so Wade goes in.

A secretary's desk, typewriter covered, lamp off.

A black boar's head hangs over an open door.

Inside, in a wash of lamplight, a man sits at a desk made of sawn pine logs. He wears a dark suit, tie loosened at the throat. He's a big man, but still his chair seems to swallow him. He's pouring a glass of amber booze. "Wade Gardner?" he says.

"Right-o."

Wade gets waved in.

The office is cool and dim and smells faintly of cigars. Lonnie Baxter rises and reaches across his desk. Wade shakes the man's hand, aware, as always, that his smile belies the distaste Wade feels when touching another man's skin. Maybe it goes back to Wade's preacher daddy, a man who liked to touch skin an awful lot. But there are rituals, he recognizes. Rituals and rites and we must observe them.

Baxter's grip is light, distracted. He's halfway to drunk. He offers Wild Turkey. Wade makes a polite smile, shakes his head. "Never touch the stuff."

"Straight arrow." Baxter gestures for him to sit.

The chairs are leather. The carpet a rich, money green.

"I apologize. I'm not my best self today."

Wade crosses a leg over a knee, folds his hands in his lap. "Who did you bury?"

"Pardon?"

Wade points at a piece of paper, resting beneath the booze. A funeral program.

"Oh. Yeah. My, um, my father." Baxter collapses into his chair.

"Very sorry."

"Sure. Listen, thanks for coming."

"Thank you for contacting me. I can't tell you how relieved I was to get your call."

"Relieved." Baxter watches him. "Look. Why don't we just put all our cards on the table here. What do you say?"

"I'd like that."

"Good. So, the truth is, Mr. Gardner, I don't really give a shit whether you and your wife and son are happily reunited. For me, this is a business entanglement. I can hand you a bag of cash as soon as your wife signs this property transfer deed over to me." Baxter produces the document from a drawer, slides it across the desk. "Perfectly simple, perfectly legal."

Wade leans forward, inspects the paper. Makes no move to pick it up. "Won't we need a notary for this?"

Baxter smiles. "I know a guy."

Wade leans back in his chair, smiles, and hooks a thumb over his shoulder. "Is that your E-series out there?"

Baxter's smile slips. "It is."

"I've read those are quite the machines. Car phone and everything."

"I guess, yeah."

"I have to say, I can't imagine ever needing to phone someone from the car. I'm not a fan of telephones in general, to be honest."

"Well, they do bring bad news more often than good."

"You have a taillight out, you know."

Baxter gulps the rest of his drink. Pours more bourbon from the bottle.

"It's funny. The same thing happened to my Mazda a few years back. Exact same light."

Baxter swallows, lowers his glass. "That a fact."

"The thing is, Lonnie, if this 'entanglement,' as you called it, has escalated to the point at which my wife is busting taillights, well, take it from me: you might as well go ahead and forge that signature."

"Forge it."

"Yes, sir. Because I can't imagine there will be any convincing her to sign anything. You have obviously rubbed her the wrong way."

"You can't convince her."

"You keep repeating what I say."

"Son, even if I did forge a signature, I'd still have to pay somebody to keep it aboveboard. And I still need her the hell off that land. Now. I thought you were the man for the job, but the longer we sit here gabbing, the more it seems to me you're the wrong man. Hell, maybe you've been the wrong man ever since you two got married, and that's why she left you. What do you think?"

Wade keeps his hands clasped in his lap. "You mentioned a number over the phone."

Baxter laughs, rocks back in his chair. Pulls his tie all the way free and tosses it on his desk. "Here it comes."

"Like you said, Lonnie, let's put our cards on the table. You want me to drag my wife out of her own house by the roots of her hair, kicking and screaming—and believe me, that is what it will take—so, it seems only fair that I be compensated appropriately."

"So?" Baxter growls.

"I want twice what you're offering."

"Twice." Baxter clutches his tumbler with both hands and stares into it.

Pure lead crystal, if Wade isn't mistaken. "Twice. Half now."

"Half now." Baxter's eyes stray over Wade's shoulder. "That it?"

"That's it."

Baxter knocks back the last of his bourbon, smacks the tumbler down, and walks around his desk to a painting on the far wall. A dog with a duck in its mouth.

Wade shifts in his chair to watch.

The painting is hinged, a wall safe behind it. Baxter works the dial.

"Do you love your son, Mr. Gardner?"

"What?"

"I have a son. I love him. But there are days I'd give up anything, even my boy, to have another chance at forever."

Wade turns back to the desk to hide the sudden flush of anger. Give up his son? Wade would never give up his son. Wade's own father might have said something like that, like some latter-day Abraham prodding Isaac up the hill at knifepoint. Wade picks up the funeral program. On the outside flap is a church, clouds parting to reveal two disembodied hands clasped in prayer. It makes him want to vomit, just to look at it, and suddenly no amount of money this Baxter creep can offer Wade is worth the price of his own dignity. He picks up the heavy crystal tumbler and stands and walks up behind Baxter, and when Baxter turns, a stack of banded bills in one hand, the other closing that shitty, hinged motel art, Wade brings the tumbler down on Baxter's head. The crystal shatters, drives shards into Baxter's scalp, and he staggers into the wall.

The money cascades to the carpet.

Baxter sits down on the floor, blood coursing over his face, into his eyes.

From the desk blotter, Wade snags the property transfer deed. He bends over Baxter and waggles the paper. Then he tears it in half and lets the pieces flutter down to the floor, among the money. He snares Baxter's shirt and hauls the man up into his fist. Once, twice, three times, until he hears a nice, bright crack beneath the skin. A cheekbone maybe.

"You don't talk to me about my son."

With that, Wade walks out of the office and leaves Baxter bleeding on his rich green carpet.

Right knuckle red and swelling, Wade drives around, jumping with adrenaline.

At six o'clock, he stops at a hardware store downtown and buys duct tape. A man in a pearl-snap shirt rings him up. He asks the man if he knows how to get to the address he read on the transfer deed. The man says sure, that's Redfern Hill. He asks Wade if he knows that nice young girl and her boy just moved in. Says they've been in a couple times. Swell pair. Wade says he does know them. So the hardware man tells him how to get there, and Wade thanks him.

Then he goes across the street to the pawnshop.

An old-timer perches on a stool behind the register, reading *Lonesome Dove*.

"Do you have knives?" Wade says.

Out of the blue depths of the chest and into the studio in the little blue house in Conway. A canvas set vertically upon the easel, on it, a woman's face, Nellie's own, half in shadow, floating in a pool of midnight behind a white slash of skin and cheek. Upon the cheek in shadow, veins blue and vessels red and each becoming hair and the hair becoming something else, a kind of slick and pulsing vine that reaches beyond the borders of the canvas and covers the sheetrock. Sweat beneath her arms, Nellie steps back and looks around, takes in the dream wreckage of her studio. Every canvas in tatters, every frame smashed. She drops her palette and palette knife and kneels before one of the larger pieces, lifting a ragged flap back into place and seeing, with a shock, the western view from the top of the fire tower at Redfern Hill. A nighttime rendering, in which the moon, a silver crescent with a rind of cadmium red, rises over a saw-toothed tree line low in the foreground.

The door to the studio creaks.

She freezes, listening for footsteps in the hallway, hearing only the thump of the refrigerator's compressor.

Along the far wall, a portrait of Max at six or seven smiles at her. He's missing a tooth. The work is warm and happy. The boy's face is slashed to ribbons.

"Max?" she calls, into the darkness.

She peers around the doorway, across the hall to his room.

He sits on the edge of his bed, wearing galoshes and a yellow raincoat. A little blue suitcase between his feet. "I'm going to run away from you," he tells her. Propped beside him is her painting of the eye, trailing its optic nerve. On the other side, Lonnie Baxter's crude cunt turned sideways. Both, she realizes, are the same. Neither eye nor cunt but an island, rising out of an inlet flowing off the river.

At the center of each, a deep, dark hole.

In the kitchen, the phone begins to ring.

The dream rolls on.

Wade misses Redfern Road, has to double back, the turnout narrow and overgrown. Driving slowly, he opts not to turn in but instead cruises on by to the bridge that spans the river, and here he pulls off the road into the grass and parks under the overpass. He tucks his knife into its scabbard and loops his belt through the scabbard, then crosses onto the property from beneath the bridge. He moves through the edge of the woods, parallel to the road, until the highway's out of sight. From here, he follows the gravel, keeping close to the ditch so he can duck into the trees if need be, but no one comes, and after about forty minutes or so, he's made it to a stretch of trees through which he can see the old farmhouse on the hill, the day's light waning.

He crosses into the trees and comes up behind the Winnebago in the long grass and squats at the front fender until twilight falls, so he can safely cross the field without being seen. The windows of the house are dark. He creeps close to the porch, then onto it, to peer in.

No one's home.

He sits down on the porch steps. His knife—a ridiculously large hunting knife—finds its way into his hands, and he jabs it idly into the porch planks as the world around him plunges into night.

The night lamps stutter on.

A dog sits out by the edge of the barn, watching Wade.

Wade swallows heavily. "Hey, girl."

The dog cocks its head.

Gripping his knife, Wade gets to his feet. He whistles.

The dog lopes a few yards toward the house, then sits.

It's a crippled thing, Wade sees. "Here, girl," he calls, and takes a step in the dog's direction.

It darts away into the long meadow grass. After a dozen or so yards, it stops and turns, tail switching.

"You want to play? Sure. Let's play." Wade goes after it, ducking through the barbwire fence.

Again, the dog runs. Slides beneath the front of the Winnebago.

Wade approaches the RV slowly, cautiously. Bats swoop out of a twilight sky, and he can just make out the shapes of the shed, the old chair beneath it, the stove. Near the front bumper, he gets down on hands and knees and makes kissing noises. He can't see it, but something scrabbles in the shadows. The dog. Huddling behind the front left tire of the Winnebago.

"Come on now."

Knife in hand, he walks around the driver's side of the RV, then drops down behind the tire and reaches for the dog, but the dog scrabbles away, lopes to a back tire and hunkers there.

"Son of a bitch."

Max always wanted a dog. Had begged for one, years back, but Wade shut that shit down right quick. Dogs are dirty, smelly mouths to throw money in. It figures, Nellie would have gotten the kid a mutt, right off the bat. *We'll see about that, Sneaky*

Nellie. We'll see. He puts his knife away in its scabbard on his hip and moves through the grass, inching as far beneath the chassis of the Winnie as he can. He talks sweetly to the dog, coaxes it. Tells it how pretty it is. Then he reaches into his shirt pocket and takes out a square of half-melted chocolate, the last of a Hershey's bar he'd bought on the road that day.

He waves it at the dog, and the dog's ears prick up.

It crawls on its belly toward him.

"That's it, that-a-girl."

The dog stretches its neck, licks at the chocolate in Wade's hand—

. . . wade . . .

He starts and jumps up, bangs his head on the bottom of the Winnebago hard enough to see stars. "Goddamn it!"

The dog is gone.

. . . wade . . .

A voice, over his shoulder.

"Who's that?" he calls, on his belly.

But he knows. Of course he knows. He'd recognize that Baptist, brimstone baritone anywhere. It was the voice of his father. Stern, harsh. Unforgiving, like the time he caught Wade doing those things to the kittens and steered him down the aisle of the empty church, forced him onto his knees to pray—

(you ask forgiveness for the terrible thing you did)

—and suddenly he's back there, beneath that narrow wooden bridge down by the river, when he was twelve, where he found the cardboard box of kittens mewling, one already stiff and dead, the others sightless. Abandoned. He takes the first kitten from the box and holds it under the water, feeling it thrash weakly, and he's weak, too, a weak and terrible boy, he knows it, because no boy should ever be so weak as to hurt things small and helpless—

Something growls behind him. He tries to turn, to see, but he can't, he's still on his belly beneath the RV and the space is too small. He can't maneuver. "Get!" he cries, and kicks, but the growling only turns into snarling, barking, and now the dog's teeth sink into his right ankle and it feels like razors slitting skin, and Wade has no time to register the pain, because suddenly he's yanked, hard, from beneath the RV. Instinct kicks in, and he claws at the earth, but he's yanked a second time into the deep johnsongrass in back of the Winnie, and now he's screaming, as whatever has him has clamped onto both legs, wrapped him, and dozens of tiny razor blades are slicing through his jeans, into his legs. Nipping at him, biting deeper. He twists and writhes and turns to see it, even as its grip eases.

A dog that is not a dog rears over him, its muzzle a long black eel—

His knife. In its scabbard.

He fumbles for it, manages to unsheathe it, even as the dog-thing falls upon him and long, rough tentacles unfurl from its belly, each bristling with a thousand tiny legs that sprout tiny teeth spinning like circular saws. Something slithers up his leg, tearing open the fabric of his jeans, just below his crotch to wriggle wetly into his pants. Wade Gardner opens his mouth to scream, but a tendril thick and fat plunges down his throat. He convulses in the grass. Tastes blood, dirt.

Then pain.

Black becoming red. Red becoming white.

White flaring into stars that dim and die.

1932

✦

OCTOBER 3

EARLY MORNING. DEWY WEBS BETWEEN THE LONG GRASS STALKS. The cabins in the meadow, deserted, boards overgrown with lichen. No smoke rises, the chimneys all crumbling and clogged with wasps. Gone are the pigs, the goats, the chickens. Gone are Daniel Two Fists and his bees. The life left here now is wild and rambling, forgotten.

A lone Ford Model A stutters through its gears up Camp Road. Jamming, grinding, lurching to a stop where the rough gravel thins out into the meadow. Behind the wheel a boy, fourteen, a head of chestnut hair and freckles and a frame that seems to hold more gristle than meat. In the passenger seat, August Redfern, not yet forty-two and already graying at the temples, the yoke of tragedy and grief and violence heavy across his shoulders. "That's one way to stop," he says, and reaches a dented metal flask from the crack of the seat. He drinks.

"I can do better," the boy says, spindly hands on the spindly wheel.

"Couldn't we all," is Redfern's answer, spoken through the passenger window, to the river. "How is it that a man can wither in a season, but a river will not change its course in a lifetime."

"P-P-Papa?"

Redfern looks back at his son, eyes misted. He smiles, holds out the flask.

Hank surprises himself by taking it, drinking. The whiskey goes down hard, leaves him coughing and spitting. But there's a fire, too, in his belly, a kind of reassurance, where before there was not.

"You're leaving soon," Redfern says, taking back his flask.

How does he know? Hank looks away quickly, to the empty meadow, the deserted cabins. The grassy knoll where his mother's old cemetery holds a scant five, six unmarked graves.

"It's okay. I won't stop you. I'm just sorry it's come to it."

Hank puts his hands in his lap, intertwines them. Spreads his fingers on his thighs. "She's mean to you. And to Aggie."

"Well. Your sister's willful. Like you."

"She's mean to all of us."

"She's kept this place going, I reckon."

"Kept it going? Look out there, Papa. She made it a g-g-graveyard."

"Times are hard. They'll be just as hard on the road. You know that, don't you?"

"We ain't n-n-never known n-n-nothing but"—Hank freezes on the word, then pushes it out with all his breath—"hardscrabble."

"When you go, go in the night. While your mother's sleeping."

"Why don't we go t-t-together? Y-you and me and Aggie?"

Redfern takes another drink, a long one. He thinks of his wife, whispering to herself in the library at her desk, poring over account ledgers and balance sheets and stock reports. The old bond between them of blood and earth, hard and fixed as red

Georgia clay. "I can't." Then: "You'll come with me, later today, to the prison? One last time, before you go?"

Once a year, at the start of the season, Redfern drives into town to negotiate the new contract at the prison, Euphemia's grand vision to hire out the harvest to chain gangs, as the turpentine farms down in Florida do. Keep the groves bleeding. But Redfern's not a slaver. He says as much, when they argue. Which is often. He talks of dignity and what they've forgotten. How the trees will all be dead. How there's hardly money to put food on the table, let alone pay the state. Euphemia, meanwhile, keeps selling things off to keep cash in their accounts. Timberland first, pulpwood the only thing that's thriving now. This old Model A is the last of Redfern's fleet. But what's next? When the land is bare and the money's all spent? Is it the noose for Redfern, a shotgun in the mouth? Or will she save him the trouble and slit his throat in his sleep, drop his body, at last, into that dark, toothy hole, to change the course of their fortunes once more?

Or will it be one of the children? Henry, the boy she never loved? Agatha, the child they conceived that red night of horror, almost a decade ago now?

The boy nods. He'll ride out with his old man, one last time.

Redfern feels a sudden wellspring of gratitude for this broken, awkward boy. The son who lived. The son he never truly loved as he should have, always comparing him to the boy he imagined Charlie would have been. *Life is so goddamned unfair, and how we make it so.*

"Something else." Redfern reaches beneath the creaky seat. He takes out a red rag and unfolds it, revealing the Colt .45 he took from Ennis Hawley. The gun he murdered Curt Barlow with, put away these long years, kept oiled and ready for lean times such as these. Times when sacrifices need to be made. When all their good luck is spent. Redfern grips it, slips his finger into the trigger guard. He looks at his son, then flips the gun and grips it barrel first and hands it across the seat.

Hank takes it with both hands, cradles it.

"I want you to take this with you."

Questions behind the boy's eyes.

"I'll teach you to use it."

They get out and walk into the meadow, stand against a backdrop of dilapidated cabins. Redfern takes his flask from his pocket, drains it. Walks it over to the last of the great pine stumps that once studded the clearing. The wood is rotten, beetle eaten. He sets the flask on the flat edge of the stump. Walks back to his son and touches the boy's shoulder, and Hank stands there, looking out from beneath a shelf of brown hair, a boy on the verge of something better, or something worse, his future undecided. *Pray God, it will not be decided by this place.* Redfern takes his son's hand and lifts his arm and sights the flask. Talking him through the first gentle squeeze of the trigger. "Two, three pounds of pressure, that's all it takes—"

The crack is loud, though it fades quickly, absorbed by the watchful woods.

"Even if you won't go," Hank says when they're back in the truck, both doors shut, smells of sweat and cordite heavy between them, "I'll take Aggie with me."

Redfern goes still, his gaze drifting out to the river. Picturing it, perhaps, packing them both off. Send them floating in a little boat, mayhap, like babes in one of Agatha's fairy tales, beneath the bright, starry eyes of a midnight sky. Little sister, big brother protector. Their bark spinning like an autumn leaf in the whorls and currents, until at last it noses up beneath a willow, and out they climb through the bulrushes, onto a bank of breadlines, where they'll take their place among the sad, shuffling husks of those left behind, cut loose. Surrounded by murderers and criminals who would have at them, even as their mother pursued them, Ahab-like, to the ends of the earth. Or forced him to. He is, after all, her prisoner, too, now.

"No." The word is so flat, so empty, so final, there is no good answer to the boy's why-not. Redfern only says, "The world will do its damnedest to chew you up and spit you out. You take her, it'll do it even quicker. To both of you. Alone, you've got a chance."

"And here, what chance does she have?"

A question like a bullet, fired into Redfern's chest. His eyes water. Threaten to spill with the guilt he has carried in his heart since the girl was born, knowing her eventual fate, her mother's dark plan. Another body to drop in the ground, here at Redfern Hill.

"I'll look out for her," Redfern lies, a tremor in his voice.

Hank's eyes dart up to catch his father's. An old mistrust between second born and his father: too much liquor, not enough love, the weary piling on of secrets and defeat.

"Now"—Redfern nods at the dash—"do you remember how to start her?"

Hank nods.

"Then get to it, son. We've got a day ahead of us."

The sun is shining and the sky is piled with October cotton as Agatha Redfern thumps out the screen door, wire basket in hand, to gather eggs in the coop behind the barn. In a hidden pocket of her dress, she carries a stick of peppermint, the last of a store she's kept since Christmas, when things were a little better than they are now. Hank's Christmas Eve birthday: the last time she remembers a smile on Mama's face, before her black moods fell permanently over the house, before Papa's distillery went cold at the end of summer. Barely enough turpentine to fill a hundred barrels.

Hank says whatever heartwood runs through Mama was once rich and grained, but it's been hollowed out, eaten away. He says she'd be strong if she weren't so tired, so full of rage. Railing, then drifting days without a word for anyone. Depressions black as the long, sunless days of the Arctic. Sometimes, Mama goes into the cellar and shuts the door and talks to little Charlie in the dark. Agatha never knew little Charlie, but she knows he was Hank's twin, and if he was Hank's twin, that means Charlie was every bit as good as Hank. *Imagine it, Dog*, she sometimes says, *two Hanks instead of one. Imagine that.*

Today, Dog crawls out from beneath the shade of the porch and trots behind her. They round the barn, Agatha dancing ahead of the mutt's tongue at her fingers. The sun is warm on her cheeks and she's happy, which is not every day, but it's good when she is. She played Mozart on the piano last night after supper, and the music seemed to make everyone sleepy, Mama in her chair by the fireplace, Papa and Hank on the old blue sofa. Sleepy is a good thing, because when Mama and Papa are sleepy, they aren't fighting, and lately they fight a lot. It's a funny thing to Agatha, being a child, subject to the moon-tide pulls and pushes of grown-ups. If she thinks about it hard enough, it makes her mad, makes her want to slam all her fingers down on the piano keys until they break and the wire strings in the piano snap and there is no more music to be made.

At the peg-locked gate of the chicken pen, she draws up short.

"Back, Dog." She shoves at the mutt's stubborn, dumb head.

Inside the pen, the two-tiered coop built against the back of the barn is empty.

Eight hens huddle in a faraway corner, still and silent. White leghorns and Plymouth Rocks, beady eyes wide, heads erect. Agatha slips the peg and pushes Dog away. She goes gingerly to the cluster of birds and kneels down to stroke the back of a hen. No movement, save a twitch of the head. Even the roosters seem stunned, like birds that have struck glass midflight. She reaches gently beneath a hen, finds an egg. Blue speckled. Beneath another, and another. They've all laid, away from their nesting boxes.

She remembers last fall, when it seemed the chickens were refusing to lay. No eggs to be found, day after day. Stubborn, stupid creatures. That's what Mama said, but Agatha, who turned the hens out to range in the evenings, suspected different. She went looking, found a cache of eggs beneath a stand of blackberry bushes at the edge of the woods. After that, she cleaned out their boxes, asked Papa for fresh pine shavings to replace their moldy hay, and sure as shooting, the hens began to lay again. Not stupid animals, just finicky. They like it the way they like it.

So she checks the coop. Feels among the boxes. Finds no eggs in the shavings.

Then, in a corner box, she sees it: a chicken lies dead on its nest.

Agatha stares, frozen between revulsion and fascination.

Its beak has been forced open, and down that broken gullet twists a black vine that corkscrews up from the ground beneath the coop. Agatha sets her basket down and hunkers close. She runs a small finger along the vine. It stirs, like a sleeping cat disturbed, and the hen's body jerks as the vine pulls away, disappears quietly into the earth.

Outside the pen, Dog whines.

A voice, suddenly in Agatha's head. High and bright, the singsong voice of a child. Boy or girl, she can't tell, but the word it calls out is bold and eager.

. . . *agatha* . . .

An invitation. To play.

Dog's ears prick up. She barks.

"Hello?" Agatha says to the air.

No answer but the wind, the soft cluck of nervous hens behind her, so she bends down and reaches slowly beneath the chicken's carcass. Her fingers close around the warm shape of an egg. She draws it out. It's a color she's never seen an egg before, an impossible crimson, the color of a sunset sky. Speckled pink. She sets her basket aside and reaches into her hidden pocket, brushing aside the peppermint stick for a small box of kitchen matches. She strikes one, holds it up behind the egg. No cracks, no meat spots. Just the silhouette of a strange, burled thing. Spiny, like a spider's egg sack, and pulsing like a tiny heart.

Like her own. Small and fragile.

Up at the house, the front door opens and Mama walks out, dressed in a loose-fitting cotton shirt. The wind blows through it and makes it look like a sail. "Agatha?" she calls. "Stop woolgathering and start egg gathering!"

"Yes, Mama!"

Carefully, so carefully, she wraps the crimson egg in a handful of straw from the bottom of her wire basket, then tucks the bundle into her secret pocket.

Outside the pen, Dog is going crazy.

"Agatha!"

"Coming, Mama!"

She gathers the rest of the eggs quickly. Later, she'll fetch the shovel from the barn to bury the hen near the edge of the woods.

Papa and Hank come rattling back up the road in the Model A shortly after three o'clock, the light getting golden, the shadows getting long. Hank finds Agatha in the browning grass of the meadow, playing with her doll. Her face flushed with the sun.

"Are you hiding again?"

She shakes her head.

"Where's Dog?" Hank looks around.

"Chasing rabbits way over yonder. Poor rabbits."

"Poor Dog. She'll never catch one."

"Don't say mean things about Dog. She can't help the way she is."

Hank looks over his shoulder, back up to the house, like he's checking to see if Mama's watching. Then he drops down beside his sister, on his knees. "Look here." From the waist of his jeans, he takes out a folded red rag and in the rag is a gun. "Papa gave it to me. It's for when I l-l-leave in a few days."

Agatha says nothing, just walks her rag doll in circles in the grass. She knows what Hank means because Hank whispered his plans through the crack of the locked door between their rooms one night, a while back, as they lay belly down on the floor, deprived of supper, stomachs rumbling. Mama downstairs tearing books from shelves and hurling them across the library, cussing the banks, Papa shut away with his maps, lost in the crinkle of old paper. Neither brother nor sister able to sleep for hunger or fear, and that odd scrabbling in the walls. They've heard it a lot lately, in all the rooms, especially when Mama's upset, and Agatha can't help wondering if something is growing in there.

It's just mice, Hanks tells her.

Why do you want to run away, Hank?

Because.

Because why?

Because there's no l-l-love here. Don't you feel it?

But where will you go? How will you eat?

I'll get by. Maybe I'll go to Savannah.

Papa says Savannah's full of bad folks.

Everywhere is b-b-bad folks. We got bad folks right here.

I'm scared, Hank.

Don't be scared. Maybe I'll join the m-m-merchant marines. Or the French Foreign Legion.

What happens to me when you go?

What do you mean, what happens to you?

There won't be anyone to stop her.

Shamefully he admits, *I don't always stop her.*

But you try.

One day, she starts in on me, I'm g-g-gonna g-g-grab that s-s-strap and hit back with it, and that'll be the end of me.

I hate Mama.

Hate's a b-b-big word for a little kid.

I hate her, and I just know I'm going to hate her even more when you go, so you better not go, Hank Redfern, you better not go!

Behind them, Dog pushes through the grass and nuzzles Hank's arm. She's been in the creek and reeks of bog water. He shoves her away, says, "Get," and folds the gun back into the rag and tucks it away, in the band of his trousers.

Agatha pouts. Picks at a thread on her doll's dress.

Hank scoots next to her. "I love you, b-b-baby sister."

"Don't call me a baby. Papa and Mama fight every night. They'll fight all day, too, when you leave."

"It's always w-w-worse when the new season starts. You know that."

"Take me with you, Hank. Please."

"P-P-Papa says I can't. He says the world's on the brink of starvation. At least here, you got food. How am I supposed to provide for you, out there?"

"It's not safe here. I have bad dreams and the bad dreams are always about Mama. I'm afraid if you leave me here, alone, something awful might happen."

"You'd starve to death out there. Or worse."

"Most days, I'm hungry here, ain't you?"

He lifts his shirt, thumps his flat belly. "Ripe as a m-m-melon, I am."

He laughs.

Right then, it's on the tip of her tongue to tell him about the egg she's carried in her pocket all day, about the hen she buried beneath the blackberry bushes. To tell him about the voice in her head. How it was like her own, a child's voice, playful and friendly. But a big cloud passes and its shadow rolls over them, and she figures he won't believe her, he'll laugh at her. Call her a liar and run away even sooner to some place where little sisters don't matter because they're all just whipped and helpless. So she keeps her secret, even as the warmth of the sun fades from her cheeks, and Hank peers up at the huge, slow-moving cloud, and she hears:

. . . *agatha* . . .

Like the shade above, it soothes, cools.

Hank gets up to head back. Before he goes, he tells her not to be late for dinner. "And remember: wash up. Mama won't like it if your hands are dirty."

Agatha watches him go. Gingerly, she takes the egg from her pocket. She lights another match and holds up the flame and looks through the shell at the small, pulsing life inside. The spiny blob is bigger than before. Size of a penny now. She peers closer, into a red map work of veins. So intent upon it that she doesn't notice the match, burning low, until it singes her fingertip.

She drops the match.

And her other hand closes, crunching the egg.

A reflex, but instantly her heart wells up with guilt.

The yolk—along with whatever grows at the center of it—bursts. And the color that spurts out is shocking, black as tar. Albumen drips through her fingers, weird and pink. Caught up in it, flecks the color of turquoise.

Dog is at her fingers before Agatha thinks to stop her, licking, lapping, swallowing.

"No, stupid Dog, no!"

Agatha pushes the dumb mutt away, but Dog only comes back for more.

She flings her hand into the grass, rubs it in the dirt.

Out of the west, October conjures up the long autumn dark.

1989

✦

JULY 9

STILL, THE DREAM. THIS NEW AND TERRIBLE WORLD OF
Nellie's making. Here, the phone is ringing in the foyer of Redfern
Hill. She's in jeans, her painter's shirt. Hair up in a red rag.
Converse high-tops. Her hand trembles over the receiver. On the
fourth ring, she picks it up, expecting Wade. But there is no voice
on the line. Only a man's heavy breathing. "Lonnie?"

"Get ready to pay the piper, cunt," Baxter says. And the line
goes dead.

Behind her, Max speaks: "Where were you, that day?"

He sits on the stairs, fourth riser up. Elbows on his knees. His
legs are saplings, bare toes rooted to the floor. Ringed bark where
his tube socks end, just below his knees. His fingers hang like
twigs. His skin is pale, his eyes are yellow. *Like the backyard in
Conway*, Nellie thinks. The swing set there. How he used to wait
out the screaming. All he lacks, a book to distract him—

"Where were you when Dad hurt me?"

"I went to see a lawyer. I told—" But she doesn't want to say
your dad. It makes her gorge rise. "I told Wade I was going to
look for a job, but that wasn't true."

"I dream about that day." Max's voice is dead, flat. "Dad

said he wanted me to be tough. It was after Leon Miller, at recess. Do you remember that."

She nods.

He cocks his head, and the pose is animalistic, horrible. Those yellow eyes. "What were you seeing a lawyer for?"

Her throat is dry. "You know what."

"You should say it. Say it, you selfish bitch."

"Don't talk to me like that, Max."

"I'm sorry, Mom."

The apology comes automatically, a kind of empty reflex. As if some other mind were indexing the appropriate response and spitting it out. For the first time, Nellie notices that the stairwell's banisters are made of rope.

"What did your grandfather think of your bridge?" she asks brightly. A tremor in her voice. "Did you tell him about it?"

"Please don't change the subject. Bitch."

This is not your son. This is not your son. This is not your son.

She stammers out the rest. "When I came home that day and you were gone, I was afraid. I was afraid your . . . Wade . . . knew where I'd been, that he'd taken you away, to hurt me. Then the phone rang."

And, of course, the phone on the little table by the front door rings.

She picks it up. "Hello?"

The boy-thing watches her from the stairs.

"It's me," Wade says. "I'm at the hospital. Kid had an accident."

Nellie covers the receiver with her hand and says to the thing that is not Max, "I knew he was lying. I knew instantly. And I should have taken you straightaway and left, that very day. I'm sorry I didn't. I don't know why I waited."

"We're coming home as soon as we can . . . Nellie? Hello?"

"Sometimes I think we'd still be there, if it wasn't for this place." She lets the receiver drop back into the cradle, cutting Wade off midsentence. "Listen, I'll see you—"

"Soon." The boy-thing grins. He darts from the stairs, tearing up wood and carpet as he goes.

Nellie follows him to the long gullet of the cellar stairs, where the door hangs open and a brilliant blue light plays over her like the sun through seawater. She takes a deep breath and plunges in.

Max wakes in the house on Elm, on his pallet of quilts at Nellie's bedside. He gets up off the floor, sees her in the same unmoving position, and goes off down the hall to pee. He goes to the kitchen to get a drink of water and finds Mr. Hank staring out the window over the sink, eyes vacant, like there's nothing out there to see. The Ranger is parked along the curb, in front of the house where the wrecker left it. Mr. Hank has an empty glass in hand. On the kitchen counter, there's a bottle, tall and slim and full of whiskey. The seal is not yet broken.

Mr. Hank turns, like he's startled, eyes big and wet.

"I needed a drink," Max says.

"You needed . . ." Hank looks down at the glass in his hands.

"Water."

Slowly, Mr. Hank turns on the tap and runs water in the glass he's holding. When it's full, he hands it to Max, and Max drinks it down in three long gulps. "That's good water."

"Soft water." His grandfather blinks at Max for a second, and Max gets the weird feeling the old man is somehow grateful to him. But it doesn't strike him what for.

In the musty, oil-smelling garage. Back wall lined with homemade wire bins, each heaped with aluminum beer and soda cans. A plywood workbench, bolted into the studs. Mr. Hank clicks on a cobwebbed lamp and shoves aside a litter of screws and washers and bug turds. From under the bench, he hauls out a heavy cardboard box. Inside are pocket watches, wristwatches, even an old mantel clock buried in the bottom. Some are clearly broken, faces smashed, bands missing. Others have simply wound down, their gears exhausted. All silent, all stopped.

"Pick one," Mr. Hank tells Max.

Max, who's never owned a watch, reaches into the box and sifts through them.

"Gotta have a watch. Else time gets away from you."

"They're all busted," Max says.

"Maybe we can fix it."

"Where'd these come from?"

"My old store."

Max settles on a pocket watch made of brass, the casing etched with the image of a winged horse. "It's Pegasus."

Mr. Hank takes it and holds it, turns it in his thick-knuckled hands. He sets the watch on the workbench. From the far end of the bench, he pulls over a wooden box that opens onto a series of tiered wooden trays. Each tray holds an assortment of odd tools Max has never seen before—silver picks and tiny screwdrivers, tweezers and weird, specialty pliers. It all smells vaguely of oil. Mr. Hank trains the light close to the watch and sets a tiny glass piece into his eye, then pops open the casing. He rummages amid a handful of dead watches and opens these, too. His hands, dry and chapped and wrinkled with age, move deftly, as he lifts tiny gears from the guts of the watches with his long, jagged nails.

Max's attention strays to the rest of the garage. Eyes wandering, he sees an old bicycle hanging on the wall by its spokes. A spindly, copper-colored Schwinn. With a girl's angled bar.

"Was that Mom's?"

Mr. Hank grunts. Snaps the pocket watch shut and winds it. Presses it to his ear.

"Is it working?"

"Not yet."

He opens the watch and shucks its casing like an oyster. Keeps at it.

Max edges closer, so that his shoulder is almost touching the old man's arm.

"Shit." Mr. Hank looks around at his tools, leans forward to rummage in his trays. "Where's that goddamn oil?" he mutters, then gets up and walks off, out the open garage door.

Max hears the kitchen door slap shut.

Alone in the garage, he picks up the Pegasus watch and presses it to his ear. Hears nothing but the heavy silence of time standing still. He sets it back on the table and hunkers down and drags the cardboard box of watches out into the light. Sifts through the old tarnished timepieces, lets their chains fall through his fingers. There's a ticking, somewhere in the box, and he starts digging for it, taking out watches and stacking them on the concrete floor.

That's when he sees it: something that is not a watch, buried among the dead timepieces. Something long and slender and made of iron. He pulls it out and blows the rust and dust from it. It's a key. A long black key.

Mr. Hank walks in through the open garage door, tiny oilcan in hand. He freezes when he sees Max hunkered there, holding the key. Mr. Hank starts to turn back to the house, then to the garage, like he's a compass without a pole, like he can't point true. His eyes fix on the key, then on Max, and slowly, without a word, he sets the oil on the workbench and takes the key and puts it back in the box. Max backs away as Mr. Hank slides the box back under the bench.

"I'm sorry," Max tries, "I was just—"

But in truth, he doesn't know what to say.

His grandfather switches off the lamp and disappears through the open garage door, and Max is left alone.

Wade Gardner, in the ashes of his chrysalis, the dry remnants of his becoming.

Daylight, filmy and dim among the trees.

He wakes, half his face crawling with ants. The Winnebago just visible, some fifty, sixty yards away. He pushes up weakly and sits back against a pine, brushes absently at his cheek and neck. His throat is swollen and raw and hurts when he swallows. His skin hangs cold and sallow from his frame. On the ground where he's lain are the broken pieces of a papery husk. Like a wasp's nest in texture, they crumble to powder between his fingers.

. . . wade . . .

Daddy's voice, again, from everywhere and nowhere.

He opens his mouth to answer, but he has no breath, no voice.

A sensation passes through him, like ropes yanked taught. He herks and jerks, is dragged upright out of the long green grass like a marionette. His heart should be racing, but he can't feel it, can't feel a heart beating in his chest. Can't sense the ground beneath his feet, or the sunlight upon his skin. Nothing at all feels connected to him anymore. No control, no control, a prisoner in his own skull, a madman leaping at the bars of his own mind—

(Wade Wade Wade I'm Wade I'm Wade I'm)

. . . wade . . .

Gentle, persistent, like the lapping of waves against the hull of a boat. Given time, that voice will wear away all things.

Silence.

. . . see the man's body . . . the man's hands . . .

The right hand moves to the empty scabbard on the dead man's hip.

Immediately, it knows where the lost blade is, the knowledge having traveled from one node of itself to another, so it turns and sees the blade being lifted up by roots that sway and coil, and the thing inhabiting the shell of Wade Gardner smiles as it plucks the blade from just one of its many long and searching hands and holds it in the man's.

I have to open that cellar door, Max thinks. *There's something terrible behind it, and I have to fix it. If I can fix it, then Mom will wake up. Because that's how we take care of each other.* It's like in the fairy tales. A maiden under a spell, a prince riding out to slay a dragon. But this is no fairy-tale monster; he remembers the bear, the bunny, that awful wriggling root-thing. Whatever the monster is, it's very, very real.

Standing in the open garage door, he stares at the Ranger, parked in the drive. No, it's no good. After that long, horrible mile of grinding gears in the dark? In daylight, a cop would stop him for sure. Or he'd wreck it.

His eyes wander around the garage, land on the bike that hangs on the nail. Nellie's old Schwinn. The one she'd ridden out to Redfern Hill, all those years ago.

The tires will be flat. It's been hanging there longer than you've been alive.

But when he reaches out and squeezes the rear tire, it's solid. The front, too. *Mr. Hank must keep it up*, he figures. After all, an old man who's a recovering alcoholic? He'd need a bicycle in good working order, wouldn't he? No matter how many cop-friendly bumper stickers you plaster on your pickup. Not a nice thought, but it's the truth.

Max lifts the bike down from the nail—it's heavier than it looks—and sets it roughly on the concrete. Rolls it outside. He stuffs the black iron key in the pocket of his sweatpants and climbs onto the bike. He's never ridden an adult's bike, only his BMX back in Conway. Grass growing up around it now, no doubt, where they'd forgotten it in the backyard.

The Schwinn wobbles, but Max manages to steady himself pretty quickly, and after a circle or two in the driveway, he pedals out into the street. He stops at the Ranger and opens the door and takes out the ax, still on the floorboard. He lays it across the handlebars, but the balance is off, he can't turn, so he dismounts and goes into the garage and comes back out minutes later with a three-foot extension cord, which he uses to lash the ax to the seat tube. Then he swings the bike around and rides fast and hard for Redfern Hill.

In a rocking chair on the back porch, Lonnie jolts awake from a nightmare in which Todd is a child again, able to walk, to speak, to reason. Lonnie's teaching him to ride a bike, one hand on the seat as the boy struggles along through a meadow, and soon enough the meadow slopes down to a wide sideways mouth and the bike begins to wobble as the mouth opens and there are teeth and tendrils and the boy begins to cry, as Lonnie pushes him faster and faster toward those gnashing blades, and Todd begins to frantically thumb the bell on the bicycle and cry out for his mother, only his words are inarticulate shrieks—

Inside the house, the phone is ringing.

Lonnie sits up too quickly and pain lances his head. Sweating through his T-shirt, he leans forward in his chair and listens for Linda to pick up the call. Bob Barker's chattering in the living room; *The Price Is Right* is Linda's only hour of must-see TV, so she ought to be around, but the phone doesn't stop, so he struggles up stiffly to get it himself. In the panes of the French doors that open onto the back porch, Lonnie catches a glimpse of his face. He looks like a mummy. Nose in a splint. Hair shaved, eleven stitches in his scalp. Wrappings all over.

Perfect end to a perfect week.

That's what he said at the emergency room last night, all smiles with the nurse. "Fell down the stairs with a tumbler of bourbon. Perfect end to a perfect week." She called him a poor thing, asked how on earth he'd managed to drive himself all the way there. To which Lonnie answered, "Well, darling, I just got behind the wheel and turned the key. The rest was like riding a bike." Later, when everything was sewn up, he called Linda to come get him. She cried when she saw him. "Oh, boo-fucking-hoo," he growled. "Just get me home and put a Bloody Mary in my hand and then leave me the shit alone. I gotta make some calls."

And make some calls he did.

The first was to Tommy Stallknocker, sheriff of Baxter County. A man whose gut was easily the size of a no. 10 washtub, which is how big a washtub you'd need to float all the cash Lonnie'd thrown that sumbitch's way, last election. "Tommy boy, I got a problem. Of the no-questions-asked variety."

Whereupon the good sheriff, to his credit, had shut up and listened while Lonnie talked.

The second call was to Jim Meadows, and by then Lonnie was so goddamned drunk and high on painkillers he can't be sure what all he said, except the part where he threatened to walk Jim Meadows into the woods and cut his dick off and drop it down a dark hole with teeth, whether the land said hole was on was Lonnie's or not. To which Meadows, Lonnie's pretty sure, simply said, "Lonnie, I don't think I can represent you anymore in legal matters," and then hung up.

Lonnie steps through the door into the house and snags the kitchen phone.

"Baxter residence, go for Lonnie."

"Lonnie, this is Tommy Stallknocker. How you holding up?"

"Not too bad, I guess, for a man got rolled on the day of his daddy's funeral."

A pause. "It's one sorry state of affairs, ain't it."

"What's the word on our private APB?"

"Listen, I put two of my best on it, like you asked. One out at Redfern Hill, the other at the motel. They never saw hide nor hair of a red Mazda. That boy you said broke in on you, he must have took that money and run."

"He's still around. I know that for a fact. You keep on it, and when you find him, you throw his ass in a cell and you call me, because I want to come down there and put a boot print on his jaw."

Pause. "Um, Lonnie, look, I can't divert men for this without it being official business, so, if you want to come down, file a report—"

"You want to shame me, Tommy? You want to drag me through the mud one day after I buried my daddy? Do you know he was shitting his pants in the end?" Here, Lonnie's voice breaks, and the words pour out like water from a burst dam. "I mean, Jesus Christ, Tommy, he didn't even know who I was, and all I wanted to do was make it clear I was the strong one, me, the one who stayed, and you're telling me you're gonna let some hoodlum break in on me when I'm bereaved and whip me like a dog and you want to talk to me about the books?"

"Lonnie, there are procedures—"

"You know, I get this shit right and left these days. You, Meadows, y'all motherfuckers forgot who this county's named after!"

One last pause. "Your great-uncle, if memory serves."

Lonnie's grip on the phone draws all the blood left in his body straight to his hand, which burns like a red-hot coal. "Fuck you, you fat, fucking, glorified garbage collector!"

But the line is dead.

Lonnie slams the phone into the cradle, then grabs his wrapped head, as another pain blazes through it like a meteor. He kicks open the French doors and goes to the tiny table by his rocking chair, where Lonnie's Little Helpers yammer for attention from their little brown bottle. He snatches the bottle, pops one, then another, and starts chewing. Then he looks out at the garage. His mouth falls open, crushed pills dropping out like crumbs.

Parked in his driveway, on the gray stone gravel, is a red Mazda.

The rest of the house is dark, all lights extinguished. The dining room, the kitchen, both deserted. It's the Showcase Showdown in the living room, but no one's around to watch it.

"Linda?" he calls out.

Buoyed by a cloud of painkillers and booze, Lonnie wields a heavy pewter object from his home office: the key to the city of Empire. He holds it two-handed like a hammer, cocked and locked and ready to rock. At the bottom of the stairs, he hollers up for his wife.

No answer comes back.

He takes the carpeted stairs slowly.

"Todd?"

He pushes open his son's bedroom door.

The boy sits in his chair, forehead pushed into the heel of his hand. He sits turned away from the bedroom window, a posture that means something has upset him, that he isn't happy. Todd gives a low whimper, a whine, then lets fly a bleat that pierces Lonnie's eardrums.

"Jesus, kid, what's—"

Turning now, to the rocking chair. Where Linda sits, in her pink polyester-cotton-blend tracksuit. Both wrists taped to the chair arms with silver tape, head thrown back like she's laughing with delight. A bib of blood drying down the front of her jacket. Throat slit.

Lonnie speaks her name as he steps toward her. He takes her shoulders in hand, shakes her hard enough to send her head dropping forward onto her chest. "Linda, get up. Come on, Linda, get up!" He kneels in front of the chair. Moves his hands over her arms, the tape binding her wrists. "Oh, Linda." He puts his face in her lap and moans.

Over by the window, Todd begins to hum, a snatch of made-up song.

Outside, in the hallway, a light comes on in the bathroom. Lonnie lifts his head and stares through the open door. The faucet belches air, retches water.

A sound begins, deep inside him, a rumble that becomes a spitting roar.

Lonnie rushes into the hallway and through the open bathroom door, swinging the key.

No one.

The sink is plugged and water is spilling over onto the lavatory. The shower curtain is drawn back, no one there. So he shuts off the water. And listens.

Firm grip on his key, he steps back into the hallway.

Something slides into his gut.

Thanks to the painkillers, he hears it more than feels it, a pop and squish.

He looks down and sees the steel haft of a hunting knife and three inches of blade protruding from his stomach. A hand attached to it, and the hand is attached to an arm, the arm to a shoulder, and above the shoulder a head that belongs to Wade Gardner—or a far-out, fucked-up nightmare that might once have been Wade Gardner.

Lonnie's eyes grow wide at the bizarre, chevron-shaped head before him, twin horns of bark where the ears once were, eyes flashing golden, blue, golden, blue. Things wriggle beneath the surface of his skin, black veins bulging. "Hello, Lonnie," the Gardner-thing says. One hand on the knife, the other reaches up and grips the back of Lonnie's head, as if to kiss him. Only he—

(it)

—swings Lonnie around to the head of the stairs, as if they were dancing.

A muffled thump as the key to the city of Empire drops to the carpet.

Lonnie's arms and legs are tingling, his vision clouding. Taste of blood—

The Gardner-thing opens its mouth and Lonnie sees into its throat and something is there, the head of a thing that rears and flashes shards of teeth that spin, and Lonnie understands, suddenly, that his birthright has come to call.

"Lonnie fucking Baxter," the Gardner-thing snarls, black ichor leaking from its nose. "Always taking more than you give, always asking more. More money, more land, more blood. This is not a servant's heart, you sad, greedy fuck-stick!"

The knife turns. It turns on every word that follows, opening Lonnie's belly wide.

"You. Are. Not. Worthy!"

Then the blade leaves his gut and he's falling, pitching backward down the stairs, down the long carpeted stairs of Frankenstein's mansion, and along the way he has a vision of how it all should have ended, after the land passed to him, and Linda and Todd were hurled by his own hands down into that hungry black pit. Lonnie stands in a three-piece suit beneath the sun-spangled dome of the state capitol, and there is no one else but Lonnie, the world is Lonnie, and he is old and happy and sonless. All he ever wanted to be, and this is the simple, fleeting vision he has, before he rocks up against the wainscoting at the bottom of the stairs and slumps there, a long smear of blood on the pale-yellow wall behind him.

Upstairs, poor Todd Baxter lets rip one last peal of anguish.

Max sticks to side streets as long as he can, until finally he's forced onto the narrow shoulder of the main road out of town. He passes a Dairy Queen, a laundromat, a furniture store, then veers onto the two-lane blacktop that runs west. Here, cars shoot past like bullets and the shoulder is rough and broken. The old Schwinn's tires bleed air. He's forced to walk the last half mile beside open pastureland, the blacktop burning through the thin soles of his moccasin slippers. A big rig rockets by as he crosses the river bridge, shaking the ground beneath him. By the time he reaches the turnout to Redfern Hill—the gate he and his mother first entered only ten days ago—his feet are killing him and he's soaked through with sweat and sunburned.

The shadows along Redfern Road are long and reaching and help to cool him off, but the relief is short-lived. The rocks roll and bite beneath shoes that were not made for walking. He figures he'll make better time if he doesn't have to fool with the bike, so he unfastens the ax and leans the Schwinn against the distillery gate. Then, to spare his soles, he walks between the ruts in the grass, ax slung over his shoulder like he's Johnny Appleseed.

Eventually, he crests the hill that looks down on the South Creek wash. He stops to catch his breath. Overhead, a white jet tail slashes a cobalt strip of sky. It's hours before dark, but the woods here make it feel like the sun's already gone. And is it his imagination, or have the woods quieted? Not even the buzz of a single mosquito.

Max sets off quickly down the hill, ax in both hands now. He tries a little whistling to drive back the gloom, but he glances over his shoulder every few steps. At the bottom, he slows to catch his breath. He can still see the Ranger's tracks from that first night, wide ruts three, four inches deep. The boards Nellie brought from the stack of old lumber behind the shed, now laid as a makeshift bridge across the wash. He crosses these, each plank groaning under his weight.

Halfway across, he hears a heavy, ragged snort.

Down the gully, at the end of a bending tunnel of saplings and low branches and bracken, the bear stands in dappled shadow. Ten, fifteen feet away, scenting the air. Max feels something in his head short out at the sight of it, this thing that cannot be.

Its shoulders and haunches are knotty patches of hairless, rotting flesh. Out of its eye sockets, rootlike tendrils twine back along its jaw, its throat, down into its chest. It shakes its head, drops to all fours, and takes one lumbering step toward Max before it bellows, huge and tuba-like.

Max runs. Up the hill, full out. Heedless of the rocks beneath his feet. Ax clutched to his chest, he runs like he's never run before, and every step of the way, he can hear it, pounding after him, breathing hoarse and jagged.

And then it begins to cry: *"MmmmMMAHHHHHHCK!"*

Somewhere in this horrible sound, Max hears his name. It would be enough to unmoor his sanity, if he lets it in. But he doesn't. He just runs until his lungs burn and the road curves up to the drive, the house looming ahead. Only then, within reach of the barn, does he dare throw a backward glance, and what he sees—or doesn't see—brings him skidding to a halt.

The bear is gone.

There's only the empty road.

All the flight goes out of him and he drops, gasping, to the ground, sucking in big raw lungfuls of air. He coughs, spits. Collapses onto his back and stares up at the clouds, torn and golden.

Max leaves the ax on the porch, by the locked front door, then limps around back and climbs the magnolia tree. He considers climbing the tower—the ladder there would make the ascent so much easier on his poor, sore feet—but his stomach pitches at the memory of his rope-bridge fall, so he takes his time, branch to branch, until at last he crosses to the tin porch roof and shoves up the bedroom window and throws himself, exhausted, over the sill and into the house.

When he finally sits up, the first thing he does is take off his moccasins. They're trashed, the balls of his feet red and raw and bloody. He changes into a pair of jeans, then reaches socks and sneakers from the armoire and pulls them on.

He fishes the heavy iron key out of his crumpled sweatpants and slides it into his hip pocket, then digs through the cedar chest for his Craftsman. Clicks it on, clicks it off.

A deep breath, and he heads downstairs to grab his ax from the porch, and after that, he opens the cellar door and descends into the dark.

Dreaming her way down, now, and the cellar stairs are not the cellar stairs but her grandfather's Winnebago, canted at an angle as if it's a ship cresting a high wave. Nellie thrusts out both arms to stay upright, as the Winnie rocks and heaves. Silverware and dishes slide out of the sink and crash to the floor. Beyond the windows, an endless blue sea.

August Redfern sits in the dinette booth, holding his stenographer's notebook and a ballpoint pen. A cup of coffee steaming on the table, sliding to and fro. Sitting across from him, Euphemia Redfern wears a man's shirt and man's slacks, and when she turns, Nellie sees she's bleeding from the left side of her head. She looks like the pictures from the album, young and beautiful, big bright eyes. Nellie could be looking into a mirror. The crescent ax slides on the table between them, until a sudden lurch sends it and Redfern's coffee clattering down the long length of the Winnebago, to the far end, a dark square that can only be the cellar itself.

"That is where the pictures we paint are shaped," Redfern says to her. "The things we fear. The things we love."

Again, the RV pitches like a ship on a storm-tossed sea. Nellie's hip socks hard against the corner of the dinette, and she bounces like a pinball, all the way down into the dark.

And just like that, she wakes.

Midday. Branches and long grass scrape the BMW's chassis as it creeps north along Camp Road, having broken through the distillery gate. Plowed right over the Schwinn. The car comes to a halt at the clearing at the end of the trail, where the old cabins are strangled in wisteria. Behind the wheel, the Wade-thing cuts the engine and sits, listening. Craggy, rough hands yet bloody from the Baxter boy. What's left of the tape from the hardware store is on the passenger's seat, bloody knife in its scabbard there, too. In the trunk—the Beamer's big, spacious trunk, so much room!— are the fruits of an afternoon's labors.

The Wade-thing passes through the woods with bodies, one by one, on its shoulder—first the wife, next the boy, and finally Lonnie—and with each trip its consciousness deepens its communion with the life around it: mushrooms sprouting from the rich earth; sightless fat grubs working to aerate the soil; pine resin shifting slowly through the veins of the oldest trees yet living. All of nature is a terrible, beautiful song of competing voices, with one low, bass rumble that draws the Wade-thing along like a current of water. Tiny green buds sprouting from neck and ears and pushing back into flesh and thickening within the walls of dead arteries, hundreds of fibrous tongues extending to leech nutrients and memories, to consume the organism entire. This, it has done for eons, to plants, animals, humans.

Humans—

(with their tenuous grasp of immortality, their flimsy notions of the soul, their limitless capacity for suffering)

—always taste best.

Afternoon thunderheads are massing by the time all three Baxters are heaped at the mouth of what George Baxter once called the Hollow. The place it first found shelter, not much more than some forest animal's burrow back then. This is where it retreats for the long sleep, to dream fitfully, sometimes waking in the night to roam the woods unseen and howl its loneliness into the void, as it did back when old August Redfern went searching for it. How it loved to watch him, from its million eyes, to regard him with the cold, curious gaze of a jungle cat. What was it the old man sought? Its destruction? Laughable.

Years upon years after the fire, years upon years after Redfern's child fled. Euphemia burned—

(she who named us, named us well)

—twisting through the empty house, night after night, year after year, a haunter in the dark. The old man its unwitting companion as he stalked these woods like an Eve-less Adam, searching for his god. Or the devil who betrayed him. Theirs a kind of dance, a kind of courtship, old as time itself: archenemies, ancient friends.

Then came the girl, with her heart full of suffering, rich as the black earth along the river, and it remembered. Deep in its old worm's heart. It recalled the taste of grief. And now the girl is a woman and the woman brings pain and suffering tenfold to make the meat so sweet and tender.

Poor Lonnie, what could you offer so fine as this?

Out of the Hollow: by the dull, slovenly sounds of a gargantuan thing eating, the dank, hungry breath of a being no earthly mind can fathom.

The Dweller, Euphemia named it.

Of all its names, in all the universes it has known, it likes this one best.

Little brown mushrooms spring out along the Wade-thing's neck as its own jaws work in tandem, the servant taking sustenance from the master in a kind of holy, parasitic communion. And when its meal is finished, the Wade-thing gets up—thin, fibrous runners tear loose from the ground, rip away the knees of its jeans—and staggers away, into the trees, headed for the house, where the evening's reunion awaits.

The Dweller will be there.

A long-welcomed return to the only house it ever called home.

The cellar.

Flashlight in hand, Max drops his ax through a belt loop, just like Nellie wore it the day she trashed that asshole's taillight. Next, he takes the key from his pocket. But his light catches on the rag doll, still on the floor where he dropped it last night, and he pauses long enough to pick it up and tuck it in his waistband. Then he slides the iron key into the lock, and the coal-closet door gives a heavy metal clank and breaks open like a sealed tomb, flakes of rust sifting from the hinges. Max jerks his hand back as the spider in the keyhole, black and shiny, drops out on a gossamer strand.

The room is small, the floor bare earth. The walls are heaped with scraps of cut wood and discarded, broken bricks. Long wide planks speckled with mold once formed a frame beneath the chute itself, a bin to keep the coal from spilling out onto the floor. But most of these have rotted through, and the coal is banked in big black drifts against the walls and the chute itself, a narrow black stone gullet angling up the foundation wall and crisscrossed with thick gossamer webs.

At the foot of the coal drift is a galvanized metal pail, and on this pail, a girl sits.

Beside her is the three-legged dog Max hasn't seen since the distillery. The girl's hand—coal smudged, fingernails black with dirt—tangles in the scruff of the dog's neck. Max shines his light at the girl's bare feet, black with dust. She's slim, dressed in a blue homespun dress, the dress from his dream, he realizes. Only in his dream the dress was pristine. Here, now, it's grimy. Torn. But the girl's face—her face is horrible. Its shape is jagged, like a rough sketch. Slash marks up and down the cheeks. Black veins stand out along her scalp and her hair is brittle moss. Her throat and ears are scaled with bark. Little ants work through the cracks.

The flashlight in Max's hand trembles.

"This is Dog," the girl says. "She's a good Dog, aren't you, girl?"

She scratches the dog's ear. The dog has patches of fur missing. Ears bent like new leaves.

No, Max thinks. *Not* like *leaves. They* are *leaves*.

"Is that my doll?"

Max hands her the toy. She takes it with blue-black fingers and stares down at it, as if trying to place it. Then she looks up. Her eyes flash golden. "I'm Agatha. You're Max."

———

Thunder, as the Wade-thing stands before the locked front door of Redfern Hill and closes its right hand over the doorknob, feeling the rotting flesh of its palm open like a torn clod of dirt. A thin, fibrous tongue pushes into the lock. When it turns its hand, the door opens and there's a snap, as what remains of a key juts briefly from the lock before flaking away. The Wade-thing enters, not bothering to lock the door again.

It walks from room to room and sees with eyes no longer human the evidence of new life lived, here in this house where once it dwelled in the heart of a woman, her many sacrifices mere husks to be conjured at will from the deep blue sea of its own memory. Imbued with a passing semblance of life to carry out the Dweller's bidding. Fun and games, when it wants. The Wade-thing stands perfectly still in the foyer. Its tennis shoes burst open as shoots extend, merge into the boards beneath, and in this way it travels below, into the dark, slipping in long strands through the cracks in the floor, the very grain of the wood itself.

Down, into the cellar.

Max swallows, throat thick with coal dust and the threat of a nosebleed. The closet's cramped and hot, and he's sweating through his already soaked T-shirt. "You know me?"

"I like your music."

"Who doesn't like Dolly," Max says stupidly.

Agatha's left nostril drips white, sluggish sap. She hugs her doll against her breast.

Overhead, a sound: the front door opening in the upstairs hall.

Agatha's eyelids—fleshy little funguses, the kind that grow on trees—flutter as she looks up.

She stands from her bucket, smooths her dress. The slash

marks run up and down her legs, too, each oozing fresh resin. Layers of hardened sap stuck with dust bunnies and dirt and bits of dead bugs. The doll dangles at her side as her eyes track the creaking boards upstairs.

A whispering from the joists outside the iron door, like the sawing of dry leaves in a breeze.

"He's here," Agatha whispers.

"Who?" Max whispers back.

She drops the doll and her hand clamps hard around his wrist. Her skin is coarse and cold, so cold it burns. "Papa," she says. Max drops the flashlight, fumbles for the ax in his belt loop, but he only manages to work it free and lose it in the dirt. "We know that blade." Agatha grins. She opens her mouth, and long sticky lashings of sap-saliva are between her teeth. "Maybe when your mommy gets here, Max, we can use it on her. We'll be a big happy family, and Mommy can watch us eat you from the inside out. Won't that be nice?"

Max tries to jerk his hand away, but Agatha's grip is iron tight, and there's a sudden bright pain in his wrist, as something sharp and hard wriggles out of her and punches through his skin. He cries out and kicks away from her and feels whatever it is slip right out of him. The coal rolls beneath his feet. He goes down hard against the brick wall, gobs of mortar gouging him through his shirt. The flashlight pinwheels away.

Sound of earth shifting in the dark. A thing burrowing away. A clatter of rock. Then silence, heavy. She's gone, and he's alone in the coal closet.

Until sneakers appear in his flashlight's slanting beam, a dark silhouette in the doorway. A garbled voice says, "Son," and Max Gardner looks up into the lumpish face of a thing that was once his father.

———

Nellie sits up in bed late in the afternoon, drenched in sweat. A washcloth falls away from her forehead. Curtains wafting, fresh air from a window, scent of rain on the wind—

But not her window. The light is strange, spilling in from the wrong direction. A score of scratches and gouges in her flesh, all red and angry. She wears a clean T-shirt featuring Ziggy—no more hers than the window, that's for sure—and a pair of soft cotton sleep pants. The tag is still on the pants, itching at her waist. She plucks it free. Wal-Mart.

Queasiness, in the pit of her stomach. Fragments of dreams still swimming in her head.

She puts her feet out of bed, winces at the pain that shoots up through the ball of her right foot. Around it a blood-crusted wrapping. She eases up, holding on to the bed frame, careful not to put any weight on her foot. Every joint, every muscle, stiff and hurting.

On a table by the window is her father's picture of Agatha Redfern, sitting on the porch steps, a chicken in her lap.

"Dad?" she calls out.

She works her way one step at a time into the hallway, the kitchen.

"Max?"

The living room. Where the TV scrolls Floyd Cramer's *Treasury of Favorites*, plus *World Famous Love Songs*, for $12.98 (NOT SOLD IN STORES), and Hank Redfern sprawls unconscious on the couch. On the carpet where his knuckles rest, a half-empty bottle of whiskey. A second bottle beneath the couch, nothing but air inside.

"Jesus, Dad."

Then, a beat later, panic.

"Max!" she yells.

She limps out the kitchen door, down the steps, into the open garage. Spins around. Her pickup's parked down the drive, along the curb. No Max to be seen. Into the backyard, hollering his name. Turning her gaze across two, three backyards, as the wind whips the trees and a chill descends, presaging hail, a storm.

Christ, how long was she out?

Back into the house, where she dumps old coffee from the pot into the kitchen sink and runs the pot full of cold water. This she slings in Hank Redfern's face. Tosses aside the coffeepot and gathers up handfuls of his coveralls to shake him until his eyes open long enough to find even the smallest focus, so that she can slap him and cry, *Where is my son?* But that doesn't happen because Hank doesn't wake, just lolls in her hands. She drops him, hobbles back into the bedroom, sees her purse on the table beneath the window. Finds her keys inside.

She looks around for shoes, doesn't see any under the bed, behind the door. So she goes across the hall into her old bedroom, starts tearing open boxes. Spilling their contents onto the floor until she finds a pair of cracked Converse trainers she wore in high school, beneath these a store of gold-ringed Wigwam socks. Her right foot's already bleeding again, so she doubles up on the knee socks, then pulls on her sneakers.

There, on the floor, among a litter of old cassette tapes, is Ruth Redfern's Zippo lighter. She grabs it.

A minute later, she's at the Ranger's cab, is about to crank the ignition, when she sees, in the bed of the pickup, the gallon jug of gum turpentine. She'd left it there, the other day. When they first got back to the house, before—

She remembers.

The island, the black maw.

Her grandfather's tree-zombie double.

These things were not delirium. These things were not nightmares.

She grabs the turpentine, tosses it on the seat beside her, and as the Ranger screeches away, the first fat drops of rain burst upon the pavement.

1932

✦

OCTOBER 15

IT'S EARLY MORNING WHEN HANK FINDS DOG BEHIND THE azaleas, beneath the parlor window. The autumn has been mild, and the leaves are not yet brown. The last of summer's blooms have clung to the bushes through September and still litter the pine straw bedded over the roots. He's standing on the porch, staring out at the meadow, the trees beyond, wishing for a boat so he could float the Altamaha south—it would be faster, safer, than walking. There's always the Model A, but Papa needs it. Even if he sells it come Christmas, it's better to leave it here, let Mama bank the cash. These are Hank's thoughts when he happens to hear a fly and look down.

"Shit," he breathes.

Beneath the bushes, a black-and-tan haunch, a withered paw.

He hops the balustrade and pushes back the azalea's branches.

"What—" is all he gets out. The sight of it steals the rest.

Dog lies on her side, a hole in her ribs the size and shape of a canning jar. Her insides have burst onto the ground, are slicked with green flies. Exposed ribs, their ends splintered. And out of this hole, like tongues unfurled, a twisted heap of fat brown roots. Her corpse is desiccated, her eyes gone. More roots there, like a nest of worms growing out of her. A fly crawls into her ear.

Hank stumbles away, around the corner, and puts one hand on the house to steady himself, as he vomits.

Later.

He wraps her in an old feed bag from the barn, then goes inside to find Agatha, who's in the parlor at the piano, playing a series of chords and scales, her daily practice. He clears his voice and she turns on the bench, dark hair pulled back in a ponytail. Little blue gingham dress rising just above her knees. She hates dresses, but Mama makes her wear them.

"What is it?"

Hank swallows. His saliva tastes of stomach acid. "It's Dog."

Agatha helps him dig the hole, out beneath the black walnut tree at the far edge of the meadow. It's shady there, and in the summers, the ground is always littered with green walnut balls. "She loves to fetch them," Agatha says, kicking at a ball that's lain on the ground since July. It disintegrates in a black puff beneath her shoe. She's still wearing her dress, but she's changed into her mud-hoppers, an old pair of lace-up brogans.

"I'm sorry," Hank says.

The soil is mounded and tamped down, the grave a shallow two feet.

Hank's palms are red and raw from the effort.

They hold hands beside the grave.

"She was a good girl," he says.

"It's my fault."

"Ain't no one's fault," he says, though he isn't sure. "It wasn't natural, whatever happened to her. It wasn't—"

"It was the egg."

"The egg? What egg?"

She tells him how Dog licked the yolk from her fingers, a few days back.

"That don't make sense, Aggie."

"I dreamed about her last night. In my dream, she was right where you found her. And she was wriggling and jerking and it was terrible, Hank, how much she suffered."

"How could you dream that?"

"It's the voice. It's in *my* head now, like it's been in Mama's head. And Papa's head."

Hank takes a knee beside her, turns her to face him.

"What the hell are you talking about? No f-f-fooling."

"I don't know what it is. Mama calls it the Dweller. Little Charlie, he's in her head, too."

Hank opens his mouth to speak, but the word lodges in his throat like a stone. It won't come until he finally shuts his eyes and pictures his shovel breaking through the hard earth and lifting it out: "Ch-Ch-Charlie?"

She nods. Then bursts into tears.

He pulls her against his chest, and her arms lock around his neck.

"I didn't mean to, I didn't mean to break the egg, I wasn't trying to hurt Dog—"

"Shh. Hush now."

He holds her close.

In the dream, she tells him later, when all the tears are gone, she walked a ways beyond North Creek by moonlight, to a sandy ridge and through a wire-grass meadow, passing three lone pines. Over moss beds and into the cypress swamp. She came out wet to her armpits, and ahead was a risen mound like a turtle shell at the center of a creek, and it had a hole in the center of it, she said, like the long black sleeve of Papa's winter coat turned inside out, and there the Dweller spoke her name and promised her she was a good, faithful girl, its praise enfolding her like the arms of—

"Arms of who?" Hank says.

"You."

They're sitting with their backs against the walnut tree, facing the distant house.

"I'll take you with me," he says finally.

"You will?"

"Tonight, after supper, you'll play the piano. One last time. Do you understand?"

She nods.

"Then you'll go up and get your bath and go to bed. Like always. And I'll sit up awhile with Mama and Papa. Once Mama's gone to bed, I'll go up and get my bath. And we'll wait until everyone's asleep and the house is so quiet it roars. Then we'll go."

"Do you think she'll miss us?"

"No." But secretly he knows this is not true. Euphemia Redfern will miss both of her children. By the time she discovers what they've done, they'll need to be miles and miles away. A boat. That'd be the ticket.

"Then again," he says, thinking out loud, "maybe Papa taught me how to drive for a reason."

"What, Hank?"

"Nothing."

"Where will we go?"

"Anywhere but here," is all Hank Redfern knows to say.

V

1932

✦

OCTOBER 15, STILL

A PURPLE DUSK AS PRETTY AS ANY IN RECENT MEMORY. THE light in the parlor, soft and golden, hurricane lamps aglow. Agatha sits at the piano stool, hands dancing over the keys, feet working the pedals. She plays a soft, lilting hymn, one she's been learning since summer: "Leaning on the Everlasting Arms." At first, it's a series of high-struck notes like the tinkle of fading stars, and then, on the chorus, she drifts down into lower, full chords, and the effect is like light falling through the room, as if she and Hank and Mama and Papa are all anchored deep beneath the surface of a dark ocean, and the sun itself has somehow dropped down among them, to buoy them up through the water to break the surface and touch the sky.

Euphemia sits in her chair by the fire, which crackles like her eyes. They're bright and dancing, a far-off memory tugging at her heart. Redfern slumps at the far end of the couch, tears cradled in his eyes. One slipping slowly down his cheek, through a forest of salt-and-pepper grizzle. Hank sits at the opposite end of the couch, listening for all he's worth to his sister's last song. These times, he realizes, have been like some communal family prayer. Reverence and silence forming a precious, precious thread, spun anew with each sitting, severed at each rising. He swallows thickly, sits on his hands to keep them from shaking. His spirit like a struck tuning fork, humming until the last of the hymn fades, and they can each hear the clunky, mechanical thump of the pedals working beneath Agatha's feet, and after this, the silence closes in like a shroud and they drown in the dark of their hideous, separate hearts.

Hank unplugs the upstairs tub and waits until the water drains completely before edging out into the hallway, a towel cinched around his waist. He pads barefoot past his parents' room and into his own, where he dresses quietly in fresh clothes from the armoire—a cotton shirt with long sleeves and a pair of patched jeans and boot socks. He glances, briefly, at the lace-up boots he sometimes wears and, instead, pulls on a pair of dirty white Keds. He goes softly to Agatha's door and knocks, and when she doesn't answer, he eases open the door and whispers her name.

The room is lit by moonlight, curtains billowing in the cool night breeze.

Agatha sits on the edge of the bed, dressed in the clothes she wore that day. Her feet not quite touching the boards. She wears her mud-hoppers. She sits very still.

Beside her, a dark, adult shape.

"M-M-Mama?" Hank says.

Euphemia moves quickly, launching herself from the bed and dragging Agatha by the arm. In her other hand is the leather strop used to sharpen kitchen knives, folded into thirds and held like a blackjack. Hank retreats and stumbles over the threshold into his own room, goes sprawling on the pine boards. Mama steps over him, and he turns and scrabbles after her, calling out, "Mama, please, please wait!"

But she doesn't.

Agatha is crying and pulling at her mother's arm, and Euphemia is strapping her legs, all the way down the hall, down the stairs, until at last Agatha hangs limp in her mother's grasp and Euphemia rounds the stairwell and yanks the cellar door open.

She drags Agatha down into the dark.

Hank thunders into his father's map room, crying out, "Papa, she's gone crazy, she's—"

But Redfern's stretched out on the map table, a bottle by his head, another empty on the floor. Maps scattered at his feet.

Hank pounds down the cellar stairs, alone.

Outside the coal closet, he seizes Euphemia's arm, tries to pry his sister's wrist from Mama's grip. But Euphemia shoves him so hard he smacks the board shelves and brings a whole shelf clattering down on top of him. Next, the iron lock clangs and Mama stalks past him, back upstairs, where she pours herself a glass of liquor from the parlor sideboard. Hank, sitting on the earthen floor, dumbfounded, hears the tromp of her boots, the cabinet door that sticks, the clink of the stopper leaving the crystal.

It's happened so fast.

He bangs on the heavy iron door until he hears his sister, sobbing so hard she can't form words. "Aggie? Aggie!" His hammering a frantic drumming that rings up through the iron pipes in the walls and echoes in his skull.

"Hank," comes her voice at last, through the keyhole. Faint.

"I'm s-s-sorry, Aggie, I'm so, so sorry . . ."

"Hank, Mama knew, she knew . . ."

"We'll g-g-get out of here, you'll see, I p-p-promise . . ."

"Hank . . ." Her voice is fading. Fading away. A candle burned low. "Do you suppose she dreamed it, like I dreamed about Dog?"

"Aggie, don't you fret." His own voice is barely a whisper. "Aggie?"

The next thing she says chills his heart: "My friend is in here, Hank. In here with me . . ."

As beneath the door, a faint blue light begins to glow.

Hank finds Mama upstairs, sitting on the edge of his bed, holding a red rag. Bruises on her arm where Aggie fought her, where Hank fought her. Her dark hair hangs in sweaty strings about her face. Agatha's button-eyed doll lies on the bed beside her.

"Mama," Hank says from the hall door.

She looks up at him with eyes that hold no hope, are dry as sand. She holds out the red rag, as if demanding an explanation. Unfolds it, and there upon her palm is Redfern's pistol.

"We have no secrets in this house," she says flatly.

"G-g-give me the k-k-key." He thinks to himself that this is the day, the day he will seize the strop and tear it from her hands. Indeed, there it is on the bed, coiled beside her like a snake.

"No." Euphemia sets the gun on the cedar chest at the foot of his bed. Folds the handkerchief around it. Gets up, bedsprings creaking, though she is not big. She never has been. She is not big and yet, to the boy she is a giant. Her head among the stars and the ragged night wisps.

"It spoke to her. Did you know that? Here, I've kept this family alive by doing its will, putting food on the table, money in the bank. The rest of you, what did any of you *ever* do? But it speaks to *her*. If you want to leave, Henry, then leave. I won't stop you. But your sister was born to die here. That's her place, her purpose. She stays!"

A breath of silence between them, until Hank says, "No," and Euphemia's face twists up in a snarl and she strides forward and grabs a handful of her son's hair and pulls, and he yelps in pain and claws at his mother's arm, even as Euphemia raises the strop like it's the torn-out-by-the-root tongue of some creature, and the leather falls once, twice, catching him on the shoulder, the ear, and he seizes her wrist and bends it, viciously, and Euphemia screams and the leather drops to the floor, and Hank is about to snatch it up and swing it back, split her lip with it or break a tooth, when he sees the key in Euphemia's shirt pocket.

With all the strength he has, he balls his fist and strikes a glancing blow to the side of her face. She reels, and in a flash, the key is in his hand. She dives after him, drags him down, is on top of him, hissing words that lose their shape as soon as they leave her mouth. Gibberish and rage. He scrabbles and kicks his way from under her, gets as far as the edge of the stairs, when she's on him again. Straddling him. Her strong hands around his throat, squeezing. Squeezing until the edges of his vision begin to darken, and the key slips free of his hand and he hears it go thumping down the stairs, to clatter on the boards of the hallway below.

"Muh—"

Capillaries in his eyes bursting.

His mother's face red and changed, her eyes blue, impossibly blue, like a hot gas flame—

Aggie, oh, Aggie—

A thunder of boots on the stairs, and Euphemia looks up and there is a moment, one second, no more, though it will seem an eternity in Hank's memory, when recognition flashes in her eyes, the realization of what's to come, and in the microseconds before it happens, a whole story unfolds upon her face—the story of a woman's long triumph, betrayal, defeat. Then the moon ax strikes her in the left temple, and the force of the blow hurls her against the wall. Hank sees it happen, the blade whisking through the air to lodge in her skull, a lurch as her weight leaves him. He hears her body *whump* the baseboard at the top of the stairs, but he cannot turn, he will not look. In the seconds that follow, he manages to keep breathing, hair plastered to his head with sweat, pale as a catfish belly, until finally, he rolls to his right, hangs his head over the top stair, and spits bile. Then, at last, he looks up.

"Pah—Pah—"

Redfern grabs the banister for support, his legs go weak, and he slides down onto a stair, to turn away from the thing he has done. Redfern's sleeveless undershirt spattered red. Whole frame shaking as he puts his head in his hands.

Hank's eyes slide past him, to the key at the bottom of the stairs. Unable yet to stand for fear of toppling over—his legs are weak, so weak and trembling—he begins to crawl, to skate down. On his belly, still, he closes his right hand around the key.

Which is when, in the cellar, his eight-year-old sister screams.

Redfern hears his daughter cry out beneath the floor, hears his son scramble down. Slowly, Redfern looks over his shoulder. Euphemia lies on her right side, back to the wall along the landing. The crescent ax is lodged above her ear. Her left eye has rolled up and the right is leaking blood. The ax juts like a pump handle. The world swims as his eyes fill. He pulls himself up and steps over the pool of blood now dripping over the lip of the stairs and goes into the boy's bedroom and sees the Colt pistol, on the cedar chest. He takes it. On his way past Euphemia, he stops. Gloved hands trembling, he snags the ax and shuts his eyes and cries out as he yanks, and the blade comes free of his wife's head with a sucking crack.

Hank lopes through the dim cellar toward the coal-closet door, good hand gripping Mama's iron key. Doorframe glowing, he staggers against it, rams the key home, is about to turn it when August Redfern says behind him, "Son."

Standing at the foot of the cellar steps, bloody ax in hand, Redfern holds out one hand, as if inviting the boy to take it. "Don't ever open that door."

A command that Hank, who knows his sister yet lives, refuses to obey.

He turns the key and drags open the door as his father springs at him.

The whole cellar is subsumed in a blue void, and out of that void, Hank sees the silhouette of his little sister suspended in a web of monstrous, writhing arms, slick and dark and undulating, a fly at the center of a living web of nerves and teeth. He feels the presence of some other thing beneath the ground, that brilliant blue light the herald of its coming, his sister nothing more than a tawdry cloak thrown in its path—

Redfern drags him back, out of the closet, and slams the door. Locks it.

Hank pushes free, grabs the key.

Redfern seizes the boy around his middle and hauls him away. The key comes out in Hank's grasp, and that's when he feels it, an impact in his breast, like a massive spike driven through his sternum. The sensation of his heart cleaved in two, each half unraveling, string by string.

Agatha is dead.

He slumps in his father's arms and howls.

The moon is nowhere to be found, the sky overhead black and star-flung. Redfern staggers with his wife's body out of the house and sets it gently into the bed of the Model A pickup in the drive. Hank climbs into the passenger seat, shivering, windshield fogging with his breath. Papa leans for a breath against the hood. Bare arms quivering. When he gets into the cab, Hank notices, absently, that his father has found the Colt pistol upstairs, tucked it into his waistband at the small of his back. Hank looks out at the house where he was raised, one last time.

The road, the rocking motion, the clank and jerk of the Model A. Pain in his wrist, a slow shock spreading up his arm and into his chest, wanting to stop his shredded heart. He fights it. He doesn't know why, but he fights it.

The distillery.

The truck squeals to a stop.

Redfern lays Euphemia on the corded wood pile near the furnace. He lights a kerosene lantern and hangs it from a pillar and bends over his wife's body, whispers to her. Chilled night air quaking through him. He shuts his eyes, listens. A wind moans through the pines. But the pines don't speak. There is no voice.

Hank's shadow stretches behind him in the lantern light.

Redfern feels the pistol leave his waistband, as the boy slips it free. He doesn't even glance at Hank, who steps back, gun at his side. The boy makes no effort to raise it, only to hold it. Considering, perhaps, its use in the moments ahead.

"Go away from here, Son."

When Hank speaks, his words don't stumble, don't tremble. His voice is cold, sharp. Choked with nothing. "How did she know?"

Redfern's gloved hand traces his wife's cheekbone. He does not answer his son.

"Was it like Aggie said? Did Mama dream it? Did that, that *thing* tell her? Or was it you?" Hank raises the pistol, levels it at his father. "It was you, wasn't it. You told Mama we were running away."

At last, Redfern faces his son. Pulse in his throat ticking.

"I thought you *wanted* us to."

"You," his father says softly. "Only you."

Hank remembers his mother's words: *Agatha's place, her purpose, to die here . . .*

"I was always," August Redfern says, "a coward before your mother."

"But she was my sister," Hank says. "Your daughter!" he screams.

At this, Redfern's hands ball into fists. He steps toward his son and yanks him forward, jamming the pistol's barrel against his own chest. Father and son stare at each other and Redfern says, "This is my heart. All you have to do is pull the trigger, Hank, and it's over. It's all over. Do this for me, Son, then leave. Leave here and never come back. Can you do this? Please, Hank. Do this for me. This one thing. Please, Son. Please."

But Hank's finger moves away from the trigger, as all the love he's ever felt for his father bleeds out of him like vented steam, and nothing is left, not even hatred. Only an emptiness. He lets go the pistol and leaves it in Redfern's hands. He staggers to a cask of hardened rosin, where he sits. Staring past his father, at his dead mother.

Redfern, chest rising and falling like a bellows, lowers the gun and sets it gently on the cask by his son. Then he upends a barrel from beneath the condensing tank, just enough turpentine left in it from the last brew to soak Euphemia's body. When the barrel's empty, he rolls it away among the other casks of runoff. He gathers wood to feed the furnace.

Hank, meanwhile, holds the gun and, after a while, snugs it in his waistband and gets up and begins to help his father stoke the fire in the brick kiln, bring it to blazing.

They work in tandem, eyes red rimmed with smoke. They roll a barrel of raw gum up the rails from the loading deck, then crack it open, dump it into the cooker, then roll another, scraping it out until the kettle is full of raw pine sap and the fire is burning hotter and hotter beneath it. With his leather gloves, Redfern sets the tall metal cap over the kettle. They climb down, theirs the work of an hour, the slow undoing of everything August Redfern has built. Redfern throws more wood on the fire. In the kettle above, the rosin grows hot. The solvent boils away, the turpentine and water separate, rise.

And when Redfern turns to tell him to go, the boy is already sliding behind the wheel of the Model A. It cranks, the headlights flare, and Hank Redfern drives away.

Redfern listens until he can't hear the truck's engine anymore. After that, he climbs the stairs to the upper deck and peers down into the kettle, where the gases build amid a swirl of telltale foam. He kicks the cap off the kettle with his boot, sends it tumbling over the edge of the platform. Off-gases flood the deck and gather like doom beneath the shingled roof. Moving quickly, Redfern drops down into the dirt, snatches up the kerosene lantern from its hook, and walks out into the gravel lane. He hurls the lantern onto the deck, shuts his eyes, and waits for the flames to ignite the gases.

He waits beside his wife and looks upon her and wonders at the mysteries he never grasped, those moments when the woman she was, the woman she wanted to be, eluded him, or he was too myopic to see. In his heart, he loves her still. The secret truth he harbors: she was his better at every turn. Discord and spilled blood did not break them upon the rocks, but bound them on a single course, each lashed to the other's mast. He will always—

The blast rips open the furnace, the roof, and Euphemia in a spray of fire, hurling Redfern backward, into the brambles, amid a shower of bricks and wood and fire.

1989

✦

JULY 9, STILL

HANK REDFERN WAKES OUT OF A THICK, WOOL-WRAPPED FOG. All around him, the house is dim and full of menace. An anvil on his chest. He tries to sit up, can't move. God, it's killing him, this coldness through his undershirt, right over his heart. In the deepest corner of the living room, a shadow grows, at the center of it a girl's shape, the last vestige of his nightmare. He lifts his arm—he's trapped in a vat of sand—and fumbles for the lamp string.

The light comes on.

Alone.

Where the shadow stood, a narrow corner cabinet with a missing door.

He sits up gasping on the edge of the couch. Jagged chunks of tombstone granite knock against the walls of his skull. The television runs at low volume, wrestling. From the window over the couch, the AC blows high. He dips his head into the stream, runs a trembling hand over a clammy neck. He glances at the floor, between his bare, knobby feet the twin bottles of Old Crow.

In the dream, Mama chased him and his long-dead sister through an endless maze of burned-out, dilapidated rooms. She chased them with an ax. That weird, moon-shaped ax Papa kept. The one he—

(no)

In the dream, Agatha was still eight but Hank was old and she ran on ahead, doll in hand, because she was faster now, so much faster, and soon Hank lost her in a warren of doorways and staircases, only to round one or climb another into a moonlit clearing, and there stood little Aggie at the wide flat altar of a pine stump, and Euphemia stood over her, a pillow in hand instead of an ax. And the stump was not a stump but the rough, pebbled orbit of a blue eye that opened and rolled wide and dream-Hank cried out, and in the far corner of a small dark room his sister stood, getting bigger, getting darker.

(the boy where is the boy)

Nellie. Shaking him. How long? Minutes ago? Ten, fifteen at the most. Her voice like the voice of a soul trapped way down in some cavern past all light. She was looking for the boy. Which means the boy is—

He staggers into the bathroom, where he lifts the toilet lid and heaves into the commode. He flushes and puts his lips against the running tap and gulps water. Stands upright, stares in the mirror at his dripping, grizzled face.

The boy. You lost him. Just like you lost her.

Old fool. Old fucking fool.

He goes outside into a driving rain, the garage door up, the workbench light shining.

The boy is nowhere to be seen.

His eyes light on the box of dead watches, dragged from beneath the bench. Hank picks it up, something in his back cricking. Staggering. Yet drunk, sweating booze through his shirt, he sets the box on the workbench and rummages. The key—

(what's in that coal closet?)

—is missing.

From the wall, Nellie's old Schwinn is gone. The Ranger, too.

The temptation is almost as strong as the first wave that drove him there, earlier: just crawl back into that bottle. And another after that, and another. There's a few still around, hidden here and there. A cubby beneath the kitchen sink. The bread box on the counter. Crawl into them and never come out. Hank wipes his lips with his knuckles.

Then, Ruth's voice, as clear as October sky: *They're going to die, Hank. If you don't go.*

"Maybe they'll die anyway," he says to the empty garage. "Me along with them."

Coward. She needs you. The boy needs you.

Oh, God, the ache of memory. He looks down at the box on the bench. In it the story of his life: a heap of lost and broken time.

Nellie passes the city limits, heedless of the speed zone, a knocking in the little truck's innards, one windshield wiper loose and flapping. Certainty growing in her mind that whatever is happening is happening now and she is too late.

"Dad?" Max stammers.

Wade speaks out of the shadows, words that chill Max's heart—and not only because it sounds like Dad's talking around a handful of rocks gummed up and sticky, but also because these words usually mean the flyswatter, a switch, a belt.

". . . you and your . . . Nellie-mom . . . have been . . . bad . . . Maxie . . ."

Nellie-mom?

". . . very . . . very bad . . ."

Max snatches the Craftsman off the ground and traces it up, along his father's frame, over the dirty knees of his jeans, the mud that crusts his hands and arms. Dark, heavy veins stand out on his forearms, only they aren't veins at all, are they? They're runners of dark, shining resin that wrap his arms and tear through his soiled WOULDN'T YOU LIKE TO BE A PEPPER, TOO? T-shirt. And that's where the light falters, at Wade's chest, because Max can't bear to go any higher, to see what surrounds the twin orbs in his father's head that shine out ocean blue. Strange, horizontal slits at the center of each.

". . . she'll be . . . here soon . . . until then . . . you sit . . . and think . . . about . . . what you did . . ."

He backs out of the light, into the darkness of the cellar, and closes the closet door.

Max remembers, in the second before he hears the heavy clang of its turning, that the key is still in the lock. Instantly, he's up and pounding on the door. "Daddy, no! No, Daddy, please!"

But no answer comes back.

Hank goes to his bedroom, to the bedside drawer. He slides it open, and there, among yellowed letters and pencil nubs and broken rubber bands, is a plastic case. He takes the case out and sets it on the bed. Inside is the Colt .45 he brought away from Redfern Hill and took overseas to Europe, after enlisting. He came back from the war in the summer of 1948, when he was still young and trim and handsome in his olive fatigues.

The pistol in his duffel as he stepped off the bus in Empire and crossed the street and went into the Grill for lunch. There, a woman named Ruth Fountain served him a cheeseburger and a bowl of Brunswick stew. Her smile was kind. She asked him if he was from here. He said he'd just got back. Didn't know yet if he was going to stay.

"Got any family here?" Ruth asked, pouring him coffee.

"No."

"Well, that's the nice thing about coming home from over there. You boys get to start over."

Maybe he'd married her because of that. He certainly loved her for it.

(And the years went by, and he fell into an ocean of liquor and sank deep, deep down where the seabed was all black glass and the only lights were those fires burning in trenches that opened on mysterious worlds that could not have been his, no, not his own . . .)

Also in the drawer: a box of ammunition. Two hundred rounds. He puts a handful in his pocket.

Hank goes through the house switching off lights, until he finds himself standing in the doorway to the room where she died. He sees the torn, spilled boxes. Nellie's things. She'd needed shoes, most likely. Hadn't hesitated. Not just to tear open the past, to discard the things that weren't useful to her and seek out the things that were. But also to go. She had not hesitated to go.

Hank Redfern reaches into his pocket. Takes out a bullet.

He pushes the first of seven rounds into the pistol's clip.

Daylight darkens into twilight as the Ranger fishtails around the last curve of Redfern Road, the whole of the property plunged into shadow. The pickup skids to a halt in front of the porch steps. Jug of turpentine in hand, Nellie rounds the hood and leaps to the front door, yanks the screen so hard the bottom hinge tears free. The door is unlocked. She throws it wide, gasping and soaked as inside the foyer she calls for Max.

But for the rain on the roof, the house is quiet.

She calls again. Listens.

Faintly, from below her feet: "Mom! Mom, down here!"

She makes for the cellar door, rounding the stairs, and walks straight into a huge, wild thing. It fills the door of August Redfern's map room. T-shirt and jeans clinging to it in rags and ribbons. Hands that are hard and rough, not flesh at all, seize her above the elbows, its voice a harsh scrape as it dips a massive, malformed head and speaks out of a face Nellie knows. *Oh, God, it's—*

". . . babe . . ."

A fat brown tongue comes lolling out as Wade—

(No, not Wade, it can't be)

—lifts her off the floor. She drops the jug of turpentine. The thing—

(Wade-thing)

—yanks her against its chest, fingers squeezing her bare arms. Fingers that aren't fingers but tendrils, vines. Little mouths, little teeth. Nipping at her flesh. She kicks at the Wade-thing's knees, and scaly pieces snap away. That horrid tongue in her ear, a fetid, cloying reek of earth and pine—

". . . shhh . . ."

She bucks, writhes. Her fingers brush the tip of something cold, metal. A knife in a scabbard on its hip—

". . . missed you nellieee . . ."

She gets a grip on the handle, tightens her fingers. Kicks out once more and he—

(it)

—slumps beneath the blow, only for a second, but long enough. Long enough for Nellie to jerk the blade free and angle it into the thing's side. Drag it down through the kidney, push it back toward the spine, but there is no cry, no shriek of pain. The thing only laughs. Laughs and drops her. Drops her to claw the knife out of its body, which is just long enough for Nellie Gardner to believe she's free.

She snags the jug of turpentine and lunges for the open cellar door—

The Wade-thing shoves her, so hard that her head slams into the low ceiling of the stairway door, just above the ridge of her right eye. The turpentine jug goes clattering down into the dark, and Nellie drops in the stairway door, unconscious.

Slumped against the soot-black brick, Max sits ramrod straight when he hears his mother call his name. The hand of fear clutching his heart loosens, and he cries out, "Mom! Mom, down here!" Then he's up, banging on the metal door. He listens. Pounds the door. Waits. Pounds again until—

A scuffle, a clatter, the heavy thud of something striking the cellar stairs. After that, silence. A long, forever silence. Until, through the door, he hears the eerie, unmistakable sound of footsteps on the stairs, heavy and monster-movie plodding, but also another sound: that dry scrabbling, like a bird picking through autumn leaves, that seems to precede or follow an appearance by some awful thing here in Redfern Hill.

Max backs away from the door, stumbles over the ax on the ground. He picks it up, tries to imagine hacking at Dad with it, and can't. He swings his flashlight beam to the coal chute. He's thought it over already: the short, narrow shaft set into the foundation wall. Covered in webs. Just the memory of that spider, tumbling out of that keyhole earlier, makes him shudder. Besides, even if he could crawl up the steep, narrow chute, the little hobbit-size iron door set into the brickwork up there at ground level is almost certainly latched from the outside.

Beyond the door, in the cellar dark, Dad begins to whistle.

A bright, happy tune Wade used to sing when Max was little.

"You Are My Sunshine."

Soon, the door will open, and when it does, Max is sure there won't be a happy family reunion. He has to get out, no two ways about it. Get out and get help. The phone in the hallway.

Mr. Hank. He'll come. He has to.

Max clamors over the coal pile—it shifts and slides beneath him—and uses the ax to clear away the caul of webbing from the upper boards of the chute's mouth. He bends beneath the boards and cranes up the stone shaft and sees it's steep and dirty black, a playground slide for chimney sweeps. At the top, hinged in a frame of damp old wood, is a small door, shrouded in gobs of coal-black webbing. The webs hang like bunting from the floor joists overhead.

Outside the closet, the whistling stops.

Max slips the ax into his belt loop and scrambles into the chute.

Nellie wakes on the cool earth of the cellar floor. She wakes to the sound of whistling, as the Wade-thing circles the dark room, looking for the jug of turpentine. She smells him, hears him, shambling back and forth, filling the room with his stench of damp wood and tree rot. *Its* stench. Sapphire eyes drifting in the dark.

The whistling stops.

". . . ah-ha . . ." the Wade-thing says. She hears the jug of turpentine slosh as he (*it*) picks it up. Blue eyes drift above her in the dark, circle her, silent and fuming, and it seems to Nellie that something of the old Wade is still in this thing, some part of him still present, still radiating fury hot as a gas flame. ". . . we told you . . . ," it says, bending over her, the reek of it filling her world. ". . . if you ever took him . . . we would cut . . . your throat . . ."

A hand—or something like a hand—seizes her hair.

". . . best part is . . . the boy . . . gets . . . to watch . . ."

She cries out, seizes the arms that hold her. He spins her round and drags her toward the coal-closet door.

The chute is a tighter fit than Max thought. For one thing, given the angle, it's impossible to do anything but crawl up over the coal until he's at the top of the pile, and then he has to somehow work his way up the steep grade to the door. It's like climbing a tunneled slide. Plus, the chute roars with the rain outside, inky black runners of water trickling down from some unseen crack between door and frame. Max lies flat on his belly—the water's cold—and shines his flashlight up there, but the door is a good three, four feet beyond his reach.

He draws the ax from his belt loop, reaches with it. He can just brush the tip of a web ensconcing the doorframe. He rolls over and lies flat on his back. Shoves the flashlight into the waist of his jeans and lifts both legs and stamps them against the boards that cover the chute's mouth. He pushes off the boards, which scoots him farther up the chute, so he gains a foot, maybe two, and there, almost horizontal now, he slips the ax from his belt with his left hand and reaches up to the door. He runs it along the edge until the blade snags in some metal lip, nook, or cranny, and this gives him leverage to roll over and pull himself up the shaft, so that his back is wedged against the left wall, and his feet are wedged against the right. Holding on to the ax, he takes out his flashlight with his right hand and clicks it on and shines it on the door. His face, the door, a swirl of dust—all that's visible in the dark shaft. With the flashlight, he pushes at the door.

It does not budge.

Below, the sound of dry hinges screaming as the closet door opens.

He's coming.

Ax arm beginning to quiver, Max plays his light over the wooden frame that holds the chute door in place. It's old and rotten. If the door won't push out, maybe he can pull it in, tear the whole thing away from the wall. He thinks he can stay wedged here, without gripping the ax. He holds the flashlight against his shoulder with his cheek and slowly lets go of the ax. He doesn't fall. He's stuck. So he grips the ax with both hands and yanks it.

Something seizes his ankle. Jerks him prone.

He cries out and the flashlight drops away, goes tumbling to the coal below. There, in the slanting beam of the light, he sees a face, inhuman, scaly with bark and lichen and oozing resin from open slashes up and down its cheeks. Eyes that flash cerulean. His father's eyes.

"...you're being...a real pain...in the keister, Maxie..."

Max jerks his foot out of the Wade-thing's grip and cries, "Mom! Help, Mom, please!"

". . . she can't talk now . . . pardner . . ."

Rough hands seize his feet and pull.

Max yelps, but his double-handed grip on the ax holds, and the ax holds on the frame, but the frame and the metal door don't hold. They rip free and go thumping down the chute, cuffing Max on the ear. Max slides after them, as the Wade-thing dodges the heavy door and the ax, and Max brings his legs up and stops his fall on the boards at the mouth of the chute. Pushes himself back up the wet, inky chute.

The flashlight flickers below, as the Wade-thing picks it up.

On his back again, Max can see only the joists above, the dark webbing there.

The beam plays slowly among them.

". . . ooh . . . what's that . . . look up there . . ."

In the coal-dusted webscape six inches above Max's head, eight space-black bodies glisten in the flashlight's beam.

Below, the Wade-thing, in its broken, inhuman voice, warbles out, ". . . the itsy-bitsy spider . . . climbed up the closet chute . . ."

The spiders are so still.

Max holds his breath. Doesn't move. Tastes blood in the back of his throat, feels it begin to trickle out of his nose.

As a rumble begins, deep beneath the house.

". . . oh, Maxie . . . do you hear it . . ."

The walls tremble. Dust whorls.

". . . we've been waiting for this . . ."

Overhead, a spider skitters.

Max jerks in fear. Blood flowing over his lips.

". . . we're coming to eat you, Maxie . . ."

Another tremor, bigger this time. The distant roar of something massive, churning, digging. Like a train barreling up from below.

More movement among the spiders, a few dislodging from the dark, descending toward him on thin, invisible strands. Their bellies fill his world, those red hourglass abdomens. The first of them mere inches now from his gushing nose.

He wants to scream, but his throat is full of blood.

Night has all but fallen, the world silvered with rain, when Hank's pickup eases to a stop at the bend in Redfern Road. Wipers sheet the water away and reveal, up the hill, near the house, something huge lumbering back and forth in the yard. It looks like a black bear, but its fur is matted and knotted, its muzzle deformed— shredded into long, fleshy flaps. Hank feels a momentary loosening of reality's strings as he watches the creature pace back and forth in front of the house, shaking its big shaggy head, as if to rid itself of a pest in its ears—

(Everything comes back, the horrors of that night. He's wrestled with it in dreams and terrors and night sweats all his life, tried to drown it with booze, but you can't drown a thing as all-encompassing and vast as the sea itself, that shimmering blue light that rose up from the cellar, the tentacles that plunged into his sister's body when he opened that door—)

His hands are shaking. His bladder wants to let go. The old Hank, a coward and a failure.

He shifts into reverse and rolls backward, silently, into the woods, grass whispering beneath the Dodge's chassis. He could shift into drive and roll left, get the hell out of here, never come back, as he did once before. Or he can do something. He can try. He looks down at the pistol in the holster on the seat beside him.

He should have put it into his mouth long before he ever took up a pillow with thoughts of mercy. Mercy for whom? Ruth, maybe. Himself, for sure.

Goddamn fucking coward.

He puts the truck in neutral and cuts the engine in the brambles outside the cemetery plot. He sets the parking brake. He gets out into the rain, which instantly soaks through his denim shirt and jeans. He wraps the pistol around his waist and snags a boxy Eveready from behind his seat and closes the door, squealing hinges lost to the downpour. A glance down the long, lonely drive to the house, where the bear-thing still marches in a crazy zigzag like a busted automaton, and then he sets out. Making his way north through the woods, stopping every so often to catch his breath. The rain slackens, becomes a drizzle. Once, beneath its patter, he hears a rustling in the underbrush. He waits, and when the sound doesn't come again, he moves on. Soon enough, he comes out behind the barn, just beyond its circle of blue magnesium lamplight.

He edges along the back of the barn to scout the house from its corner.

The bear is gone.

Hank judges the distance between the barn and the front porch, so much shorter than he remembers it. The difference between a child's eyes and an old man's. He can make it. He has to, only where's that goddamn bear?

Something nudges his shoe, and when he looks down, he finds himself staring into the face of his long-dead sister's long-dead dog. It sits back on its haunches and looks up at him and pants happily in the wet grass. "Dog?" Hank says, unbelieving. "My God, is it really—"

A low, soft woof. Nub of a tail switching.

Hank takes a step back.

Dog whines at a peal of thunder.

Hank puts his hand on the butt of his pistol, puts his back against the barn wall.

Dog coughs. A harsh canine hack, all tongue and teeth and eyes. A wad of something thick and white drips in a long lashing onto the ground. Hank finds himself staring at the mutt's rear leg, the one that used to hang limp against its body. It's not a leg at all now. It's a wet, knotted appendage all twisted together, raw skinned and ending in a shredded mouth.

Hank draws his pistol. He takes aim, hand shaking.

Dog darts away, into the trees.

A tremor passes through the earth, sudden and low, which gives way to a rumble, a growl, and Hank turns, and there, in the long grass at the end of the shed, is the bear-thing, its wide, flat head dropped low. Its lower jaw a beard of tentacles, its eyes wide black sockets leaking the same white sludge as Dog. When it takes a step toward Hank, the bear's paws actually tear free from the earth. Hank swings his pistol round but the bear-thing closes the gap between them in two bounds and swats him.

The paw hits him like a tree trunk, sends him rolling on the slick grass. He struggles up on hands and knees, and the bear-thing butts him with its head, pitches him flat on his back. It roars, a pitiful anguished sound, part bear, part dog, then drops to all fours, whimpering and whining, and begins to circle Hank, slowly, as Hank struggles to move, the pain in his back so intense.

"ANK," the bear-thing spits wretchedly.

The sound of his name in this creature's mouth freezes Hank's blood.

"ANK ANK ANK!"

Despite the harsh, terrible, alien sound of it, another voice is beneath it. Familiar. A girl's voice. Weak, heartbroken. The way she spoke his name, that awful night—

"Aggie?" Hank says.

"ANK! ANK OHHH ANK!"

It's mocking you.

A thought that cancels out all fear, balances everything with rage.

"You bastard," he growls.

The bear-thing shoves itself against the side of the barn, leaves hair and skin and white sticky slime behind. It shakes its head and snorts almost human laughter, then sneezes a great gout of white.

Hank pushes up on hands and knees and gets his feet under him and runs—old man or not, he runs like a fifteen-year-old boy—for the back door of the house.

The bear thunders after him.

Above Max's nose, the spider dances at the end of its thread. Below him, in the cellar, a train roars up from somewhere deep in the earth, and suddenly, the Wade-thing's knotty, spongy hands whip like lariats into the chute, as Max, drenched in sweat, gulps back a mouthful of blood. The fingers lash Max's ankles, yank him down and bite into his flesh with their razor-sharp teeth, reel him kicking and thrashing like a hooked fish—and then the first of the spiders drops into his hair.

Max screams.

The earth is shaking when Nellie comes to in the dark, and Max is screaming inside a cave. No, not a cave. The coal chute. She sits up on her elbows and sees the Wade-thing bent low, arched into the chute, a flashlight beam flickering. There, in a fleeting glint of light, beside his ropy, awful leg, the ax amid the coal. She gets up and staggers over the coal and seizes the ax, shores up her grip, and brings the blade down into the center of the Wade-thing's spine. It shrieks and she screams and she strikes again and again and again, tearing away flesh and bone and wet writhing things that scrabble away in the dark. She strikes until there's nothing left in her, until the entire lower half of the thing that was her husband has been severed, a knob of white spinal cord trailing out and twitching.

Then she drops to her knees and picks up the flashlight that clatters out.

Angles it into the chute and shines the light on her son's face.

Their eyes lock, but before she can say anything, the Wade-thing's blue eyes open beside her, and it smiles, and the smile is full of leaves and needles and white sap and the Wade-thing seizes her by the throat, and she smashes the light into its face, but the Wade-thing's hideous mouth only smiles, as its body reknits itself and it drags her out into the dark closet, as Max, above her, watches, frozen in terror.

Hank never makes it to the back door. A thing steps out of the shadows at the northwestern corner of the house. Part of it is a broad-shouldered man wearing a crumbling bowler hat. Hank aims his light and sees with horror that the side of his face is blasted away, in its place a flowering of mushrooms and odd appendages that wriggle and flap. In one hand, the thing carries a moldering blackjack. His other hand is missing two fingers. From the nubs grow two red-stemmed sprigs of Virginia creeper.

Below the waist, the thing doesn't even resemble a man. It shifts and dances—

(holy weeping Christ)

—on eight legs of devil's-walking-stick. Each studded in spiny black thorns.

The spider-thing steps toward him, rears up, and raises its sap in a sluggish, half-remembered posture.

The pistol bucks in Hank's hand. Three, four shots scatter chunks of its undercarriage into the grass. It shrinks away, circles around, and Hank dances with it, moving for the back door, which will take him into the kitchen. But the spider-thing dashes sideways to cut him off, and now the bear-thing, too, is at the corner of the porch, growling, and Hank realizes they've got him flanked. Behind him, the magnolia tree. Beside it, the fire tower. He whirls and leaps for the ladder and climbs.

The bear-thing and the spider-thing lunge at once.

They strike each other, and some ragged piece of one snags Hank's right calf. The pain is white-hot as it rips his flesh. He feels a piece of himself tear away, warm blood begin to flow, and still he hauls himself up, rung after rung. Once, he glances down through the crook of his elbow, sees the spider-thing and the bear-thing tangled up in knots and merging into one massive nightmare creature.

Atop the platform, pistol still gripped in his trembling hand, Hank rolls over onto his back and lies gasping. He draws his torn jeans up over his calf, inspects the jagged slashes in his pale, vein-shot skin.

The tower begins to shake. Hank cries out, grabs the railing.

The bear-spider-thing slams into the pylons below. Out of its bloated body, eight spiny legs flail furiously. The tentacles at the end of its face grasp at the rain-wet steel, finding no purchase.

It gives out a shriek of frustration, and suddenly the creature's whole bulk unseams itself with a sickening rip—tail and legs and spine and ribs and claws and skull—and out of that cracked skull, a single horrible eye burns bright and blue as a summer sky. The eye bounces at the end of a long wavering stalk, the essence of the monster now unraveled like a length of apple peel, becoming a mass of thorny vines all climbing, stretching, reaching for Hank Redfern in grotesque tandem.

In the grass below, a trampled bowler hat and moldy blackjack.

Shards of a bear's broken skull.

Hank takes aim through the trapdoor at that blue, wobbling eye. He fires.

The bullet pocks into the eye, is absorbed like a pebble in a pond. The vines, the eye, all of it keeps climbing, and now Hank realizes he's made a terrible mistake. He's trapped atop the tower, nowhere to go. He remembers the rope bridge he once made, when he was a boy. A flimsy thing. But, oh, how he wishes it were—

A Postman's bridge spans the gap between the tower and the magnolia tree.

"Well, I'll be dipped in shit."

He steps to the rail, checks the knots. Hopes to God it will hold a grown man's weight. He throws his good leg over first, then drags the other, which is little more than dead weight. He turns and something pops in his back. He grimaces, keeps moving. Standing outside the rail, hanging on with both hands, fifty feet of air beneath him, as he grasps the upper rope. Both hands tight around it, he puts his left leg out and steps onto the bridge, begins to inch left.

The tower lurches, the eye at the end of that huge stalk burning like a blue flame.

Hank inches. And inches. Holding his blood-soaked leg as steady as he can.

Then, from somewhere beneath the house, the earth begins to shake, and the tower and the rope begin to sway, and just as Hank steps off onto the wide bough of the magnolia, the lower rope drops away and the tower bends as the ground sinks beneath it, and then the world goes still, just before the tower falls. Metal screams. Wood splits. Glass shatters as it crashes into the western wall of the house, caving in the back door, the breakfast nook, the butler's pantry, the old map room. The wooden platform at the top breaks apart when it strikes the sloping yard, just below the coal-chute door and the twin crape myrtles.

Hank clings to the tree until the earthquake passes. Until all is silent.

Out of the dark, his mother screams, "Get out, Max! Go!"

And his paralysis breaks.

He channels all his strength into his legs and pushes against the joist above the chute. He grabs the top edge of the brick opening, and suddenly, his head is through, and he heaves himself up and out, just as two, three spiders drop onto his jeans. He pushes into the fresh night air. Falls on his side and rolls around in the grass like a boy on fire, crushing the black widows.

He lies on his back, staring up at the purple sky.

And then the rumble that began deep below the house shakes everything.

Suddenly, a scream of metal. When Max sits up, he sees the whole of the fire tower, wrapped in some terrible writhing vine and plunging earthward. The ground beneath it falling away. He scrabbles to his feet, slips in the damp grass. The tower hits the roof of the house. Windows explode, shower Max with glass. He runs for the porch, as behind him the map room's outer wall collapses in a cataclysmic roar.

Hank edges along the branch, and from there to the bough that reaches like a friendly arm to the slope of the porch roof, and up the roof to the open bedroom window, dragging his wounded leg in after him, and once he's inside and the window is shut, he collapses, holding his chest, thinking he might just have himself a heart attack or two. But the tightness soon lets go. At which point he looks around his old room and thinks: *I'm home.*

Coal cascades to the center of the closet, where the earthen floor is sinking, swirling, spiraling out greater and greater until the walls, too, are avalanching into the hole, the same hole that's opening up beneath the tower. A brilliant blue ocean of light blazing out of it, as the Wade-thing holds Nellie over it. Not just light but energy, a hum and crackle in the air that's living, conscious. A source of power, a fearsome strength, a blinding terrible—

The Wade-thing drops her into the light.

Max yanks open the screen door and runs for the phone. He fumbles the receiver from its cradle, but it's dead. He looks up and sees the collapsed wall, the ruins of the fire tower lodged in the house like a fallen ship's mast. August Redfern's maps fluttering like scraps of sail. High up, in the corner, near the old master bedroom, he can see purple starlight shining down. Water sprays from a pipe in the bathroom. The stairwell itself is canted sideways, precarious. For an instant, Max feels a jubilant sense of victory. They cannot live here now! Not now—

The floor begins to vibrate. The bell in the phone gives out a false jingle. Slats fall from the exposed wall as the whole house trembles once more. As if it hangs yet over some chasm.

Below his feet, in the cellar, a massive rumble.

Max edges around the stairs, to the top of the cellar steps, up from which shines a stroboscopic blue light. The Wade-thing appears in silhouette at the bottom. They lock eyes, briefly, before the monster lunges at the boy, and Max hooks left, around the stairs, headed up for his bedroom. Stairwell rocking and creaking beneath him, he's made the second-floor landing—what's left of it, anyway—when the vines snag his leg and he falls face-first onto the floor. He rolls onto his back and kicks at the scrabbling tendrils with their razor-sharp teeth, aware that the Wade-thing is still ascending the stairs, arms outthrust like some horrible wizard firing snakes from its fingertips. In the flickering light of the hallway pendant, Max can see, clearly, for the first time, that his father, Wade Gardner, is gone. In his place some hybrid zombie born of man and tree and something else, something alien, and Max feels, briefly, a sharp twist of grief, but then he remembers the pitch of his mother's scream—

(she can't talk now, pardner)

—and shoves those feelings down and kicks until the vines nipping at his flesh tear free.

He scrabbles into his bedroom and slams the door. Jams a chair beneath the knob.

A weak voice behind him says, "Hey."

Max whirls, heart in his throat.

His grandfather sits on the floor, against the wardrobe, legs stretched out before him, right calf bleeding. He wears an army belt and a holster on his hip. The pistol that belongs in the holster is in his lap. "Just taking a rest."

A flood of relief as Max drops to his knees and throws his arms around the old man.

Hank laughs. Puts one arm around the boy. But the arm slides away. Weakly the old man says, "Got a belt I can borrow?"

Max rummages in the trunk at the foot of his bed. He tosses out Legos, books, the shard of rosin brought back from the distillery, until he finds a red-and-blue Spider-Man belt and drops to his knees beside his grandfather and tears the old man's pant leg free of his wound. "Where do I put it?"

"Above," Hank says. "Here."

Max wraps the belt around the old man's thigh.

"Tight as you can make it."

Max draws the belt tight.

"What's this now?" Hank picks up the rosin. He hands it to Max.

"It came from the distillery." Max turns it in his hands.

Something heavy hits the door.

"It's my dad," Max says.

Strangely, Hank Redfern laughs.

The Wade-thing shambles up the stairs. Its shirt and jeans hang in tatters. Its body ripples with new growth coursing beneath the skin, green stalks bursting, flowers blooming, dying. Its heart pumps sap. Its feet splay into ten, twelve, twenty runners, each sprouting teeth that chew the hardwood floors at every step. The last of Wade Gardner's flesh falls away in glops, and out of its skull breaks a crown of twigs and thorns, and when it strikes the door, it becomes a part of the door, and its body melds with the wall, and inside the room where the boy is hiding, it begins to grow, finding the sap that runs in the heartwood pine frame of the wall and oozing into it and out of it and eating through the insulation and into the clapboard wood and buzz-sawing its way out of a single hairline of grain, then a hundred hairlines, stripping through frame boards until it's nothing but a singular column of tentacles and mouths ready to devour, there in the center of the room, but the room is empty, and so it draws knowledge of its surroundings as a taproot draws nutrients, letting its tendrils be messengers and the wood itself tell the story, and, oh, the stories this wood could tell—stories of sadness and pain and human suffering so ripe, stories of loneliness, of twin siblings playing, of a baby crying in the nursery as its soul-sick mother tends it, stories of a woman who had come here and won its heart with her sadness, stories of an old man whose blood it had, this very day, tasted for the first time, having already tasted his sister's, his brother's, his father's, a man whose presence here was unexpected but sweet, an old man who is, right now, limping into the hallway from the room next door, hand upon the balustrade to support his weight as he and the boy try to slip past. The Wade-thing coalesces, draws itself into a creature six, seven, eight feet tall with a single, cyclopic blue eye, then swings its pine-branch arms and bursts out of the bedroom door and snatches at the boy, plucks him up, and the balustrade becomes vines and the vines have teeth and now the old man's pistol is in his hand, raised, but he cannot fire, for the boy dangles in the monster's grip, and the creature is laughing, laughing at Hank Redfern through rosin-hard teeth, its blue eye sparking madness.

Hank's pistol wavers, dips. Tentacles tighten around the boy.

No clear shot.

He takes aim at the blue pool in the center of the monster's face. He knows it won't do a thing, but there's no other target, no other shot—

A sound, behind him. Out of the twisting, creaking, groaning of the house and the monster, a scraping.

Hank turns.

A girl—*Miss Frannie, that was her name, Frannie Sullivan*—approaches slowly along the foyer. She wears a plain homespun dress with a lace collar, but the lace is not really lace. It's fungus, spongy and white. Her skull is caved in and her jaw hangs crookedly. With her left hand she drags a shovel. In her right, she holds the hand of Agatha Redfern, who walks beside her, clad in the blue dress she died in, a bib of old blood spreading out from a hole in her tiny chest, the blood dried in long beads of resin. Clutched in her arm, her little rag doll. Aggie's jaw opens, hardened amber where her teeth should be, and a voice comes out of her, nothing like the voice of the child Hank remembers, the sister he loved—

". . . hannnnnnk . . ."

It's like the long, slow sound of that scraping shovel.

He raises his pistol.

Miss Frannie's head bursts in a spray of dirt and skull.

Agatha's hand jolts free and she hugs her doll to her chest, blue eyes wide with terror.

"I'm sorry," Hank whispers. And fires again.

His sister's face shatters like yellow glass. Shards fly along the hall as Agatha collapses into a roiling knot of black worms. They break over the floor, burrow between the boards and cracks, and disappear.

Meanwhile, all around, the house erupts with vines and roots and runners of long, fibrous arms. Out of the walls, the long, slow-moving scratching-scratching bursts forth and reaches up and around and over floor and ceiling.

Hank's grandson cries out.

The boy hangs over the broken stairs, feet scissoring air. The long twisting tentacle that wraps him tracks back to the Wade-thing's arm. Above the shoulder, an inhuman visage, a wound where a face should be, framed by a head of thick, hard bark. At the center of that cat face with its sap-oozing hacks, a single, shimmering, blue-sea eye.

Hank lifts the Colt.

The floor in front of him bursts open and the knot of black worms wells up and wraps his wounded leg. A thousand tiny needles pierce his flesh at once, and he screams and tries to dance away, but all he can do is stumble backward and fall.

Nellie opens her eyes to the blue. A light like no other light she has ever known. Warm and nourishing, a rich forever sea. It fills her vision, becomes another world. She hears a gentle tearing, feels something like the kiss of cobwebs across her face, and it's as if she's passing through some translucent membrane, her spirit being drawn from her body, out of a chasm in the void of space, straight into the heart of a brilliant, flaming star—

not a star, an eye
    our own beautiful, blue eye opening upon a spheroid of unfathomable size, unending, its curvature unseen, in us the

*warm liquid bath of the universe, pockets and holes and tunnels
sunk in space and time*

and you, Nellie, floating and seeing, in the blue forever

*and we, cast down from eternity upon some plot of sand to
delve into the hidden channels of the earth, where old things
slumber among woods and winds and lesser gods dwell deep,
deep down, where sacrifices are made and the blood runs like
roots to knit all things together, from the lowest boatman in a
faraway swamp to the wreckage of this house this home this
shimmering vortex of wood and metal and wiring and old maps
blown like leaves in this blue realm*

your *blue realm where bleed the bodies of men and women
and children*

(max)

*for you are greatest among those we've loved
the sadness, the pain you've long carried
we want you need you love you
stay and make us your home and we will make you ours
offer us what we crave and you will never want again*

(no god no)

your son upon the knife's edge a breath away from dying

(max's throat in the Wade-thing's grip, eyes opening as she
reaches out into the vast blue sea to find his hand, and he reaches
back for her, and oh the panic in her breast to think that she
could lose her boy to this thing this monster this ocean of hunger
with its ceaseless tides)

(MOM!)

(swimming she's swimming for her son's reaching hand)

open your eyes to the glory of our love

(MAX I SEE YOU I SEE YOU)

and give us what we want

(the boy's hand slides into hers, and hers into his, and the eye blazes all around them and whole galaxies erupt, collapse, are lost forever and born anew, as mother and son pitch apart, and the Dweller screams in fury)

The floor is consumed, as are the walls, the stairs, the fallen fire tower, and here on the second floor, the Wade-thing—the Dweller, too, inasmuch as the bear, the dog, Barlow, August Redfern, Agatha Redfern, Little Charlie, all have been it, are it, will be it forever—draws Max back from the air and blinks at the boy from behind its single mad eye, and the boy sees, deep in the shimmer, the faint shape of his mother, struggling against horrible currents. The Dweller draws the boy close to smell his fear before plunging a shoot into the child's neck, but the boy opens his fist, and in his hand is the shard of rosin taken from the ground where Charlie Redfern died, where Euphemia Redfern burned, where August Redfern sent Hank away. Max closes his fist around the shard and puts it straight through the luminescent jelly of his father's eye.

Nellie comes back to her body in the curving gullet of the red clay tunnel beneath the wreckage of Redfern Hill. Smells of coal and blood and the dank, womb-like earth. A single tentacle piercing her side, boring into her with tiny teeth, like fingers in wounds, and it hurts. *Oh, Jesus, it hurts!* She cries out the name of her son. Knows she will die, at least, having stood, having fought in the place where all is love and all is fear—

In the piled earth at her feet, a plastic gallon jug.

She sits up, a simple act made excruciating as the teeth chew—

they *chew!*—but her hands are on the jug and her thumb is on the cap and as soon as the bright pine scent of it floods the small, close space, the long wet arm ceases burrowing, and when she splashes it, it shrieks away into the wall, tearing free of her flesh like a snipped thread.

She takes calm, weary stock.

The tunnel—a kind of oubliette—has not collapsed, has not suffocated her. In fact, she can stand almost upright, which she does, grimed and bruised, jug in hand. Hole in her side, but not so deep. Her Ziggy T-shirt plastered to her skin with blood. Behind her, the tunnel rises and dwindles to a hot, rain-steamed July night, framed by the jagged wreckage of Redfern Hill.

Ahead, it curves away into darkness.

The ground and walls begin to tremble, softly at first, then louder, like doom gathering, the slow rumble of some inevitable, final act. Now is but the breath between the lightning and the thunder. She wants to turn, to crawl away toward the sky. But already the slick red earth around her is glowing with that harsh blue light.

Red dirt showers down as Nellie sets the jug of turpentine on the ground. She takes off her T-shirt and rips Ziggy right down the middle. She drops to her haunches and stuffs a strip of T-shirt into the jug. Sloshes it, soaks the fabric.

Ahead, out of the tunnel's blue throat, something roars, a sound at once like the cry of a bird or a bat or a bear, but big as the world. A dank wind blasts over her, wallops her to the tunnel floor with the stink of wet raw gum and some horrible gaseous reek. And when Nellie turns and pushes up on trembling arms to stand, jug in hand, to face the end, she sees it. She sees it and her brain simply slams a series of doors and hatches, sealing her mind away, lest she go insane.

It rounds the bend like an express train, massive blue eye burning bright with cosmic rage. Some dark, gradient center that might be a pupil, or it might be the unending void of space-time. Beneath the eye is a fat, segmented body framed by a sheath of grub-pale skin. Setae the size of anchor ropes claw the tunnel walls with teeth the size of shot glasses, spinning a hundred strong.

Bathed in the blinding, electric light, Nellie tightens her grip on the jug. Her hand slips into the pocket of her sleep pants. Her fist closes around the object there. She takes a deep breath, shuts her eyes to let it out, to hear the sound of her own breath drown the onrushing end, so the rest is—

Silence.

Nellie opens her eyes.

The Dweller idles some twenty, thirty yards away, a massive, breathing engine, eye like a giant headlamp, eager to barrel down. Wriggling, writhing limbs below it jitter with anticipation. But caution, too—

(Afraid? Is it afraid of me?)

Nellie glances at the jug of turpentine, the tongue of T-shirt over the lip.

The darkness at the center of the eye shifts down, locks onto what she holds.

"You're afraid of this," she says.

The creature shudders.

Nellie takes her mother's Zippo out of her pocket.

"It's okay." She ignites the lighter. "We're all afraid of something."

Possessed of no mouth Nellie can see, the Dweller gives out a raw, high-pitched shriek of rage and leaps forward, like a bull out of a chute.

Nellie thinks of Max, the day he was born. Warm and soft and wrapped in swaddling. She held him close and felt a stirring deep inside—abject terror. Not for her, but for him. To be born to a mother such as she. How could she ever protect him when she couldn't even protect herself?

On it comes, a thousand mouths eating its way through dirt and clay.

Nellie touches the Zippo's flame to the turpentine-soaked rag of shirt.

"I love you, Max," she breathes.

And charges forward, into the blue.

Heat blistering her hand, even as the plastic jug ignites and begins to melt. At the last second, the Dweller's eye flares bright with terror, but it slows too late, and there comes a tremendous *POP*, as the creature's momentum carries it forward into Nellie and Nellie's into it, and the eye bursts like the yolk of an alien egg, and Nellie is plunged into and through the world's foulest pool of viscous white jelly. Pressure all around her, eyes shut, mouth closed, breath held, she grips the flaming jug for all she's worth until sheer opposing force tears it from her hand and the fire—

(It makes em scream)

—blazes like a comet's tail behind her, through the creature's innards, licking at the pine sap the Dweller has, for over a century, ingested, absorbed, assimilated into its own vascular system, the fragile engine of its long life, its regeneration, its transformation, and so, from the inside out, the god of Redfern Hill erupts, as Nellie flies ahead of the fire that blooms in beautiful slow waves like oxygen blazing through a rocket ship, and the soft, grub-like body lights up like a detonating glowworm.

She explodes through the tail in a spray of fire and foul sticky white goo and goes rolling in the churned earth. Covered in a milky, flaming caul that the dirt snuffs out as she rolls and screams, the tunnel behind her littered in slabs of worm, dirt showering down as the whole long burrow rocks and shudders.

Nellie staggers up, stunned and numb. Her left shoulder, which took the full brunt of the creature's momentum, is broken. Her arm hangs limp at her side. Her skin is blistered, her hair crisped to the scalp. Charred and oozing, she wades through the leftovers, and when she reaches the bend in the tunnel, the coal that skitters down makes a treacherous slide she doesn't have the strength to climb, so she collapses. Overhead, stars shimmer in the void of night, water from a burst pipe arcing across them. Pain from the burns just beginning to reach her nerves as the coal settles beneath her. She lies on her back, staring up at the distant ruin of Redfern Hill, washed up at last on the wide and waiting shores of a place she's never been, where there are no maps to guide her.

After a while, her father's grizzled face appears above.

At his side, her boy.

Together, they lower a rope. It's a simple bowline knot.

Nellie reaches up.

They clamber to the top of what's left of the cellar stairs. The boy's clothes and face are black with coal dust, Nellie sticky with the creature's blood and pink with her own seared skin. Still, Max hurls himself against her, and she holds him close. Hank limps ahead down the hallway, leg swollen. Stairs, walls, ceilings—all of it clattering and shimmying, as the earth beneath the foundation fails.

The walls of the house are laced with vines and roots that are not vines or roots but the many tendrils of the dead beast that has long worked its way up through earth and brick and board. Gravity and suction from the sinkhole in the cellar tugging at them now, and they, in turn, like chains, are helping to pull down the house around them. The air is clogged with a dense, pine-scented dust. A section of wall drops free near the dining room (*We never used that room*, Nellie thinks oddly), exposing studs built from heart pine seventy years prior, weeping, like the wood in the cellar, pine resin. Little amber beads. The art deco pendant lamp in the hallway smashes to the floor, as boards above begin to crack and buckle. Nellie and Max and Hank shove out onto the porch, just as the ceiling caves in behind them.

A heavy, terrible rumble, as the earth draws breath.

Hank pulls open the Ranger's passenger door and scoots Max in, across the bench seat. The old man has to lift his shredded leg into the cab before he can shut the door. Nellie scrambles into the driver's seat and cranks the ignition. She works the shifter, lets Max steer one-handed from the middle as they pull away. Behind them, a calamitous eruption, like the apocalyptic crack of a whole forest felled at once.

Out near the Winnebago, Nellie brakes, and they all turn and watch Redfern Hill sink like a harpooned leviathan.

It's a good end to every story they've ever called their own.

And a fitting prologue to the next.

Somewhere with water, bright and green, Max hopes.

ACKNOWLEDGMENTS

✦

The first draft of *The Hollow Kind* was written in the summer and fall of 2020. That summer, Crystal and I hunkered down with our cats and watched a lot of Netflix, in particular *The Great British Baking Show*, which may have saved our sanity, if not our waistlines. To burn off calories from our versions of Mary Berry's Victoria sponge or Paul Hollywood's cinnamon rolls (damn, those were good), we started day hiking in and around Middle Georgia. Those hikes—through the woods and swamps of Georgia's Sandhills Region, in particular—are the bedrock of this book.

If you're ever on the Golden Isles Parkway between McRae and Jesup, you can hike the Little Ocmulgee State Park's Oak Ridge Trail, which, by the second draft, had pretty much become August Redfern's spread above North Creek (keep your eyes peeled for indigo snakes and gopher tortoises—and alligators; they're there, trust me). Also, we visited the Georgia Museum of Agriculture's historical village, a wide-open space where you can see a steam train, a sawmill, a gristmill, and one of the state's last working turpentine stills. In truth, most of the historical details in this book are owed to that museum, which is run by the good folks at Abraham Baldwin Agricultural College. If you're passing Tifton on I-75 and need to stretch your legs, it's just the ticket.

I also owe a debt to Robert B. Outland III's book, *Tapping the Pines: The Naval Stores Industry in the American South*. His is a comprehensive portrait of turpentining, from its frank assessment of the economic and ecological impacts of the industry to its heartfelt examination of the day-to-day lives of the men who worked the fields. Any inaccuracies with regard to turpentining are mine alone, either by fault or fabrication.

The people who supported me in the writing of this book, and who support me in general, are kind, generous souls, and it's a privilege to know them and call them Team Davidson: Elizabeth Copps of Copps Literary, my fearless and brilliant agent; my impeccable editors, Daphne Durham and Lydia Zoells; Sean McDonald, for his continued support; the whole amazing, talented crew at MCD × FSG Originals; Sean Daily, my film agent; Martha Guzman and Maria Carvainis; and Dr. Eugenia Bryan, my incisive, diligent beta reader and the world's foremost scholar on the works of Andy Davidson.

And Crystal. Where would I be without you? You kept me going through this one. You'll keep me going through the next. You make every book the dream it should be.

Lastly, thank *you*, Dear Reader, for your time and your heart.

The final draft of *The Hollow Kind* was finished in our Florida room on December 19, 2021, as all the cats lay sleeping in the sunlight.

A NOTE ABOUT THE AUTHOR

◆

Andy Davidson holds an MFA in fiction from the University of Mississippi. His debut novel, *In The Valley of the Sun*, was nominated for the 2017 Bram Stoker Award for Superior Achievement in a First Novel, *This Is Horror*'s 2017 Novel of the Year, and the 2018 Edinburgh International Book Festival's First Book Award. Born and raised in Arkansas, he now makes his home in Georgia with his wife and a bunch of cats.

If you loved *The Hollow Kind*, you'll love...

THE

BOATMAN'S

DAUGHTER

◆

IT WAS AFTER MIDNIGHT WHEN THE BOATMAN AND HIS DAUGHTER brought the witch out of Sabbath House and back onto the river. Old Iskra sat astride the johnboat's center plank, wearing a head scarf and a man's baggy britches damp with blood, their iron reek lost to the night-fragrant honeysuckle that bowered the banks of the Prosper. In her lap: a bread bowl, wide and deep and packed with dried eucalyptus sprigs and clods of red earth broken around a small, still form covered by a white pillowcase. The pillowcase, like the old woman's clothes, stained red.

They angled off-river at the mouth of a bayou and were soon enclosed by the teeming wall of night. Cries of owls, a roar of bullfrogs, the wet slopping of beaver among the stobs. Miranda Crabtree faced into the wind, lighting Hiram's way with the Eveready spot mounted on the bow. The spotlight shined on branches closing in, cypress skirts scraping like dry, bony fingers along the johnboat's hull. Spiders in the trees, their webs gleaming silver. A cottonmouth moccasin churning in the shallows. Miranda held up arms to guard her ears and cheeks from the branches, thinking of Alice down the rabbit hole, one small door opening upon another, and another, each door smaller than the last.

"Push through!" the old witch cried.

Branches screeching over metal, they did, the boatman breaking off fistfuls of dead cypress limbs until the boat slipped free onto the wide stage of a lake. Here, Hiram cut the motor and they drifted in a stump field, a preternatural silence descending over frog and cricket and owl, as if the little boat had somehow passed into the inner, sacred temple of the night itself.

To the west, purple lightning rolled thunderless in the cage of the sky.

In the water were the twisted, eerie shapes of deadfalls. They broke the surface like coffins bobbing in flooded graves.

"What is this place?" Miranda asked, angling her light all around.

But no one answered.

Ahead, a wide muddy bank stretched before a stand of trees, tall and close, and when the boat had nosed to a stop in the silt, the old witch got up with a pop of bones, stepped over the side, and staggered off along the path of the light, bowl in her arms. Her shadow long and reaching.

Hiram brought up a shotgun and a smaller flashlight from behind the stern seat. Miranda knew the double-barrel to be her grandfather's, the only gun Hiram had ever owned. She had never seen him fire it. They were bowhunters, the Crabtrees. Always had been.

"She needs me to go with her," he said. "You stay put."

"But—"

He stepped out of the boat into the mud and came around to the bow, where Miranda could see his face in the light. Long and narrow, sadness in his very bones, it seemed, the first touches of gray at his temples. Drops of moisture swirled thick in the light between them.

"Stay," he said. "The light will guide us back."

He took her chin in hand and brushed her cheek with his knuckles and told her he loved her. This frightened Miranda, for these were not words Hiram Crabtree often said. They struck her now like a kind of incantation against something, some evil he had yet to fathom. He kissed the back of her hand, beard rough against her skin. He said he would be back. He promised. "Leave that light shining," he said, and then he left her, following the witch's humped form into the trees. Their deep tracks welling up with water, as if the land itself were erasing them.

The spring night grew hushed save for the far-off mutter of the coming storm, which had been threatening since twilight, black clouds like a fleet of warships making ready to cannonade the land with fire, water, wind, and ice.

Hours before, when Hiram woke her, Miranda had been dreaming of stumbling through woods and brambles onto a path that brought her out of the trees and into a clearing, where the land sloped up to a hilltop draped in flowering kudzu, little white blossoms aglow in the moonlight. Cradled in her arms, a black bullhead catfish she had only just pulled slick and dead from the bayou. Atop the hill: the witch's cabin on stilts, one yellow flame burning in a window. Miranda went up the crooked, red-mud path, up the wide board steps of the porch, and into the cabin, where the old witch stood waiting. She dropped the fish in the old woman's bread bowl and the witch took her filleting knife from her apron and slit the fish's belly. Miranda put her thumbs in the fish's gills to lift it and the innards slopped out in a purple heap. The old witch slung the guts into her boxwood stove, where they hissed and popped in the fire, and the dead fish heaved in Miranda's hands, came alive, began to scream. It screamed with the voice of a child.

Then Hiram's hand on her shoulder, shaking her.

Now, in the johnboat, she was waiting. Chin in hand, elbow on her knee, just as she had sat waiting earlier that night on the porch steps of Sabbath House. They had fetched the witch from her cabin on the bayou, and from there upriver to that ugly, paintlorn manse.

The front door of the plantation house stood open to let in the cool, blustery air. Last fall's leaves skittered over the boards like giant palmetto bugs as, inside, the witch went about her ancient trade behind a shut bedroom door. Across the gravel lane, Hiram stood in the bald, root-gnarled yard of a low shotgun house, talking softly to a man who was not quite five feet tall. The little man listened intently, head down, hands in his pockets. Windows of the other five shacks that stood beneath the trees were lit, a few men smoking anxiously between the clapboard dwellings, just beyond the reach of their own bare-bulb porch lights. Vague, grown-up shapes to Miranda.

Within the manse, a woman screamed, freezing every soul who heard.

Another scream: the wail of something deep and true torn loose, lost to the dark.

Hiram and the dwarf went charging past Miranda into the foyer, only to halt in shock at the foot of the stairs. Miranda pushed between them and saw an old man, all legs and elbows in black suit pants and a bloody white shirt, stagger out of the bedroom to sit like a broken toy at the top of the stairs. He clutched in his hands an object, something Miranda could not see, forearms red with blood up to his cuffs, which were rolled at the elbows. Miranda felt her father's hand on her shoulder, and when she looked up she saw Hiram's face gone pale as chalk. The little man to her right was stout and strong, but she glimpsed it on his face, too: horror.

The witch came solemnly out of the bedroom. Carrying the bread bowl. She passed the old man on the stairs, whose eyes never strayed from whatever faraway place they had fixed.

Blood dripping on the boards between his scuffed wing tip shoes.

Hiram pushed Miranda toward the front door, and she glimpsed, off the foyer in the downstairs parlor, a man sitting on an antique sofa. He was young, slim, handsome, a lit cigarette between full lips and a glass of amber liquid in hand. He wore a gun, a badge.

He winked a cornflower-blue eye as Miranda scooted past.

Now, in the johnboat. Waiting still, picking at a scab on her bare knee.

Thunder boomed, closer.

Straight ahead, a white whooping crane stepped out of the trees into the Eveready's beam. It stood in the mud and seemed to glow, stark and bright and otherworldly against the black of the swamp. Miranda watched it, and it watched her. The spotlight's beam like a tether between two worlds, Miranda's and the bird's. Something preternatural crept up her spine, raised gooseflesh on her arms.

A slow, rolling rumble that wasn't thunder came out of the trees, and the crane launched itself into the dark.

The water in Hiram's bootprints rippled, and Miranda felt the aluminum boat shudder.

The distant trees swayed in their tops, though the air was heavy and still.

Miranda's heart pounding in her chest.

Then, deep within the woods: a gunshot.

It cracked the night in two.

A second shot followed, reverberating huge and canyonlike.

Miranda drew a single breath, then leaped from the boat. The mud yanked her down, but she struggled up and ran for the trees, forgetting that the Eveready at the bow shone only so far. In the woods, darkness reared up and closed her between its palms. She skidded to a halt.

Called for Hiram. Listened.

Called again.

Heart racing, blood pounding, shore and spotlight at her back, she ran.

Lightning flashed at close intervals, lit the trees bright as day.

She ran on, calling out until Hiram's name was no longer a word, just a raw, ragged sound. She struck a tree, bounced, came up hard against another, and there she hung against the rough bark, gasping.

More lightning, and in that staccato flash, the land sloped down to a maze of saw palms wrapped in shreds of mist. Beyond the maze, the undergrowth rose up in a tangled, briar-thick wall, impenetrable. Great thorny vines, woven tight as a bird's nest.

Shining deep within that nest, like a string she had followed from boat to forest, was the faint orange beam of a flashlight. Fixed and slanting across the ground. All but swallowed by the darkness.

Miranda staggered into the saw palm maze, blades nicking her bare arms and legs. She felt the wisp of orb weavers against her cheeks, webs enshrouding her as they broke against her, as if nature were clothing her in itself, preparing her for some arcane ritual. When the fronds grew too close, she went down on hands and knees and crawled in the moist earth, and the light ahead grew stronger, closer. When she finally reached the undergrowth, she saw a kind of tunnel through it, just large enough for a fox or a boar—or a girl. She pressed her belly to the ground and worked elbows and hips and legs to worm through the thick tangle, aware a sound was coming out of her, some primal grunt that made her think she might vomit up the whole of her insides and there, in the sticky pink folds of stomach, would be a pile of stones, the source of this grunting, clacking noise. Finally, she came out where Hiram's flashlight lay bereft in a clump of moss and pale, fleshy toadstools.

"Daddy," she was gasping, "Daddy."

The glass of the lens and the blue plastic housing crawled with bugs.

Covered in mud and spider silk and tiny rivulets of blood, the squished remnants of a green-backed orb weaver stuck like a barrette in her dark hair, Miranda took up the light and got to her feet. She called again for Hiram, sweeping the beam over bare, bone-white trees, like great spears hurled down into the earth. Clumps of marshy reeds rising out of black pools that sheened in the light like oil. Narrow, mossy strips of earth among the pools.

And something else, too, glimpsed in the lightning, just beyond the trees.

Miranda went carefully alongside one of the pools that branched into a stream, black and thick. Moss along the bank festooned with brown toadstools and odd, star-shaped plants she had never seen the like of in all her trips hunting, fishing, trapping with Hiram. Sticks and clumps of bark were lodged in the stream and blackened, and at what appeared to be the widest, deepest point, her light caught the shape of something large and half submerged on its side. Brown feathers speckled black. An owl.

The stream opened out into a kind of moat that circled a great wide clearing, and at the center of the clearing was the thing she had glimpsed in the lightning. A shape, huge and dark and shrouded in mist. Peering up at it, Miranda saw what looked like a head, two great horns, and two long ragged limbs ending in crooked fingers. She almost cried out, even took a step back. Then realized, in the rapid shutter of the lightning, that it was only a shelf of rock, atop it a tree, thick and twisted and dead, its trunk canting out at an angle that should have sent it tumbling from the ledge into the muck below.

A bark-skinned log bridged the black moat that encircled the rock. Miranda crossed it, balancing as she went. Sweat soaked through her shirt, her underwear. The earth beyond the moat was spongy, soft, rich. She felt it sinking underfoot with every step. She went through clumps of reeds and grass and played her light up at the rock as she came into its shadow and saw a long branch reaching like an arm from the tree, and from this arm a thick vine dropped straight down like a plumb line into a mound of freshly turned black earth, at its center a hole, deep and dark. The opening big and wide as a tractor wheel.

Among a stand of thin brown reeds at the base of the mound: the old witch's bread bowl, drawn in blood, overturned. A pillowcase in the dirt.

Miranda heard a snap in the dark, a squelch from near the rock.

Eyes were on her, she could feel them.

Bugs crawled over Hiram's light.

Her voice small and swallowed by the night: "Daddy?"

She played the light over the distant rock, its cold surface shining back, a tangle of fat roots and vines like a fall of wet hair. Her beam caught something in the mud, a glint of brass. She went to it, bent, and plucked up the red wax casing of a shotgun shell. She touched it to her nose, smelled the acrid scent of gunpowder still fresh on it. She knocked bugs from the light and cast about for Hiram's blood, a second shell, some track or sign.

Nothing.

She pushed the shell into the pocket of her shorts.

A rustling, in the clump of grass near her feet.

Miranda swung the light.

Something round and red and raw lay in the moss, not far from the upended bowl. At first Miranda didn't recognize it. Slicked with gore, more like a skinned rabbit than a baby. Its flesh a lifeless gray. She played the beam over arms and legs. They were mottled, rough and scaled, a long white worm of umbilicus twisted beneath it. Leaves clinging to a head of dark hair.

Its belly heaved. Its mouth opened.

For an instant, she did not move. Then she ran to it, dropped on her knees beside it.

Below its chin, a wide slit bubbled fresh bright blood like a second mouth as the baby gulped and sucked air.

She saw the pillowcase among the reeds and stooped for it, not looking where she was stepping. She splashed into a shallow pool of black liquid, thick and warm. It flooded her shoe, soaked her sock. Miranda gasped as her foot began to tingle, then to burn. Working quickly, ignoring her foot, she turned the pillowcase inside out and used a clean edge to press the wound at the baby's throat. But now it seemed it was not a wound at all, for the blood wiped free and the flesh there, beneath the jaw, was whole.

Had she imagined it? Some trick of shadow and gore?

She wiped her hand on her shorts, snakes of adrenaline still in her fingers as she worked her thumb into the baby's old-man palm and the digits parted. Between each digit was a thin membrane of skin, purple veins alight in the glow of Hiram's flashlight.

Webbed—

A sudden rustle from the reeds where she'd found the pillowcase.

A whiplike blur, pink tissue and fang.

She felt the sound: a tenpenny nail punching flesh.

Shocked, she fell back on her haunches. Barely caught a glimpse of it, fat and long, the color of mud. A cottonmouth, corkscrewing away.

. . . snake-bit, oh, oh, Daddy, no . . .

. . . she grabbed the flashlight, shined it on her left forearm, saw the wound welling blood, the flesh already puffing . . .

. . . stay calm, keep your heart rate down, the boat, the baby . . .

One last clamor of thunder and the rain began to fall. Big fat drops, cold and stunning.

Oh, oh no, Daddy, I'm sorry . . .

Miranda staggered to her feet, picking up the baby in her right arm, holding the flashlight with her left, right foot gone numb from the sludge that slicked it, and set off back in the direction she had come.

At the tunnel she fell to her knees, heart racing, sluicing venom, head fuzzy.

The flashlight went tumbling. Lost.

Crawling now, pushing through, slow, so slow, the numbness in her left arm reaching her shoulder, the tingling in her foot inching higher, into calf and thigh, her whole body assaulted, long thorns snagging her shirt and hair, and all the while the baby's heart hammering against her own, a fish odor wafting up.

Upright again, lurching—

Left arm tight against her side, stumbling, sharp fronds slicing, right leg numb from the hip down now, oily black sludge burning skin—

She fell.

She lay on her back and the rain pelted her face, ran beneath her in tiny rivers.

The fingers of her left hand swollen thick as corks.

The baby lay at her small, girl's breast. Alive but weak.

You are going to die tonight, Miranda Crabtree thought, staring up at the dark boughs of the trees, where the lightning made jagged shapes and turned the trees into devils come to minister. *This is your death.*

She had a sudden urge to taste the black licorice they kept in jars to sell. Catfish bait, the old-timers who came to the mercantile called it.

Oh, Daddy, where are you, I am sorry, Daddy, so sorry I was not clever . . .

The rain was hard and cold and numbing.

Then, from the dark recesses of the trees behind her, a terrible rumble, the boughs overhead thrashing. From the forest all around a cracking, a *rending*, as trees tore free from the earth and hurled themselves to the ground, and a wind blasted the cold rain sideways so that it seemed the breath of a huge thing was blowing over Miranda, and with the wind came a bright piney scent of fresh resin that stung her nostrils, and yes, something massive, something dark and horned and snarling and impossible, emerging now from the trees—

Not real, it's not real

—to lift her up in its terrible, rough-bark hand, entwining vines around arm and waist and leg, setting her afoot and nudging her over wet ground, stomach turning, hair wet against her scalp, and a fever burning in her arm and head.

Feeling had returned to her leg, she realized, the burning from the black sludge subsided, so she staggered off, soaked through, the baby against her breast chilled and silent.

Eventually there was a light, a pinhole in the darkness, and at first she thought it was the light to bring her over to another land, to the place her mother, Cora Crabtree, had gone long ago, when Miranda was only four. But it was not. She looked around and saw she stood mired in the muddy shore, where her footprints, like Hiram's, like the old witch's, were filled with water and led back to the place where the johnboat was lodged in the mud, Eveready spot still shining from the bow.

To guide us back.

But she saw no boatman in the lightning, no witch in its glare, and her left arm was hot and hard like a length of stovewood despite the cold, cold rain. She spoke her father's name. A whimper. Tears. Retching. Vomit. She collapsed in the mud, lay over on her back and let the baby rest atop her, right hand cupped around its weakly pulsing fontanel.

Out of the dark, into the weak beam of the boat light, a stooped shape came, small and hunched and peering down. Smooth chin and black eyes glittering within a head scarf. In one hand, Hiram Crabtree's shotgun, in the other an empty, bloody bread bowl.

Thunder, the whole world booming.

I'm only eleven, Miranda thought, fading. *I don't want to die—*

She felt the baby's weight against her, its faint warmth a promise. She closed her eyes. Darkness took her.

The storm poured down ruin upon the land. Indeed, it was a storm the people of Nash County, Arkansas, would remember for years to come.

It raged like a thing alive. On the outskirts of the defunct sawmill town of Mylan, the painted women of the Pink Motel stood watching the rain like forgotten sentries from their open doorways, the night's business washed away. They smoked cigarettes and hugged themselves as hailstones broke like bullets against the weed-split parking lot. The older women turned away, shut their doors, drew curtains. The young remained watchful, restless, eyes fixed, perhaps, on the position of some faraway star they had long looked to, now obscured by the storm. Miles south, where the land became a warren of gravel roads twisting back upon themselves, where the sandy banks of the Prosper gave way to stumps and sloughs, bottom dwellers came out onto the porches of shanties, long-limbed men in overalls and rail-thin women in cotton shifts. Children not clothed at all. They watched the rain pour from the eaves of their tin roofs to wear away the mud below and saw in this the promise of their own slow annihilation, their fates tied inextricably to the land they or some long-lost forebear had claimed.

And finally, along the river's edge, the congregants of Sabbath House, numbering no more than a dozen souls, this clutch of ragged youth sheltering not from the raging heavens but from the terror that was their mad, lost preacher Billy Cotton, who even now sat soaked in the blood of his dead wife and child in the old manse across the lane. Their numbers ever dwindling since the madness had first bloomed in the old man years past, they huddled in the little row of shotgun houses as the wind howled and pine branches cracked and fell to lodge like unexploded bombs in the earth. They prayed, some of them. Others wept. Come the morning, surely they would all be gone.

Inside the manse, the old preacher sat unmoving on the stairs, even as a great oak bent and crashed into the western wall, shattering glass and stoving in the copper-sheeted roof. Billy Cotton's mouth was dry, his tongue like sandpaper. His heart ticked steady as a clock. The object in his bloody hands—what the boatman's curious daughter had not seen—was a pearl-inlaid straight razor, closed. Outside, the wind roared like a great cyclone come to funnel the old preacher up and away, and now as the water began to strike him he looked up through the hole at the sky above and saw lightning crack like God's own judgment of his sins. And so he stood and went down the steps with his razor in hand, down the gravel lane and out onto the rickety dock that jutted over the stagnant water that flowed off the Prosper, where the boatman had brought the witch to deliver his child, and the child had been a monster, an abomination Cotton had held aloft by the ankle to show it to the twisted, pain-ravaged face of its mother, who would have loved it had she lived, because how could she not, this woman he had once given his heart to, whose pity and voice had moved mountains, and so the razor flashed in the gleaming light from the bedside lamp, and the old witch watched him draw it sharply, quickly. And did nothing, because she knew, as he did, that it was monstrous, this thing, this child that was not a child. And now, here, at the end of the dock, he closed up the razor that had been his since the days of his youth in a Galveston orphanage and hurled it into the water and fell to his knees and began to weep, great racking sobs, and soon he lay prostrate, bereft, a wailing banshee slicked in blood and rain, and after a while he curled up on his side and slept there on the boards, and soon the storm abated, and the air grew fresh and cool, and the dark rose up in a chorus of frog song.

For more fantastic fiction, author events,
exclusive excerpts, competitions, limited editions and more

VISIT OUR WEBSITE
titanbooks.com

LIKE US ON FACEBOOK
facebook.com/titanbooks

FOLLOW US ON TWITTER AND INSTAGRAM
@TitanBooks

EMAIL US
readerfeedback@titanemail.com